SC

**This book is to be returned on or before
the last date stamped below.**

THE THIRD LIFE

Caroline Gray

THE THIRD LIFE

Michael Joseph

LONDON

101331

MICHAEL JOSEPH LTD

Published by the Penguin Group
27 Wrights Lane, London W8 5TZ, England
Viking Penguin Inc., 40 West 23rd Street, New York, New York 10010, USA
Penguin Books Australia Ltd, Ringwood, Victoria, Australia
Penguin Books Canada Ltd, 2801 John Street, Markham, Ontario, Canada L3R 1B4
Penguin Books (NZ) Ltd, 182–190 Wairau Road, Auckland 10, New Zealand

Penguin Books Ltd, Registered Offices: Harmondsworth, Middlesex, England

First published in Great Britain in 1988

British Library Cataloguing in Publication Data
Gray, Caroline, *1930–*
The third life.
Rn: Christopher Nicole   I. Title
823′.914[F]

ISBN 0-7181-2914-8

Typeset by Goodfellow & Egan Ltd, Cambridge
Printed in Great Britain by
Richard Clay Ltd, Bungay, Suffolk

PROLOGUE

The room was quiet as the three men watched Patrick MacGinnion reading the report. Once Hart took out a silver cigarette case, but Kaley quickly shook his head – big Pat MacGinnion did not like smoking.

The office was large and sumptuous, with huge plate-glass windows. Its situation – fifty-three floors above Madison Avenue – meant that even the roar of New York's afternoon traffic was nothing more than a whisper. The chairs were upholstered leather, and big Pat MacGinnion's desk was walnut – and large enough to play billiards on. In this early spring of 1932 the whole world might be sinking further and further into the grip of the Depression, but MacGinnion and his associates continued to amass vast profits behind the shelter of this huge and respectable realty building – at least up to this minute.

MacGinnion raised his head. 'Holy shitting cows!' he remarked. Like so many Irishmen, he spoke quietly, the soft voice belying the size of the man – the immense shoulders which seemed to bulge out of his Savile Row suit, the thick eyebrows which seemed about to topple over and blind him. 'Twenty million dollars? You're asking me to believe that my oldest friend has robbed me of twenty million dollars?'

'Robbed us, Pat,' Dominic Cerdo reminded him. In contrast to the Irishman, Cerdo was small and neat. He wore a pencil-thin moustache, and looked as if he had been inserted into his suit with a shoehorn.

'You knew something was happening, Big Pat?' Kaley pointed out. 'Or you wouldn't have set up the investigation.' Kaley was tall and thin, with a hatchet face. He looked exactly what he was: the Association's watchdog.

'Every goddamned year,' MacGinnion muttered, looking at the report again. 'For ten years. Two million a year. Jesus Christ! And you guys never clicked?'

'How could we, big Pat?' Kaley protested. 'Mr Armitage was in charge of all the finances, and he was the senior partner. How could we?'

'He was trained as a bookkeeper,' Cerdo said glumly.

'He was trained as a goddamned thief,' MacGinnion replied. 'Okay. I want that money back. Where is it?'

He looked from face to face, his gaze settling on Hart. 'What did you say your name was?'

'Hart, Mr MacGinnion,' the detective said. He was a nondescript-looking man. But then, he was intentionally so. He spoke with an equally nondescript accent, pronouncing each word with great care. 'Calvin Hart.'

'And you know what's going on?'

'He works for me, permanently,' Kaley explained. 'The private dick act is just a front. But he is a dick. The best there is. So I put him in the picture. You can trust him, Big Pat. He's one of us.'

MacGinnion had kept his gaze on Hart's face. 'Convince me.'

'On instructions from Mr Kaley,' Hart said carefully, 'I investigated the habits and actions of Mr Armitage in England.'

'So where's he hidden the money? Or has he spent it?'

'As far as I can ascertain, sir, he hasn't spent the money. But I'm afraid I don't know what he's done with it.'

'And you call yourself a detective?'

'Now hold on, Big Pat.' Kaley hurried to the defence of his protégé. 'Calvin has done the best he could with the information he was given. When you think what he's turned up . . . Jees.'

'Okay. So Eddie Armitage is living a double life. Tell me again,' MacGinnion said.

'Well sir, Mr Kaley told me that Mr Armitage was in the habit of spending two months in England every summer, and every winter over Christmas. He gave me to understand that Mr Armitage had done this every year for a considerable time, and that it had always been perfectly acceptable to yourself and Mr Cerdo—'

'For Chrissake, the guy's English,' MacGinnion pointed out,

4

resenting the implication that he had landed himself in this hole. 'Why shouldn't it be acceptable?'

'And he's set up the Association over there as well,' Cerdo said. 'It's doing pretty good.'

'Yes sir,' Hart agreed. 'But now you wanted him investigated.'

MacGinnion looked at Cerdo.

'Well Pat, as soon as there was the slightest suggestion of any funny business – even before we had the secret audit – I figured it'd be a good thing for us to find out just what Eddie did in the UK. And by God was I right.'

'So?' MacGinnion looked at Hart again.

'Mr Armitage was simple enough to trace in London, sir. He maintains a most lavish apartment in Mayfair. They call them flats over there, but this is in an expensive part of the city.'

'He got a woman?'

'Not living in, sir. There's a porter who seems to double up as a general factotum, but that's all.'

'He couldn't risk a valet or a butler,' Kaley observed. 'He has too much to hide.'

'Go on,' MacGinnion said.

'Well sir, my partner and I undertook a round-the-clock surveillance of Mr Armitage from the moment he stepped off the transatlantic liner in Southampton. I followed him to London, where he went to his apartment. For the first week he lived the life of a man about town—'

'At his age,' Cerdo commented primly.

'He also saw several of his – your – associates, and I presume did business with them. Whatever funds were handed over appeared to be deposited in his bank in an entirely above-board fashion.'

'We gotta see that bank statement,' MacGinnion growled.

'I doubt you'll find anything wrong there, sir. While Mr Armitage is being Mr Armitage, he appears to conduct his life entirely in accordance with his appearance to yourselves. However, the other life . . .'

'We're waiting.'

'Well, sir, after a week, I was called by my partner, who was sharing the watch with me, to say that Mr Armitage was leaving town again, for the continent. This was a couple of weeks before Christmas.'

5

'That figures,' MacGinnion said. 'He was doing some business for us in France.'

'No doubt, sir. However, I felt he should still be kept under surveillance, so I relieved my partner, and followed Mr Armitage on the boat-train to Folkestone, but . . .' Hart had a sense of the dramatic and paused to look from face to face. 'He never went to France at all. Instead, at the railroad station, he merely caught a train back in the direction of London. This train he changed twice, and finally arrived at a town called Epsom. He had no idea he was being followed,' he added, with quiet satisfaction.

'That's the place where they run the Derby,' Kaley explained.

'They run the Derby in Kentucky,' Cerdo objected.

'So the Limeys have one too,' Kaley pointed out.

'Will you guys shut up?' MacGinnion was now definitely interested in Hart's tale. 'So he gets to this place Epsom. What then?'

'Why sir, he takes a cab from the station and drives to a house – his house. Neat little place, just outside the village on the edge of the Downs. At first I supposed this was some private country retreat, but I thought I should ask a few questions in the shops, and to my surprise I learned that the house doesn't belong to Mr Edward Armitage, but to Mr Edwin Allen. Apparently this Allen is an executive with British Petroleum who works in the desert, coming home on holiday for several weeks twice a year.'

'Holy shitting cows,' MacGinnion shouted.

'This Allen is a widower . . .' Hart paused.

'A widower? Eddie never married.'

'Edward Armitage never married,' Kaley pointed out. 'Edwin Allen sure did.'

'And she's dead. Okay. So . . .'

'There's a daughter,' Hart said.

MacGinnion stared at him. 'Living in this Epsom place?'

'Well, one presumes that's her home, sir. But she spends most of her time in Switzerland, while her father is in Arabia.'

'Switzerland? You mean she's Swiss?'

'No, sir, she goes to school there. A sort of college for young ladies, what the English call a finishing school.'

'How old is this kid?'

'She was actually twenty-one last December, sir. This is her last

6

year at this school. She finishes . . .' he paused to smile at his little joke. 'In June.'

'She ain't relevant,' Cerdo growled.

'You don't think so?' MacGinnion asked. 'So where's the dough? This Allen live like a millionaire?'

'No, sir. Mr Allen appears to live very frugally.'

'With twenty million bucks under the bed.'

'Well, he sure ain't keeping it there,' Cerdo said. 'We know the set-up now. And it can only have been made for the dough. So when he gets back here—'

'What?' MacGinnion demanded. 'You aim to stand in front of Eddie Armitage and accuse him of dipping in the till? He'd break your goddamned neck.'

Cerdo had always suspected that MacGinnion was afraid of the Senior Partner, for all his size and air of menace. Now he was sure.

'Big Pat is right, Dominic,' said Kaley. 'And anyway, Mr Armitage is still The Boss to a lot of the guys. You could start some kind of civil war inside the Association.'

'The Feds would just love that,' MacGinnion said.

'So you don't mean to do nothing?' Cerdo was horrified.

'I aim to do plenty,' MacGinnion said. 'Let me think.' He gazed at them. 'You reckon this daughter knows anything about the money?'

'It seems unlikely, sir,' Hart said, 'seeing that her father isn't spending any of it.'

'Then what the hell is he stealing it for?' MacGinnion suddenly shouted.

Hart looked at Kaley.

Kaley cleared his throat. 'May I make a suggestion, Big Pat?'

'You better.'

'Well . . .' Kaley raised a thin hand, and ticked off his fingers. 'What do we know for sure? One: we know that Mr Armitage has been embezzling funds from the Association for ten years. Two: so far as I know, that's a capital offence under the code.' He looked at MacGinnion, but MacGinnion's expression did not change. Kaley went on. 'Three: it seems almost certain that the "Edwin Allen" cover is to do with the money, or why set it up?'

'Ah . . .' Hart cleared his throat, and Kaley glanced at him. 'I'm not sure we can make that assumption, Mr Kaley. As I have said,

7

this Julie Allen is twenty-one. And she knows nothing about her father being Edward Armitage. So he set up the Allen deception at least twenty-two years ago – but he only started embezzling ten years ago.'

'You sure he isn't really Allen and not Armitage at all?' Cerdo asked.

'He was Eddie Armitage when he got out of Dartmoor back in 1900,' MacGinnion said. 'And when he went in. I know. I was there with him. For Chrissake, we shared a cell. And he was Eddie Armitage when we came across together. Steerage. Christ, that was a voyage.' He glared at Kaley. 'So now you want me to bump off my oldest pal.'

'Who has stolen twenty million dollars,' Kaley reminded him.

'But how the hell is killing Eddie going to get our money back?' Cerdo demanded plaintively.

'I think the girl would be easier to work on than Mr Armitage,' Kaley said.

'But your bloodhound here says she don't know about the dough,' MacGinnion pointed out, keeping his temper with great difficulty.

'I think she may be the one to find out,' Kaley said.

'Come again?'

'The situation is this, Big Pat. We can't do anything about Mr Armitage while he is alive without causing a monumental bust-up inside the Association, right?'

'And we sure as hell can't do anything about him if he dies. Because everyone will point the finger at us if we start hunting through his house and apartment. Then we'll have both the police and Eddie's goons breathing down our necks.'

'Agreed. But why should he die?'

'You're losing me, Kaley.'

'Why shouldn't Mr Allen die instead?'

They stared at him.

'Of course, that would involve Mr Armitage disappearing. But he's always been a secretive character . . . Nobody would know what had happened to him. At least, not until we had regained the money.'

'And how the hell does Allen dying – and Armitage disappearing – help us to do that? If we try to muscle in on his estate, or Armitage's London set-up, we'll blow the whole thing.'

8

'Think about this, Big Pat. Allen dies—'

'How?'

Kaley's eyes took on a curiously hooded look. 'Leave that to me. It'll happen when he goes back to Epsom for the summer.'

'Okay. So he dies.'

'And this girl whatever her name is will inherit. She's his only daughter.'

'She'll inherit the house in Epsom, and whatever assets Allen has,' Hart reminded him. 'Nothing else.'

'Well, we don't know that, Calvin. There is at least a chance that this chick knows all about the twenty million. If she does, we're home and dry – even if we have to burn the soles off her feet.' He gave one of his rare smiles. 'Or anywhere else we fancy.'

'And if she doesn't?'

Kaley's eyes became even more hooded. 'I suggest we let her find out. Once she's done that she ain't going to stop looking. When this sweet little girl discovers her dear old daddy was head of the biggest vice ring in England – she doesn't have to know that he was actually running the biggest vice ring in the world – she's going to start asking questions. So, we let her ask questions. As far as anybody knows – Mr Armitage's boys or the girl – we don't know nothing about Allen, right? If we find out that he was really Armitage, we're going to be as surprised as anyone. Especially anyone in the Association. So we let this girl get on with finding out about her dad's past, because it's gotta be her past too, even if she don't know it. Then we let her get a sniff of the twenty million. She'll find it. By God, she'll find it.'

'There ain't no dame could resist looking for that kind of money,' Cerdo agreed.

'And she'll be doing the looking, not us. Our noses will be as clean as they have ever been to the Association. As far as the cops are concerned, at least in England, we don't even exist.'

'Until she finds the dough,' Cerdo said enthusiastically. 'And then . . .'

'You guys are nuts,' MacGinnion remarked. 'Just how the hell do we let this girl know she's sitting on twenty million without letting on we're her old man's partners?'

'I said, we ain't gonna come into it at all, Big Pat,' Kaley insisted. 'I know just the guy to do it. He's gonna lead that dame by the nose just as far as he needs to.'

MacGinnion frowned. 'One of us?'

Kaley nodded. 'He's based in England. But he's also the ideal man for the job. He don't have a heart; there's just a slab of ice in there. But can he act – he can play any role he wants to. And think of this. This chick is going to be desolated by her dad's death, right? According to Calvin there ain't no relatives. Well, how could there be with Mr Armitage's set-up? So this daughter ain't gonna have no one to turn to. Not even a shoulder to cry on. My boy will supply that shoulder. He is going to have this chick eating out of his hand in fifteen minutes flat. Don't ask me how he does it. But he's never failed me yet. And when he's briefed, he'll just lead her along, bit by bit.'

MacGinnion gazed at him for several seconds, then looked at Hart. 'You know this character?'

'No sir.'

'But you think it'll work?'

'I think it's worth a try. If we can have this Miss Allen straddling both camps, as it were, and trying desperately to find out who and what her father really was, why, probably even the Metropolitan Police would co-operate in helping her get to the bottom of things. And if it could be done without involving the Association . . .'

'That's the point,' Kaley said. 'It'd just be Armitage's English operation.'

'They could never produce twenty million profit.'

'Maybe. But is this schoolgirl going to know that? I will bet you a year's pay, Big Pat, that not only is she going to lead us to the money, but seeing as how she's Mr Armitage's daughter – even if she don't know it yet – she isn't going to figure on sharing it with anyone, which'll make our task of getting it away from her that much easier. What do you say?'

MacGinnion looked at Cerdo.

'I'm for it.'

'Yeah.' MacGinnion looked at Kaley again. 'Okay. Give it a whirl. But I want results, Kaley. And fast. You better remember that.'

Part One

LONDON

CHAPTER 1

'Mrs Simpson will see you now, Julie,' said Frau Haussmann. She was a large, severe-looking woman – Mrs Simpson liked her staff to look severe – but this morning she was on the verge of tears. Presumably some domestic crisis, Julie supposed, carefully straightening her tie. During the day Mrs Simpson made her girls dress in what she considered correct middle-European young ladies' attire: blue skirt, white blouse and stockings, low-heeled black shoes – not necessarily laced – and a neatly knotted plain blue tie. As the most senior girl in the Academy, Julie had daringly risked gold tassels on her courts this last year, and been allowed to get away with it. She supposed she could have got away with much more than that, had she wanted to. Few of Mrs Simpson's girls stayed until the ripe old age of twenty-one; in the four years Julie had been here, the pair of them had reached a certain *rapprochement*.

This had been partly due to Julie's character, partly due to her circumstances. Mrs Simpson knew that Julie's mother had died when the girl had been just a child, and that her father's job as an executive with British Petroleum kept him in the Middle East for most of every year. As these circumstances had made it necessary for Julie to remain at the Academy during the Easter holidays – although her father always made it a rule to be home for summer and Christmas – Mrs Simpson had soon come to realise that, her life founded in loneliness, Julie was a most self-possessed as well as introverted young woman. She had made few friends at the Academy, even amongst those who had been in her own age group when she had first arrived. Now that she was in an age group of her own, she had no close girl friends at all, although she got on well

13

with most of the other pupils. Neither had she ever shown a great deal of interest in the young men who from time to time were imported for dances, and who often requested the pleasure of taking one of Mrs Simpson's young ladies to the theatre. Such permission was sometimes granted, providing the young man came from a respectable background. When Julie had first been at the Academy the invitations had clustered thick and fast, for she was an intensely attractive young woman, not beautiful, but with her crisp features, her reddish-brown hair cut short and upswept, and her full, strong figure – she was a great walker in the foothills of the Alps as well as an expert skier and swimmer – she could draw a second glance from any man. Yet she had refused to accept any of them. Mrs Simpson had often tried to find out why, but had elicited only an, 'I'd rather not,' from her pupil. A severe case of father-fixation, Mrs Simpson had decided.

Julie herself was unaware of Mrs Simpson's opinions. She had refused to be dated because she could see no point in it. She enjoyed the theatre, but not to the extent of having her hand held throughout the performance, or her body fumbled whenever the lights were down – which was what the other girls told her was the invariable routine; she preferred to attend with Mrs Simpson and the Academy *en bloc* whenever there was anything really worth seeing.

In the eyes of the other girls, this made her something of an oddball. Yet it was not that Julie disliked men. In fact she dreamed of them every night, and sometimes during the day as well; the characters who peopled her dreams were the only true friends she possessed – that they nearly always looked like Father did not bother her; she fully expected to meet the right man and fall in love and marry and have dozens of children in the course of time.

But her circumstances, of being both an only child and half an orphan, had made Julie an intensely private person. She could hardly remember her mother, who had died when she was only seven, during the Great War. Father had been away a lot even then, although he had never been in the Army, and Julie had spent her adolescence at a girls' boarding school, her holidays – except for those magic weeks when Father was home – again boarded out at the homes of various friends. She had always been an outsider, and even then had rejected male company; men were cast in Father's image, or merely cast. Father, so gay and handsome, so knowledgeable and well travelled, so gentle, and yet with a streak of the finest steel lurking

14

behind his smile, and so vaguely, romantically mysterious, was clearly going to be difficult to replace. Not that there was any hurry about that. Indeed, this summer was going to be the finest ever, because she was leaving the Academy, and Father was taking an extra month off, and they were going to travel together. Presumably, during their travels he was going to broach the subject of what she did next. He might even bring up the question of marriage. She had no doubt she would want to do whatever he suggested.

With such a vacation to look forward to – and it was only a week away now – Julie hardly gave a thought to why she had been summoned from the middle of Professor Antoine's culture class to the study. Mrs Simpson would have some bee or other in her bonnet, which could be met by a quiet smile, and an inevitable response: 'I'll ask Daddy.'

Frau Haussmann was opening the door for her, which was unusual. Julie stepped through, and saw that Mrs Simpson was standing behind her desk, rather than sitting, which was equally unusual. She was also looking quite unnaturally distressed; her lorgnette, which she used to devastating effect, had fallen to the end of its chain, and dangled between her enormous breasts in a most derelict fashion.

And there was a man in the room. Not a young man, but then, Julie realised, he could hardly be described as old either. A remarkably handsome man, she discovered with faint surprise as she took him in; they too were unusual around the Academy. This man was not as tall as Father, slim, and, although he had a good pair of shoulders, with dark hair and a somewhat aquiline face, made her think of Mr John Gilbert, who was one of her favourite movie stars. He was also terribly well dressed – suit, shirt, tie and shoes all impeccable – and there was a carnation in his buttonhole. But his face, too, was twisting with some inner anguish as she entered.

'Julie,' Mrs Simpson said, and swept round the desk. 'Oh, my dear, dear girl.'

Julie realised she was about to be embraced, and caught her breath just in time; being lost in Mrs Simpson's ample flesh – she was a large woman in every way – could be a frightening experience. She allowed herself to be hugged, the breath to be squeezed from her lungs.

'My dear girl,' Mrs Simpson said again, 'Major Roberts is here.'

15

Released, Julie gazed at the man, who took a tentative step forward. Good Lord, she thought; am I to be embraced by him as well?

But he had stopped. 'I shouldn't think Julie remembers me,' he said.

Unlike Mr Gilbert, whose career had crashed with the coming of talkies and the discovery that he had a somewhat high-pitched voice, this man spoke in a deep and resonant tone. Julie couldn't place his accent, which sounded vaguely British and yet somehow clipped. Certainly she had never seen him before in her life; she looked to Mrs Simpson for an explanation.

'Major Roberts is a friend of your father's,' Mrs Simpson said. 'A very close friend.'

'Well . . . we belong to the same club,' Major Roberts explained. 'In London.'

'Oh,' Julie said. She didn't know that her father belonged to a London club. But presumably he did.

'Major Roberts has come . . . oh my dear, dear girl.' Mrs Simpson surged forward once again, and Julie tensed herself for another embrace, but this time an arm was merely flung round her shoulders. 'My dear, there has been the most terrible accident.'

Slowly Julie lifted her head.

'Accident,' Major Roberts snorted. 'By God, the villain should be . . .'

'Please tell me,' Julie said, surprised at the calm of her voice. 'Has something happened to Father?'

'Oh, my dear girl,' Mrs Simpson said, clutching her close and bursting into tears.

Julie did something she would never have supposed possible until this moment; she pushed Mrs Simpson away. 'What has happened?' she asked, her voice rising an octave.

'Well,' Major Roberts said, looking desperately at Mrs Simpson. 'Your father . . .'

'He's dead,' wailed Mrs Simpson. 'Oh, my God, he's dead.'

Julie sat down in one of the upholstered armchairs before the desk. Her legs felt quite strong, but she wasn't sure she wanted to stand up any more; the room had suddenly become filled with sound, a huge buzz which was threatening to burst her eardrums.

'Went for a walk . . .' Major Roberts' voice drifted through the

16

hum. 'In Epsom, would you believe it? Had just arrived . . . this tramp attacked him. Hit him on the head. In Epsom.' He sat down too, next to her.

'Dead,' Mrs Simpson wailed, and then sniffed. 'Dead,' she said in a lower tone.

Mrs Simpson was a consummate actress. Julie had known this for years but had never actually hated her until this moment, even if she knew the act as an attempt to convey sympathy.

Major Roberts took her hand. She looked down at the fingers with faint surprise; no man had ever held her hand, save Father.

'I know what a terrible shock this is,' he said. 'That's why I felt I had to come myself. I knew Eddie would have wanted that.'

Julie raised her head to look at Mrs Simpson again; this man was behaving as if she wasn't in the room.

Mrs Simpson didn't seem to mind. 'You have to go home,' she explained. She had her emotions back under control. 'There's the funeral, and . . . things. So Major Roberts . . . he'll escort you.'

Julie continued to look at her; she knew she was at least thirty-six hours away from England.

'There's a train in a couple of hours,' Major Roberts explained. 'We'll be in Calais by dawn, we'll catch the ferry and be in Epsom tomorrow afternoon.'

'Of course it's irregular,' Mrs Simpson said. 'But Major Roberts is an old friend of your father's, and I know, well . . .' she flushed, something Julie had never observed before. She clearly wanted to be rid of Julie, just as soon as possible. One of her girls involved in a murder? There was no way Mrs Simpson could accept that.

But there was no way she could accept it either. Her brain just could not. Father? Dead? Murdered? Julie stood up. 'I'd better pack,' she said.

They stared at her. She had not shed a tear, or made a comment. But she knew she had to get out of the office as quickly as possible.

'Of course,' Mrs Simpson said. 'And change. You are excused class.'

'Thank you.' She looked at Major Roberts. 'I . . .'

'I have a car waiting,' he said. 'It will take us to the station as soon as you are ready. We can lunch on the train.'

Lunch? Julie thought; I don't want lunch. But she said nothing, and left the room.

'Oh, Fräulein Julie,' Frau Haussmann wailed.

Julie side-stepped another possible embrace and ran along the corridor, up the stairs to her room. As the senior girl she had a room to herself, a treasured place. But now . . . she sat on the bed. The crashing in her ears had settled to a dull grind, but now it had entered her head and seemed to take hold of her brain. Father was dead? It was not believable, not acceptable, not possible. As long as she kept thinking that it could not be true. When she got to Epsom she would discover that it was all a mistake, and he would give that funny little laugh of his, and hold her tight, and then they would have dinner and gaze at each other across the table and look forward to the weeks ahead. When she got to Epsom.

Julie gazed at herself in the mirror over her washbasin. Her face hadn't changed in the past half an hour. Her eyes were dry. The Niagara gathered behind that high forehead was still dammed – by the power of her own will.

She pulled off her tie, dropped it and her blouse on the floor, added her skirt. They would be there when she came back. But was she coming back? She packed, hurriedly, anxiously, tossing clothes into the two suitcases, changing her white stockings for flesh-coloured ones, dressing in her normal travelling outfit; a dark blue pleated skirt and a pale blue tunic top which hung past her thighs; it had a huge, floppy, dark blue collar which exposed her throat. She tucked her hair into her felt cloche, threw her coat over her arm. All she wanted was to be away from here before she broke down.

Julie paused, biting her lip, gazing at the door. She could hear sounds from out there. Opening the door, she looked out at the staff and some of the other senior girls, assembled in the corridor. Old Wilhelm the porter was there too, waiting for her bags. She was hugged and kissed and people said things to her and she heard nothing. She ran down the stairs, and encountered Mrs Simpson yet again for another bear hug.

'Now, Julie,' Mrs Simpson whispered, remembering her responsibilities. 'I know Major Roberts is a friend, but you must take care. Lock your door on the train, and . . . I'd come with you, if I could, but . . .'

Come with me? Julie thought. You? That would be unbearable. 'I quite understand, Mrs Simpson,' she said, and turned away.

18

Wilhelm and the chauffeur were putting Julie's suitcases into the boot, and Major Roberts was holding the door open for her. She didn't look at him as she got in, but gazed through the window at the faces, slowly receding as the car moved away. No, she thought with sudden decision; I shan't be coming back.

They drove in silence, the lake on their left, the mountain rising beyond it, straight up to the sky. Lake Lucerne really was a conversation-stopper in any event, and Julie was glad of that. Major Roberts moved, once or twice, and she thought he might be going to hold her hand again, but as she refused to look at him, he did not risk it. Instead he said, as they entered Geneva itself, 'It might be better to let rip.'

Then Julie did turn her head. Could he possibly understand?

He smiled at her; it was the first time she had seen him smile, and she liked it. 'I can stand it,' he said. 'If you can.'

'Is Daddy really dead, Major Roberts?' she asked.

The smile faded into a frown. 'I'm afraid he is, Julie. I'm afraid he is.'

She turned her head away again. The street was full of shops and people, but they were just a blur. 'How well did you know him?' she asked.

'We've been acquaintances for years. But recently we've seen a lot of each other. In London,' he added. 'I suppose we got on well. He liked to talk – about you, quite often, about his hopes for you. He loved you very dearly. And he was very aware of how lonely you are. That's why, the moment I learned of his death, I knew what had to be done. I couldn't bear the thought of a couple of large bobbies turning up to tell you.'

'Did you know him in Arabia?'

'No. I'm in a different business. Julie . . . I hope you don't think I overstepped the mark. In coming for you, I mean.'

She turned back to him. 'I'm awfully grateful to you, Major Roberts.' She meant it. Somehow, having the news broken by a stranger who was yet not a total stranger helped to keep her wall erect, at least for the moment.

'Then why not call me Bob?' Another smile. 'Everyone else does.'

'I think . . . may I call you Uncle Bob?'

He raised his eyebrows, then shrugged. 'Why not? Until we get to know each other.'

19

When the car arrived at the station, Uncle Bob took care of everything – just as Father had always done. Julie had to do nothing but board the train, and be shown to her first-class sleeper. Uncle Bob's was next door. 'I imagine you'd like to be alone for a while,' he said. 'Join me in the dining-car at one.'

The train started to move. Julie locked the door, stretched out on the seats and stared up at the ceiling. Father. Beaten to death by a tramp? It was the most horrible thought she had ever had. It made her feel sick; a moment later Julie was vomiting into the little basin. Almost immediately there was a knock on the door connecting the two compartments; they could be turned into a double if so desired.

'Julie? Are you all right?'

Julie wiped her mouth, sat on the seat, and gasped.

'Julie?' Uncle Bob asked again.

She got up, unbolted the door and sat down again. 'I don't feel very well.'

He took in the situation at a glance, went back into his compartment, and returned with a glass. 'Drink this.'

She peered at it, nostrils twitching. 'What is it?'

'Brandy. It'll make you feel better.'

She wasn't sure about that. She had joined Father in the occasional after-dinner drink, but hadn't really enjoyed it. But now she knew she needed something. She gulped at the brandy. It set her chest on fire, but some of the pounding began to leave her head at the same time.

'Finish it off,' Uncle Bob urged. 'Medicinal.'

She obeyed. He was really just like Father. The compartment swayed for a few seconds, but that could have been the train going round a bend.

'How do you feel?' Uncle Bob asked, sitting beside her.

'Woozy.'

He put his arm round her shoulder, and held her against him. 'My dear girl,' he said. 'My poor darling.'

Oddly, she resented neither being held in his arms nor his words of endearment. She was realising that to be held in a pair of strong arms was just what she needed more than anything else at the moment. She rested her head on his shoulder, and he pulled off her hat, and smoothed her hair. Father had done that.

'Would you like the other half of that drink?' he asked.

20

'I couldn't. I wouldn't make lunch.'

'Are you hungry?'

'No,' she said.

He released her and stood up. 'Then I think another drink would be better for you.' He smiled at her. 'I'll join you, and then you can lie down and have a good sleep. It's the best thing. When you wake up, things'll seem better.'

He wasn't entirely right. Julie woke up with a start, realised it was still daylight, and that the train was still chugging along, occasionally emitting a piercing whistle. Then she noticed that her bed had been made up, that she was in it, beneath the sheet, and . . . she had been undressed. She looked down at herself in horror. Her skirt and tunic had been removed; she was wearing her slip, and her underclothes hadn't been interfered with, or her stockings. But still, the thought of . . . or had she done it herself? She couldn't remember a thing after that second drink, except yawning, and Uncle Bob smiling at her . . .

Julie turned her head and gazed at the still open door. Good Lord, she thought; whatever would Mrs Simpson say?

She knew she should be outraged. The thought of a strange man taking off even her outer clothing, touching her – because he would have had to: she almost thought she could still feel the imprint of his fingers – should have had her ringing for the guard. And yet, somehow she was sure that she hadn't been abused in any way, nor was she in the least frightened. Uncle Bob was the most reassuring man she had ever known, except for Father . . . and Father wasn't there any more. A tear rolled out of Julie's eye, and a moment later she had turned on her face and was sobbing her heart out. There were no thoughts, just huge sobs which racked her body and soaked her pillow. And which slowly subsided, leaving her exhausted, sprawled on the bed, the sheet half on the floor.

Suddenly Julie was aware of a hand on her naked shoulder. She raised her head. 'I'm glad that happened,' Uncle Bob said. 'If it hadn't, I'd have been scared stiff.'

'Were you . . .?' she sniffed.

He gave her a linen handkerchief, and she rose to her knees, and blew, vigorously. 'I was here. It's my business to be here, until . . . well, until you find your feet.'

She turned her head to look at him, and then down at herself. The sheet was gone, the slip had ridden up to her thighs and she wasn't doing much good at the top end either; her brassière was half exposed. Hastily she tugged it straight.

'I hope you don't mind,' he said.

She shook her head. She didn't. She didn't know what she would have done without him there.

'Well, I'm going to close the door now,' he said. 'I want you to wash your face and dress yourself – there's no need to change – and then we'll go along and have a bite of supper. Hungry yet?'

Julie realised she was. 'Yes,' she said. He squeezed her shoulder, and stood up, and impulsively she held his hand. 'Uncle Bob . . . thanks.'

He raised his eyebrows. 'For what?'

'Just . . . for being here.'

'Mr Cornwall will see you right away, Miss Allen,' said the clerk, and looked at Uncle Bob, who had also got up. 'I think Mr Cornwall would like to see Miss Allen alone, sir.'

'Oh, of course,' Uncle Bob said and sat down again.

Julie smiled at him. Amazing, that she could smile at all. And yet, it was easy to smile at Uncle Bob. Had it not been for the tragedy which had lurked at the back of her mind, the journey from Geneva would have been the most memorable of her life. That was an awfully unfair thing to think, with poor Father just dead, but it was true. Uncle Bob had been like a younger version of Father come to life. They had dined, gazing at each other, and he had brushed his wineglass against hers, the way Father had always done. And later they had sipped an after-dinner liqueur – cherry brandy for her, this time – sitting together on her bunk and gazing out of the window at the night sky; Uncle Bob had been so reassuring she hadn't even wanted to lock the separating door. He had insisted she do that, after kissing her goodnight. On the forehead.

They had promenaded, wrapped up in their coats against the chill sea-breeze, as the ferry had crossed the Channel, and they had sat opposite each other in the first-class compartment as they had journeyed up from the coast.

Only during the last part of the journey had she been subdued, now that the adventure of travelling with a strange man was about to end, and the reality of being an orphan about to begin. Yet Julie had the strangest feeling that she was not going to be alone, that Uncle Bob was going to be there through all the ordeal that lay ahead. It was odd that she could not remember meeting him before, but as he had told her, it had been several years ago, when she had just been a young teenager, and he must have seemed terribly old. She had not had the nerve to ask him if he was married. A man this attractive would surely be – but she had no doubt that his wife was going to be just as nice.

She didn't think she could say the same about Mr Cornwall, who was tall and thin and severe, with rimless glasses and thinning hair. He made her think of a male Mrs Simpson, an emaciated Mrs Simpson. Now he took her hand, but his fingers were cold. 'Miss Allen,' he said. 'Julie. We haven't met before.'

'Father has spoken of you,' Julie said.

Cornwall showed her to a chair in front of his desk. 'I have been your father's solicitor for more years than I care to remember.' He sat down himself, peered at her. 'You're looking very well.' Clearly he meant, too well for a recently bereaved daughter.

She decided to ignore that. 'Can I see Daddy, please?'

'I don't think that would be a very good idea. You see, the murder took place nearly a week ago, and it wasn't very nice, and . . .'

'He was beaten to death,' she said. 'Uncle Bob told me. I would still like to see him.'

'I'll have a word with Inspector Rodham. He's in charge of the case.' He picked up his telephone. 'Get me Inspector Rodham, if you will, Toby. Thank you.' He replaced the receiver. 'Your father is still at the police mortuary, you see. But he'll be released for the funeral. That's tomorrow.'

Just as if he were a criminal, Julie thought, and suddenly felt very antagonistic towards Mr Cornwall, and the police, and everyone in the world. Everyone except Uncle Bob. 'When are they going to try the man who killed him?' she asked.

'Well, I suppose they have to catch him first,' Mr Cornwall said, placing a file on his desk.

'You mean they haven't caught him?' She couldn't believe her ears. 'But . . . isn't he a tramp?'

'It seems likely,' Mr Cornwall said. 'It seemed to be an unpremeditated attack. It isn't as if your father had any enemies. Indeed I would have said that he was well loved in the community. Oh, the police will catch the fellow. They always do. Now tell me ؛ . . .' he gazed at her. 'Did you have a safe journey back?'

She frowned. It seemed an odd way of putting it. 'Of course.'

'That man . . . well, I was very unhappy about the whole thing, Julie. But when I telephoned Mrs Simpson she assured me that you could look after yourself.'

'I don't know what you're talking about,' Julie said.

'I am talking about this so-called Major Roberts.'

Julie's frown deepened. 'So-called?'

'Well . . . I've checked the army lists and they don't seem to know anything about him.'

'But he's a friend of Father's.'

'Ah.' Mr Cornwall seemed greatly relieved. 'You mean you know him.'

'Well, no. I'd never met him before yesterday. No, that's not right. I did meet him, I think, but a long time ago. Anyway, he said he was.'

'Quite,' Mr Cornwall said, no longer so relieved.

'He knew everything about Daddy.'

'Did he now? Well, I suppose he could be genuine. Of course, I myself have no knowledge of your father's friends and acquaintances in the desert or—'

'Uncle Bob wasn't in the desert,' she explained. 'He and Father belong to the same London club.'

'Uncle Bob?' Mr Cornwall raised his eyebrows, then picked up the receiver as the phone rang. 'Ah, Inspector, look, I have Julie Allen with me; she would like to see her father's body. I know . . .' he said, frowning as he listened. He replaced the receiver. 'He'd like you to go down to the station now. If you feel up to it.'

Julie stood up. 'Yes,' she said. 'Yes. Uncle Bob can take me.'

'Uncle Bob,' Mr Cornwall said again. 'Well, if you're sure. But later I want to talk to you about your father's affairs. Look, will you give me a ring when you're finished at the station, and I'll drive over and meet you at the house. Mrs Lucas, the housekeeper, is there.'

'Yes,' she said. 'Thank you.'

'So you're going to move straight in,' Uncle Bob remarked, as the taxi drove them into the station.

24

'Well, it seems the best thing. I don't know if I have any money, or anything.'

'I'm quite sure you do, but until it's all straightened out, you're my responsibility.'

'Oh, I couldn't. I mean . . .' she looked at him. What Cornwall had said had upset her. 'Uncle Bob, how come you're a major? Are you still in the army?'

'Good Lord, no. And it was the New Zealand army.'

'Oh,' she said, relief flooding through her system. 'That accounts for your accent.'

'Do you know, I always think I sound like a true-blue English-man. Actually, I don't suppose I should use the rank any more, although I was a major when I got out. But it's good for business, you see.'

'Of course,' she agreed. How easy it was to relax in this man's company, even if the time for relaxing was over for the moment; the car had stopped in the police station yard, and a uniformed officer was opening the door for her.

'Miss Allen? The Inspector is waiting.'

Julie was ushered through the charge room, where the duty sergeant attempted to look sympathetic, and into an office at the back, Uncle Bob at her shoulder.

'Miss Allen.' Inspector Rodham was short and fair. 'I wish these were happier circumstances. But I am very glad to have you here. Major.'

Uncle Bob shook hands. 'I hurried,' he said.

'Oh, quite. I understand you would like to see your father's body, Miss Allen.'

'Yes,' Julie said.

'Oh, here, I say,' Uncle Bob protested. 'Is that necessary? I made the identification.'

'Yes, sir,' Rodham agreed. 'But you are not actually a relative. I know it will be a pretty ghastly ordeal for you, Miss Allen, but I would be grateful if you could positively identify your father.'

'Yes,' Julie said.

The Inspector picked up his cap. 'My car is waiting.' He looked at Uncle Bob. 'Would you mind remaining here, sir? We won't be long.'

Uncle Bob looked at Julie.

'I think I'd rather be alone, Uncle Bob,' she said.

He nodded. 'Of course.'

The Inspector took Julie outside to the police car, and sat beside her in the back. 'Your father has of course been kept under refrigeration,' he said, perhaps in an attempt to reassure her. When she didn't reply, he searched for words. 'It's difficult to express one's feelings in a case like this,' he said. 'I am most terribly sorry.'

'Will you catch the murderer?' Julie asked.

'Ah . . . the morgue is just along here. We'll certainly do our best to catch him, Miss Allen. But we may need some assistance. From you.'

'From me?'

The car was stopping, and he didn't reply. Instead a uniformed constable got out of the front and opened the door for her. Then Inspector Rodham was showing her into a very cold room, with an odd smell, and she was gazing at a face she recognised, and yet didn't. It was a face she didn't want to recognise. It had been washed clean of blood, but the expression was wrong, and the bruises were wrong, and she felt sick again.

Inspector Rodham held her arm and helped her outside. 'I know what an experience that was,' he said. 'But I also know that you want us to catch the murderer. Miss Allen, you simply have to tell us the truth about your father.'

She blinked at him, unsure about what he was saying.

'Miss Allen,' he repeated, urgently. 'We know that your father never worked for British Petroleum in his life.'

CHAPTER 2

Julie could only stare at him.

'Didn't you know that?' the Inspector asked, gently.

'I don't know what you're saying,' she said. Her mind was still filled with the sight of that face, so well remembered, so peaceful, so bloody.

'Miss Allen – Julie . . .' the Inspector almost took her hand, but changed his mind. 'I am sure you want your father's murderer to be brought to justice as much as any of us. But to do that, we have to have the facts. Now, your father came down here last Sunday, according to his housekeeper. Did you know he was here?'

Julie nodded. 'He telephoned the Academy when he arrived at the house. He always did that.' Father, not work for British Petroleum? She just could not understand how this silly man could say something like that.

'Where did he say he'd come from?'

'Dover. He always took the overland train from Naples. That's where the boat from Port Said dropped him, you see.'

The Inspector gazed at her for a few seconds, saw the tears gathering in the huge green eyes. 'Yes,' he said, still endeavouring to speak gently. 'Well, it appears that he went for a walk that same evening, after Mrs Lucas had gone home, and was attacked by a tramp, killed for what money he had on him. That in itself is not a very usual form of murder these days. But when we checked up with your father's supposed employers, and found that they not only do not employ him, but had never heard of him . . .'

'I don't know what you mean,' Julie insisted, her voice high. 'Daddy worked for BP. He always did.' The noise was back in her ears.

27

Inspector Rodham studied her as the car drove into the station yard. He could tell she wasn't lying. 'How well do you know this Major Roberts?' he asked.

Just like Mr Cornwall, she thought. 'He's a friend of Father's,' she said.

'You've known him for some time.'

She gazed at the policeman. Uncle Bob was the only rock to which she could hold. Daddy not work for British Petroleum? The whole world had to be upside down. 'Yes,' she said. 'He has been a friend of Daddy's for years.' And then, remembering Mr Cornwall, 'He was in the New Zealand army.'

'Ah,' Inspector Rodham said with some relief. 'So he knew your father in the desert.'

'No,' Julie said. 'He didn't. They were members of the same club, in London.' A tear trickled down her cheek. 'Please,' she said. 'Please let me go home.'

He hesitated. 'Yes,' he said at last. 'I think that would be a good idea.' He picked up a large manila envelope which lay on the seat beside him. 'You'll want these; your father's effects.'

Julie took the envelope. The last of Father, she thought.

'I've kept his passport for the time being,' Inspector Rodham told her. 'In view of all the circumstances. I have a lot more investigating to do. And I'd be most grateful if you'd think about everything I've said and whether you may be able to help us. Because, you see, if your father was not who he appeared to be, then there could be some entirely unsuspected motive for the murder. I am assuming you want the murderer caught?'

'Yes,' she said. 'Oh, yes.'

'Then I'd like you to see if you can remember anything which might give us some clue as to what your father really was. I want you to telephone me tomorrow. By then we may have some idea as to whether we're dealing with a simple case of assault and battery, resulting in death, or a very complex case, involving some fictitious life of your father's.'

'Fictitious?' she cried.

'I'm afraid that is how it looks to us. Now, I believe you've told me the truth here today. I'm sorry I had to present it so brutally. But we simply have to learn the truth, if you follow me. I know that you're as anxious to get to the bottom of this business as we are. I'd like to

28

talk to you again tomorrow.' He pulled out his notebook and scribbled a number, tore out the sheet and gave it to her.

The car was pulling into the station yard. 'But,' Julie said, 'if Daddy wasn't an executive for British Petroleum, who was he?'

'That is what we have to find out, Miss Allen,' Inspector Rodham said.

The sense of unreality grew. What he had just said was not acceptable. But then, the fact of Father's death was not acceptable. And then to suggest that Father was not what he had claimed to be . . . that was the least acceptable of all. Julie got out of the car and gazed at Uncle Bob, who was waiting for her.

'Was it terrible?' he asked.

For a moment she didn't know what he was talking about.

'Miss Allen was able to make a positive identification,' answered Inspector Rodham.

Uncle Bob ignored him. 'Was it terrible?' he asked again.

'Yes,' Julie said. 'Will you take me home please, Uncle Bob?'

'Right away.' He glanced at the Inspector. 'I assume we're free to go?'

'Anywhere you like. Miss Allen has my telephone number,' Rodham said, meaningfully.

'Oh . . . could I telephone Mr Cornwall and tell him we're leaving,' Julie said. 'He was going to meet me at the house.'

'Excellent,' Inspector Rodham said. 'I'll do it for you.'

He went into the station; Uncle Bob sat beside her in the back of the taxi, which had by now run up an astronomical figure on the meter. 'What the devil was all that about?'

'God,' she said. 'It's all so confusing. Uncle Bob, how well did you know Father?'

'We were friends. I mean, same club . . . but more than that. I told you, we sort of liked each other from the start.'

Julie stared at the back of the taxidriver's head. 'Inspector Rodham says Father never worked for BP.'

'Come again?' Uncle Bob was frowning.

She turned, wildly, anxiously. 'That's what he said. BP say they've never heard of him. Oh, Uncle Bob . . .' she threw herself into his arms. Uncle Bob had the most comforting arms in the world.

29

'That has got to be a load of codswallop,' Uncle Bob said. But his tone was not altogether convincing.

Julie's head had been resting on his chest. Now she pushed herself straight. 'But you think they could be right.'

'Julie,' he said. 'Of course I don't.'

'So tell me,' she said. 'How well did you know Father?'

'Only that we were members of the same club.'

'And he told you he worked for BP.'

'Well, of course he did.'

'But did he ever show you any proof?'

'Well, of course he didn't. I didn't ask for any. Julie, my dear girl . . .' he held her shoulders. 'This is your father we're talking about. You surely can't believe he'd lie to me? Or you? Or anyone?'

Her shoulders sagged, and the tears began again. So mysterious. That had been Father's principal characteristic, and perhaps his most attractive one . . .

Uncle Bob gave her his handkerchief, and Julie dried her eyes. 'It's all so – I just can't believe it.'

'We'll sort it out,' he said. 'But I really don't think it's a good idea for you to stay in that house all alone.'

She raised her head to look at him, and he flushed.

'Well . . .'

'I have to go there,' she said, uncertain what she really wanted him to do. Somehow, while travelling across Europe with him had been an adventure, to have him actually in the same house seemed definitely improper. And yet, she didn't want to let him out of her sight. Her world was spinning too far out of control. The taxi stopped, and she looked at her home. The garden was as neat as ever; by looking along the side of the house she could even tell that the lawn at the back had been recently mown; Father employed a local man to take care of it. The front door was open, and Mrs Lucas was standing there. She was Father's daily, and she kept the inside as immaculate as Harry kept the garden.

'Oh, Miss Julie,' she said, and embraced her. 'I can't believe it.'

Julie went inside, sniffed Father's tobacco. Uncle Bob had brought in the bags, while Mrs Lucas stared at him.

'This is Major Roberts, Mrs Lucas,' Julie explained. 'He's a friend of Father's.'

'Ah,' Mrs Lucas said, and shook hands. 'I'll take the bags, sir.'

30

She took one in each hand and climbed the stairs. Julie went into the lounge, gazed at the bar, then the rolltop desk in the corner. Father kept that desk locked. But Father had apparently kept so much locked.

'I think you could use a drink,' Uncle Bob said.

She nodded, watching another car draw up at the gate. Of course; Mr Cornwall would know. But why hadn't he said something before?

She hurried to open the door, and the solicitor peered at her. 'Pretty awful, was it?'

'Yes,' she said, closing the door behind them.

'Just pouring,' said Uncle Bob. 'Will you join us?'

'Thank you, no,' Mr Cornwall said. 'Do you feel like having a chat, Julie?'

'Oh, yes,' Julie replied.

Mr Cornwall looked at Uncle Bob.

'I'd like Uncle Bob to stay, please,' Julie said, sitting down on the settee. Uncle Bob handed her a glass of sherry; he had taken a whisky and water for himself.

'Very well.' Mr Cornwall looked around the room, decided against the desk, and sat beside her. He placed his briefcase on his knee and flipped the lid up. 'It's all very straightforward. You are your father's sole heir, and you are, fortunately, over twenty-one. Therefore you now own this house, and you have the right to all his possessions. These include . . .' he opened the file. 'The motor car in the garage.' He peered at her. 'Do you drive?'

'No,' she said. She had been going to learn this summer; there had never seemed any reason to before.

'Ah, then perhaps you should sell it. That would probably be a good idea anyway. The fact is . . .' Mr Cornwall tapped the file. 'There isn't very much cash, I'm afraid.' Again he peered at her, and she looked back uncomprehendingly. 'Your father had his salary as a British Petroleum executive, of course, which was paid into his bank account every month, less a proportion which went direct to Saudi Arabia, but I'm afraid he spent most of it. Let me see . . .' he looked into the file. 'There is four thousand pounds on deposit, and three hundred and forty-five in the current account.'

That seemed quite a lot to Julie. But she wasn't interested in money right this minute.

31

'The release of the money will have to await probate, of course,' Mr Cornwall went on. 'But I have no doubt, as there are no other heirs or bequests, that I can arrange with the bank to provide you with sufficient funds to live on for the time being.'

'So you won't starve,' Uncle Bob said. 'And as soon as the will is probated, I'll be able to give you a hand sorting out your investments.'

Mr Cornwall peered at him in turn. 'There are no investments, Major.'

Uncle Bob put down his whisky. 'I'm not with you.'

'Mr Allen had no investments,' Mr Cornwall stated.

'But that's absurd. We'll check out his safe deposit . . .'

'Mr Allen does not have a safe deposit, either. I have handled his affairs for nearly twenty years, and I can tell you that his sole possession is this house. He did not even carry any life insurance. I often raised the point with him, but he said he didn't believe in it.'

'That has got to be nonsense,' Uncle Bob declared.

'Twenty years?' Julie asked.

'Just on. He bought this house in the spring of 1912. Of course, my father handled that, but I remember your father and mother quite well.' He gave one of his frosty smiles. 'You were just a baby.'

'You mean you've known Daddy for twenty years?'

'Of course I have.'

'And has he always worked for British Petroleum?'

'Ever since I've known him. I was just coming to that. I am quite sure that he must have belonged to some sort of pension scheme. As a matter of fact, I have already written to the company informing them of his tragic death, and asking for information. As to whether such a pension will be payable after his death I cannot say, but I would estimate there should be something.'

'But . . .' Julie looked at Uncle Bob; the spinning world was gathering pace.

'The police have told Julie that her father did not work for British Petroleum,' Uncle Bob said. 'That he never has.'

Mr Cornwall frowned at him. 'But that's nonsense.'

'Quite,' Uncle Bob said. 'Everything about this business is nonsense. How do you know he worked for BP?'

'He told me that he did. Always had. And his salary arrived every month . . .'

'From where?'

'Why . . . a transfer from a London bank.'

'Oh, God,' Julie whispered. 'Oh, God, oh, God, oh God.'

'This is really absurd,' Mr Cornwall declared. 'I'll get on to it right away, Julie. If your father didn't work for British Petroleum, what did he do?'

'Quite,' Uncle Bob said.

'I think our best bet is to ask Mrs Lucas to sleep with you here,' Uncle Bob said. They gazed at each other across the lunch table. Mrs Lucas had prepared a tasty meal, but Julie had not eaten anything; she was keeping her sherry down with an effort.

'Yes,' she said. 'I must find the key to the desk.' She got up, and he caught her hand.

'Julie, you're being just magnificent. Most girls would be having the screaming heebie-jeebies by now.'

'Yes,' she said. She could have them any minute. He followed her into the lounge, and they gazed at the desk.

Then he put his arm round her shoulder. 'It's going to be all right, you know. I'm going to make sure it's all right. Because Eddie was my friend. And I just know he was on the up and up. Just as I know he was a wealthy man.'

'How do you know that?' Julie asked.

'Why . . . his lifestyle. His clothes. Besides, he told me so.'

She raised her head, frowning.

'He showed me a picture of you, once,' Uncle Bob explained, 'and said, "that little girl of mine is going to be as rich as Croesus one of these days". The key is probably amongst those effects the police gave you.'

She gave a little shudder, then emptied the envelope on to the table. There were two sets of keys, as well as a wedding ring and a pen – Father did not carry a lot. Not even a piece of string, she thought absently.

'May I?' Uncle Bob picked up the keys.

'Yes. Please.'

She stood beside him while he tried first one and then another. The fourth key opened the desk, and he rolled up the top. 'You'd better do it.'

She sat down, hunted through the pigeon holes. Father had been very neat. There was a stack of statements from his bank in Epsom, revealing that monthly figure paid in, and also, as Mr Cornwall had indicated, that most of it was utilised by the various cheques drawn against it. The cancelled cheques were there as well, in another neat pile, and also a neat pile of receipted accounts. There were also several unpaid accounts, but all recent. Father had only just arrived here when he had been killed. From Saudi Arabia. But it hadn't been Saudi Arabia.

'Would you like me to take care of these for you?' Uncle Bob asked.

She shook her head. 'I can do it. I have an account of my own.' She shrugged. 'There's not much in it.'

'We'll have that four thousand released just as soon as we can, or at least enough of it for you to live on. But . . . we have to find those investments.'

'We have to find Daddy,' she said.

He rested his hand on her shoulder. 'We're going to do that, Julie. I am going to do that. What about the drawer?'

But the drawer contained only a few old envelopes, addressed to Edwin Allen, containing letters from various local authorities. She flicked through them hurriedly. One was from the Golf Club. But none of them was personal. Julie had the oddest feeling that Father had in fact never lived here.

'Let's go upstairs,' Uncle Bob suggested.

Julie had not wanted to go into Father's room. But she followed Uncle Bob, watched him as he opened the wardrobe and the drawers, peered at the suits. 'Every one Savile Row,' he said.

Julie sat on the bed, suddenly aware of a creeping exhaustion. 'What am I going to do, Uncle Bob?'

'You're not going to worry.' He sat beside her, putting his arm round her shoulders. 'I am going to sort everything out. I said I would. Now I tell you what I'm going to do. Tomorrow, after the funeral, I'm going to go back up to town, to the club, and start checking. I'm going to find out everything about your dad, and then I'll come back down here and we'll work everything out. How does that sound.'

She raised her head. 'You're spending so much time . . . your family?'

'What family?'

'Don't you have a family?'

'You're all the family I have, right now,' he said. 'Or want.' He kissed her on the lips.

It was a perfectly chaste kiss, and yet she was surprised. Perhaps he was too; he moved his head back to gaze at her. But he wasn't embarrassed. 'I mean that,' he said.

'Oh, Uncle Bob.' She was in his arms, held tightly, while his hands stroked her shoulders and back. She could feel the passion in his fingers, felt there were things he wanted to do, and they were sitting on a bed, but she still did not fear him. She knew he would never harm her. She just knew it. As for whether she wanted him to *become* passionate, she wasn't prepared to think about that right now. For one thing, he was so much older, and for another, she wasn't prepared to feel passion herself, with anyone, until she had had a chance to think, and understand. That Father was dead, and had been living a lie. That she should be mourning desperately, instead of feeling betrayed and angry.

But she didn't want him to let her go, either.

'I think you had better have a rest,' he said. 'I must be off.'

It had not occurred to her that he would not be staying at the house; his overnight case had been brought in with her bags.

'Will you come back?' she asked. 'For dinner?'

He stood up, looked down at her. 'If you'd like me to.'

She grasped his hand. 'I would like you to, Uncle Bob.'

'Then perhaps you'd drop the uncle.'

'If you really want me to.'

'I really want you to.'

She stood up, and he took her in his arms. I don't really want this, she thought. I don't. But yet she did. Here in his arms was the only sane place on earth. And perhaps the only safe place as well. She turned up her face and he kissed her again. But this was not chaste. She had not been tongue kissed before, and she was again surprised, so surprised she involuntarily stepped backwards; her knees struck the mattress and she fell over, carrying him with her. He was lying half across her, and suddenly she could feel him against her. He wants to make love to me, she realised. But he can't want to do that; he could be my father. She couldn't possibly have a lover, now. And Uncle Bob . . . he was still kissing her, and his

35

right hand was sliding down her side to the curve of her buttocks and then up again, moving gently over her brassière as if to make sure she was wearing one. What will I do, she wondered, if he starts to undress me? She simply did not know.

His head moved away suddenly. 'I am terribly sorry.'

He looked genuinely contrite, but she was so out of breath she couldn't speak.

He pushed himself up, straightened his tie; the carnation had fallen from his buttonhole. 'I just – you are so absolutely adorable. But at a time like this . . .' He stood up, and looked down at her. 'Do you still want me to come to dinner?' he asked.

She licked her lips; they had gone numb. She felt as if her brain had suddenly fallen into two parts. One part was saying, no, I don't want you to come for dinner, not if you're going to do anything like that again. But the other was saying, I mustn't let him go, no matter what is involved, because if he lets go of me I am going to crumple up and die.

'Yes,' she said. 'I'm sure.'

Mrs Lucas had consented to spend the night, and perhaps tomorrow night as well. She was doubtful of any time after that; her husband wasn't too pleased at the idea. But Julie was relieved that she was spending this night. Because she had no idea what was going to happen, and even less than this afternoon of what she wanted to happen. It occurred to her that she was more frightened than ever before in her life. She would have been frightened anyway, by Father's death. But in addition, by this sudden suggestion that he had been living a lie . . . why? And now Uncle Bob – Bob!

She put on a cocktail dress and added a little make-up; a touch of powder and a hint of scarlet lipstick. Mrs Simpson never allowed her girls to wear make-up, but Father had liked her to use it when she was home.

Bob arrived with a cold bottle of champagne, and mixed them each a cocktail. 'Correct seduction procedure,' he said, smiling at her and handing her a flute. She gazed at him, and he flushed; he had kissed her forehead as he came in. 'I'd like to apologise for this afternoon.'

He sat down beside her on the settee. 'It was unforgivable, taking advantage of you like that. It would have been unforgivable at any time, but right now . . .' He held his glass to her lips, brought hers to his. 'But oh, how adorable you are,' he whispered.

She sipped, and immediately felt more in command of herself; there was an awful lot of brandy in the cocktail.

She licked her lips. 'You're being so kind. I don't know what I'd do without you—'

'But right now you have more important things on your mind. That's entirely understandable. And I was terribly forward. It's just that you are so utterly lovely. So utterly desirable.'

'Me?' She was incredulous.

'Didn't anyone ever tell you that before?'

'Of course not.'

'Then I'm just lucky. I would like . . .' he gazed into her eyes. 'When you feel like talking about it.'

Julie drank some more champagne. 'Now.'

'I would like to devote a lot more time to looking after you,' he said.

'Would you?' The idea sounded entrancing, but it was less entrancing if it involved him making love to her.

'You don't like the idea of a slightly older man? I'm not quite forty, you know.'

'Oh,' she said again. She had put him down as more than that. But she couldn't decide why.

'Does the idea not appeal to you at all? I thought, this afternoon . . .'

She fell back on the oldest of defences. 'We've only known each other three days.'

'I've known you much longer than that. I've told you, your father spoke of you all the time, showed me photographs. I feel I've known you all your life.'

That just didn't sound like Father. It wouldn't have sounded like Father anyway. But if in addition he had been living some kind of double life, then it just didn't make sense to go telling comparative strangers all about this life. But she couldn't believe that Bob would lie about a thing like that.

He put down his flute, took hers from her hand and put that down as well. He's going to kiss me again, she thought. And then? It was incredible. Had any other man made this kind of advance she'd have slapped him so hard she'd have blacked his eye. Yet with Bob she was only aware of not wishing to offend him. Even if he stretched her out on this settee here and now? Her brain began to spin again.

'Ahem,' said Mrs Lucas from the doorway.

Oh, thank God for Mrs Lucas.

Mrs Lucas remained in close attention all evening, and the mixture of the champagne cocktails, the wine with dinner, and her own emotional exhaustion had Julie yawning at nine o'clock. Bob did not seem offended and kissed her goodnight. 'I'll collect you tomorrow at ten,' he said.

'Oh, Lord. I've nothing to wear. I just don't have anything black.'

'Leave it with me,' he said, as reassuringly as ever.

'Was he really a friend of your father's, Miss Julie?' Mrs Lucas asked after the door had closed.

'Yes. Yes, he was.'

'Hmm,' commented Mrs Lucas. 'Strange he never visited here before. I think you need a good night's sleep, young lady. Would you like a couple of aspirins? It won't do you any good to lie awake brooding.'

Julie thought there was no chance of that, but took the aspirins anyway, and then discovered that however tired she was, sleep wasn't going to be that simple. She slept very heavily until about one, and then was suddenly wide awake, her brain seething. There was so much to think about, but she had nothing to think with. Her mind was a mass of images; of Father's face, of Father's lies – if they were lies – the possibility that the crime was not just a robbery.

She felt guilt that she was not lying here weeping her heart out all over again. Father had now been dead for a week. But he had been a stranger before then, obviously. She knew she was angry about that. Her entire life had been built around that man, but he had only given her a tiny portion of his. Yet she wanted him . . . avenged? Or simply, the mystery of what he had really done to be solved?

But most of all she found herself thinking of Bob. She owed him more than just her sanity; he had also helped to drive aimless thoughts about Father into the back of her mind. But what he had done . . . She had not allowed herself to think about it before, in case she had hysterics all over again. Now, in the privacy of her bed, she wanted to. She could still taste his kiss. It had been experienced as well as passionate – well, he was thirty-nine after all. He would certainly have kissed lots of girls. But it had been the most exciting thing that had ever happened to her, and the excitement had been compounded by the feel of him against her, the touch of his hand . . . she touched her own breast, and shivered. She knew she was somewhat backward as regards sex. It had been a personal choice, part of refusing to be dated at Mrs Simpson's. Thus she had never known a touch like that before, and if Mrs Simpson's marriage classes – which she had always taken herself – had gone into a wealth of detail, most of it, as expressed by Mrs Simpson, had been made to sound rather unpleasant. Certainly not the least exciting. Although some of the girls had managed to get quite aroused by it all.

She had not. Excitement with a man, she had always been sure, would come from being with him, looking into his eyes, watching him smile. That she and her husband would have sex together was obvious, but it would flow out of that strong romantic attraction. The idea that a man she hardly knew could seize her and kiss her and stroke her breast and actually touch her bottom, and that she would be excited by it, was the most frightening thing of all.

And yet she could not help thinking: if only it hadn't been Uncle Bob, but someone younger, and – she didn't know what else.

Eventually she slept again, and awoke feeling quite rested, and perhaps because of the aspirins, much calmer than yesterday. She had a hot tub, looking down at her long, slender body as if she had never seen it before; the boyishly narrow hips, and then the surprisingly large breasts, normally flattened by the fashionably tight brassière. You are so desirable, he had said. How did he know that? Of course, he had undressed her on the train. She sat up at the memory of it, leaping out of the bath a moment later. She had never been embarrassed by her own body before.

She dressed in the most sombre clothes she possessed, a grey suit to which she added a white blouse. Bob was there punctually at ten. As reliable as ever, he had bought a black headscarf for her to wear, and a black armband for himself. 'You look a lot better,' he remarked, and kissed her forehead.

There was a surprisingly large turn-out for the funeral; Edwin Allen had become a well-known and well-liked figure in Epsom over the past twenty years. The rector was there to shake her hand,

and she was shown to the front pew, where she sat between Bob and Mr and Mrs Cornwall. Then after the service, before she, Bob, and the Cornwalls drove to the crematorium, there were more than a dozen people waiting to shake her hand. Some of them were vague acquaintances; most were strangers.

'My dear girl,' Mrs Cornwall said, when they left the crematorium. 'If there is anything I can do, anything at all you need . . .'

'Thank you very much,' Julie said.

'I'll be in touch as soon as I hear from BP,' Mr Cornwall said.

Julie nodded, glancing at Bob.

'You'll be going back up to London now, I suppose, Major,' Mr Cornwall said.

Bob nodded. 'I'm catching the twelve o'clock train. I plan to do a little investigating of my own.'

'Yes,' Mr Cornwall said. 'Well, no doubt you'll be in touch.'

Bob dropped Julie and Mrs Lucas back at the house. 'The service took longer than I had expected,' he said. 'I simply have to rush.'

'Yes,' she said, standing beside the car. Mrs Lucas had already gone inside, but she was waiting by the door.

'I think she thinks she's protecting you,' Bob remarked.

'Yes,' Julie agreed.

'Do you feel you need protecting? Because of yesterday? God, if you knew what a heel I feel. But the sight of you, so adrift and yet so beautiful . . .'

She didn't want to offend him, so for the first time, she kissed him, gently on the lips. 'You are forgiven, really. Now, I'd like you to hurry back,' she said.

'Julie . . .' his hand was tight on hers.

'Let me think, Bob,' she said. 'Please. And I can't do that until I know something about Father.'

He nodded. 'I'll hurry. You just have a good rest.'

She waved the car out of sight and then went inside.

'I think you want to watch him,' Mrs Lucas said. 'He has lecher written all over him. Are you *sure* he was a friend of your father's?'

'Yes,' Julie said.

Mrs Lucas shook her head. 'Then he has no business behaving like that.'

'Behaving like what?' Julie asked; Mrs Lucas couldn't possibly know what had happened in the bedroom yesterday afternoon.

40

'Like that,' Mrs Lucas said again, and went into the kitchen.

Julie went into the lounge, and looked around her. She still felt a stranger here. But it was hers. It was actually the only thing she owned. That and four thousand pounds. She supposed she could live comfortably on four thousand pounds. At least for a while. Certainly a year or two. And then . . . she had no idea. No doubt Bob would know. A lecher? Was it lecherous to make love to a girl? How could it be? Perhaps it was only lecherous if you were eighteen years older.

Julie stood above the bar, realised she could drink anything she wanted. In the past she had always waited for Father to offer. Even yesterday she had left the pouring to Bob. But now this too was all hers, and Father had a well-stocked bar. She chose a medium sherry, walked to the window, and saw a car stopping at the gate. Oh, Lord, she thought; she really had had all the sympathy she could take for one day. But she frowned as she saw the man getting out. He was no one she had ever seen in her life before, tall, with heavy shoulders, made to look heavier by the sports jacket he was wearing, youngish, maybe about thirty she thought, with an extremely rugged face; it might have been good-looking, except that at some stage he had broken his nose, while his chin jutted like the bow of an ice-breaker. It was an aggressive face, on an aggressive man.

She turned, and gazed at the door with her mouth slightly open, waiting – for an aggressive knock.

'I'll get it, Mrs Lucas,' she called, and opened the door.

'Miss Julie Allen?' the man asked.

'Yes.'

He took what looked like a small wallet from his pocket, flipped it open. 'Detective Sergeant John Baldwin, Scotland Yard. I'd like a word.'

Julie goggled at him. A Scotland Yard detective? In Epsom?

'With me?' she asked lamely.

'With you. Are you going to let me in?'

No, she thought. I don't want to let you in. You're just going to tell me something else awful about Father. But she stepped back, and he came in, closed the door. 'I have a warrant here,' he said. 'Giving me the right to search these premises.'

41

Baldwin felt in his pocket again, and produced the document. 'You'd better read it.'

Julie glanced at it, but could make little of it. 'Search here?' she asked. 'But why?'

'The fact that I have a warrant is sufficient.' He took it back, replaced it in his pocket. 'I wish you present throughout the search. Understood?'

Julie found herself becoming angry. 'Mrs Lucas,' she called.

Mrs Lucas came to the kitchen doorway, wiping her hands.

'This man wants to search the house,' Julie said.

'He what? Be off with you,' Mrs Lucas snapped. 'Here's Mr Allen scarce in his grave and you're wanting to pester Miss Julie? Be off with you.'

'I have a warrant which I intend to execute,' Baldwin said. 'Obstructing a police officer in the course of his duty is an offence.'

Julie had got herself back under control. 'So search,' she said. 'You didn't need a warrant. All you had to do was ask. If it's anything to do with Father, you won't find a thing. Because I haven't been able to find a thing.'

'We'll see,' Baldwin said. 'You'll both accompany me on the search.'

'I am cooking lunch,' Mrs Lucas announced.

'Then turn it off. I won't be long.'

'Well, really.' Mrs Lucas looked at Julie.

'Turn it off, Mrs Lucas,' Julie said. 'And please get on with it,' she told the policeman.

He glanced at her in surprise, but she was now definitely angry. 'We'll start upstairs,' he said.

They followed him through the house. He was very thorough, checking everything with great care. 'Well, really,' Mrs Lucas commented as he sifted through the drawers containing Julie's underclothes. But she was even more scandalised when he searched her room as well, and then downstairs. He left the lounge until last, then he said, 'Thank you, Mrs . . .?'

'My name is Lucas.'

'Well, you can get on with your lunch. You stay here, Miss Allen.'

Julie had no intention of leaving. She waited while he hunted through the lounge. Then he pointed at the desk. 'Where are the keys?'

'In my handbag.' She had thrown it on the settee when she had come in from the funeral.

'I'll need to have a look in there as well,' Baldwin said.

Julie shrugged, gave it to him. He emptied the contents on to an occasional table, picked up her passport, and opened it. 'Excellent work,' he remarked.

She sat on the settee and watched him open the desk, sift through the papers. His back was turned to her, but as he was a policeman she presumed he wasn't stealing anything. Then he closed the desk again. 'Well?' she asked.

'Your father was a smart operator,' he said. 'I didn't really expect to find anything. But it had to be done.' He turned in the chair. 'Now, suppose you tell me how much you know about it?'

'Know about what? I don't know about anything. Inspector Rodham told me yesterday that Father apparently had a different job to the one I thought he had.' Inspector Rodham, she thought; she had promised to telephone him, and forgotten. But she would do so now, and make a complaint about this great oaf.

'That's putting it mildly,' Baldwin said.

She frowned at him. 'You mean, you know what his job really was?' She was desperate to find out, however much she disliked this man.

'Don't you?'

'Of course I don't.' She discovered her sherry glass still at her elbow, and took a sip. Baldwin watched her.

'You expect me to believe that?' he asked.

'I'm not in the habit of lying,' she snapped.

'Aren't you?' He picked up her passport again. 'Do you realise this is a forgery?'

'A . . .' her jaw dropped. 'I've had it for four years.'

'Quite. Did you apply for it yourself?'

'Of course not. Father did it when I first went to Switzerland.'

'Quite,' Baldwin said again.

'But . . .' the fear was back, swamping her anger, as she felt herself again slipping back into that whirling vortex of uncertainty.

'Do you have a birth certificate?'

'A . . .' she'd never seen one. It had never seemed necessary.

'I think you'll find that you don't. Unless it too is forged. This is an excellent piece of work,' Baldwin said. 'But then your father only employed the best. So come on now. Tell me your real name.'

'My what?' she shouted. I am going mad, she thought. I am going *mad*.

'Miss . . . Allen,' he said, leaning forward. 'You are either a very good actress or a total innocent.' He glanced down at the passport. 'You have no doubt at all that you are Julie Elizabeth Allen?'

She could only stare at him. 'Who else do you think I am?' she whispered.

Baldwin gazed at her for some seconds, then he stood up. 'I suggest you take a trip to London, Miss Allen,' he said. 'Go to Somerset House. You'll probably find quite a few Edwin Allens there, because it isn't all that uncommon a name. But you won't find any Edwin Allen corresponding with your father. And you won't find any Julie Allen at all. Miss Allen, you don't exist, officially.' He put the passport in his pocket. 'I am confiscating this.'

Julie thought she was going to faint; the entire room was heaving up and down.

Baldwin went to the door. 'Think about what I've said,' he recommended. 'I'll let myself out.'

Julie sat absolutely still, listened to the door slam, and then the car engine start. Her brain seemed to have solidified. There was nothing there except terror.

'You ought to complain about him,' Mrs Lucas said from the doorway. And frowned. 'Miss Julie? What's the matter? That man . . .'

Julie took a long breath. 'How long have you worked for Father, Mrs Lucas?'

'Oh, going on six years now.'

Julie knew it hadn't been all that long. But Mrs Lucas was an Epsom woman. 'But you knew him before?'

'Well, in a manner of speaking.'

'Do you remember my mother?'

'Can't say I do. Don't you?'

'Only a face, really. And sometimes a voice. I was only seven.'

'You poor girl,' Mrs Lucas said. 'You really have been unlucky. But that man . . . I'd complain. Really I would.'

'Yes,' Julie said. She wished Bob were here. And she didn't even know how to get in touch with him. Odd, she thought, he had never

44

even told her the name of the club he and Father had belonged to. But then, with so much else going on, she hadn't thought to ask.

But there was Inspector Rodham. She got up, went to the telephone in the hall, found that her hands were trembling. But that was shock, and outrage. She knew that whatever that man had told her had to be a lie. And just to walk away with her passport without even a by-your-leave. He had wanted to shock her, to frighten her – into doing what? She picked up the phone, gave the number on the slip of paper, and asked for the Inspector. He was on the telephone a moment later. 'I thought you'd forgotten,' he remarked. 'Have you anything for me?'

'Inspector . . .' she drew another long breath, then told him of Baldwin. Just the visit and the manner and the search warrant to begin with.

'Hmm,' he commented. 'Well, I'll be damned. Now I wonder what . . .'

'You mean you didn't know he was coming?'

'I'm afraid Scotland Yard regard themselves as a cut above the ordinary copper, Miss Allen. No, they don't often inform us what they're doing. Although technically they have no jurisdiction in a local case unless invited, so . . . One must presume that your father's death is related to some London or national crime.'

'National crime?' she cried. 'Then what was he doing here?'

'As I say, deuced odd. It would have to be something pretty important . . . I'll get in touch with them, of course, but I'm not at all sure they'll co-operate. I wouldn't let this man Baldwin upset you.'

'Upset me?' she shouted. 'He took away my passport. He told me I don't exist.'

There was no reply.

'Did you hear what I said?'

'Yes,' Rodham said. 'I'm afraid there does seem to be some uncertainty about that. It's just come to our notice that for some reason your father's birth was never recorded at Somerset House. Neither was yours. I'm quite sure there's a perfectly sound explanation for this, and I have one of my men looking into it. But, I suppose, looked at in the letter of the law, well . . . you don't exist, Miss Allen.'

Julie replaced the receiver before he had actually finished speaking. I have *gone* mad, she thought. I have gone *mad*.

'Lunch is just about ready,' Mrs Lucas said. 'I'm not promising it

45

won't be spoiled, thanks to that lout. I hope the Inspector is going to give him a right talking to.'

Julie looked at her. Had she heard the conversation?

Mrs Lucas gave no sign of it. But she was frowning again. 'You really don't look well, Miss Julie', she said. 'I think you're suffering from delayed shock. Would you like me to call the doctor?'

Julie continued to gaze at her for several seconds. Do I know this woman? she wondered. Do I know myself? No, of course I don't, because I don't exist. I've been told that, twice in fifteen minutes.

'Miss Julie?' Mrs Lucas was asking again.

'I really don't need a doctor, Mrs Lucas,' she said. 'As you say, it's probably a case of delayed shock. I think I'll have lunch and then lie down.'

'Now there's a sensible girl,' Mrs Lucas said. 'I've kept all the papers, you know.'

Julie blinked at her. 'Papers?'

'Covering the crime. Your father's death. Would you like to look at them?'

Julie shuddered. 'No. Burn them. No,' she said. 'Don't do that, Mrs Lucas. I . . . I'll look at them in a day or two.'

'Of course you will. Do you think I could have the afternoon off? My old man is a little upset about the present arrangements, and I'd promised to go to the pictures with him. I'll be back in time to cook dinner.'

'Of course you must have the afternoon off, Mrs Lucas,' Julie told her. 'All I want to do is rest. I just have one more call to make first.'

But Mr Cornwall was with a client. His clerk took her number and said he'd have the solicitor call back immediately after lunch. He didn't, but Julie wasn't too unhappy about that, because she did want to rest. Rest, and not think, until Bob returned. She slept very heavily, and when she awoke found it was just past three. The house was quiet, even the street outside was quiet. She lay in bed staring at the ceiling, feeling quite calm again. Whatever the mistake over the entry of her birth, there had to be an explanation. That lout Baldwin had been attempting to frighten her into doing something. Into rushing up to London, obviously. She couldn't imagine why. Maybe he just wanted her out of the house so that he could search it again, take up the floorboards. Well, she wasn't going to be panicked into rushing anywhere. She was going to wait for Bob, and

46

together they could get to the bottom of whatever was going on. Until then she mustn't even think about it. When Cornwall finally called her back she'd just put him in the picture.

She had lain down fully dressed, save for her jacket and shoes. Now she had a hot shower – few English homes had showers, but Father had always showered, never bathed – then looked out of the window. It was a perfect June afternoon, with not a cloud in the sky, and without a breeze it was even hot. She pulled on a pair of shorts and a jumper, went downstairs and took a deckchair from the garage. She hefted it the length of the lawn and to the edge of the apple trees which fringed the end of the property, where it abutted on to the Downs, and lay back with a sigh. The sun on her face and her legs felt so good; she left the back door open so that she would hear the telephone if it rang. But more than ever she was hoping it wouldn't. She would just lie here for an hour, she thought, and think about Bob. Lying in the warm sun made it attractive to remember his kiss, and his hand . . . it had certainly excited her. Therefore it would do so again. And he obviously knew so much about it, he would never disgust her, or frighten her . . . but hadn't there been a touch of both of those which had led her to reject him? That was silly. That was sheer innocence, and—

'Hi!' said a voice.

Julie sat up, startled, and saw a man leaning over the garden fence. Although there were houses all along the street, behind was the beginning of the Downs, on the top of which, some distance away, was the famous racecourse. This man must have been walking on the Downs, and now he had the cheek . . .

'You'll be the girl whose dad had just died,' he said.

Julie stood up, wished she was wearing slacks. But he was looking at her face rather than her legs, and the more she looked at him, the less annoyed she became. He was very tall, and somewhat thin. He wore a cap, but she could see that his hair was fair and his eyes were blue. His trousers and pullover were unexceptionally English, but he spoke with an American accent; she didn't know anything about America except through the movies, but she rather felt he was a northerner rather than a southerner. Ye the mere fact that he was not English gave him a boost in her eyes; she had encountered too many of her own countrymen who were hostile in the past couple of days.

47

More important than any of those things, however, he was young. She felt he couldn't be very much older than herself. And he had the most delightful grin, somewhat crooked, as if he was afraid to let his whole mouth go, and it was a wide, generous mouth. He had good manners, too; he was taking off his cap.

'I guess you think I've one hell of a cheek,' he said. 'But I wanted to say how sorry I was.'

'Thank you,' she said.

'You know, one reads about guys getting murdered, and that kind of thing, but you never expect to have it happen on your own doorstep.'

'Do you live in Epsom?' she asked.

'Right now, yes.' His grin was back, spreading wider. 'I'm a student.'

She nodded. She had guessed that.

'At Oxford,' he explained. 'So when it came to vacation time, I thought I'd go live in a real English country town.'

'And ran into a murder,' she said.

'I guess I did, Miss Allen.'

'I don't know your name,' she said.

'Longman, Miss Allen. Fits, eh? Edward Longman the Third. But you can call me Teddy. Everyone else does.'

'The Third?'

'Well, I guess the family likes continuity. It helps the business, see. So every firstborn Longman is called Edward. Have been, since the Revolution.'

'What sort of business is that?'

'Oh, law. Always law. That's what I'm reading at Balliol. Boring. But it's the firm, right? The firm lives forever.'

'Yes,' she said, and thought how wonderful it must be to belong to something as permanent, as established, as safe, as a family firm of lawyers. Edward Longman the Third. She was not even Julie Allen the First. She was Julie Allen the nothing.

'Well, I guess I've intruded enough,' Teddy Longman said. 'Maybe I'll see you around. I just felt I'd like to have a word. You see, I was the guy discovered your father's body.'

48

CHAPTER 3

'You what?' Julie cried, utterly taken aback.

'Say, I didn't mean to upset you, Miss Allen. It's just that it gave me a personal interest in what happened. If I only could've come along just five minutes earlier, maybe—'

'Mr Longman,' she said. 'I'd like to talk to you.' Because he might be able to tell her something. Something important.

'Well, gee, Miss Allen, if you think I can be of any help. I've told the police everything I saw, of course. They and me don't exactly agree on what happened. Maybe because I'm not British . . .'

'Would you tell me everything you saw? Please.'

'Sure. If you'd like me to.'

'Can you climb over this fence?'

'No problem.' He virtually vaulted it, one hand on the cross timber, landing beside her. She presumed he was an athlete, and liked him the better for that.

'We'd better go inside,' she said. 'You know what neighbours are.' She led him to the kitchen door – Mrs Lucas had taken the front door key – and showed him into the house.

'You all alone?' He seemed concerned.

'Oh, no. There's a housekeeper. She'll be back just now.' For a moment she wondered if she'd done the right thing in allowing a stranger into the house. But he seemed so very nice, so frank and open, and if he had virtually witnessed Father's death . . . She led him into the lounge. 'Will you tell me, please? Oh, do sit down.'

Teddy Longman looked around the room, chose a straight chair, and sat down, somewhat gingerly. Julie sat on the settee. 'Well,' he said. 'I spend quite a lot of time walking over the Downs, you know,

49

and I guess I was coming back from one of my walks last Sunday afternoon, and there he was, lying by the side of the road.'

'Where, exactly?' Because while everyone had been telling her all about herself and how she didn't exist, no one had actually thought to tell her where Father had died.

'That lane, not a hundred yards away.'

'Oh,' she said. 'Yes, I know it. Was he . . .' she bit her lip.

'He was dead, I think. If not he died a few seconds later. But I'm pretty damn sure the attack hadn't taken place more than a couple of minutes before I came along. I'll tell you why. I guess I was kind of shocked, and for a moment I just didn't know what to do. There's so many things you should do, in those circumstances. But then I thought, maybe he isn't dead, so I knelt and tried to find a heartbeat, and to stop the bleeding, because he'd taken a terrible crack on the head . . . and I heard a car engine start up.'

Julie frowned at him. 'Where?'

'Well, I think it must have been on the road. This road, in fact. The lane runs into it. Well, I guess I was still pretty distraught. I left your dad and ran along the lane, because I thought the car would get help quicker, but by the time I got there it'd already turned the corner. So I never even saw it. Then I returned to your dad, but he was definitely dead. So I came back to the road and started banging on doors until someone opened up and let me use the telephone. Funny thing, I never got as far as this house. I didn't know he lived here.'

'But . . . the police said it must have been a tramp.'

'Yeah.'

'Even when you told them about the car?'

'Well, like I said, Miss Allen, I'm not sure they believed me. They kept saying, now, if you had a number . . . they did put out some kind of radio message asking anyone who had driven along this road that afternoon to check with them, and nobody did. And nobody else seems to have seen or heard the car. Heck, sometimes I wonder if I actually heard it myself. Yet I know it was there.'

Julie gazed at him. He looked genuinely distressed. And she could not get over the fact that he was the last person to have seen Father alive. Maybe. But he had wanted to help. Tried to help. 'The police said Father had been robbed.'

'Oh, sure, he'd been robbed. His jacket pockets were pulled inside out, and his wallet was gone. They found the wallet, on the Downs, not fifty feet away. Empty, of course. But as nothing else had been taken, not even his passport, which was in his pocket as well, they figured it had to be a robbery gone wrong, maybe interrupted by my turning up.

'But . . .' Julie's brain was spinning again. 'If the wallet was found on the Downs, and you had just walked across the Downs, you'd have seen the murderer.'

'Well, that's what I thought. But they said, not necessarily. Their theory is that this guy assaulted your dad with a brick . . . they found the brick, it was lying right there beside the body. Maybe he didn't even mean to kill him, they think, just lay him out. Anyway, he must've been going through his pockets when he heard me coming, so he darted behind a tree or something. There are a lot of trees on that lane. Kind of makes my skin crawl to think he could've been there, watching me. Then when I went to the street after that car, he ran off.'

'Only you don't believe that.'

'Well . . . I'm sure I heard that car. So maybe it was just a coincidence. Trouble is, according to the police, there's just no motive for anyone to kill your dad. Seems he was a well respected and liked man. Never troubled anybody. So why should anyone kill him? Save as part of a robbery. Seems it was also known he was pretty well heeled.'

Julie got up, walked to the window, looked out. The police were spending more time hounding her than looking for Father's killer, she thought bitterly. Yet by now they clearly knew there was a lot more to Father's death than had first seemed apparent. And they, both Inspector Rodham and the Scotland Yard sergeant, felt that she had an idea what had really happened. Thus she, and Bob of course, would simply have to get some kind of an idea. Not only for her own sake. She was aware of a growing determination to avenge Father as well.

'I didn't mean to upset you,' Teddy Longman said again.

'You haven't. I'm all through being upset.' Julie turned back to face him. 'Mr Longman . . . may I call you Teddy?'

'I'd kind of like that.'

'I'm Julie. I can tell you that the police don't really think it was a tramp, either.'

51

'Come again?'

Julie hesitated. Once again she was about to trust a complete stranger. Only this man *was* a complete stranger, where Uncle Bob had been a friend of Father's. Would Uncle Bob think she had done the right thing? Probably not. But she simply had to share her frightening predicament with someone, and it wasn't as if she had anything to hide, or that she *could* hide; the police were going to tell everyone about her, whenever they felt like it, and she had the strangest feeling that this man would be able to help, perhaps just because he wasn't emotionally involved. Yet she hesitated, and the telephone jangled in the hall. 'Oh . . . excuse me,' she said, and ran to answer it.

'Miss Allen? John Cornwall here. I imagine you've heard from the police.'

'The . . . yes. About Somerset House?'

'Yes,' he said. 'I must say, it's the oddest thing I've ever heard. I have handled your father's affairs for twenty years and it's never occurred to me that he could not have been— but of course, he was probably born abroad, even if his passport does say "born in Sussex".'

'So where was I born, Mr Cornwall?'

'Well . . .'

'My passport, my forged passport, says born right here in Epsom.'

'Does it? Good Lord!'

'The police tell me I don't actually exist,' Julie said, her voice rising an octave. She had intended to remain very calm – even disinterested – until Bob came back, but the very thought of her situation made her want to scream.

'My dear Miss Allen, I do assure you that the police, and myself, are going to leave no stone unturned to get to the bottom of this just as quickly as we can. But I felt I should warn you that there may well be a slight delay in having your father's will probated. You see, if he . . . well . . .'

'If he doesn't exist, he can't leave me anything,' Julie said.

'Well, of course it's not like that . . . the difficulty is proving you are his daughter where we can't obtain a copy of your birth certificate. I don't suppose you have one?'

'No I don't, Mr Cornwall. And if I did, it'd be a forgery, wouldn't it?'

'Bless my soul. I suppose it would. Look, let me call you back later.'

'Thank you, Mr Cornwall.' She hung up, gazed at Teddy Longman, who was standing in the lounge doorway.

'Seems to me you have a problem,' he remarked. He didn't look embarrassed at having overheard. But then, how could he have avoided overhearing? She had been shouting.

'Yes.' She sighed. 'I have a problem trying not to go mad.'

'Anything I can do to help?'

She gazed at him. If only Bob were here. But he wasn't, and this young man – how nice the thought of that was, this *young* man – had actually been with Father just before he died. If Father had been alive at all, then. And suddenly she realised how she could dispel her lingering uncertainty. She picked up the telephone again and redialled the number of the solicitor's office.

'Yes, Miss Allen?' Mr Cornwall sounded just a little bit tired.

'I just wanted to ask you one thing, Mr Cornwall. Who found Father's body?'

'Who . . . let me see, it was some American student. What was his name now? I have it here somewhere—'

'Longman?'

'That's right. But it's in the paper.'

'Yes,' she said. 'Thank you.' She hung up, looked at Teddy Longman.

Who grinned, with his whole face this time. 'Pays to be sure,' he agreed.

'I'm sorry, but there's so much . . .' she went back into the lounge. 'Would you like a drink?'

'I wouldn't say no to a beer.'

'A beer.' She opened the cupboard door and found a bottle of brown ale. 'This?'

He peered at it. 'You wouldn't have anything lighter? And maybe cold?'

'Cold?'

'Like out of the icebox.'

'Icebox,' she said. 'I don't think we have an icebox, Mr Longman.'

He took the brown ale, opening it expertly. 'I thought we had gotten around to Teddy.'

53

'Oh. Yes. You must think I'm an absolute fool. But I think my brain is about to explode.' She sat on the settee, her head in her hands.

'Can I get you something?'

She raised her head. 'Yes. Yes, I'll have a – a Scotch. And water.'

He raised his eyebrows, and she listened to a clock chiming five. Maybe it was a bit early, but she desperately needed something. Because she knew she was going to tell him, and she also knew that she shouldn't. Bob was going to be furious. But Bob wasn't here, that was the trouble. She was facing a quite impossible situation. And this young man was genuine, and wanted to help.

He sat beside her, gave her the glass. 'I think you need a shoulder to cry on.'

Her head jerked. But he was making no effort to touch her. If he did that she'd knock his block off, she thought. But she hoped he wouldn't. She needed all the friends she could find. Just as long as they didn't turn out to be mashers, and he certainly was not one of those. 'I need a brain to help mine,' she said.

'Try me. I'm going to be a fully-fledged lawyer, one day.'

'Are you? Oh, boy, then do I need you.'

'Pretend I'm there now. Just lie back and close your eyes and tell me what the problem is. Oh, sure, I got some of it from what you were saying on the phone. And it sounds pretty grim.' He got up, moved across the room, sat down again. 'Shoot.'

She hesitated. Then told him, everything she could think of. He hardly seemed to blink as he listened, and his expression never changed.

'So,' she finished. 'Then you turned up. And here I am telling you my life story. Such as it is.'

'Well, it sure beats anything I ever heard before,' Teddy Longman said. 'But it also makes me more certain than ever it wasn't any tramp. That car must've had something to do with it. But if, as you say, the police know about your father not being what he seemed . . . heck, I can see that must be one sock on the jaw for you.'

'Yes,' she said. She thought a kick in the stomach would have been a more appropriate description of the way she was feeling.

'This fellow Roberts?'

'He's in London now, seeing what he can uncover. Through the club, I suppose. But if he can't . . .'

'Yeah. What a mess. But I can't believe a guy would keep a secret like that from his daughter. No, sir.'

'Yes, but supposing he did mean to tell me? That's what's haunting me. Because he didn't know he was going to die, like that. He was perfectly healthy. If he does – did – have this secret identity, maybe he was waiting until I was twenty-one before telling me.'

'Aren't you twenty-one?'

'Yes, I am. I became twenty-one last December. But then I had to go back to the Academy for the last time, and maybe he was waiting for that, too. We were going to take a long holiday together, this summer. Maybe he was going to tell me then.'

'I see what you mean. He got bumped off first. Yeah. But still . . . I'll bet there's a letter or something around someplace waiting for you, which'll tell you everything. I mean to say, a guy may not expect to be bumped off, but everyone runs the risk of stepping under a bus, or something like that.'

'Yes,' she said, suddenly totally relieved. Why hadn't she thought of that before? Of course there would be a letter for her. But . . . 'Where?' she asked. 'There wasn't a deposit box. There wasn't anything with the solicitor. There wasn't anything, anywhere.'

He frowned at her. 'Have you looked?'

'Uncle Bob and I virtually took this house apart.'

'Sure?'

'Of course I'm sure. I . . .' she checked herself, frowning.

'Aha,' Teddy said.

'The suitcases,' she cried.

'What suitcases?'

'Daddy's suitcases. We never looked in there. We . . .' she flushed as she remembered how they'd become sidetracked.

'Well, maybe it'd be an idea to do so.'

Her face fell. 'But Detective Sergeant Baldwin did.'

'Were you there?'

'Well, yes.'

'So what was in them?'

'I have no idea. I was standing by the door, and I saw him open them on the floor, on the other side of the bed. But he didn't say anything.'

'Yeah, but he may not have been looking for the same kind of thing you were. I think you should have a look in those suitcases, Miss Julie.'

'Come with me,' she cried, wildly excited.

'Me?'

'Please.' She dashed upstairs, and he followed more slowly. He'd probably never met anyone quite so forward, she thought, and here she was, running into a bedroom with another strange man. But she just knew that this shy, somewhat bumbling young man was a gentleman.

The cases weren't locked, and still lay on the floor, where Baldwin had left them. She threw the lids up, and paused in surprise. The first two were filled with neatly folded clothes – poor Father had not even got around to unpacking. But the third was stuffed with equally neatly folded newspapers. 'What on earth are those?'

Teddy Longman was standing above her, sipping his beer. 'Your dad sure liked reading,' he commented. 'But there could be something hidden there.'

She took the papers out, one after the other, opened them. 'The *New York Times*. They're all copies of the *New York Times*,' she said wonderingly.

'Did he just come from there?'

'Good heavens, no. He had just come from Arabia.' But how did she know that? she suddenly wondered. Desperately she tossed the newspapers to and fro and she hunted through them. But the case contained nothing else. Then she tackled the clothes. But there were only clothes and personal effects. Yet, she thought as she knelt and gazed at the untidy heap to which she had reduced everything, there could have been a whole lot of documents in there . . . and Uncle Bob had not troubled to look.

'Seems like we've drawn a blank,' Teddy Longman remarked. 'Well, it was a long shot, anyway. I guess your best bet is some other bank.'

'According to Mr Cornwall, there isn't any.'

Teddy scratched his head and finished his beer.

'There's another,' she said.

'Ah . . . no,' he decided. 'But I wouldn't say no to joining you.'

'Help yourself.' She led him back downstairs. She was desperate

56

for him to stay at least until Mrs Lucas came home. She didn't want to be alone any more, and besides, it was so reassuring to feel that someone else was thinking about her problem. And he was such a reassuring man. Even more reassuring than Bob? Somehow he was, because of his air of detachment perhaps. And because he was young? That was unfair to Bob.

He poured. 'Seems to me what you . . . we – do you mind if I help you?'

'I need help from somebody.'

'Well, it seems to me what we need to do is to keep our feet very firmly planted on the ground, here, and our brains real cool. Okay?'

She nodded.

'Well, let's accept that your dad, for some reason, and I'm sure it was a very good one – is a very good one – found it necessary to live a double life. And had been doing so for some time. You have to accept that, however unpleasant it is. You have to accept that you may have been born outside England, and arrived here as a small kid, without anybody knowing. Okay?'

She nodded.

'Now, you've never doubted he's your dad?'

'You mean he needn't be?'

'We have to make every assumption under the book, Julie. If you can face it.'

Julie drank some whisky. 'I can face it.'

'Okay. And even if he was actually your dad, he could have a wife and other children someplace. But he brought you up as his daughter. And you reckon he loved you.'

'Yes,' Julie said. 'Yes,' she repeated fiercely. 'We were very close.' She had to keep reminding herself of that, even if they obviously hadn't been close enough. Father – with another wife and children? She'd read books about that happening. But she didn't want it to happen to her.

'Okay. Then there is no way, as I said before, that he would take the risk of dying without leaving you in full possession of the facts. No way at all. There has to be a letter. Or a pointer to a letter.' He looked around him. 'And I would say it has to be in this house.'

'We've searched the house,' she repeated.

'Ah, but looking for what?'

57

'Well. Bob was sure there would have to be some investments. You know, stocks and shares.'

Teddy was frowning. 'That was what he was looking for?'

'Well, in the main, yes.'

'You sure this character is on the up and up?'

'Well, of course I am. I—'

'He breezes into your life, claims to be a great pal of your dad's, who's just died, sweeps you off your feet, becomes the old Dutch uncle type . . . but all this is on his say so.'

He's done more than that, she thought; she hadn't told Teddy about Bob's advances. But oddly, where Mr Cornwall's doubting of Bob had angered her, Teddy's didn't. And there was that curious business with the suitcases. Uncle Bob had known there was nothing worthwhile in those suitcases. But how had he known that?

'I think you want to think about him very carefully,' Teddy said. 'Coud be he just wants to get his hands on your father's dough.'

'Oh, but . . .' she checked herself. If that were true, she'd not have a friend in the world. Anywhere.

'So maybe I'm sticking my nose in where I shouldn't,' Teddy went on, 'but I'd sure hate to think of a pretty girl like you being fleeced. And it can happen. And does.'

'Yes,' she said. 'Yes.'

'I reckon that's what he's looking for now,' Teddy said. 'I'd reckon he knows more about your dad than he let on.'

'Oh, my God!' Julie exclaimed in horror.

'But I also reckon he isn't going to get anywhere. Because your dad would have thought of that possibility too. And you say you were looking for shares. Those are bulky things. But suppose your dad had left you a message. Could be a deposit box number. Could be anything. Something only you would understand. It could be right here in this house.'

She stared at him.

'Can't do any harm to have another search.'

'But where? Through those newspapers again?'

Teddy considered. 'Nope,' he said at last. 'That'd be too risky. He'd have to reckon that anyone opening that suitcase would throw the newspapers into the trash can without even looking at them. No, I think it'd be in his papers.'

'All his papers, and there aren't really any papers, are in that desk.'

'So go through the desk again. Only this time, read everything.'

'Will you help me?'

'Me? Heck . . . I don't think I should do that. I mean, I felt bad about the suitcases. You don't know me at all. You sure don't want me prying into your dad's affairs. You know, you shouldn't be so trusting, Julie. I don't like the idea of your trusting this guy Roberts so much, and you sure as hell shouldn't just have trusted me.'

'But . . .'

'There's something going on which you don't understand. That means there's someone trying to hoodwink you. Could be anyone. So you don't want to trust every Tom, Dick and Harry that comes along.'

'But I have to trust someone,' she said.

He made a face. 'I guess you do. Heck, I've never been in that position. But make sure it's someone you can check out.'

'Can't I check you out?'

'Me? Well . . .'

'You say you're a student at Balliol College. I could call them and ask them.' Suddenly she was desperately anxious to do that; he had frightened her all over again.

He grinned. 'I guess you could at that. Here, I'll give you the number.' He took out his wallet, looked in his address book. 'As it's vacation time, there'll only be some old stuffed shirts there. But the porter should answer the phone.'

'Oh. Oh, yes.' She went into the hall, asked for the Oxford number and waited. Teddy Longman leaned in the doorway, arms folded, while he watched her.

'Balliol College,' said a voice, speaking with an impeccable Oxford accent.

'Oh,' Julie said, taken by surprise. 'I'm enquiring about a Mr Edward Longman. He's a student there.'

'The college is presently on vacation, madam.'

'But Mr Longman is one of your students.'

'Longman. Longman . . . an American gentleman?'

'That's right.'

'Yes, we have a Mr Longman with us.'

'Can you give me his holiday address.'

'I don't think I can do that, madam, without his approval.'

'It's terribly important I get in touch with him,' she said, gazing at Teddy past the phone. Now he was grinning from ear to ear.

59

'Well . . . the address he left with us was care of a Mrs Smith, in Epsom. That's in Surrey, madam.'

'Yes,' she said. 'Yes. Could you describe Mr Longman for me?'

'Madam?' The man sounded scandalised.

'Well, I want to know it's him when I catch up with him, don't I?'

'Mr Longman is an American, madam,' the man said, conveying that she need know nothing more.

'Yes, but . . . is he tall, or short? Dark, or fair?'

'Mr Longman could be described as tall and fair, madam. Now, if you will excuse me . . .'

'Yes,' she said. 'Oh, yes.' She replaced the receiver, gazed at him. 'I hope you don't think I went too far.'

'I think you were just magnificent. Am I going to pull Bates' leg when I get back.'

'I feel like some kind of secret agent,' she said. 'But now you can help me look for whatever it is I'm looking for.'

He glanced at his watch. 'Heck, Julie, I can't. I'm supposed to be someplace in half an hour.'

'Oh.' Her face fell. She kept forgetting that all the other people in the world had lives to live; only she was left stuck in limbo. A nameless limbo, she realised.

'Tell you what,' he said, and scribbled another number for her. 'That's Mrs Smith's number. I'd sure as heck like to know if you find anything.'

'You shall,' she promised. 'The very moment.'

'I'll look forward to that. Out here, is it?' He walked to the back door, checked. 'Now remember, you examine everything.'

'Yes,' she said. 'I will.'

'And lock this door,' he recommended. He closed it behind him, and she gazed at it for a moment, then did as he had said. Then she went back to the front of the house, watched him leave the garden and stride down the road. Teddy Longman. What a strange encounter. But presumably, no more strange than Uncle Bob.

Uncle Bob! She went back into the lounge and picked up her drink. Had she really been a fool there? She didn't want to think that, but the fact was that she didn't have any proof of who he was; he hadn't suggested ringing him at his home in London or wherever it was – he had to live somewhere. And she had let him make love to her. Well, sort of. She wondered what it would be like to have

Teddy Longman throw her on a bed and start interfering with her clothes. She wondered if she'd enjoy that.

But Bob was going to come back. What was she going to do then? Well, that would have to depend on what information he brought her, if any. Teddy thought what she wanted to find was right here in this house. She gazed at the desk. It could only be there, unless there was a secret safe or something hidden away beneath the floorboards – and she was sure there wasn't.

She sat at the desk, opened it, took out the bank statements and the cheques and the accounts and began going through them again. She looked at both sides of every piece of paper, reading the writing. Father's handwriting. Everywhere. Oh, Father, she thought, how could you do this to me? A tear rolled down her cheek; she was keeping off another crying fit only by not letting herself stop to think. And anyway, she told herself fiercely, there had to have been a reason. A very good reason. Which she would soon discover.

Or would she? When Mrs Lucas returned from the pictures she was still at it, without having found anything.

'Drive yourself mad, you will,' Mrs Lucas said. 'Going over his things like that.'

'Has to be done,' Julie said.

'I'll get tea,' Mrs Lucas replied.

Julie had just reached the last of the items in the desk when the meal was served. Mrs Lucas sat with her. 'I'm not sure how much longer I'll be able to stay nights,' she said. 'My Bill isn't happy, sleeping all alone.'

Do you think I'm happy, sleeping all alone? Julie felt like asking. But she said, 'Of course, Mrs Lucas. I think it's awfully sweet of you to have stayed this long.'

'Don't you have relatives?' Mrs Lucas asked. 'Everyone has relatives.'

I don't even have a name, Julie wanted to scream at her. 'No,' she said. 'I don't have relatives, Mrs Lucas. But I can manage.' Besides, she thought, Bob will probably be back tomorrow. Only she couldn't possibly have him in the house overnight. Anyway, she was no longer sure she wanted him to come back at all. She was so confused she thought her head would burst.

'Well, I'll see if Bill will agree to one more night,' Mrs Lucas said, and began clearing away.

61

Julie returned to the lounge, stared at the still open desk. Teddy had been wrong. There was nothing. She had checked everything. Everything . . . she sat down again and opened the drawer. Just various envelopes, the ones she'd looked at yesterday. She picked them up, sifting through them. She'd done this before as well, had even looked inside each one. Now she began tearing them open. One after the other. Mr Edwin Allen, from the Golf Club. Mr Edwin Allen from the bank. Edwin Allen, Esquire from the electricity board. Mr Edwin Allen from the telephone company. What a lot of people had accepted Father as Mr Edwin Allen.

Edwin Allen, Esq., from Cornwall, Cornwall and Everton. Mr Edwin Allen, from the gas company. Strange there was nothing from this London club Bob said they'd belonged to. She frowned as she continued. Mr Edwin Allen, Mr Edwin Allen, Mr Edward Armitage . . .

Julie sat absolutely still, staring at the envelope. For a moment she thought her heart had stopped beating. She closed her eyes, and then opened them again. Mr Edward Armitage. The address was a flat in Mayfair, London. Edward Armitage? Only yesterday she had been right through these envelopes with Bob . . . With Bob!

She ran to the telephone and dialled the number Teddy had given her. 'Oh, Mrs Smith,' she gasped. 'Is Teddy, Mr Longman, there?'

'Yes. Who shall I say is calling, please?'

'Just tell him Julie.'

'Julie,' Mrs Smith repeated, and went away.

Moments later Teddy was on the phone. 'Julie! You've found something?'

'Yes,' she said. 'Oh, yes. Listen . . .' but she knew Mrs Lucas could overhear from the kitchen. 'Can you come over? It's terribly important.'

'Five minutes,' he promised, and hung up.

'Who was that?' Mrs Lucas asked.

'A friend.'

'Who's coming over? It's past eight o'clock, Miss Julie.'

'We're just going to have a little chat. There's no need for you to wait up.'

'Hmm,' Mrs Lucas commented. She seems to think I'm still a schoolgirl, Julie thought. And Mrs Lucas certainly stayed up until

62

Teddy arrived, surveying him from the kitchen doorway. 'I know you,' she said. 'Your picture was in the newspaper.'

'That's right, Mrs Lucas. Teddy found Father's body,' Julie explained.

'And he's a friend?' Mrs Lucas asked in disgust.

'Yes,' said Julie. 'Good night, Mrs Lucas.' She escorted Teddy into the lounge and closed the door.

'Rather a dragon, isn't she?' he remarked.

'I'm going off her quite rapidly. Teddy . . . look at this.'

He took the envelope, frowning. 'Edward Armitage. Who's he?'

'I found it in the drawer, along with a whole lot of other letters Father had kept.'

'Father? Mr Allen?'

'That's it. Edwin Allen, Edward Armitage.'

'Holy Cow! You think the letter could really have been meant for him?'

'I don't know what to think. Except . . . Teddy, this envelope was not there when I last went through that drawer.'

'Come again?'

'Just that. I told you, I searched that desk yesterday. Went through everything. So maybe we were searching for something bulky, but I still looked at all the envelopes. There was nothing addressed to Edward Armitage then.'

'You positive?'

'I'm certain. Anyway, there's nothing in it. All the other envelopes contain letters. That's why Daddy kept them. He wouldn't have kept an empty envelope. Somebody put it there, today.'

'Well, heck . . . but who?'

'Uncle Bob was helping me. And he was by himself from time to time. Why, only this morning, he was alone down here when he collected me for the funeral.'

'Uncle Bob,' he said thoughtfully. 'Nobody else?'

'No,' she said. 'Nobody else. Except . . .' she frowned.

'Who?'

'Well, that Scotland Yard man. He went through the desk as well.'

'Carefully?'

'It seemed so to me.'

'Then he would have spotted the envelope.'

63

'Oh, my God!' she gasped. 'And he didn't say anything.'

'Just like he didn't say anything about that suitcase filled with newspaper.'

'But . . . you don't think he planted it? A policeman?'

'How do you know he was a policeman?'

'Well . . . he flashed some kind of badge at me.'

'Easiest thing in the world.'

'But he had a warrant,' she cried, now truly alarmed.

'If you can forge a badge you can forge a warrant.'

And he was such an unpleasant beast, she thought. 'But why?'

'Two possibilities. One, he could really be a policeman, who has tracked down your dad's true identity, and wants to get a reaction to it, seeing how you claimed not to know it. The second is that he wasn't a policeman at all, but someone to do with your father's other life – and maybe with his death – and again he's trying to stampede you into doing something.'

'Well, he's going to stampede me straight down to Inspector Rodham, first thing tomorrow morning. Or Monday, anyway.' She frowned at him as he gave a slow shake of his head. 'Why not?'

'It seems to me you should be wary of trusting the police too far. You probably won't be telling Rodham anything he doesn't already know, anyway.'

'So what do I do?'

'Well, if it were me, I'd go up to London and take a look at the apartment belonging to this Edward Armitage.'

'But isn't that what they want me to do?'

'Maybe it is. But sometimes it pays to do what the other guy wants, so long as you understand that.'

'Go to London,' she said uncertainly.

'It'd only take a couple of hours. You'd be back for lunch.' He studied her. 'Like me to come with you?'

'Oh, would you?' Her face lit up. 'But . . . you have other things to do.'

'Nothing which can't wait. I'm as interested in this set-up as you are, you know. I've never come across anything like it. Listen, we'll leave here on the early train tomorrow, nip up to town, check this place out, have lunch together, decide what we're going to do, and come back down in the afternoon. How does that grab you?'

'It sounds wonderful,' she said. Because a day out in London, with someone as effervescently attractive as Teddy Longman, did.

'Okay. I'll pick you up at eight.' He finished his drink and got up. 'And don't mention this envelope to anyone. Anyone, right?'

She nodded. 'Must you go?'

'I think an early night would be a good idea for both of us.'

'Oh. Yes.' He was just as masterful as Bob had been. But how she wanted to be mastered, by someone, right this minute. Someone she could trust. She went with him to the door. 'It's awfully good of you to go to all this trouble.'

'No trouble at all, little lady,' he said, and gave one of his crooked grins. 'Besides, I want to know what to call you, properly.'

She wondered if he would try to kiss her, but he didn't, just gave her a wave from the gate and disappeared down the road. Teddy Longman. She had never met anyone quite so nice. And thanks to him she was getting somewhere. Of course it had been a stupid reaction to want to go rushing off to the police. They weren't really on her side, and as Teddy had said, they probably knew all about Edward Armitage already. It was up to her to find out something about him as well.

She called goodnight to Mrs Lucas, went upstairs, undressed and got into bed, then sat up with her arms clasped round her knees, staring out of the window. Edward Armitage. Did that mean her name was really Julie Armitage? Was it even Julie? She simply had no idea. Yet somehow that fact no longer bothered her quite as much as before. She was sure she was on her way to finding that identity.

She lay down. It had been a very long day. And she had hardly given a thought to Father. She wasn't at all sure how she felt, how she wanted to feel, about Father. He had been living a double life, without telling her. She had no idea what she was going to find, tomorrow. Sergeant Baldwin had said something about national security . . . no, it was Inspector Rodham who had said that. But now she didn't know that Scotland Yard actually were involved. And if they weren't, then who was Baldwin? And who was he working for?

She realised she was going to drive herself into another brainstorm and wondered if she should take two more aspirins, when she heard the telephone jangling. She leaped out of bed, pulling on her dressing-gown. Mrs Lucas called out, 'It's your friend Bob.'

'Oh.' She had supposed it might be Teddy. She went down the stairs, slowly. 'Bob?'

65

'Julie! Are you all right?'

'Of course.'

'You sound a bit odd.'

'Well, I was in bed.'

'Good Lord. At this hour?'

'I was tired.'

'Then it was the sensible thing to do. Julie . . . I've turned one or two things up.'

'Yes,' she said. 'Like that I don't exist.'

There was silence on the other end of the line.

'The police were here to tell me about it,' she said.

'Oh, my dear girl. My dear, dear girl. I wish I'd been there. Look, are you sure you're all right?'

'I've got over the shock, if that's what you mean. When are you coming back?'

'Tomorrow.'

'Oh. When?'

'Well, there are one or two things I still have to check out which will hopefully shed some light on this mess. Is it all right if I come back tomorrow afternoon?'

'Yes,' she said. 'Yes, that would be fine.'

'Julie . . . I adore you.'

'Yes,' she agreed. 'Bob . . . where are you staying?'

'That doesn't matter, my dear. I'll explain it all tomorrow. Julie, have you thought about, well . . .?'

'Yes,' she answered truthfully.

'And?'

'We'll talk about it tomorrow. I really am most awfully tired, Bob. I can't wait until tomorrow.' Which was also no lie, she thought as she hung up. But now she was deceiving him. Well, that made a change from him deceiving her. If he was doing that. God, here she went again, rushing from one possibility to another. And she had to be fresh tomorrow. 'Do you think I could have another couple of aspirins, Mrs Lucas?' she asked.

She really was exhausted, and the combination of the aspirins and the whisky made her sleep heavily, for the first time in several nights. But she set her alarm, and was up at seven, to have a shower and dress in her grey suit with the black headscarf and have a quick cup of coffee and some fruit juice with an alarmed Mrs Lucas.

'London?' she inquired. 'You never told me about this.'

'It's to do with Daddy's Will,' she explained. 'But Mrs Lucas, if anyone calls, don't tell them where I've gone. Just tell them I'll be back this afternoon.'

'What you want to do is go to church,' Mrs Lucas recommended, but fortunately before she could elaborate Teddy arrived in a taxi. The sight of him made Mrs Lucas look even more critical, but Julie felt happy for the first time in days as they drove away.

As Teddy noticed. 'You look a whole lot better than last night,' he commented.

'Well, I slept well, for a start. Teddy . . . Bob called.'

'Oh?'

'He's found out about Daddy not being Daddy . . .'

'Or he knew all the time.'

'Yes. Teddy, he's coming back down this afternoon.'

'Well, maybe by then we'll know more than he does.'

'Teddy, will you come back to the house this afternoon? Be with me when he gets there?'

'If you want me to. There could be quite a bust-up.'

'I'd like you to be there.'

He grinned. 'Okay.'

He insisted on buying the tickets. He bought second-class, but that was fine with her; Bob had insisted on giving her twenty pounds, but she didn't know if she should spend any of it, if she was no longer going to accept him as her guardian. Especially as she didn't even know if she was going to reject him. She was praying something would turn up today which would solve her dilemma.

They sat and gazed at each other as the train hurried into London. It was only forty-five minutes from Epsom to Victoria Station.

'We'll take a cab,' Teddy decided.

'Oh, but—'

'Don't worry,' Teddy told her. 'I've checked it out in my guidemap. We'll stop a couple of blocks away, and just stroll by the house as if we were tourists. If there are any policemen about, we'll just sidle off and think about it. Okay?'

'Yes,' she said, feeling more like a *femme fatale* than ever. They

67

lined up at the taxirank, and were whisked through the streets of London. It was still early in the morning, and as it was Sunday there was no rush hour, but there was still a lot of traffic and people about. She had not been to London all that often, but Teddy apparently had, and pointed out to her Apsley House, where the Duke of Wellington had lived, as they drove up Grosvenor Place, round Hyde Park Corner, and then turned left on to Park Lane.

'That's Hyde Park,' he told her, pointing at the huge green area on her left, where the trees were nodding in the breeze, and some very smartly dressed horsewomen were walking their mounts. 'You ever read *Peter Pan?*'

'Oh, yes,' she said.

'Well, that's where he hung out, on that lake. Called the Serpentine. I'll take you rowing on that, after lunch, if you like.'

'Would you?' She had never had a more romantic offer.

'Sure. Then along there, at the end of this street, is the Marble Arch. They used to hang people there.'

'Hang them?'

'Sure. That's where Tyburn Tree stood, where all the highwaymen were hanged.'

'Good Lord.' She gave a little shiver. She didn't want to think about hanging, right this minute.

But the taxi turned off well before they got to Marble Arch, down Stanhope Gate, with the majestic bulk of the Dorchester across the street, and then stopped on the corner of South Audley Street. 'This where you wanted to get off, gov'nor?' the driver asked.

'Here will be fine,' Teddy said, and paid him. Then he walked Julie along the pavement, her arm tucked under his. His touch gave her an immense feeling of security. 'It's down here on the right,' he told her, as they crossed at the next lights. 'Now remember, a real nonchalant walk, only we study the numbers as we go by, right?'

'Yes,' she said, nearly bursting with excitement.

They strolled down the sidestreet, looking casually from left to right, while Teddy talked, about nothing in particular, although he kept the particular very much in mind. 'Thirty', he said.

'Twenty-nine over there.'

'Twenty-eight. Twenty-six. There it is.'

'It looks awfully grand,' she said. On the other side of the street the house rose several stories, and looked very well kept. The front door was open, and a porter was sweeping down the steps.

'Guess what,' Teddy said. 'This is an empty street.'

Julie gave a quick glance over her shoulder. He was right. There was no one in sight.

'I think we just have to chance our arm,' he said.

She licked her lips. 'Okay.'

They crossed the street. 'Say,' Teddy said.

The porter straightened, slowly. He was grey-haired, in his sixties, Julie thought, but had quite a well-built body.

'I wonder if you can help us,' Teddy said. 'We're looking for a Mr Edward Armitage, and we were told he lived at this address.'

The porter looked him up and down. 'He does,' he agreed. Then he looked at Julie. 'My word,' he said. 'You'll be Miss Julie.'

CHAPTER 4

'What did you say?' Teddy asked.

Julie was so amazed she couldn't speak.

'Miss Julie,' the porter said, peering at her. 'You are Miss Julie, aren't you?'

Julie was still speechless, but Teddy came to her rescue. 'This is Miss Julie Armitage, yes. Mr Armitage's daughter.'

'I knew it,' the porter said, and hastily dried his hands on his apron. 'I'd have recognised you anywhere, Miss Julie.' He squeezed her hand. 'Mr Armitage said you'd be coming here one day. Come in, come in.'

Before she could gather her wits he was showing her in to the lobby, Teddy at her heels. 'He isn't here right now,' he said. 'Went off to Paris on business. But as you're here, I expect he'll soon be back. Oh, yes, indeed. I'll take you up.'

'Take me up?' Julie said in a faint voice.

'He said any time you came here you were to be admitted.' The porter took a key from one of his hooks, ushered them into an open lift which mounted beside the stairs. 'Name's George, miss. George Gardner. Been here for ten years, I have. Not as long as your dad, of course. But he's been good to me, he has.'

Julie dared not look at Teddy. But fortunately Teddy was far more in command of himself. 'And he's gone to Paris?' he remarked. 'Mr Armitage.'

'That's right. Left last Sunday. But you must've known that.'

'Actually, we didn't know the exact date,' Teddy confessed. 'Miss Armitage has been travelling, you see, and I met her boat this morning. She knew her father was going away, but not this soon. This is very unfortunate.'

70

The lift stopped, and they stepped out on to a carpeted floor. 'Well, I'm sure he'll be back. I certainly hope so. What with the burglary and everything . . .'

'The burglary?' Teddy asked.

'Terrible it was. No bags, Miss Julie?'

'I . . . ah . . .'

'We checked in to an hotel,' Teddy explained.

'Ah, well, your dad'll want you to move in here, Miss Julie,' George asserted, unlocking the door for her. 'After what happened last week, why, it'll be a tonic.'

She stepped inside, blinked, while her brain did another of its spinning-out-of-control acts. She had not actually encountered such elegance before. The entry hall was thickly carpeted, with a gilt-framed mirror on her left and a mahogany table on her far right, on which stood a vase of flowers and a silver card tray. And a large silver-framed photograph – of herself. She remembered when it had been taken, at Christmas when they had celebrated her twenty-first birthday together. Just the two of them, at a hotel restaurant in Epsom.

She took a few steps further, looked into a double bedroom on the left, sumptuously furnished, and with an en suite bathroom. On the right there was a large kitchen, fitted in the most modern fashion. Teddy will like this, there is a refrigerator, she thought irrelevantly.

An archway gave access to a huge lounge at the end of the hall. This was again exquisitely furnished with leather upholstery, a deep pile carpet, glass-topped tables and a splendidly stocked bar. On the right there was a dining-room, with an open service counter between it and the kitchen, while on the left a door led to a second bedroom. She went towards it, looking at another huge room with an enormous double bed, built-in wardrobes, and a splendid bathroom beyond.

Even Teddy was taken aback. 'Some spread,' he remarked.

But Julie was lost in the photographs; on the mantelpiece, on the tables, and on the bedside table in the bedroom – all of her.

As Teddy had noticed. 'Your dad sure is fond of you,' he commented.

'Oh, he is that,' George agreed. 'When my little girl comes home for good, he'd say, then, George, I am really going to begin to live. Now, Miss Julie, if you'll tell me which hotel you're checked into, I'll telephone them and have them send your bags over.'

71

'Oh, ah . . .' she looked at Teddy.

'We can collect them,' Teddy said, easily. 'That's no problem. You were saying something happened last week.'

'Oh, sir, it was terrible. The place was broken into, and ransacked. How they got in, nobody knows. The police think they must have got hold of a duplicate key. But from where? Funny thing is, they didn't take anything, so far as I can make out. Strange, it was. And very disturbing. When Mr Armitage is away, I'm supposed to be in charge. But he'll sort it out when he comes back, I know. And you are going to stay here, Miss Julie?' George asked anxiously. 'Mr Armitage would be most upset to know that you'd come, and gone again, if you follow me.' He looked embarrassed. 'He has explained the circumstances.'

'Oh,' Julie said, waiting for Teddy to come to her rescue, as usual.

'Oh, she certainly means to stay here,' Teddy assured him. 'After having been away so long.'

'And you'll be able to stay awhile? That would make Mr Armitage so happy. Your mother won't object?'

'Julie is twenty-one now, George,' Teddy told him. He seemed to have a brain like a razor; hers was still rotating out of control. 'She can do what she likes, live where she likes.'

'Oh, Mr Armitage is going to be happy about that,' George said. 'Well, I'll leave you the keys. There's not much in the refrigerator, but there's Shepherd Market just round the corner. If there's anything you want, just give me a ring.' He went to the door. 'It is so very good to have you home, Miss Julie.'

The door closed, and Julie and Teddy stared at each other. Then he stepped impulsively towards her, and threw both arms round her waist to sweep her from the floor and whirl her round and round. 'Wheee!' he said. 'Our lucky day.' He kissed her on the mouth. 'Your lucky day. But you carried it off very well.'

She held him tightly; he could keep on doing this forever. But he set her down, and she gasped for breath. 'Do you really think so?'

'I do. That old bird really thought you were surprised. Well, heck, so did I, at first.'

'But . . . I am totally confused.'

'Oh, come on, Julie. You still going to pretend you didn't know all about this place? To me, at any rate. That's what hurts. Envelopes planted . . . you put it there, didn't you?'

She could only stare at him. 'I didn't. Why should I? If I knew this place was here, or what Daddy's real name was, all the time, why should I have told you anything?'

He frowned. 'You're on the level?'

'Of course I'm on the level,' she shouted. 'If you'd think for a minute you'd see that I have to be on the level.'

'Then there sure is a bit of unravelling to be done.' He went into the kitchen, opened the fridge, took out a cold lager. 'Now that's what I call beer. You drinking?'

'I don't think I'd better. It's awfully early, and I didn't have any breakfast.'

'Then breakfast it shall be,' Teddy said, producing some eggs, which he proceeded to boil with great expertise, popping bread into the toaster and coffee into the percolator as he did so.

'Teddy,' she leaned on the counter to watch him. 'What are we going to do?'

'Do? Why . . . don't you like the idea of being Miss Julie Armitage?'

'Julie Armitage,' she repeated. She was most relieved that her name was really Julie. Taking on a new surname was like getting married; but she didn't think she could have coped with a new Christian name. 'Am I really Julie Armitage, Teddy?'

'Now that is something we are going to have to check out, right away. First thing tomorrow we'll mosey down to Somerset House and see what they have to offer. By then we'll have had a look around in here.' He placed the eggs on the counter, together with toast and two steaming mugs of coffeee. 'Voila!'

She sat down at the dining table. He had even found place mats and cutlery. Silver cutlery. 'Can we, Teddy? Look around in here? Somebody else's house?'

'Whose, do you suppose?'

She gazed at him. 'We'll have to tell George.'

'Not on your sweet life. Not yet. Listen to me, my darling girl. This is the biggest stroke of luck you can ever have had. Your dad obviously has been telling George all of these years that he is divorced and that you are in the custody of your mother, but that one day you'll be coming here to stay with him.' He peered at her over the rim of his coffee cup. 'You sure you didn't hatch that one together?'

'Teddy . . . '

'Okay, okay. The important thing is that George accepts that story, and here you are.'

'But Daddy is dead. George has to know that.'

'Why?'

'But . . .'

'Daddy Allen is dead. As far was anyone knows, Daddy Armitage is still alive. I think it might be an idea to keep him that way until we find out just what Daddy Armitage was doing for a living.' He looked around him. 'It must have been something pretty rewarding. And it's yours, my darling.'

This was the second time he had used such a term of endearment. And she liked it. But it was making it difficult to think. 'But, Teddy . . . my God!'

'What?'

'It wasn't a stroke of luck. Don't you remember? *Somebody* planted that envelope. And someone has already been looking.'

'Damnation,' he said. 'I had forgotten that. About the envelope. Either your friend Bob, or the police. Or the pseudo policeman.' He went to the window, stood half behind the drapes, and looked down at the street. 'I'll swear there's no one watching the house.'

'They don't have to. They know we're here.' She finished her eggs; despite her agitation she had really been hungry. 'What are we going to do?'

He continued to look at the street for a moment. Then he turned back into the room. 'Just as I said. Play it straight, and wait for the other side to show their hand. And we're gonna begin by having a look around in here.'

'Teddy . . .' she seized his hand. 'This could be very dangerous. If someone killed Daddy . . . someone who knows about this place, and therefore about what Daddy really does, who he really is . . .'

'I know,' he said. 'You could be in the firing line.'

'I was thinking about you.'

He grinned at her. 'But I was thinking about you.' He leaned forward and kissed her again, lightly.

'Were you, Teddy?'

74

'That's why I'm here. And that's why I'm staying. As close as you'll let me.'

'Oh.' She had never heard anything so reassuring in her life.

But he was away again, into the bedroom, flicking through drawers, looking into closets . . . 'Your old man sure had a good wardrobe,' he said. 'He must've changed his suits every day. But that's what we want to get into.' He pointed at the desk in one corner of the lounge.

The lock was broken. Teddy glanced at her. 'I guess the burglar did that. Or burglars. You feel like taking a look?'

'No. But I will.' She sat at the desk, opened the drawers. As with the roll-top desk in Epsom, everything was very tidy, albeit on a somewhat different scale. There were bank statements in the name of Edward Armitage, which showed biannual deposits of some hundred thousand pounds.

'That's a lot of money,' Teddy commented, peering over her shoulder. 'I wonder what he spent it on.'

'Look.' She pointed to the regular monthly withdrawals, exactly equivalent to the amounts shown on the statements in Epsom as being paid into Edwin Allen's account.

'So that's the money he claimed was paid to him by BP,' Teddy said. 'It's those other withdrawals that interest me.' For every so often, whenever the account reached six figures, there was a debit for seventy-five thousand pounds. All the others were for small amounts, clearly living expenses. 'He's been salting away seventy-five grand a year, approximately. But where?'

Julie flicked through the other statements. These were for 'Mr Armitage and Others', and also showed biannual deposits of some hundred thousand pounds. On these there were no small debits at all, but every year the hundred thousand was withdrawn.

'Another stashing job,' Teddy commented. 'Your father has one hell of a lot of money hidden somewhere.'

'There's quite a lot in the account now,' she pointed out. Because the balance was five thousand pounds.

'Yeah. It'd be nice to be able to get our hands on that – I mean, your hands. But it'd be even nicer to find out where the real loot is.'

'Umm.' But Julie's mind was racing away again. There was so much to think about – and a lot of it she didn't want to think about. Father had obviously been a very wealthy man, which was what

Uncle Bob had suggested. But . . . 'Are we really going to stay here?'

'I don't see why you shouldn't. Here's where you are going to find out what your father really did.'

'What about my clothes?'

'We'll just have to nip back down to Epsom and pick them up. Old George won't know whether we've been back to your "hotel" or not.' He watched her expression. 'Don't you want to do that?'

'No,' she said. 'But we have to, anyway.'

He looked at her. 'For your friend.'

'I have to see him, Teddy. And there's . . .' she bit her lip.

'Tell me.'

'Well . . . I don't really have any money. I mean I have an account of my own in Epsom, but there's only a few pounds in it. Daddy left me several thousand, but it can't be released until the Will is probated, and the Will can't be probated until I can prove I'm his daughter. The bank were going to let me have some on account, as it were, but even that's been stopped now, with this identity thing. So . . . Bob lent me twenty pounds to tide me over.'

'That figures,' Teddy said grimly. Then he grinned. 'You're in a kind of Ancient Mariner situation, only with money instead of water; you're surrounded by it, but you can't spend any of it. You spent any of the loan?'

'Well, no. But I owe you for the tickets.'

'Forget it. Today is on me. As for Bob, just hand him back his money.'

'And then what?'

'Leave it to me.'

'Teddy, I couldn't.'

'What the hell? Think of it as a loan. Listen, sweetheart, my old man has more money than he knows what to do with, and he gives me an allowance I can't spend. Let me lend you a little of it.'

'Oh, Teddy . . .' she gazed at him, and felt tears spring to her eyes.

'A loan,' he repeated. 'And just so you won't think I'm going into white slavery, I promise not to touch you again until it's paid back.'

'Oh,' she said. He hadn't really touched her yet at all. But how she wanted him to.

He grinned. 'Unless you ask me to, of course.'

76

She stepped up to him, put her arms round his neck, and kissed him.

It was the first time Julie had had the pleasure of surprising a man, both by her action and by the vehemence of her kiss. Their tongues touched, and she moved her body against his, and felt him respond – even as she thought, what am I doing? But she had to have him at her side, always, she knew. At least until things were sorted out. She just could not face what might lie ahead without him.

He moved his face back. 'I have an idea you might've meant that.'

'Umm,' she said.

'You ever been with a guy before?'

She shook her head.

'Then you want to think about it. Listen to me,' he said, as she would have spoken. 'You're all shook up. Who wouldn't be? You could even still be in shock. That wouldn't surprise me either. You don't really want to go rushing into anything you could regret in a big way.'

'Will I regret it, Teddy?'

He grinned. 'Not if I can help it, baby. But listen, seriously. We have a lot to do. Let's go do it. Then, when we get back here, and the world has settled down a bit, we'll see if you still feel like it.'

'But you'll be here.'

'I'm not going anywhere. There's a promise. Unless you go too.'

'I'm going to hold you to that.' But she released him. The momentary madness was past, even if she knew, and hoped, it would come back. But it was something to think about, although she had no doubt she had at last made the right decision. 'Okay,' she said. 'What do we do first?'

'Lunch, I think. Then we'd better skedaddle back down to Epsom for your things, and to sort Uncle Bob out, and then . . .'

The telephone jangled.

They looked at each other. 'Maybe you'd better answer it,' Teddy said. 'You're the boss as regards George. And remember, you don't have a care in the world.'

Julie took a long breath and picked up the receiver.

'Oh, Miss Julie,' George Gardner said. 'Sorry to disturb you, but there's a man here asking to see you.'

'Oh?' She looked over the phone at Teddy, who had heard what was said.

'Ask his name,' he whispered.

'Does he have a name, George?'

'Oh, indeed, Miss Julie. Detective Sergeant Baldwin, from Scotland Yard.'

Julie opened her mouth and then closed it again.

But Teddy did not look alarmed. 'Let him come up,' he whispered.

Julie had to take another long breath. 'Would you . . . would you show him up please, George.'

'Right away, Miss Julie.'

She replaced the phone, gazed at him. 'What are we going to do?'

'We're going to get to the bottom of this guy, that's what.'

'But . . . suppose he's armed?'

Teddy grinned at her, and moved his hand. She wasn't quite sure what he did, but a moment later she was looking at a small automatic pistol, hardly larger than the hand which held it.

'Teddy!' She stopped herself from screaming with an effort.

'Always carry it,' he said.

'But people don't carry guns in England.'

'They do in America.'

'Yes, but if the police catch you . . .'

'If he's a policeman, sweetheart, he won't ever know about it, unless you tell him.'

'Oh, Teddy.'

'But if he isn't, you might be glad I have it. You gonna let him in?'

The apartment bell was ringing. She went to the door, gazed at Sergeant Baldwin, and George behind him. 'Miss Armitage?' Baldwin raised his hat.

'Mr Baldwin.' Her voice was surprisingly calm. 'Thank you, George.'

'My pleasure, Miss Julie.' The janitor returned to the lift.

'You'd better come in,' Julie said.

Baldwin stepped past her. 'Miss Julie, is it?' He gazed at Teddy. 'Who are you?'

'A friend of Julie's,' Teddy said. 'A very good friend.'

'Is that so?' Baldwin asked, looking him up and down.

'I'm here because right now I think she needs a friend,' Teddy said. 'Don't you?'

'I would agree with you.' Baldwin went into the lounge. 'Some place you have here, Miss Armitage.'

'So, if you don't mind, Baldwin, I'd like to see your ID.'

78

Baldwin looked at him again, then put his hand in his pocket and brought out the wallet.

'I meant, look at it,' Teddy said.

Baldwin handed it to him, then turned back to inspecting the apartment, and Julie, who was hovering by the telephone. 'What was the point in lying to me yesterday?' Baldwin asked.

'Lying? I . . .' she looked at Teddy.

'Seems in order,' he said.

'Thank you.' Baldwin took the wallet back. 'Now, Miss Armitage, as I was saying, it was pointless to lie to me when you intended coming up here today. Didn't you think I'd have this flat watched? So why not . . .' he glanced at Teddy. 'Come clean, as our American cousins would say.'

'Come clean?' Julie snapped, taking refuge in a genuine anger at his cheek.

'Well, obviously you weren't telling the truth when you claimed you thought you were Julie Allen, or you wouldn't be here today. Therefore, you must know all about your father – as he really was, I mean. That means you have just got to co-operate with us, or you could find yourself in serious trouble.'

'Let him have it, Julie,' Teddy said.

Once again she had to get her breathing under control. 'I have no idea what you are talking about,' she said. 'I am here because someone . . . you . . . planted that envelope in Daddy's drawer. And you have the nerve—'

Baldwin frowned at her. 'Just what are you talking about?'

'You! When you were pretending to search my house yesterday, you . . . you thug, you planted the envelope with this address on it, trying to lead me—'

Baldwin looked at Teddy. 'Has the young lady been drinking, sir?' he inquired.

'I'm on her side, buster,' Teddy said. 'We know, Baldwin. We know.'

Baldwin looked from one to the other. Then he said, 'I assume this is all part of your very funny little game, Miss Armitage. But I'm not going to play. I'll warn you again – unless you stop this foolishness and co-operate with the police you are going to find yourself in very serious trouble. At the very least you have benefited – are benefiting – from your father's mysterious activities. Well, let me tell you something: we have a pretty good idea just how much profit Armitage made over the past few years. That is criminal money, Miss Armitage. And we also have a pretty good idea that you know where it is. Unless you co-operate to the extent of handing it over, and giving us all the other information we require, you could wind up in the dock on a charge of being an accomplice in your father's crimes. I suggest you think about that. I'll be in touch.' He looked at Teddy. 'I would think about that too . . . what did you say your name was?'

'I didn't,' Teddy said. 'But as you've asked, it's Longman.'

'Longman,' Baldwin said, obviously making a mental note. 'Well, Mr Longman, mud sticks, as the saying goes. I'll bid you good day.'

He went to the door.

'Presumably your goons are going to be following us for the rest of the day,' Teddy said. 'Just to save you the trouble, I'll tell you: we're going back to Epsom, returning here this evening. And tomorrow we're going to Somerset House.'

'Quite a busy day for you, sir,' Baldwin remarked. 'But I wouldn't waste your time with Somerset House. Armitage is there all right. He really does exist. But you won't find your lady friend. She doesn't.' He looked at Julie again. 'I would think about that too, young lady.' He closed the door behind him.

'Heck, what a character,' Teddy remarked, and frowned at Julie. 'You okay?'

Julie stared at him. 'He called Daddy a criminal.'

'Yeah, well . . . they must think he's done something wrong, or they wouldn't be involved. If they are involved. I'm just going to check that guy out.' He flicked the pages of the telephone directory, and dialled the number he wanted.

'A criminal,' Julie said. 'Oh, my God, Daddy . . . a criminal?'

'Ah,' Teddy was saying. 'Scotland Yard? Oh, good morning. I'm trying to get in touch with a Detective Sergeant Baldwin . . . oh, that can't be right . . . but he gave me . . . yes. Okay, officer, you're the boss.'

'Daddy can't have been a criminal, Teddy,' Julie said. 'I know he wasn't. And that thing about my birth not being registered . . . God, I thought we were getting somewhere.'

'We are getting somewhere,' Teddy said. 'But it's not very nice.'

80

She stared at him; his face was grim.

'Scotland Yard have just told me they have no Detective Sergeant named Baldwin working with them.'

Julie could only goggle at him.

'Therefore he certainly planted that envelope,' Teddy said. 'And that means there is something very deep going on. I hate to say it, Julie, but just suppose your dad was involved in some underworld activity, and had stashed away some of the loot, and his old partners felt he had robbed them, well, that would explain everything, wouldn't it. Every single thing that has happened.'

'Oh, my God! Teddy, I'm frightened.'

'Well, it's a pretty hairy situation. But we have certain things going for us. One is, if that's true, then the police really don't have a clue what's going on. That is, they don't know anything about Armitage; the guys who searched this apartment must've been pals of Baldwin. So the cops aren't going to be pushing us about. The second thing is that the goons are obviously not sure whether you know about your father's second life or not – that is, whether you do know where he's got his money. So they can't let anything happen to you, until you, or they, find it.'

'But that man Baldwin, suppose . . .'

He nodded. 'Suppose you had been here alone. I reckon finding me on guard was the nastiest shock Baldwin has had in a long time.' He grinned. 'Well, he's going to find me here every time he calls. If that's okay by you.'

'Oh, yes,' she said. 'You promised.'

'I was thinking about the neighbours.'

'Oh. Blow the neighbours. But Teddy . . . we can't live here, if these people know about it.'

'Sweetheart, they also know about the house in Epsom, and Julie Allen.'

'Oh, my God! Of course they do.'

'But the police obviously don't know about this place yet. So I reckon we'll be better off here than there. Besides, George is obviously on our side. So I suggest we just skedaddle back to Epsom, pack you a couple of bags, and move in here without telling anyone where we're going. Those goons want us to find their money for them, well, by gum, we'll do just that. Only

I reckon that money is yours, if it was your dad's. They're not going to see a penny of it.'

'But . . .' there were so many thoughts rushing through Julie's brain she couldn't separate them. 'Is he . . . was he, my Dad, Teddy? That man said I wasn't registered, not even under Julie Armitage. For God's sake, who am I?' Her voice was rising, and she was near another breakdown.

He sat beside her, putting his arm round her shoulders. 'Now just take it easy. In the first place, Baldwin may just have been trying to frighten you. I'll check Somerset House out. But I'll tell you this; if your name isn't there, under Julie Armitage, it's because your dad had a darned good reason for keeping it out. You just have to trust his decisions, what he did, up to the day he died.'

She raised her head; tears were rolling down her cheeks. 'Even if he was a crook?'

'He was still your dad. Whatever he did, he did for you. And we don't know he was a crook, yet.'

He was contradicting himself, but she didn't mind. He was trying to help her, to reassure her and she needed that more than anything else in the world. She put up her face, and he kissed her on the lips. This was a long, slow, deep kiss, where the others had been brushes. But he made Bob's deep kiss seem like a brush too, while his hand, on her hip, moved up and down her body, again as Bob's had done, but much more gently, hardly seeming to touch her thighs, and then the side of her breast, like a caress or breeze, but the more exciting for that. 'Teddy,' she whispered, as his head moved away.

'You haven't thought about it,' he said.

'Yes, I have,' she insisted. 'I want . . . God, how I want you.'

'You want reassurance, and support, and protection,' he said. 'You have to stop wanting those things, and want just me.'

She gazed at him. It had never occurred to her that a man could be so forbearing. Bob had not. He had found her similarly adrift, and had tried to take the fullest possible advantage of it.

He grinned at her, and kissed her again. 'Just in case you think I'm a eunuch, I'm not, I'll prove that I'm not. But I have to have you, Julie, not just a chunk of you that's come apart from the rest. Now . . . lunch, and Epsom?'

*

82

It was totally absurd to be happy in such a situation, Julie knew. Her father had recently been beaten to death. She had just discovered she had no identity, did not even legally exist. She could no longer doubt that she was in physical danger as well as penniless – and the physical danger would increase with every step she took to find whatever wealth her father had left her, and in proportion to that wealth. She was also entirely alone in the world, except for the man sitting opposite her in the train. But that was the reason for her happiness.

It was not just that he was a man close to her own age, who by his confidence and his personality had made her feel that there was someone in the world who cared about her. It was the way he seemed able to cope with every situation, even explain every situation. In Teddy's presence, everything fell into place, because he had such a clear, logical mind. What had fallen into place was frightening, but how much more frightening it would have been just to blunder from mishap to mishap, trusting the wrong people.

And the thought that – if she wanted to – perhaps tonight . . . but that was the key to everything. *If* she wanted to. Yet he would be there whether she wanted to or not, she had no doubts about that, now. He had put her back in charge of her own destiny again. If he never did anything else, she would be grateful to him for that.

The train was slowing, and he was smiling at her. 'Scared?'

'Yes,' she said.

'Don't be. I'll be there.'

'Yes,' she said. 'I know that.'

He leaned forward to squeeze her hand, and a moment later they were stepping on to the station, and he was hurrying ahead to summon a taxi. If he really was only a couple of years older than she, he was far more sophisticated. But that was because she had always left everything to Father. It was such a comforting thought that she could now leave everything to Teddy Longman.

How quiet the street on the outskirts of Epsom seemed. 'I think you had better wait,' Teddy told the driver. 'We don't mean to be very long.'

Julie hurried up the garden path, but the door was opened long before she reached it. 'Oh, Miss Julie,' Mrs Lucas said. 'Inspector Rodham has been ringing, and Mr Cornwall, and . . . that Major Roberts is here.'

83

'Yes,' Julie said.

And Bob at that moment came out of the lounge. 'Julie? Where in the name of God have you been?'

'Out,' Teddy said. 'You'll be Bob.'

Bob stared at him with his mouth open.

'This is Teddy Longman,' Julie explained. 'He's a friend.'

'A friend,' Mrs Lucas snorted. 'He's the one found the body of Mr Allen.'

'I thought his face was familiar,' Bob said. 'Well, thanks for entertaining Miss Allen, old man, but she's home now.'

'Is she?' Teddy asked, pleasantly.

Bob looked at Julie.

'I think we should go inside,' she suggested. 'I'm sure the neighbours are interested enough in my affairs.'

She walked past Mrs Lucas and Bob into the lounge.

'Well,' remarked Mrs Lucas, 'I'm not going to stay, you know, Miss Julie. My Bill—'

'Oh, quite, Mrs Lucas,' Teddy said. 'In fact, you can pack up whenever you like. Miss Julie and I have to hurry on this evening, so she won't need you any more.'

'Well!' Mrs Lucas remarked.

'Mr Longman is right,' Julie said, from the lounge doorway. 'I'm most terribly grateful, Mrs Lucas. But I won't need you to sleep in any more.'

'Well!' Mrs Lucas said a third time, departing for her kitchen.

Bob looked from one to the other. 'Just what the hell is going on?' he inquired.

Julie turned to face him. 'I am going away with Teddy for a little while,' she said.

He stared at her. 'Going away? With him?'

'Yes,' she said, aware that Teddy was framed in the doorway.

'Are you out of your mind? You can't do that sort of thing.'

'Who's going to stop me?'

'Well . . .'

'Not you, Uncle Bob,' she said. 'Because you'd prefer me to go away with you, wouldn't you? Or let you move in here with me.'

'Well . . .' he flushed.

'So let me ask you this: how well *did* you know Daddy? What was this mysterious club to which you both belonged?'

'The Travellers', as a matter of fact.'

'And was he ever more than a casual acquaintance, who one night maybe mentioned to you that I had no relatives apart from him, and that I would be well off when he died?'

'Do you know what you're saying?'

'Yes,' she said, suddenly just as angry as she was pretending to be. 'I'm saying that you realised, the moment you read of Daddy's death, that you could make something out of it. You came rushing down here pretending to be his best friend, and then hurried off to Geneva to pick me up, making love to me shamelessly all the way back and wanting me to sleep with you the moment we arrived here . . . And all the time were hunting desperately for the money Daddy is supposed to have left me.'

His mouth was open in surprise. This was a Julie he had not seen before.

She opened her handbag, took out the twenty pounds he had lent her. 'So, thank you very much. I haven't spent any of it.'

'Julie . . .'

'Bob,' she said. 'There isn't any money. Even the four thousand in the bank isn't going to be mine for a very long time, because I don't exist, remember? Daddy doesn't exist. So you're wasting your time.'

'Julie! Do you really think . . .' he checked, looked at Teddy. 'Do you think we could be alone for a few minutes?'

Julie hesitated. But she owed him that much. 'All right. Teddy?'

'You sure?' Teddy asked.

She nodded.

'I'll be in the hall,' he told Bob. 'Just don't try to lock the door.'

'Quite the tough guy,' Bob remarked, as the door closed. 'Just how long have you known him?'

Julie could not prevent a flush when she thought of it. 'Since yesterday.' Hadn't she known him forever?

'Yesterday? For God's sake—'

'How long have I known you, Uncle Bob?'

'Your father and I—'

'You keep saying that. But I have no proof of it.'

'You're calling me a liar.' His face was stiff.

'I would prefer not to do that. I know you must have been at least acquainted with Daddy. But you must admit that you have taken advantage of me.'

'I happen to have fallen in love with you.'

'Oh, really, Uncle Bob. I'm twenty-one, and you're . . .?'

'I'm thirty-nine.'

'Well . . .'

'It can happen.'

'But it's not very nice when it does.'

He gazed at her. 'I thought you rather enjoyed it.'

'I hated it. But I needed a shoulder to cry on.'

'And now you've found a younger shoulder, is that it? What do you think *he's* after?'

'Teddy is after nothing, Uncle Bob.'

'Not even you?'

Once again Julie could not control her flush.

'But because he's young and virile and exciting, you're going to jump into bed with him and not worry about the cost until after, is that it?'

Her face froze. Because that was exactly what she wanted to do. Except that she *had* counted the cost. 'You're being disgustingly vulgar.'

'And you're being a little whore.'

She swung her hand, again her anger compounded by the knowledge that he was speaking no more than the truth. But he caught her wrist and swung his own. The slap was sharp, and as he let her go, she tumbled backwards on to the settee, arms and legs scattered.

Instantly he was contrite. 'Oh, Julie . . .' but he checked as the door opened and Teddy came in. 'You've had your fun, little man,' he said.

Bob gazed at him. 'She deserved it.'

'Then I deserve it more. So why don't you take a swing at me?'

Bob looked him up and down. 'I doubt you're worth it.'

'Yeah?' Teddy said. 'Well, I sure intend to take a swing at you, buster.'

He stepped forward, but Julie had got herself sitting up. She could taste blood inside her mouth, yet the anger had evaporated. Perhaps it had always been manufactured. 'No,' she said.

Both men looked at her.

'I'd like you to leave, Uncle Bob,' she said. 'You gave me a shoulder to cry on when I needed it. Whatever your motives, I'm grateful for that. Now, just leave.'

86

'And leave you to him,' he said.

'Leave me to myself,' she said.

He gazed at her for a moment, then at Teddy.

'Let him go, Teddy,' she said.

Teddy let his hands fall to his sides.

'You,' Bob said, 'need your head examined.' He stepped past Teddy into the hall.

'Take our taxi,' Julie said. 'We can call another.'

'You are far too generous,' Teddy commented as the door closed. 'I certainly didn't want you fighting over me. God, my mouth hurts.'

'That swine. You should've let me poke him one. Just one. Is it cut?'

'Inside,' she said.

'I'll get something for it.' He left the room, returning a moment later with a glass. 'Salt and water,' he said. 'It'll burn like blazes. Don't swallow it; just gargle a bit and then spit it out.'

She nodded, went to the stairs, and encountered Mrs Lucas, wearing her hat and coat. 'I'll say goodbye, Miss Julie. Brawling! You know where to find me when you've come to your senses.' She looked Teddy up and down and went to the door. 'Mr Cornwall will know how much I'm owed.'

Julie hadn't actually meant her to quit, but she wasn't in the mood for arguing at this moment. 'Of course, Mrs Lucas. And thanks for everything,' she said. Then she went upstairs, gargled as Teddy had instructed her, biting her lip against the sting. There were tears in her eyes. She had been very rude to both Uncle Bob and Mrs Lucas. But there was a surging feeling of freedom, too. She had never been free before. The realisation of that was only just sinking in. She was long past the age when most girls sought freedom, but it had never occurred to her to do so before. It had taken an unthinkable catastrophe to jerk her out of her rut of complacent reliance on the formula Father had dictated as her lifestyle. So, was she now going to rely on Teddy? If she wanted to, she reminded herself. If she wanted to. Even if, at this moment, she had to want to.

He came up the stairs, stood in the bathroom door. 'Okay?'

'Just wearing off.' She smiled at him. 'I suppose I should telephone Mr Cornwall. And the inspector.'

'I wonder if that would be a good idea.'

'They may have turned something up.'

'Such as what? Which we haven't turned up for ourselves? They mustn't find out about the apartment.'

'No,' she agreed. 'But I can't just vanish.'

'For a day or two mightn't be a bad idea.'

'Won't they start looking for me?'

He grinned. 'I don't think you're quite that important in their eyes.'

She hesitated, then shrugged. 'You're the boss. I'll just pack.'

'And I'll call a cab, and go along to Mrs Smith and pick up my gear. I'll be back in half an hour.' He held her shoulders. 'Don't open that door to anyone, Julie. Except me. And don't answer the telephone. Just sit tight until I come back. Okay?'

She nodded, and slid into his arms. 'But do hurry,' she said, as he kissed her, and their bodies pressed against each other.

'I'll hurry.'

He released her, went down the stairs, and she heard him on the phone. She leaned against the wall. She knew she was still whirling through space, but the speed was slowing, and soon it was going to stop. In his arms. Did she know what she was doing? But it was not something she dared reason about. Reason would scream at her that she was a fool, and worse. Reason would tell her that well-bred young ladies did not have lovers before they married, that they did not fall in love virtually at first sight, that they did not feel happy within a few days of their father's death, that they did not borrow money from strange men – but reason knew nothing about it. Because well-bred young ladies did not find themselves in a situation like hers, either.

'It's coming right along,' Teddy said. 'I'll wait outside. You come down and lock this door.'

She went down the stairs. 'Do you realise we're all alone in this house?' Reason didn't understand the wild excitement which was racing through her system, either. That kind of excitement wasn't a reasonable emotion. But it was there. And until it was put to rest she doubted she'd be able to think straight.

He took her in his arms again, held her close, while his hands moved from her shoulder blades down to her buttocks, and stayed there. She shivered. Everything he did to her was a first. And she wanted them all. 'At this moment, my dearest little girl,' he said. 'You're not quite sane.'

'I know,' she said. 'That's what I'm looking for. Sanity.'

He kissed her mouth. 'And you're gradually driving me insane too.' He half lifted her from the floor to bring her against him, and her arms went round his neck. She would have put her legs round him as well if her skirt hadn't been too tight.

From outside there came the toot of a horn. 'Your lucky day,' Teddy said. 'Five more seconds and I wouldn't have been able to let you go.' He put her down. 'Half an hour.'

'Teddy . . .' she caught his hand. 'Is it my lucky day?'

He grinned at her. 'If I have anything to do with it. Yes.'

She bolted the door, leaned against it, and found herself breathing very hard. Then she went into the lounge, and looked around her. Part of her excitement was the thought of getting out of here. This house had only ever been acceptable because it had been Father's. She had never been in it without him before. Without him, it was a hateful place.

She went upstairs, and pulled out her suitcases. She had not actually had time to unpack properly. Now it was merely a matter of taking such extra clothes from her closet as she thought she might need. She had no idea when she would be coming back, and added a third case. Yet there again, a sense of freedom, because she *could* come back whenever she chose.

The telephone jangled. Instinctively she hurried to the stairs, and then stopped. Teddy had said not to speak with anyone. And as he had pointed out, what could anyone have to tell her that she did not already know? Except what Father had actually been – and she wasn't too sure she wanted to find that out, unless Teddy were at her side. Besides, it could be that hateful man Baldwin, with more of his lies and threats.

She went back into her room, closed the suitcases and carried them downstairs one after the other. The phone continued to ring for some minutes, then it stopped. Julie discovered that she was trembling, went to the bar and poured herself a short whisky. It was only four o'clock. But time seemed as mixed up as everything else.

She saw the two bunches of keys lying on the table and dropped them into her handbag almost absentmindedly. Then she sat down, got up again, and moved restlessly to and fro. She didn't want to think, because all thought was horrifying. Yet she couldn't stop. Baldwin had said that Daddy was a criminal. Of course everything Baldwin had said had been lies, or nearly everything. Yet Teddy believed that one, she could tell. It was the only logical explanation, in Teddy's eyes, for what had happened – for what was happening. That was horrifying. The thought that there might be other criminals following her, waiting for her to lead them to some goal, was even more horrifying. Left to herself she knew she would simply have run away. She would, in fact, have run away with Uncle Bob, just to be able to stop thinking about it. And what a disaster that would have been. Teddy had known instinctively that she couldn't run. She had to face them out. And she could do that, with him at her side.

A car engine, and a moment later a bang on the door. She ran to it, threw it open, and herself into his arms.

'Whoa,' he laughed. 'You didn't check that it was me, before opening the door.'

'I knew it was you. Oh, Teddy, I've been scared stiff, in there, alone.'

'Yeah. Well, we're gonna make sure you're not alone any more. The cab's waiting.'

He carried all three of her suitcases together, and she locked the front door. Then they were together in the taxi and driving to the station. She felt she was eloping and held his arm tightly. Here was the only sanity she knew.

'We must make up a list of things to be done,' he said seriously. 'First thing tomorrow morning I'll go along to Somerset House and do some hunting. Right?'

'Right,' she agreed.

He grinned at her. 'We may turn you out to be a millionairess.'

'What would you do then?'

He shrugged. 'Sidle off into the sunset, I guess. You wouldn't need me any more.'

'I'll always need you, Teddy.'

Another grin, this time with only half his mouth. 'That's what they all say.'

George was pleased to see them back. 'I'll take the bags, Mr Longman,' he said. 'You go on up. Oh, and I put the case just inside the door.'

'Case?' Julie and Teddy spoke together.

'It's for Mr Armitage. He gets cases fairly regularly. Just put it in a corner. He'll handle it when he comes back. Do you know when that will be, Miss Julie?'

'Ah, not exactly,' Julie said.

'Well, he sometimes stays away several weeks, although he usually telephones pretty regularly, just to keep in touch. But as he knew you were coming I'd expect him back any moment. Is he going to be pleased to find you moved in. It may make up for the burglary. He isn't going to be happy about that.' It was obviously much on his mind.

They hurried up to the apartment, unlocked the door and gazed at the large brown suitcase waiting in the lobby.

'This came by hand?' Teddy asked, as George staggered in with the other four suitcases.

'Oh, yes, sir. They all come by hand.'

'Who brought it?'

'This one? It was delivered by a young lady.'

'Did she give a name?'

'No, sir.'

Teddy nodded thoughtfully.

'I'll leave you to it, Miss Julie,' George said, and closed the door.

Teddy hefted the suitcase on to the dining-table. 'It's as heavy as hell.'

Julie licked her lips. The excitement was building again. 'Do you think we should open it?'

'Well . . . it's yours. You're damned right we should open it. But carefully, mind. It could've been left by our friend Baldwin, or someone working for him.'

'But you said they wouldn't harm me until he's got what he wanted.'

'Why, so I did. Okay.' From his pocket he took a penknife, flipped open the large blade. 'Will you pry, or me?'

'I'd like to try these.' She took the two bunches of keys from her handbag.

'Holy cow! Are those his?'

'They were found on his body.'

'Good God. And they don't belong to the house in Epsom?'

91

'These do. But these don't.' She stood in front of the case, looked at them. The key which would fit was obvious.

'Let me do it,' he said. 'Just in case there's any funny business.'

'Be careful,' she begged, bit her lip as he inserted the key and turned it, then stood beside him as he slowly lifted the lid. 'Paper,' she said. The suitcase was filled with what appeared to be folded letters, very carefully stacked. 'Just like the one in Epsom. But those aren't newspapers. What can they be?'

'I can tell you what they are,' Teddy said, and now his voice was excited as well. He took one of the letters out, and unfolded it. Julie gazed at a huge five-pound note.

'Oh, Lord,' she said. 'Are they . . .'

Teddy pushed his hands into them, raised a heap and let them fall again. 'They are all five-pound notes,' he said. 'Heck, there must be thousands of them.' He raised his head, gazed at her. 'Tell you what, you can start lending me money, now.'

Julie sat down, staring at the cash. 'I don't understand.'

'I'm beginning to get the drift. Hello, there's something else.' Tucked into the pocket in the lid of the case was a sheet of paper. It was rather like a bill of account, a series of neat figures; first a date, which extended from the first of April to the end of May; then a series of multiples, such as 110×2, 150×1, $170 \times \frac{1}{2}$, and at the end of each line a total: on this first line, 455. The amounts fluctuated, most totalling considerably more than the first. This last column was totalled at the bottom, £58,703 15s. 4d. Beneath this there was a deduction, Expenses £8703 15s. 4d., leaving a total of £50,000 0s. 0d. exactly. Then there was a neat note, 'Certified correct, Alma Briden, 19 June 1932.'

'Holy Jumping Jesus,' Teddy remarked. 'Fifty thousand pounds. I've never seen so much money.' He looked at her. 'And George said they come every couple of months. You know that totals three hundred thousand pounds a year. What does it feel like to be rich?'

'But that's not my money.'

'It was sure intended for your dad. Those have got to be the amounts paid into his account twice a year. Remember? George said he accumulated the suitcases and your dad sorted them out whenever he came – twice a year.' He grinned. 'And you know what, it's tax-free.'

'But who sent it?'

'There's a point. Alma Briden.'

'But who's she?'

'I think it might be an idea to find out. You gather up that dough while I have a look.' He sat down with the telephone directory.

'You think she'll be in there?'

'Why not? Almost everybody is. Even your dad.'

Julie looked at the money. Fifty thousand pounds. And hers? If she dared touch it. But if she didn't, what was she going to do with it? Take it to the police? That would be to admit that Daddy was a crook. She raised her head. 'Do you think this is what Baldwin came for?'

Teddy shook his head. 'If it were, why didn't he come before? I don't think he was looking for this fifty thousand. But if your dad had been collecting something like three hundred grand a year for God knows how long . . . where he's keeping it must be of interest to a few people.'

'Could be it's simply in a bank account.'

'Could be. But your dad sure doesn't keep the statements here.' He snapped his fingers. 'Unless the burglar did take something after all. George wouldn't have noticed one complete set of statements missing.' He frowned. 'But I don't see how knowing where it is is going to help them. Unless . . .' he glanced at her.

'They think they can force me to hand it over.'

'They'll have to get through me first.'

She blew him a kiss. 'But even I can't touch it until I can prove I'm Edward Armitage's daughter. And according to Baldwin I can't do that.'

'Good point. That's why he's pushing you along, maybe.' He was still turning the pages of the directory. 'Here we are. Alma Briden. Lives not far from here.' He carried the book to the telephone.

'You mean you're just going to telephone her?'

'Why not? But we won't let on who we are.' He dialled.

'Hello,' said a woman's voice, softly.

'Miss Briden?' Teddy asked.

'I am she.'

'I'd like to drop in and see you, if I may.'

'Of course. When would suit you?'

'Ah . . . fifteen minutes?'

'You *are* an early bird. But I should think that will be all right. May I have your name?'

'Teddy Longman,' Teddy said.

'And you're an American gentleman,' Miss Briden suggested.

'Right first time. Oh, there'll be two of us.'

'The more the merrier,' Miss Briden said. 'Third floor, and ring the bell.'

The phone went dead, and Julie, who had heard the conversation quite clearly as she was standing at his shoulder, said, 'What an odd woman.'

'Yes,' Teddy said, looking a little odd himself. 'I wonder if it wouldn't be a better idea for me to handle this on my own.'

'No,' she said. 'We're partners, remember? And if this woman knows who Daddy really was—'

'But we're not going to let on who you are or why we're there until we're very sure of the set-up, right?'

She nodded.

'So pack up that dough.'

'And put it where?'

'Well . . . I'd take about fifty pounds with you, just in case. The rest . . . well, I guess under the mattress is as good a place as any.'

'I hate to think of all that money just lying about.'

He grinned. 'Sweetheart, down to half an hour ago you didn't know you had it.'

She flushed. 'Well . . .'

'That burglar isn't going to come back at half past five in the afternoon,' Teddy pointed out. 'And we'll be back by half past six. Right?'

'Of course. I'm being a fool.' Teddy lifted the mattress in the master bedroom for her while she carried the money in and spread it around. Ten of the notes she put in her handbag. 'So let's go.' She was on the trail again. And surely now they were going to get somewhere.

They walked, as Alma Briden's address was only three streets away. It was the oddest sensation to be strolling hand in hand along a London street, on her way to what? A shadow from her father's past? Or something real and perhaps dangerous?

'Here we are.' Teddy stopped in front of another quite imposing building, and led her into the lobby.

94

'Yes?' The porter was less friendly.

'We're here to see Miss Briden.'

The porter stared at Julie. 'Both of you?'

'She knows we're coming.'

The porter continued to look at Julie for a few moments, and she felt her cheeks grow hot. Then he shrugged. 'Third floor.'

Julie almost ran into the lift. 'I don't think he liked the look of me,' she whispered as they ascended.

'I think it's his business to be suspicious of people,' Teddy said. 'Ready?'

The lift had stopped.

'Ready,' she said. She wasn't scared. Not with Teddy beside her.

They stepped in to a carpeted lobby. In front of them was a white painted door, with a bell. Teddy pressed this, and a moment later a voice said, 'Who is it?'

'Mr Teddy Longman,' Teddy said. 'I telephoned.'

What sounded like several bolts were drawn, and the door swung inwards, although it remained held by two stout chains. They gazed at a middleaged woman wearing a maid's uniform, who looked Teddy up and down, and then looked at Julie, and started to close the door again.

'I told Miss Briden there'd be two of us,' Teddy said, putting his hand on the wood to stop it closing.

The maid looked at Julie again, then shrugged. 'Takes all sorts,' she commented, and released the chains. They stepped inside, into a world of subtle odours, half attractive but, strangely, half repellent as well. And it was a world of subtle sounds, too, although Julie could not identify any of it.

'It was Miss Briden personally we wanted to see,' Teddy said.

'She's expecting you. You can wait in here.'

They were shown into a comfortably furnished sitting-room. 'Would you like something to drink?' the maid asked.

Julie looked at Teddy, who shook his head. 'Better not.'

The maid looked at Julie for a third time, then withdrew.

'Teddy,' Julie said. 'This is the oddest place.'

'Isn't it just,' he said. 'Now remember, leave the talking to me, and just follow my lead. Right?'

'Right,' she promised.

They sat down together on a settee, and rose together as the door

95

opened. Julie felt her jaw dropping. She hadn't really known what to expect – but she had not expected this. The woman who entered was tall and statuesque, with deep golden hair cascading past her shoulders, and big, handsome features, which went with a big, handsome body. She was wearing a deep blue lurex evening gown, early as it was, and very high-heeled shoes – and nothing else, Julie was certain, except for an expensive diamond ring on her finger.

She glanced at Teddy to see if he had noticed. He certainly seemed surprised, but not less so than Miss Briden – who was looking at her. 'I thought Watson was pulling my leg,' she said in the deep contralto they had heard on the phone. She came further into the room.

'I'm Teddy Longman,' Teddy said.

'Delighted to meet you, Teddy,' Miss Briden said, and squeezed his hand. 'And the young lady?'

'My fiancée. Amanda Richards.'

Julie shot him a glance. But presumably that had been for the purposes of this investigation.

'Amanda.' Miss Briden stood in front of Julie. 'My dear, you are one of the best sights I have seen in years. All you need is a little grooming, and you could be a raving beauty. Why with a figure like yours . . .' Julie was still wearing her grey suit, and to her consternation Miss Briden now opened the jacket, and without a by your leave gently caressed her left breast. 'And it's all real, I do believe,' Miss Briden commented.

Julie shut her mouth with a snap, and stepped backwards, while she looked at Teddy. He had said to *keep* her mouth shut and do whatever he did, but he wasn't doing anything, and there were limits – which this woman had just overstepped in a big way.

'And shy, too,' Miss Briden remarked. 'I suppose that's the trouble. I think what we need is a foursome, and you may leave Miss Richards to me. But I must tell you that yours is a very unusual requirement, Mr Longman. Very unusual. I have had it before, but only once or twice. It's expensive.'

Julie found herself panting, as the most alarming suspicions started roaming through her brain.

'How expensive?' Teddy asked, to her horror.

'Well, *I* am expensive, to begin with. I don't go with anybody I don't fancy, nowadays. And then, another girl, and what you need . . . it'll cost you fifty pounds.'

96

'Fifty?' Teddy demanded.

'Well . . . as your girlfriend is such a poppet, and it's not busy yet, I could make it forty.'

'Done,' Teddy said.

'I'm afraid it has to be in advance.'

'Mandy has the money.'

'Has she now. I would say Mandy has everything.' Miss Briden stood in front of her again, and Julie took a deep breath. If she touches me again, she thought, I am going to hit her. But Miss Briden this time only stroked her head, very lightly. 'I like your hair. I'd grow it, though. My dear, I am going to enjoy you.'

Julie got her breath back, side-stepped smartly, and got the settee between them. And she couldn't wait on Teddy any longer. She was more angry than scared now. 'There seems to have been a mistake,' she said. 'I . . . we thought you were an accountant. We'll leave now.'

'Leave?' Miss Briden raised her eyebrows.

'Ah, yes,' Teddy said. 'There *has* been a mistake. I do apologise, Miss Briden. Some other time, perhaps.'

'Just what the fucking hell is going on?' The gentle charm suddenly left Miss Briden's voice, as it also vanished from her face.

'I said I apologise,' Teddy said. 'The fact is, I don't think my fiancé really wants to, ah, have a foursome at all. It would upset her. I think we had better leave.

Miss Briden pointed. 'You,' she said. 'Are trying to play some kind of game with me. I don't like that.'

Suddenly Julie sensed trouble. She looked at Teddy, and saw that he had sensed it too. He put his right hand in his pocket, held out his left. She clasped it. She was furious with him, because she had an idea he had known from the start what they were getting into . . . but she also knew only he was going to get them back out.

'Now Alma,' Teddy said. 'Just be reasonable.'

'Jerry,' Miss Briden said. 'Step in here.' She hadn't raised her voice, and Julie realised that there must be hidden microphones which conveyed their voices outside. The door behind Miss Briden had opened, and a very large young man stood there. 'Jerry,' Miss Briden said. 'Take this long streak of misery upstairs and beat the hell out of him.'

'Oh, my God!' Julie gasped.

'Hold it right there, Jerry,' Teddy said, and produced his pistol.

'Well, kiss my ass,' Miss Briden remarked.

As she spoke there was a rustle behind them. Julie had assumed the drape was over a window, but it had been an open door, and before she could even scream a small bag of sand had slammed into the back of Teddy's head. His knees gave way and he hit the floor without a sound other than the thump of his body on the carpet.

Then Julie did scream. At least, she intended to, but, in almost the same movement, the man had thrown one arm round her waist and clapped the other hand over her mouth; she was too terrified even to bite him.

'If you cause trouble,' Miss Briden said, 'I am going to let the boys have you. Think about that. Let her go, Roddy.'

The fingers released her, and she panted for breath, her brain a whirling mixture of outrage and terror. 'If you've killed him . . .'

'With a little bump on the head? I would hope we've knocked some sense into him. Doesn't he know it's illegal to carry a gun in this country? Call Prudence and Amelia, Jerry.'

The first man went ouside, and Julie dropped to her knees beside Teddy. He was breathing, if stertorously.

'Now perhaps you'll tell me just what you're at,' Miss Briden said.

Julie raised her head. 'I told you. It was a mistake. I thought you were an accountant.'

'You really are a twit,' Miss Briden remarked. 'But I'm glad you're such a stubborn twit. Girls, don't you think we are going to have a bit of fun with this one?'

Julie stared at the two women who had entered the room. One was a brunette of what looked like Hispanic origin, the other a redhead. Both wore evening gowns, like their mistress, and both were large, strong young women.

'Oh, she is cute,' said the brunette.

'She came here for a lesson,' Miss Briden said. 'And then changed her mind. I don't think we should let her do that.'

'Oh, no,' said the redhead.

Julie straightened. 'If any of you lays a finger on me,' she said in a low voice.

'And she's always threatening. You come along with us, Mandy. I know you're going to enjoy yourself.'

The two women moved forward. Julie reached for a chair to use as a weapon, but had it wrenched from her hands by the man called Roddy, who had remained behind her. She gasped and tried to hit him, and had her arms seized by the women. She tried to kick them, and one of her shoes came off. She panted, and shouted for help as loudly as she could, and was dragged through the doorway. Here there were more young women, and the maid. Julie ran out of breath as she was pushed through another doorway and found herself in a bedroom. A very beautifully furnished bedroom, the motif being gold and white. But she had no time to admire it as she was hurled across the coverlet, held on her face while her jacket was taken off, rolled on her back for fingers to unfasten the buttons of her blouse.

'Stop it!' she shrieked. 'Let me go. Let me . . .' she looked past them in amazement as Miss Briden entered the room, and with a simple sort of shimmy, caused her gown to slide from her shoulders, past her hips, to the floor. As Julie had surmised, she was naked underneath, and had the sort of figure which would have been admired in Valhalla.

'Let's have a look at her,' Miss Briden said, standing beside the bed.

Julie's blouse was pulled off, and her brassière released. She was thrown down again for her skirt to be removed. 'The police', she screamed.

'Are you really going to go to the police?' Miss Briden smiled. 'I wonder what you'll tell them.'

Julie was forced flat again as her knickers and suspender belt were removed together, her stockings dragged over her toes. She tried to sit up again and the brunette held her wrists, extending her arms above her head to keep her pinned to the bed. She tried to kick, and the redhead grasped both her legs and held them tightly, while she watched Miss Briden coming closer. Miss Briden was smiling. 'You are even better than I had hoped,' she said. To Julie's consternation she climbed on to the bed herself, and then swung one of her legs over, to sit astride, on Julie's naked thighs. She was a heavy woman, and Julie was absolutely helpless, while her arms were still being held above her head, and the other girl was still grasping her ankles. 'Now you listen to me, you little bitch,' Miss Briden said pleasantly. 'I am going to have you, either way. Whether I hurt you or not depends on whether you co-operate. And co-operation begins with telling me just what your long streak of misery and yourself came here for.'

Julie gasped for breath. She could only think, I am about to be raped – by a woman. Teddy had said no one was to know why they had come. But he might be being beaten up at this very moment, and she . . . 'We . . . we came to see you,' she gasped. 'The money . . .'

Miss Briden stopped smiling, and stopped stroking Julie's breasts. 'What money?'

'The money you sent to . . . to Father. The suitcase. We wanted to . . .'

Miss Briden's face suddenly changed, from contempt to horror. 'Just who are you?' she whispered.

'Julie,' Julie gasped. 'Julie Armitage.'

Miss Briden stared at her, and seemed to shrink before her eyes. 'Oh, God,' she said. 'Oh, Jesus.' Her body slithered away, and the hands holding Julie down were also gone. 'Oh, Christ in Heaven,' Miss Briden said, and fell to her knees beside the bed, her face buried in the coverlet. Then she looked up, seized Julie's hands. 'It was just a joke, Miss Armitage, just a joke. Please believe that. I didn't . . . I wasn't . . .' she licked her lips. 'You mustn't tell your father.'

Julie sat up. If she was still whirling through space, she realised that she had suddenly become the sun itself.

CHAPTER 5

'I would like to get dressed,' Julie said, carefully omitting the please.

'Of course.' Miss Briden snapped her fingers, and the girls began gathering Julie's clothes. 'I do hope they aren't torn. I'll replace them, of course. I—'

'I would also like Mr Longman brought here, and given whatever assistance he requires.'

'Right away. Prudence . . .'

The redhead hurried from the room, and Miss Briden began holding up Julie's clothes for her.

'He'll be quite all right, you know. Just a little bang on the head . . . it was all fun . . .'

Julie clipped her suspender belt, added her blouse, and began to feel better. 'Just what do you think my father would do to you, were he to find out about today?'

'But you aren't going to tell him, my dear. Are you?' Miss Briden seized Julie's hand, releasing it again as Julie looked at her.

'That depends,' Julie said. She had never been in such a position before. Her anger at what had been done to her and to Teddy, made her want to watch this woman squirm. But more than that, she understood that she might not command quite such strength again – and there were so many things to be found out. 'Tell me what he would do.'

Miss Briden looked at Amelia.

'He'd slash her, for a start,' Amelia said.

'Slash her?'

'Carve her cheeks for her.'

'Father?' Julie could not believe her ears.

'He's such a violent man,' Miss Briden said.

Father? Julie thought. The most gentle man on earth, she had always thought him.

'Oh, he wouldn't do it himself,' Amelia said. 'He'd have one of his goons do it. Then he'd laugh. I saw him once, laughing at a girl, while the blood ran down her cheeks. "You're on the street at half a crown a throw, now," he said. "Then it's the dung heap."'

Julie gave a little shiver. Oh, my God, she thought, Daddy?

'You don't know him very well, dear,' Miss Briden said. 'You don't ever want to cross Eddie Armitage.' Then she frowned. 'You *are* his daughter? By Christ, if I thought this was another game you're trying to play with me . . .'

'Of course I'm his daughter. If you doubt that, telephone George Gardner.'

'He know you?'

'For Heaven's sake,' Julie said, with a confidence she did not feel. 'I'm living in my father's flat, aren't I?'

She was fully dressed, and Amelia handed her a hairbrush. It smelt clean, so she used it.

'So how come we haven't seen you before?' Miss Briden asked.

'I've been living with my mother,' Julie explained. 'She and Daddy split up years ago, and she didn't want me to know him. Well, I'm twenty-one now, so I thought I'd pay him a visit.'

Miss Briden considered, but Julie was sure Father would have told her the same thing he had told George Gardner – if he had told her anything.

'So why are you here?' Miss Briden inquired. 'With that man.'

'Teddy is my fiancé,' Julie said, deciding it was best not to complicate matters by changing that story either; there was too much else on her mind. 'He met me when I arrived back from Switzerland, and we went to Daddy's flat, as usual. Only George told us Daddy'd gone across to France for a few days on business. And then your suitcase turned up. It seemed rather a lot of money to be carried around in cash, and Daddy had left no instructions, so we thought we'd ask you where it came from.' She paused for breath; she had never actually told a lie in her life, before – now she didn't seem able to tell the truth. Fortunately, at this moment Teddy came in, walking somewhat uncertainly, with two of the 'girls' hovering at his shoulder. 'God, my head,' he said, and gazed at Miss Briden.

102

'It's all right,' Julie told him. 'Miss Briden has discovered who I am. She's very sorry for what happened, aren't you, Alma?'

'Oh, yes,' Alma said, and stroked Teddy's brow. 'You poor boy.' Teddy was still staring at her, and now she realised why; unlike Julie she had not bothered to put her gown back on. 'He needs a drink,' she said. 'Fetch him a brandy.'

Prudence hurried off again, and Teddy sat on the bed. 'Will someone tell me what's going on?' he asked.

'Just stop worrying,' Julie told him. 'Now, Alma, the money.'

"Don't ask me, dearie. My instructions were to deliver it to the flat every two months. I don't really think you should have opened the case. You don't want your daddy getting mad at *you*.' Her expression suggested she would rather enjoy that.

'But it all comes from here?'

'Oh, no, dearie. Even my girls aren't *that* good. It comes from all the houses. We just collect it here.'

All the houses, Julie thought. And he would have slashed this woman's face. Oh, my God!

'Not that we're more than a drop in the ocean,' Miss Briden went on. 'When I think what the Association controls in the States . . .'

'In the States?' Julie asked feebly.

Prudence had returned with the brandy goblet, and Teddy was clearly feeling better.

'I think we'd better go home,' he said.

'Shall I call a taxi?' Miss Briden asked.

'I think we'll walk,' Julie decided. 'Can you walk, Teddy? The fresh air will do you good.'

'I can walk,' Teddy said

'You owe him his gun,' Julie said.

'Prudence!' Once more Prudence hurried off, but Miss Briden was shaking her head. 'You want to be careful with guns, in this country. Your dad wouldn't approve of that.'

'Daddy approves of anything I do,' Julie said. Until she could have a moment to think, she simply had to keep riding this wave.

'I'm sure he does, dearie.' Miss Briden put her arm round Julie's shoulders and hugged her. 'You are a perfect poppet. If you're ever at a loose end . . .' she allowed her gaze to drift over Teddy, contemptuously, 'give me a ring. I think you and I could have real fun together.'

'Yes,' Julie said. 'I'm sure.' She held Teddy's hand, made herself move with relaxed confidence, at least until they were in the lift. Then she leaned against him. Her knees felt weak.

His arms went round her. 'Would you mind telling me just what happened? I don't remember a thing after that thug came into the room. And you weren't going to let on who you were.'

'I didn't have any choice.' The lift reached the ground floor and they nodded to the porter and walked out into the afternoon air. The sunlight hurt her eyes, but the tears were more real than that. 'Oh, Teddy. There was another thug, who hit you with a sandbag. Then they took me into a room, and . . .' she decided not to tell him what had actually happened. 'They threatened to torture me if I didn't tell them what we were after. Maybe I lost my head. Anyway, I thought you might be dying or something, so . . .'

'So you blew it,' he commented.

'Oh, Teddy. Teddy, the things they told me. Daddy is – was – a crook. He's running a whole chain of . . .'

'They're called brothels,' Teddy told her, as she searched for the word.

'And he has men at his command who'd cut a woman up, and – oh, Teddy. I can't believe it. Father?'

'I'd keep your voice down,' he said. But they were nearly back at the apartment building, and a moment later were inside.

'You all right, Miss Julie?' George asked. 'You look as if you've seen a ghost.'

Yes, she thought. That's just what I've seen. A quite hideous ghost.

Teddy hurried her upstairs. 'I think you need a drink as much as I do,' he said, and poured.

Julie went into the bedroom and gazed at herself. She did look a sight. Her clothes were crushed and a button had come off her blouse. Her hair was rumpled. And she desperately felt like a bath, while there were tearstains on her cheeks and she had lost all her lipstick. But it was her face itself which she wanted to look at. It was her face, the face she had looked at for twenty-one years. Suddenly it was the face of a stranger. It was the face of the daughter of a man who operated brothels and who would cut a woman's cheeks open. God, she thought; I have that blood in my veins.

Teddy stood behind her. 'Did they hurt you?'

104

She shook her head.

'Then drink this, and tell me what's on your mind?'

She gulped the whisky. 'On my mind? For God's sake, Teddy. My father is a criminal. Was a criminal. A really nasty, vicious criminal.'

'If what that woman said is true.'

'How can it not be true? There's the money under that mattress, and believe me, when she found out who I was she was terrified. She said Daddy would have his people slit her cheeks for her.'

'It's the old punishment for a whore who misbehaves.'

'So it has to be true. Teddy, we have to go to the police.'

'Now hold on there. And tell them what?'

She sat on the bed, shoulders hunched. 'Everything.'

'What good would that do? You'd blacken your dad's memory, and have yourself plastered all over the newspapers. And make a lot of unpleasant enemies. And really, alter nothing. Once the underworld knows that Eddie Armitage is dead, there'll be too many people just waiting to try on his shoes.'

'But—'

'And to get their hands on his money.' He sat beside her, his arm round her shoulders. 'I have a notion there could be one hell of a lot of it lying around somewhere. I would say finding that is our number one priority. It's your money.'

'It's criminal money.'

'Okay. But as you can't give it back, it would be stupid just to *leave* it lying around.'

She gazed at him, eyes wide. 'Give it back,' she said. 'I could give it back.'

He frowned at her.

'Don't you see? We'll find the money. All of it. Then I'll give it all to charity, and I'll tell the police, and . . .' her eyes filled with tears. 'I have to clear Daddy's name, my name, somehow.'

He took her in his arms and kissed her. 'You are just too good for this world, my dearest child,' he said. 'Just too sweet.'

She fell backwards across the bed, and he fell with her. Then he rose on his elbow, and looked down at her. She had seen the look before, in Bob's eyes. He wants to make love to me, she thought. And knew that this time it was going to happen. Because she wanted it too.

And he could tell that. His head came lower, and he kissed her mouth, slowly, deeply, longingly, while his leg flopped across her thighs. Then he raised his head again. 'If you don't slap my face, right this minute,' he said. 'I am going to be a terrible cad.'

'I'm not going to slap your face,' she said.

He gazed into her eyes. 'Certain sure?'

She inhaled. Certain sure? She wasn't certain sure of anything right this minute. She only knew that the girl she had supposed she was, the virginal innocent the world had supposed she was, had never really existed. She was the daughter of a big-time criminal. A world-wide criminal. They hadn't discussed the implications of that yet.

He was smiling his crooked smile. 'I guess you're not. You'd better start swinging.'

'Certain sure,' she said. 'It's just that . . . could I take a shower first?'

He raised his eyebrows. 'Whatever turns you on.'

'Those women, manhandling me . . . I feel filthy.'

He nodded. 'I can understand that.' He moved his leg and sat up. 'It'll give you time to change your mind.'

He was such a perfect gentleman. He was the only good thing about this whole horrible business. 'I'm not going to change my mind,' she said. 'You can share the shower, if you like.'

'Now, do you know, that sounds like a most attractive offer,' he said.

She stood up, taking off her jacket. 'This suit is ruined,' she remarked. She was desperately trying to keep her nerves under control, to approach whatever was going to happen with utter calm, because if she let go for a moment now she was going to have hysterics.

'So throw it out,' he said. 'I think you can just about afford a new one. Or two. Or three.'

She glanced at him, fingers on the buttons of her blouse.

'Would you like me to leave while you undress?' he asked.

'I'd like you to stay,' she said. With him actually looking at her, she couldn't think of anything save his presence. She stared at him as she took off her blouse, and released her brassière.

He was sitting up, staring back. Now he said, 'May I?'

She didn't know what to do, had a tremendous urge to say no. But

106

she wasn't going to turn back now. She moved closer, and his arms went round her waist, bringing her against him. His face rested against her breasts, and his lips went between, and then moved over the mound to suck her left nipple between his teeth. She gave a shudder, but what had started out as a mixture of alarm and even revulsion was now becoming pure ecstasy. His hands slid down over her buttocks and held them tightly, and she put her own arms round his neck to hug him against her.

He released her, moved his head. 'I think we had better hurry,' he said.

She released her skirt, allowing it to slide past her thighs, and took off her knickers and suspender belt. He was still watching her, but now he was on his feet, and undressing in turn. She stepped out of her shoes and as she stood in front of him, wondered if he found her as attractive as Miss Briden had done. She certainly hoped so. And remembered that she should be angry with him, because she was sure he had known exactly what Miss Briden was before they ever got there, and had been enjoying the suggestion that they should make up a foursome to teach her the facts of life. Well, he had certainly accomplished that, even if in a way he had not anticipated.

And how could she be angry with him, if she was going to let him make love to her? She gazed at his chest, remarkably strong and smooth, and his strong legs as he dropped his trousers. She instinctively wanted to look away as he let his drawers fall behind them, but then she didn't. He was certainly ready for her. Mrs Simpson's 'facts of life' classes had included books with pictures of the male anatomy, but always flaccid, and Mrs Simpson's tone as she had explained – 'It has to harden to force an entry, of course' – had as usual suggested only pain and humiliation. And for some reason the illustrations had never included hair. She felt quite frightened, as she looked at him, but very excited as well.

He took her into his arms, and it was actually against her naked stomach. His hair is mingling with mine, she thought. Somehow that seemed more intimate than what was about to happen. He kissed her mouth, allowed his lips to wander all over her face and hair. 'Most people shower afterwards,' he said into her hair.

'Yes,' she said. She didn't want this to stop, or she'd never have the courage to let it start again.

He lifted her from the floor and laid her on the bed. He covered

107

her, kissing her mouth and eyes, caressing her breasts, while she felt him, ever more insistent, on her groin. She opened her legs and he was between, and pressing into her. There was more discomfort than pain, at first; then he slipped off her. 'I don't want to rush you,' he said. 'Let me play with you a little,' he said.

She didn't know what he meant, wanted to close her legs tightly as his hand slipped between, made herself lie still, while he stroked her with infinite care, and she felt a sudden warmth, combined with a growing feeling of anticipation. He smiled at her. 'Now, I think,' he said, and entered her. This time the pain was sharp, and she gasped, but then it eased a little before there was even more warmth, and his body sagged on hers, leaving her only the still growing feeling of anticipation.

She gasped again, and he rolled off her. She sucked huge breaths into her lungs and gazed at the ceiling. Julie Allen had ceased being a girl, and become a woman. But then, she had also ceased being Julie Allen, and become Julie Armitage.

'Heck,' Teddy said. 'I didn't figure you were a virgin.'

She turned her head. He had risen to his elbow, and his expression was anxious. 'Or you wouldn't have done it?'

'I . . .' he flushed. 'I sure wanted to.'

'So did I. Does it always hurt like that?'

He shook his head. 'Shouldn't. Only the first time. There's a protective membrane I've just penetrated.'

'Oh. I'm glad of that.' She sat up, looked down at the blood.

'Again, just the first time,' Teddy said.

'I'm glad of that too.' She went into the bathroom, showered for a long time, soaping and soaping and soaping. It was more than a desire to be clean; it was also a desire to be aware of herself, to increase the awareness he had induced.

The curtain parted and he stepped in beside her. He took the soap and massaged her all over again, and then gave it back to her. She knew what he wanted, and soaped him in turn. She held him and felt him harden again, and a moment later they were on the bed again, still wet. She was still hurting from the first time, but as he had promised there was no increase of pain, and this time the anticipation was even greater.

'I love you,' Teddy said. 'Oh, my God, how I love you.'

And I could love you, she thought. When I know who I am.

They showered again, dressed, and went out to dinner at the first restaurant they found. They gazed at each other across the glowing candle, and sipped claret. 'I wish we could forget everything else,' he said. 'And just do this, and that, all day and all night, for the rest of our lives.'

'But we can't,' she said. 'I can't, anyway.'

'I know. So . . .' he reached across the table to squeeze her hand. 'First thing tomorrow I go to Somerset House and get all the information we need. Then . . .'

'We should open a bank account for that money.'

'Not a good idea, I think. We want to keep as low a profile as possible for a while, and twenty-one-year-old girls opening bank accounts with fifty thousand pounds in cash might just cause eyebrows to be raised.'

'I hadn't thought of that. Anyway, I'm going to need some of it, to get us to the States.'

'To do what?' He nearly spilt his drink.

'Didn't you hear what that woman said? This is just a minor operation compared with what Daddy has in the States.'

'I wouldn't take that too seriously.'

'I do take it seriously.'

He gazed at her for some seconds. 'And just what do you intend to do about it? Take on the mob?'

'I have to find out about Daddy,' she said stubbornly. 'I have to know all about him, Teddy. I have to, or I'll never sleep again.' She didn't know if she was ever going to sleep again, anyway.

He raised his shoulders and let them fall again in a gesture that was more expressive than a mere shrug. 'And the money?'

'That isn't as important as finding out what he's done. Everything.'

Teddy considered this for several seconds. Then he said, 'But you can't make amends until you find the money.'

'God, it's all so confusing. But there'll be more money in the States.'

'I wonder,' he argued. 'Your daddy was English. I think it's most likely he'd have stashed his loot in England.'

'How do we know he was English?' she asked. 'He could've been anything. I could be anything. I could have been born anywhere in the world.'

'I'd take odds against Tokyo or the Congo,' he said, but he could see

109

she was again close to tears. 'Listen. We don't do anything until I've checked out Somerset House. Come to think of it, we can't do anything until then: you don't have a passport.'

She'd forgotten that. 'Teddy!'

He squeezed her fingers. 'Come on home to bed, and stop thinking about it until tomorrow. We'll sort something out.'

'I'll say goodnight, Miss Julie, Mr Longman,' George said. 'Will you be staying long, sir?'

'Ah . . .' Teddy looked at Julie.

'Well, when you come down, sir, as I probably won't be here, just make sure you close the outer door firmly behind you. You'll hear the latch snap. Then the house is secure. All right?'

'Sure,' Teddy said. 'I'll do that.' He closed the door of the apartment, leaned against it. 'Those were the clearest marching orders I have ever received.'

'Well, I hope you're not going to take any notice of them.'

'Julie . . .' he held her shoulders. 'You just can't do this sort of thing.'

'Who's going to stop us?' she asked.

'Well – the neighbours, George . . .'

'You're forgetting who I am,' she said. 'At the moment, I'm Julie Armitage. I could be the heiress to the greatest criminal organisation in the world.' It was slowly sinking in.

'Just how much of that wine did you drink with dinner?'

'Couldn't I?'

'It's possible, I suppose. In a manner of speaking. But Julie – those characters play rough. I'd have thought you'd have got that message this afternoon.'

'Yes,' she said. 'So maybe I'll have to start playing rough, too. If I'm going to survive.'

'Do you know how to?'

She shook her head. 'I need someone to teach me.'

He held her against him, kissed her lips. 'Sometimes you frighten me.'

'I'd like to frighten a few other people. I want you to stay, Teddy. I don't want you to leave my side.'

'Well . . .' he grinned at her. 'I guess I'm under orders.'

*

110

Sunlight, drifting through the half-drawn drapes, cascading across the bed, bringing with it the growl of Monday morning traffic. Immediate warmth, wakefulness and awareness. Julie thrust her feet beneath the sheet. She had never slept naked before. Now she thought she was never going to wear pyjamas or a nightdress again.

She rolled on her side, thumped the empty mattress, and sat up in alarm. Then she heard him in the bathroom. He was half dressed. 'Where are you off to?'

'Somerset House, remember?'

'But . . .' she thrust her hands into her hair. 'Breakfast?'

'I've had a cup of coffee. We'll brunch when I get back. I really have this on my mind, Julie.'

She lay down again. Well, it was on her mind too. But not as much as before. How many times had they made love? At least six. She was surprised he had any energy left at all. And each time had been better than the time before, even if there had always been the anticipation of something even more, each time, as well. She had been utterly wanton, as if she had been on her honeymoon . . . only she wasn't. But she was Eddie Armitage's daughter. Eddie Armitage! The very name had a sinister ring to it.

Teddy came in and bent over to kiss her. 'I shouldn't be more than a couple of hours. You just sit tight, and don't let anybody in. I'll leave you this.' He put his automatic pistol on the bedside table.

'What am I supposed to do with that?'

He grinned at her. 'Be tough, if you have to prove a point. But you won't, if you don't open the door. See you.'

He waved at her, and a moment later she heard the flat door bang. She stretched, slowly and luxuriously, reaching as far as she could with both arms and legs. She had never felt like this before, at once exhausted, sated and utterly complete. Why had she waited so long? Simply because up to a couple of days ago she had been Julie Allen, and Julie Allen had been a well-brought-up young lady.

So what exactly was Julie Armitage? It was very important to be sure. Last night she had been riding a wave and been afraid to look down into the troughs. This morning she was just relaxed – for the first time since she had walked unsuspectingly into Mrs Simpson's office – could it possibly have been only four days ago? But the relaxation was part of the understanding that she was embarking upon, a way of life totally different to anything she had known

111

before. She didn't want to think of Julie Armitage as a bad girl, a criminal, yet she had to acept the fact that she might be, that there were things she might have to do, situations she might have to face, which would have sent Julie Allen into hysterics. But which Julie Armitage would have to take in her stride. So think. Imagine. Cutting a woman's cheeks, or watching it being done – that made her feel sick. Well, then, being made love to by a woman, by Alma Briden – she just couldn't imagine that. But then, four days ago, she had never been able to imagine actually being made love to by a man, either.

So think about that, and Teddy. Because that was important too. Teddy had fallen in love with her, wildly, romantically, delightfully. As she was being honest with herself she supposed she should accept that the fact that she was surrounded with some mystery, and perhaps even a lot of money, had probably helped. But no more than the fact that he thought she was beautiful. Odd, she thought, she had never considered herself beautiful before. But now, in rapid succession three people had told her how much they desired her. So maybe, if she wasn't actually beautiful, she was intensely desirable. She threw back the sheet and looked down at herself, touched herself. This was all part of being Julie Armitage, a girl who feared no one and nothing, who was going to seek out her father's past, and his fortune, and then . . .

Then maybe Julie Armitage could fade away, like a female picture of Dorian Gray, and Julie Allen could live again. But Julie Allen would never be innocent again.

A key turned in the latch and she gave a gasp and leaped out of bed, looking wildly to and fro. She ran into the bathroom, plucked her dressing-gown from the hook, dashed back into the bedroom to pick up the pistol, and heard George's voice. 'Miss Julie? Miss Julie? Are you in?'

Now her gasp was sheer relief. 'Oh, George, you did give me a start. Just a moment.' She put the gun in the drawer of the bedside table, tied the dressing-gown tightly, ran a brush over her hair, and went into the lounge. 'I'm afraid I was still in bed. Is there anything the matter?'

George stood in the archway to the lobby, and looked embarrassed. 'Miss Julie . . . that young fellow, Mr Longman . . . did he spend the night here?'

To Julie's annoyance she could feel heat gathering in her cheeks. But now it was very important to be Julie Armitage. 'Why, yes, George, he did.'

George looked even more embarrassed. 'You're not married, are you, Miss Julie?'

'No.'

'Oh.'

'But we are engaged.'

'Ah.' George seemed slightly relieved, but not entirely. 'Still, it weren't proper, Miss Julie. Why, if the neighbours were to get to know of it – or your father . . .'

Julie sat down and crossed her legs. She wished she could light a cigarette, in keeping with her new image, but she had never smoked and had no idea how to set about it. But her dressing-gown fell away from her knees and George's embarrassment was back. 'How long have you worked for my father, George?'

'Oh, ten years now, miss.'

'I see.' How incredible, she thought, that it had not occurred to them to begin their search at home, so to speak. 'I know very little of him. Having been living with my mother, you see. Sit down, George. I know, I'll make us both a cup of coffee. But I really would like to know about him.'

'Well, miss . . .' George cautiously lowered himself on to a straight chair.

Julie filled the percolator. 'Do you know how long he's had this flat?'

'That I couldn't say, miss. He had it when I came to work here.'

'And how often does he use it?'

'Why, only four weeks in the year, really, miss. But regular as clockwork. A week at the beginning of the summer, and a week at the end. Then a week at the beginning of December, and a week about the middle of January. Empty the rest of the time, but it's my job to keep it spick and span, ready to be occupied at a moment's notice. He always knew you were going to come here, one day.'

'And now I'm here,' she reminded him. 'Did . . . I mean, does my father entertain a lot?'

'Oh, no, miss. He never entertains.'

'Not even a woman? I mean, a lady?'

'Good heavens, no, miss. That's why . . .'

113

Presumably, if he wanted sex, he'd just telephone Alma Briden, Julie thought. She interrupted. 'What about those suitcases?'

'Well, Miss Julie, I always just leave them here in the flat until he comes. He sorts them out then.'

My God, she thought: there would have been about two hundred thousand pounds just sitting here, from time to time. 'Don't you ever wonder what's in them?'

'Of course not, miss. And you shouldn't, either.' He stood up. 'I really must get downstairs.'

Julie offered him a cup of coffee. 'Drink this first. George, is my father a violent man?'

George frowned. 'Violent, miss? Not to my knowledge. Always sunshine and light, is Mr Armitage. Mind you, he can be upset. I mean, he's going to be upset about the burglary. But then, he's going to be so happy you're here. But that young man will upset him. I'll move his case downstairs, shall I, Miss Julie?'

Julie put down her coffee cup. She might as well start being Julie Armitage, she supposed. It was a shame to hurt poor old George, but she had to begin somewhere. 'You'll do no such thing, George.'

'But Miss . . .'

'Mr Longman is staying here with me, George. And that's final.'

George opened his mouth and then shut it again, put down his coffee cup. 'I'd best be getting downstairs,' he said.

It was surprising how easy it was. And how satisfying, even if it left her feeling a heel. But as Teddy had said, she was moving into a society which played rough, and therefore she had to be rough too, all the time.

She turned on the radio, and then she ran her bath, and sank into the water with a sigh. She certainly needed a hot bath. She also needed to think, but she wasn't sure she was ready to do that yet. She had to assimilate her new image, her new personality, come to grips with the fact that while she was now her own boss for the first time in her life, she also had no back-up except for Teddy. Darling, delightful, Teddy. She was surprised she felt so little different to before, save for the soreness, so little remorse, so little fear for the future, in the sexual sense. How could she? He had told her how much he loved her, and she believed him. He was like a dream come true. But . . . she frowned. He had proved curiously inept in

114

Alma Briden's brothel. He had in fact never provided the solid feeling of security she had known when Father had always been there, standing between her and the world. Even Uncle Bob had actually suggested more certain protection. She wondered about Uncle Bob. About whether he was actually after her money, or just her body. About whether he could really have been a friend of Father's. Because if he hadn't been, and yet knew so much about him . . . she raised her head with a gasp as the radio was switched off. Because there he was, standing in the bathroom doorway, looking at her.

Part Two

NEW YORK

CHAPTER 6

'Uncle Bob!' Julie drew up her knees and hugged her breasts against them. For the moment she was too outraged to be afraid. 'You . . . get out of here!' How in the name of God had he got *in*?

He came into the room, and she hugged herself tighter yet. 'Just what are you doing here?' he asked.

'You . . .' she licked her lips. He was standing immediately above her, looking down at her, and she didn't like his expression. The gun! She had to get into the bedroom. 'I live here,' she said.

'So I gather, from George.' He took a towel from the rail, held it out. 'You'd better come out. You and I have to have a serious chat.'

Julie had lost control of her thought processes again. From George? He knew George. Of course he'd know George, if he was a friend of Father's. But George only knew Father as Edward Armitage!

'Come on,' he said.

'Not with you in the room,' she said.

He shook his head. 'I'm not letting you out of my sight, Julie. You're just too slippery. And if what George has been telling me is true, you're in no position to resume the shy young virgin act. Out!'

Julie realised he was deadly serious, and also very angry. 'If you touch me,' she warned.

'If I touch you, Julie, you are going to squeal. Do you want me to start now?'

He had laid the towel on the toilet seat. She got it into her hand and let it unfold as she stood up. Water ran down her shoulders and hips, dripped from nipple and pubes.

'Dry yourself,' he told her. 'I don't want you catching cold.'

119

'And you're going to watch?'

'Yes,' he said.

She wondered why he didn't fall down dead as she got all the hatred she could into her glance. But she stepped from the bath and towelled, while he leaned against the wall with his arms folded. 'Where is lover boy?' he asked.

'Out,' she snapped. 'But when he comes back . . .'

'I may have to teach him a thing or two,' Uncle Bob agreed.

Julie's head jerked; because suddenly she realised that Uncle Bob could very probably teach Teddy a thing or two. But now he was holding out her dressing-gown. She wrapped herself in the clinging cloth and tried breathing again.

'Outside,' Uncle Bob said.

She stepped into the bedroom, wondered if she should make a dive for the gun, but he was too close behind her.

'The lounge,' Uncle Bob commanded.

She walked in front of him, her bare feet still leaving damp patches on the carpet. If only she could think, could try to work out . . . but she was too conscious of his presence.

'Sit down,' he invited.

Julie sat on the settee, knees pressed together, body hunched. Uncle Bob sat opposite her, quite relaxed. She wondered if he was armed.

'Now tell me how you found out,' he said.

'Found out what?'

'That your father was really Eddie Armitage.'

She stared at him, again seeking all the hostility she could command. 'You didn't tell me, did you, Uncle Bob?'

'I couldn't. I promised your father I never would.'

'Well, you can now, because I know. Right?'

'I don't break promises, Julie. My only concern is that you have been foolish enough to stick your head into a situation where you might just get it chopped off. You have to get out of here, and fast.'

'You . . . oh, I get it. You don't want your lovely crime empire torn apart, is that it? Forget the sweet words and the pseudo concern, Uncle Bob. I know all about it. I know all about the brothels and the American end. So what are you? Daddy's second-in-command?'

Uncle Bob gazed at her for several seconds. Then he said, 'You're in more danger than I supposed.'

120

From you, she thought. Because I have talked too much and you are going to have to . . . kill me? It was an incredible thought to be having in a Mayfair flat, especially when wearing only a dressing-gown, but that was how these people behaved. Therefore she couldn't afford to wait any longer.

Heart pounding, she stood up.

'Sit down,' he said.

'I have to go to the toilet,' she said, and went to the bedroom door. She knew he was going to follow her, but he had been slow getting up. As she reached the doorway she leaped forward, throwing herself at the bedside table. But he was right behind her. She got the drawer open, reached the gun, turned, praying that she would not actually have to fire it, and was struck a paralysing blow on the arm. The gun flew from her nerveless fingers and banged against the wall, and she was hurled on to the bed, arms and legs scattered. Before she could push herself up he was kneeling astride her, like Alma Briden, she thought, only she was on her face and he was fully dressed.

She gasped, and he drove his fingers into her hair to raise her head. 'You unutterable little fool,' he said. 'I should bust your ass. Maybe I will, if that's the only way I can get any sense into you. Whose idea was the gun? Don't tell me: your American boyfriend. I have an idea you want to think very carefully before you let that character into this apartment again.'

'You . . .' she tried to twist, and he held her flat.

'All you have to do is listen, Julie. Very carefully. Your father and I were friends. Closer friends than you can imagine, or than I have told you. No, I was not involved in his criminal activities, but I knew about them. I couldn't tell you who he really was because he made me swear that I never would, but as you seem to have found out, there are some other things you should know. Eddie Armitage is – was – a very big wheel indeed in the underworld. He was senior partner in something called the Association, which runs all the bootlegging and vice rackets in New York and New England. This London operation is just a sideshow. Therefore it seemed to me that this talk of him being attacked by a crazy tramp and dying by accident is just so much bullshit. He was deliberately murdered. But he was murdered as Edwin Allen, and Edwin Allen didn't have an enemy in the world. Therefore he was really murdered as Eddie

121

Armitage, and that means he was killed either by someone from within his own organisation, or from some rival group. But the strange thing is, although he's been dead now for a week, not a word, not a whisper, not a sentence, has escaped – anywhere that I have been able to find out – that Eddie Armitage is dead. Therefore whoever killed him wants him to stay alive, officially, at least for the time being. Does any of that make sense to you?'

'No,' she gasped. 'I can't breathe.'

He got off her, and she rose to her knees, hugging herself, keeping her back to him.

'Not even the police seem to have any idea about your father's true identity,' he said.

She turned her head. 'Don't they?'

'Why, have they approached you?'

She hesitated. But there was no reason for her to tell him anything, and anyway, Baldwin wasn't a policeman – Teddy had checked that. Which made it extremely likely that Baldwin was the murderer. 'No', she muttered.

'So tell me how you found out about this place.'

She got off the bed, went back into the lounge, and then the kitchen, poured herself a glass of water. He was at her shoulder the whole way. Should she defy him again? She simply didn't know what he might do; her right arm was just regaining its feeling.

'There was a man', she said. 'Came to the house in Epsom just after you had left, last Saturday. He pretended to be a policeman, but he wasn't. I didn't know that at the time, so when he produced what looked like a search warrant, I let him get on with it.'

'Oh, Christ,' Uncle Bob said. 'I knew I shouldn't have let you out of my sight for a moment.'

'He didn't find anything,' said Julie. 'He didn't come to find anything. He came to leave something. An envelope with this address on it. He stuck it in the middle of Daddy's letters while pretending to look through them.'

'You saw him do that?'

'No. But it was there next time I looked. And I know it wasn't there before. I thought you must have planted it, but then I realised you that couldn't have, or this man Baldwin would have found it.'

'Baldwin,' Uncle Bob repeated, thoughtfully. 'So who did find the envelope? Your friend?'

122

'No,' she snapped. 'I did.' She went back into the lounge and sat down; her knees were weak.

This time he sat beside her. 'So you came up to have a look, and George recognised you. Well, he would.' He pointed at the various photographs. 'So what did you tell him?'

'Nothing. I went along with what Daddy had apparently been telling him, that I had been in the custody of my divorced mother all of these years.'

'Well, thank God for that. So how many people do know that you are Julie Armitage?'

'Well, the man Baldwin must do so.'

'Nobody else? You didn't inform Rodham or Cornwall about that mysterious envelope?'

'No, I didn't.'

'You thought you could take on London's underworld on your own.'

She made no reply. She certainly wasn't going to tell him about her encounter with Miss Briden – that would involve telling him about the fifty thousand pounds under the mattress on which he had thrown her.

'But your friend Teddy Longman certainly knows,' he went on.

'Well, of course he does.'

'Just how did you accumulate him?'

'We met. And liked each other. Very much.'

'You couldn't have met before Saturday. And by Sunday night you were in bed together.'

She glared at him, because his criticism was so very justified. 'Are you jealous? We clicked. Something you wouldn't understand.'

'I suppose not. Have you done any checking into his background?'

'Of course I have.'

'What?'

'Well, I know his father is a big lawyer in Boston, and . . .'

'How do you know that?'

She stared at him, hating her flush.

'I see. He told you.'

'All right,' she snapped. 'But he's at Oxford. At Balliol. I checked that out.'

'How?'

'I telephoned the college, that's how. And they identified him.'

123

He leaned back, studying her. 'I think he's as crooked as everyone else connected with this business. Julie, oh Julie . . .' he held her arm and pulled her back against him. 'How adorable you are. I'm sorry I manhandled you just now. But when people point guns at me I tend to react a trifle strongly. Julie . . .' he was kissing her ear, and his other hand was sliding round her waist. My God, she thought: I am about to be raped. 'Julie, listen to me. Please believe that I cannot tell you everything I know, because I promised your father that I would not. But Julie, I also want you to believe that Eddie Armitage was not quite the thug people thought he was. He was a loner in a world of organisations, and he made enemies. He also made a lot of money. A hell of a lot of money. Some of that money may have been funds he was not entitled to. It is my belief that it is that money his murderer is after, and the men who paid his murderer. And if they killed him before getting it, it has to be because they believe you know where it is, and because they feel that getting it out of you is going to be simpler than getting it out of Eddie. Julie, listen to me. These are men – and women – who will take you apart, bone by bone, if they feel that will get them what they want. You're just not in their league.'

What he was saying was quite terrifying, but it was defused by his hand, which had now slipped inside the dressing-gown to caress her breast. She daren't move, because if she moved she was going to start fighting him again, and she knew now she couldn't do that.

'It's a miracle you've survived so far,' he told her. 'If you have, it's because they are playing you like a fish, waiting for you to move in the direction they think you are going to, eventually. Now I tell you what we are going to do. You are going to dress yourself and pack a bag, and you and I are going to walk out of here and you are going to just disappear, until I can sort something out of this mess.'

Now she did turn; she couldn't stop herself. 'Disappear where?'

'Somewhere safe.'

'Where only you would know.'

'That would be the idea.'

'And where I would be your mistress, until you were ready to kill me yourself.'

'Oh, Julie . . . I love you. I told you, I must have loved you even as a girl – Eddie would talk to me about you, and show me your photographs. I know every photograph in this apartment by heart, every line and every smile.'

124

'Do you seriously expect me to believe that?'

'Oh. Julie . . .' his hand was in her armpit now, under the dressing-gown, and he was drawing her forward. Her legs unravelled themselves and she was lying on his chest. 'Please trust me, Julie. I'm the only chance you have. Please believe that.'

Their faces were very close. He was about to kiss her. 'I'd sooner run away with a rattlesnake,' she said.

He gazed at her, his face slowly hardening, and then his fingers relaxed. She put her hands on his chest and pushed herself up.

'So get out of this apartment,' she said. 'Or do you mean to try your hand at kidnapping, as well?'

He got up, and she braced herself for another attack; she could tell he was very angry.

'I'm just stupid enough,' he said, 'and in love enough, to say that when you start screaming, I'll try to be around. But I may not be.' He went to the door, looked over his shoulder. 'The inquest on Edwin Allen is to be held tomorrow. I imagine Inspector Rodham has sent official notice of that to your house in Epsom. I would be there, if I were you, or the police really will be interested in what you are up to.' He opened the door, looked at her. 'I'll try to keep an eye on you,' he said, and closed the door behind himself.

Julie discovered she was trembling all over. She went to her father's bar and poured herself a brandy, waited for some calm to overcome the tension. It was less the physical manhandling she had suffered, for the second time in two days – after never having been touched, aggressively or offensively, by a human being in her life before – than the clouds of doubt which were again rising up about her. Uncle Bob didn't want her to trust Teddy, Teddy didn't want her to trust Uncle Bob, they each accused the other of being a crook, and they both wanted her, apparently. But why? And what was she to do? What Uncle Bob had suggested was terrifying – but it was virtually what the man Baldwin had told her as well. Daddy had not only been a crook, but a double-crossing crook, one who had been executed by his own kind. Who would now be coming after her . . . there was a knock on the door and she jumped so violently she spilt her drink. She got up, went into the lobby. 'Who is it?'

'Teddy. Open up.'

'Just a minute.' She ran into the bedroom and picked up the gun.

This time she was going to use it, she was determined, if it was anyone she didn't like the look of. She returned to the door, opened the latch and stepped back, the gun levelled.

'Whoa there. This native is friendly'. He looked flushed and happy, but the look was slowly fading as he took her in. 'Julie?'

'Oh, Teddy.' She was in his arms, and he was holding her tight while closing the door behind him.

'What happened? That George been giving you trouble? He gave me the oldest of old-fashioned looks when I went out this morning.'

'George,' she gasped. 'Oh, yes, and—'

'But we're all friends now.'

'Are you?' Something else that didn't make sense.

'Tell me.' He half carried her to the settee, then sat down beside her, holding her hands.

She told him both about George and Uncle Bob.

'God damn,' he said when she'd finished. He went to the bar and refilled her goblet, taking one for himself. 'At least they're coming out into the open.'

'The way Uncle Bob put it, it's something bigger than just money.'

'To these characters, there's nothing bigger than money. Although I suspect it's likely that your dad put aside something pretty big, to start with. But I agree, it has to be much bigger than a mere couple of hundred thousand a year.'

'You think Uncle Bob and Baldwin are working together?'

'I should say it's almost certain. It's the oldest game in the world. One issues nothing but threats; his partner offers nothing but sweetness and light.'

'Oh, God,' she said. 'What are we going to do? Me, I mean. I don't want you to be involved, Teddy. It's too dangerous.'

'But I am involved, sweetheart. From here on I'm involved in anything that involves you.'

When Teddy said things like that Julie felt she wouldn't care even if he was after her money himself. She would give him half anyway, just to be reassured. But there wouldn't be half, because there wasn't any. 'But Teddy . . . I don't know where the money is. I don't have the slightest idea. I don't even know if Daddy kept another bank account.'

'It's not in a bank,' Teddy said. 'I've been thinking about it, and I

126

reckon you can bet your bottom dollar on that. If it's the sort of loot that would get every crook in London into a tizzy, it's somewhere a lot more secret than a bank.'

'But where?' she wailed.

'Well, we just have to figure that out. If your friend Bob is right, and your dad was stealing the money from his own organisation, it would have had to be in cash. And it would have had to be done over a period of years. So, let's make an assumption, that every time he came to England he was bringing a lot of cash with him. We can be pretty sure it originated in the States, not only because of those newspapers, but because from what Bob told you he had a much bigger organisation over there. What we have to do is trace his movements from the moment he got off the boat. Now I've had this in mind, and I've been doing it. And it seems to me that it all points to Epsom. Because so far as I've been able to find out, he always took the boat train to Victoria, and from Victoria took a cab straight here.'

'How do you know all this?' she asked.

He began pulling slips of paper from his pocket. 'I took the liberty of looking at these old steamship tickets, which were lying in that desk, and relating them to George's book downstairs. He records the arrival and departure of every tenant, you see.'

'And George let you look at his book?'

'Well . . .' Teddy grinned. 'I had to offer him a couple of your five-pound notes. I hope you don't mind.'

'Not if it helps us get to the bottom of this. But—'

'They all tie in, exactly. Now, as far as George knows, and has recorded, your dad spent his usual week here, and then left for the continent. He arrived with three suitcases, and he left with the same three suitcases. George seems to think they were all pretty heavy, so they each could have contained money. The point is, he's pretty sure they never left the apartment before your dad's departure for Paris, and your dad only went along to this club of his two or three times during the week. Several people came to see him here, but from George's descriptions they all sound like members of the mob, including your friend Bob. I think it's very unlikely he would have trusted anyone else in the organisation.'

'So you think he took the money to the continent?'

'No, because he never went to the continent. He went to Epsom,

127

remember? Like this last time. George has him checking out of here at noon on the Sunday to catch the Folkestone–Boulogne ferry. And at six o'clock that same evening I find him dying in the lane not a hundred yards from his house.'

Julie had clasped both hands round her neck. 'And there was a suitcase at the house filled with newspaper.'

'Right first time. I have to say I thought that was a dodge at first, that the case must've been emptied here and just taken down there to cover his tracks. But now I'm pretty sure he didn't unload the stuff here. So, if you'd like to get dressed we'll nip down there now.'

'But . . . If he took it down to Epsom, and immediately went for a walk, that must have been to hand the money over to someone. This so-called tramp.'

Teddy shook his head. 'Nope. Because the tramp would either have taken the suitcase with him, or left it lying by the body. Instead it was home where it should've been. But empty, except for the paper. And the sort of dough which needs to be carried in a suitcase sure can't be concealed in a couple of pockets.'

She felt there was something wrong in his reasoning. But she also knew what he was getting at. 'So you think it's at the house.'

'Has to be. And you have to be at the inquest tomorrow anyway, so no one can raise an eyebrow if you turn up there this afternoon instead. Save that I'll be in tow. But they'd raise an eyebrow about that anyway.'

'But where in the house?' she persisted.

'Somewhere. Has to be, somewhere.'

'If he left here at twelve,' Julie argued, 'and went all the way down to Folkestone . . . do you think he did that?'

'If he was setting up so elaborate a cover, I would say yes.'

'Well, then, he wouldn't have got to Epsom until about three at the earliest – and he was killed about six, three hours later.'

'Lots of time to hide the loot.'

'But not to conceal its hiding place. If he'd buried it in the garden or something there'd be signs. Freshly turned earth, that sort of thing.'

'I think your dad was a bit more sophisticated than burying money in the garden.'

'I think he was a bit more sophisticated than taking it down to

Epsom at all,' Julie said. 'I don't think that money ever left the States.'

'Then we'll look there, after we've looked at Epsom. You said you wanted to go there anyway.'

'Yes. But how can we, without a passport?' There were so many things weighing her down.

Teddy laughed, and kissed her on the cheek. 'I forgot to tell you the good news. Julie Armitage is alive and well and recorded at Somerset House.'

She stared at him. 'Honest?'

'Would I lie about a thing like that? But I have proof.' He took an envelope from his jacket pocket. '*Voilà!*'

She opened it slowly, took out the folded parchment inside, and gazed at a copy of a birth certificate. Her birth certificate: Julie Armitage, born Lewes, Sussex, 12 December 1910, daughter of Edward John Armitage and Mary Elizabeth Armitage, née Goodwin. She realised she had never known her mother's maiden name before. Mother had never really existed, for her, and Father had never wanted to speak of her.

She felt as if she were holding all the wealth in the world in her hand. She actually did exist.

'Oh, Teddy,' she said. 'Thank you so very much.'

'That's why I took so long,' he explained. 'I had to wait for them to make that up. But I brought something else as well.' He laid the form on the table. 'That's an application for a passport. You fill it out now, and we'll stop by a photographer and have a couple of snaps taken. As we're going down to Epsom anyway, your friend Cornwall can sign the back to attest that it is really you, and we'll pop it in the mail. They told me you'll have a passport back in forty-eight hours.'

'Will I?' That sounded awfully quick. But she was too ecstatic to care. 'Oh, Teddy.' She threw her arms round his neck. 'I do adore you.'

They made love, then went out, had her photograph taken, lunched, and returned to the apartment to pack. 'We can't just leave all this money under the bed,' she said.

'We'll carry it with us,' Teddy decided. But it really was impossible to conceal more than a couple of thousand on their persons. The rest they divided between their two suitcases. That meant carrying very few clothes, but they were only going for a couple of nights, anyway.

This time they travelled first class, and smiled at each other. Because they shared so many secrets, and they were all of them big. Julie had half expected the house to have been broken into, but it was exactly as she had left it, save that Mrs Lucas had apparently not been in. There were a couple of letters on the mat below the letterbox. One of them, predictably, was from Inspector Rodham, informing her that the inquest was tomorrow morning. The other was from Cornwall, asking her to call him the moment she got back.

Teddy shrugged. 'Why not? He may have turned something up.'

But he hadn't. 'Julie,' he said. 'Where on earth have you been?'

'I'm sorry, Mr Cornwall,' she said. 'I felt I just had to get away for a couple of days.'

'With that American fellow?'

Julie hesitated. She wanted to ask what business of his that was, but she didn't want to quarrel with him as well as everyone else.

'I've had Mrs Lucas here,' he went on as she didn't reply. 'With a tale as long as my arm.'

Julie sighed. 'It's probably mainly true, Mr Cornwall. Yes, I did go away with Teddy. I simply couldn't face being on my own.'

'Bless my soul. I really don't know what to say. I mean, really! I know your father would not have approved.'

'Do you think I approve of my father living a lie?' she retorted. 'Lying to me? Leaving me without an existence?'

It was his turn to be silent for a moment.

'Or have you managed to find something out?' It was important to establish that.

It was his turn to sigh as well. 'No. No, I'm afraid I've met nothing but brick walls. As the police told you, British Petroleum have never employed an Edwin Allen, and in fact there is simply no record of him having an existence anywhere, except for about three months in every year, right here. I am most awfully sorry . . . but Julie, as everyone in Epsom knows you are his daughter, and whatever his true identity the money in the bank is his, I have persuaded them to allow you twenty pounds a month from his account until I can get to the bottom of this business. I will, believe me.'

'Twenty pounds,' she said. There were a thousand in the handbag hanging from her shoulder.

'I think that is extremely generous of them,' Cornwall said. 'I had to give my personal guarantee, of course . . .'

'I am ever so grateful, Mr Cornwall. Will I see you at the inquest?'

'Oh, indeed. By the way, is, ah, Longman still with you?'

She glanced at Teddy, who was grinning at her from the doorway. 'Yes.'

'Hmm. He is required at the inquest too, you know.'

'Oh. Yes. I suppose he is. Well, he'll be there. And there is something I want you to do for me afterwards.'

'My pleasure. Do be careful, Julie.' He hung up.

'I am the original scarlet woman,' Julie said. 'And your name is mud for having seduced me. But at least Cornwall doesn't have a clue about the truth. Which must mean the police don't either.'

'Yes,' he said thoughtfully. 'And we aren't going to let on, remember? Not a word about our proposed jaunt to the States.'

'Oh, Teddy . . .' she put her arms around his neck. 'Are we really going to do that?'

'If we don't find anything here.'

'But what about Oxford? Won't the new term be starting soon?'

'Blow the new term.'

'But your parents will be furious.'

He kissed her. 'Not after they've met you. I thought, as we're going across anyway, we'd take a trip up to Boston to say hello.'

'Oh, Teddy! That would be heavenly.'

'Maybe we could announce our marriage at the same time.'

'Marriage?' Her voice rose to a squeak.

'Don't you want to marry me? I think you'd better.' He swept her from her feet and carried her to the stairs. 'Because we sure are honeymooning.'

He was more interested in making love than in searching the house, which made sense; she was sure there was nothing here. 'Teddy,' she said, lying on his chest. 'Are we really going to get married?'

'I think it's the best thing,' he said. 'Especially if we're going to the States pretty shortly. One has to be on the up and up.'

She squirmed on him with sheer delight. 'Oh, Teddy . . . but if we're going to the States, what about the banns, and—'

131

'No problem. We'll get a special licence.'

'A special licence? But aren't they frightfully expensive?'

'Oh, they are.' He grinned at her. 'You may have to lend me the money.'

She kissed him. 'Silly man, if we're going to be married, what's mine is yours.'

'I never thought of that. You grow more and more lovely with every second.'

She knew he was joking. But then, it was sometimes difficult to decide when he wasn't joking. And there was something on her mind. 'Teddy,' she said. 'Would you have gone along with that Briden woman, and well . . . made love to her and me at the same time?'

'I think you have it backwards. She and I were going to make love to *you* at the same time. With a little additional help.'

'Teddy!'

'I think it was a great idea. Turns me on just to think of it.' He grinned and kissed her. 'Nope, of course I wasn't going to go along with it. I wanted to give her enough rope to hang herself. It never crossed my mind that simply telling her you were Julie Armitage would do the trick. Not that I think it was a good idea, really. I mean, it's obvious that she got on to your friend Bob right away. That's how he knew where to find you.'

'Umm,' she said.

'No matter. We're just going to disappear without anyone knowing. I've reserved us cabins on the *Bremen*.'

'The what?'

'A German liner. She leaves Southampton a week tomorrow. First class for us. I hope you don't mind. She really is a superb ship. Fastest thing afloat.'

Julie had heard of the *Bremen*; she had never supposed she would ever sail with her. 'It sounds tremendous.'

'We'll really honeymoon, right across the Atlantic.'

'But the passports . . .'

'Won't bother a soul, especially if we hand out a few tips in the right direction. Movie stars do it all the time. Stewards and pursers on board these transatlantic liners are like the three monkeys – you know, hear no evil, see no evil, speak no evil. And they do very well at it, too. Anyway,' he added, almost as an afterthought. 'We'll have our marriage licence.'

132

She was so excited she could hardly speak.

'I've also sent a wire booking us into the Plaza Hotel in New York.'

'The Plaza?'

'It's our equivalent of your Savoy.'

'Oh, Teddy!'

'Well – you've got the cash.'

'Yes,' she agreed. 'Yes. And what then?'

'Don't you have any ideas?'

'Yes,' she said. 'I do have a plan. I thought I'd put an advertisement in the *New York Times*. Something like: "Miss Julie Armitage would like to meet any friends of her father, Mr Edward Armitage, who may be in town."'

It was the first time she had ever seen Teddy totally taken aback. 'You what?' he gasped.

'Well, it seems to me that we don't have any time to lose, and that a direct approach to these people would be best.'

'And that sure would be a direct approach,' Teddy said. 'My God, it would. What's your next plan, when half the mobsters in New York turn up on your doorstep? Especially if your friend Bob, and your other friend Baldwin, are right, and he has been embezzling their profits?'

'Well, I can prove I had nothing to do with it,' she argued. 'And I want to find that money as much as they do. If we were to pool our knowledge of Daddy's habits and movements . . .'

'You do realise they aren't going to want to give it back, or give it to you?'

'I want to find it,' she said stubbornly. 'And I want to find out the truth about Daddy. That's even more important. I have to do that, Teddy. I have to.'

He gazed at her for a moment, then pulled her down on to him. 'Sure, I understand that. But I also understand that you need protecting, from yourself.' He kissed her. 'Now let's take this place apart.'

There were fewer people at the inquest than Julie had feared, but those who were there were certainly interested in her. At Teddy's suggestion in London the previous afternoon they had bought her a black dress, and with this she wore the black headscarf Uncle Bob had given her. She still couldn't think of him as anything else but Uncle Bob, however much of a crook he might be.

Needless to say, he was there, but he didn't immediately greet her. Mr Cornwall did, and escorted her to a seat, leaving Teddy to follow. Inspector Rodham was also there, and shook her hand, a trifle stiffly, she thought. Does he know the truth yet? she wondered. She had been brought up to believe the police always knew the truth. But she had also been brought up by Father, and he had known different.

The proceedings were surprisingly brief. The coroner heard the facts of the case from the Inspector and a police sergeant. Teddy was called to give evidence of finding the body. Major Roberts was called to give evidence of identification. 'Were you in Epsom at the time of the incident, major?' asked the coroner.

'No, I was in London, but I read of it in the newspapers, and came right down,' Uncle Bob said.

This seemed to satisfy the coroner. And a few moments later Julie's name was called. 'Your name is Julie Elizabeth Allen?'

She stared at Inspector Rodham. 'Yes,' she said.

'And you are the daughter of the deceased?'

'Yes,' Julie said.

'I must ask you this, Miss Allen. Can you think of anyone who would have wished your father dead?'

'No,' Julie said, continuing to stare at the spectators. And becoming aware that one of them was staring back at her. It was no one she had ever seen before in her life, that she could recall, and in fact he was rather a nondescript-looking man; she would have been hard put to describe his face. Yet he was gazing at her with an intensity which was disconcerting; she had a most peculiar feeling that he knew she was about to lie. She turned away, and for the first time gazed directly at the coroner. 'My father, Mr Allen, did not have an enemy in the world.'

'The court extends its deepest sympathy, Miss Allen. Thank you.'

It took only five minutes for the jury to bring in a verdict of robbery and murder against a person or persons unknown.

'Well, that's over,' Inspector Rodham said. 'I understand you've been away, Miss Allen.'

'Yes,' Julie said. She looked into the people who were still milling around – one of the journalists had flashed his camera at her – but

134

could not see the nondescript man. 'I find the house gives me the creeps.'

'Oh, quite. Will you sell it?'

'How can I, Inspector? I don't own it, until you people tell me who I am.'

'Ah, yes.' The Inspector looked embarrassed. 'We are working on it, I do assure you, Miss Allen.'

'Thank you. Did you get in touch with Scotland Yard? About that man Baldwin?'

'Ah . . .' he looked more embarrassed than ever. 'They were not very helpful, I'm afraid. But I am sure they are working on the matter as hard as we are down here.'

'Bully for them,' she said, and gazed at Uncle Bob.

'Staying in Epsom for a while, Julie?' he asked, pleasantly. Only yesterday he had held her virtually naked in his arms.

She answered as nonchalantly as she could. 'Very probably. Teddy will be staying with me. Oh, by the way, we're engaged to be married.'

For a moment she thought he was going to explode. Then he got himself under control, glanced at Teddy, standing at her elbow. 'I'm sure you know best. My congratulations, Longman.' He turned away.

'The perfect squelch,' Teddy whispered.

'Teddy, there was a man . . .'

'You said there was something you wished to see me about, Julie,' Mr Cornwall said.

'Oh, yes. Would you sign a couple of photographs for me? Certifying that they are me, if you see what I mean.'

He frowned. 'Do you need that?'

'Well, I do. I can't do anything, Mr Cornwall, because I can't prove who I am. The police have taken my passport . . .' If Rodham wasn't letting on to her that he had discovered John Baldwin had not after all worked for Scotland Yard, he would hardly have let on to Cornwall, she calculated.

'Oh, yes, rum business that. But I suppose they had to do it.'

'And Teddy and I want to get married, and—'

'Married? You and – this gentleman?' He was obviously flabbergasted. 'That's impossible.'

'He has asked me, Mr Cornwall, and I have accepted.' No I

135

haven't, she thought with delicious pleasure; he just told me we were going to.

'But, my dear girl, you have only known Mr Longman a few days. I'm sorry, Longman, but that is true.'

Teddy shrugged.

'I am not your dear girl, Mr Cornwall,' Julie snapped. 'I am twenty-one years of age, and I wish to get married. Now, I can't prove who I am without some identification. So I need someone to identify me, am I right?' She glared at him.

Mr Cornwall hesitated, then shrugged. 'All right, Julie, I'll sign your photographs for you. Have you got them?'

'Right here.'

'Well, I'm going back to the office now. I'll give you a lift, and I can put my stamp as a notary on the back. It's not very regular, of course, as, well . . . but in the circumstances I suppose . . .' he peered at her. 'You wouldn't be thinking of applying for a new passport, I hope.'

'Good heavens, no,' she said. 'How could I? I don't have a birth certificate.'

'Of course,' he agreed, relieved. 'I'm sure the police will let you have yours back as soon as is practical. Well, shall we go?' He looked at Teddy.

'Oh, Teddy's coming too,' Julie told him. She glanced over the crowd to see if she could spot the man who had upset her, again could not find him, but found herself gazing at John Baldwin.

'Teddy,' she gasped. 'That—'

He squeezed her arm, and shook his head, quickly. She bit her lip; of course, to start blurting out about Baldwin in front of Mr Cornwall would blow the whole thing, and Baldwin, who was standing right at the back of the little group – she was sure he had not been inside the courtroom – turned and walked away the moment he saw that she had spotted him. But she was equally sure he had waited only to make sure that she did see him. She found she was trembling again; he frightened her more than anything else connected with this whole affair. She could hardly wait to get back into the house and bolt the door. 'Oh, Teddy, I'm so scared . . .'

'It figures – where Roberts is, so will Baldwin be. As I said, it's a well-known pattern. Constant pressure. They figure you know where the money is, and that if they keep frightening you enough you're going to make a grab at it.'

'Pour me a drink, please.' She sat down, shoulders hunched. 'That isn't what Uncle Bob said.'

'Come *on*.' He gave her a Scotch and water; he'd taken one for himself. 'Does it matter what he said? It's what he wanted that matters. He wanted to get you out of the apartment and alone with him. In other words, away from me. Then you would really have needed to be scared. What I have read about the methods some of these mobsters use to get what they want would freeze your blood.'

She drank, felt better. But she couldn't accept what he was saying. Because the odd thing about Uncle Bob was that while he had terrified her more than once with that streak of violence which seemed to lie just below the surface of his personality – and even more by the apparently irresistible sexual attraction he felt for her – she had never, not even yesterday morning, felt he was really going to hurt her. But maybe she was again just being innocent. And then there was the other man. She told Teddy about him, and he listened patiently.

'Probably just a reporter,' he commented. 'You're letting this thing get to you.'

'Shouldn't I?' she asked. 'This is my life we're talking about. Not just whether I go on breathing. It's my past, my future, my everything.'

'I know,' he said, and put his arm round her shoulders. 'My own sweetheart, I know just what you have been going through. My dearest . . . you wouldn't like to pack the whole thing in, and just be Mrs Edward Longman the Third?'

'Mrs Edward Longman the Third,' she said. 'Oh, I do want to be her, Teddy. But I'm the daughter of a criminal. A master criminal. A man who . . .' Uncle Bob had contradicted Alma Briden's appraisal of Father. Or had he? He had merely said Father hadn't been as bad as some people would paint him. That covered a lot of ground. 'May have been really wicked,' she continued. 'I have to find that out, Teddy, I simply have to.'

He kissed her. 'I think I can understand that too. What happens if . . . well . . .?'

'He turns out to be even worse than anyone says? I guess I'm naive

137

enough to feel that, as he was my father, he won't. Is that very stupid?'

'That is very loyal,' he said tactfully.

They spent the next day in Epsom, completing their search. But there was no sign of any patch of earth, any floorboard, any wall panel, having been tampered with, and although they covered themselves with dust hunting through the attic they came across nothing but her old toys, which amused Teddy but left Julie feeling very blue.

The delay was necessary because Teddy insisted they mustn't arouse any suspicions as to where they were intending to go while he made the arrangements for their marriage, but it was a grim period for Julie, especially when he went up to London to arrange for the licence. She alternated between the determination to be Julie Armitage, Eddie Armitage's daughter, who would avenge him and then atone for his crimes, and total doubt as to whether she had the guts to be that; between a creeping sorrow that she would never see Father again, and a creeping feeling of betrayal that he should have left her in ignorance of something which could consume her entire life. And also felt that somehow she had treated Uncle Bob very badly. Which was a joke. Even if Uncle Bob had been telling the truth when he claimed to have been a close friend of Father's, it was he who had treated her very badly – and it was Teddy she was going to marry. But she was desperate to get away from England, even if that meant braving the greater dangers of New York.

To her surprise, Julie was not troubled in any way at Epsom, not even by Mr Cornwall or the police, and she saw no further sign of either Uncle Bob or Baldwin – or the nondescript supposed reporter, and Teddy came back that night with the licence, a most official-looking document. 'I hope you don't mind,' he said, 'but I ran into an old chum of mine in town. He was at Oxford with me, and in fact only went down last Christmas. He's been ordained as a priest . . . so I asked him to marry us.'

'Oh, Teddy,' she screamed.

'Well, the fact is, he's never married anyone before, and he was a bit dubious about the whole thing . . . but I talked him into it. God knows he needed the money. Is it okay with you? He can do it in our own lounge, at the apartment, if we have the witnesses.'

138

'I think that's the most romantic thing I have ever heard,' she said.

Next morning they caught an early train to London, and Teddy, who was obviously having the time of his life, made the taxi from Victoria drive round for half an hour before taking them to Mayfair, just in case they were being followed. But at last even he was satisfied, and there was George, absolutely delighted when they told him they were getting married the next day and asked him to produce a second witness. When he had stopped congratulating them he was able to tell them that there had been no callers at the flat, but he had put the mail inside for her.

The mail! She raced into the lounge, and tore open the heavy rectangular envelope. Her passport. *Julie Elizabeth Armitage*. 'I'm alive!' she cried, and threw herself into Teddy's arms.

Next morning was the great day. At Teddy's suggestion they went out early, to church. They had some difficulty in finding a Protestant church open, but they did eventually, and knelt together in silent communion, before hurrying back to the flat. At ten o'clock George and his wife, a rather large but very jolly woman, arrived, and at eleven a nervous young man in a dog collar named John Stevens, who was Teddy's friend. His nervousness grew as he began the ceremony, and from time to time he even required prompting by Teddy, who was very impatient, but then it was done, and she was Mrs Edward Longman the Third. Teddy had laid in champagne the previous night, and the five of them toasted each other, Stevens becoming more and more relaxed until Teddy whispered to her, 'We'd better call a halt; he never could hold his liquor.'

They went out by themselves for a wedding lunch, and then returned to the apartment. There were still four days to go before the departure of the *Bremen*. So they honeymooned, endlessly and ecstatically. Making love was not only something she was amazed she had managed to exist for twenty-one years without experiencing, it also precluded thought. At least for her. Teddy did a lot of thinking, and she was content to let him do hers for her, because as usual he thought very clearly and coherently.

They went out for a couple of hours every day, with several thousand pounds, and at various banks bought travellers' cheques, never in large enough amounts at any one bank to arouse suspicion. By Friday they had managed to change all of the money except for a few thousand pounds. 'Now it really is safe,' he told her.

But he had also been planning their moves when they reached New York. Her earlier ideas he dismissed as both absurd and too dangerous to be considered. 'What we shall do is,' he told her, 'roughly what we've done here. Only we hold more cards now than when we began here. So, we shall go to the Plaza and we shall stay there, just like a couple of tourists. We will go shopping and we will do the sights. And while we are doing that, we will – I will, anyway – do a little investigating. We want to really smell out the land before we make a move.'

'And then?'

He grinned. 'Let's see what we find, first. We don't want to stir a bee's nest until we're sure we can cope with it. But think of this: your dad has to have had a home over there, or at least an apartment, sitting empty just waiting for him to come back.'

'And it could be full of photographs of me. Just like this one.'

'I never thought of that. Now that would be something.'

'Or full of a beautiful wife and beautiful children who don't know I exist.'

He gazed at her in genuine alarm. Obviously he hadn't thought of that one either. 'I'd say that's very unlikely. If ever a man was a loner, that's your dad. Hasn't it struck you as odd, that someone who was obviously as rich as Croesus, and living a fairly dangerous life, should travel all by himself, without even a valet, much less an entourage of bodyguards?'

Now that hadn't occurred to *her*.

'I think it's far more likely that we'll find the apartment full of thugs waiting to get their hands on you.' He grinned at her. 'Don't worry about it. If it comes to a crunch I have lots of friends over there, so we won't lack for support when the time comes. It may mean letting them into a little of the secret . . .' he paused.

'If they're friends of yours, that's fine by me,' she said. 'But Teddy . . . once we go, won't Baldwin or Uncle Bob alert the people in America that we're coming? If they're all in the same organisation.'

'I don't think they will, for two reasons. One is, I have a strong hunch they'd like to find that money all for themselves, and the other is that they first of all have to find out where we are. And how're they going to do that?'

Because as usual he had thought it out. They were due on board

140

Monday night, so he told George that they were going back down to Epsom for a few days. They carried only one suitcase each; then, instead of catching the boat train to Southampton, they took the Epsom train, leaving as before just after breakfast, only Teddy bought tickets for a station considerably further on; from there they kept changing trains, slowly working their way to the south, at the cost of a good deal of waiting around stations, which was wearying, but intensely exciting as well. 'This whole thing is like something out of John Buchan,' Julie said.

'Well, fact is stranger than fiction,' he agreed.

It was six that evening before they finally arrived in Southampton, and took a taxi to the docks, where the great liner lay alongside, having only berthed a couple of hours before. At that they were an hour before the boat train was due in, and were shown to a luxurious cabin on the upper deck. Their passports were taken off to the purser's office without comment, although Julie kept gazing at the door awaiting the knock which would say, 'You are not married and cannot therefore share this cabin,' and they would have to produce their marriage certificate. But it never did, and gradually she began to relax. Teddy had by then rung for a couple of whiskies and soda, and given their steward, whose name was Hans, a ten-pound tip, which was clearly going to ensure that they received the best treatment for the duration of the voyage. The steward told them that it was not necessary to dress for dinner on the first night on board, as only a cold buffet was served, which gave Julie another shock.

'Teddy,' she said when the man had left. 'Do we have to dress for dinner every other night?'

'In first class, yes.'

'I didn't bring one with me. I only have the one, anyway. But you said we'd buy what clothes I need in New York.'

'Quit worrying.' He hugged her. 'They'll have a boutique on board. Several, in fact. We'll buy what you need right here. We'll have to pay through the nose for it, but I guess you can afford it.'

The excitement was back. It returned every time he reminded her that she could now do all the things she had never been able to afford in the past – or had the nerve to attempt. They went upstairs to watch the main body of passengers arrive by the boat train, which came right on to the dock itself, but he made her stand well back in the shelter of the superstructure, just in case there was anyone

141

watching from the shore. Then they enjoyed a most delicious buffet, in the midst of terribly well-dressed and obviously wealthy people – 'But I'll bet they don't have fifty thousand pounds in their handbags,' Teddy whispered – before returning to the upper deck to watch the huge ship cast off and be manoeuvred by her tugs into the mainstream of Southampton Water, while whistles blared and streamers flew and the ship's band, which was of course German, for some reason known entirely to themselves played 'Over the Sea to Skye'.

It was two o'clock before they went to bed, and by then the liner was slipping out of the Solent into the English Channel, and beginning a long, slow roll. That made Julie sleep heavily, and she awoke to breakfast in bed, served by Hans with a benevolent smile. 'The first day out,' he said. 'Not always very good for passengers. You need seasick pills, just ring for Hans.'

Julie was far too excited to feel seasick, and after they had dressed they began their shopping spree. She spent over a thousand pounds, on day-dresses and sun-dresses as well as evening-gowns, and in addition Teddy talked her into a white mink jacket, which seemed an unimaginable extravagance, but everyone, having by now made up their minds that this young couple was eloping, was anxious to help, and when she was finished she thought she was the best-dressed woman on board. Except for jewellery. But here Teddy stepped in, and on his own, and with his own money, went off and bought her a sapphire and diamond engagement ring to add to the plain gold band he had given her when they were married. 'Oh, Teddy,' she said when he slipped it on her finger in the privacy of their cabin. 'That is the loveliest thing I have ever seen.'

'Well, there'll be lots more like that,' he promised.

They were the happiest four days she had ever spent. There was dancing every night after dinner in the huge salon, and Julie was just about the belle of the ball – few of the first-class passengers were only twenty-one, and she was in constant demand. The passengers were mainly American, to her relief, and even if they confused her by asking, with great seriousness, 'You're not backing Roosevelt, I hope?' she found them all splendidly full of life and amazingly wealthy, when she considered everything she had read about how poverty-stricken America was. But then, England was supposed to be poverty-stricken as well, as indeed was the whole world, and she

142

had never seen any personal evidence of it. Because she was the daughter of a mobster, as Teddy called him. A horrible word. But then, it was a horrible thought. She wondered what her new acquaintances would think if they knew the truth. But not even reflections like that could impair her happiness. Because on the ship she was isolated from fear and horror, in a world of her own, of which she was very nearly queen.

Teddy had of course been thinking about the situation, and had refined their plans still further, as he confided to her as they stood on the upper deck on the fourth night. They had all worn fancy dress for the captain's ball so that Julie was dressed as Boadicea while Teddy was a Roman centurion. 'I think I should nip up to Boston and fill in the folks about what's going on. I'll also raise some help while I'm there, have it on stand-by, eh, for when we need it.'

'That sounds a great idea,' she enthused. 'But aren't we booked into the Plaza?'

'Sure. And we'll go there, drop our bags, and you can stay there while I'm away. You'll be quite safe. Nobody will know that Mrs Edward Longman is really Julie Armitage. They're not going to look at your passport or anything like that.'

'Oh, but . . .' she bit her lip. The thought of being in New York – of being anywhere – without Teddy at her side was terrifying.

'Listen.' He put his arm round her shoulders. 'I won't be gone more than forty-eight hours. The fact is . . . well, I reckon I should see the folks on my own, first. There's likely to be an initial resistance to the whole thing.'

'A gangster's daughter as a daughter-in-law,' she said sadly.

'It's not just that. It's my quitting Oxford.'

'Can't you go back?'

'Maybe. I haven't thought about that. Heck, that's only tradition. Why shouldn't I graduate from Harvard Law School? But you know what parents are.'

Julie didn't reply. Because she didn't know what parents were. She had only ever had one, and he had turned out not to exist.

'So I reckon our best course is to let me sweet-talk them a bit first. They'll come round, believe me, but the fact is . . . when I said I had a lot of friends, well, they're really friends of Dad's. Tough old Irishmen who worship the ground he walks on, I guess

143

because he's bailed them out of gaol so often. They're the guys we need at our back when taking on the mob.'

She had never known him so nervous. For the second time she realised that he was a thinker rather than a doer, and she guessed that while the thought of facing his parents was frightening enough, the idea of facing her father's associates without a lot of power behind him was impossible. But she knew he wasn't actually running out on her. She was his wife. She kissed him. 'Just as long as you come back,' she said.

Her first glimpse of the skyscrapers confirmed her preconceived opinion that New York was the most exciting city in the world. She found everything about it exciting, even the long delays as their bags were taken ashore and the slow progress through customs. She couldn't help wondering if there would be any comment about the enormous amount of money she was carrying in travellers' cheques, and braced herself, but the customs officer merely remarked, 'Enjoy yourself,' having looked into her handbag.

'Can we spend pounds here?' Julie whispered as they waited for a taxi, or cab, she supposed she should get used to saying.

'They'll give you dollars whenever you cash them,' Teddy said. 'And you'll feel better, too. You realise that fifty thousand pounds is just about two hundred thousand dollars?'

She hadn't realised that, and it was no longer quite fifty thousand pounds, but it was still an awful lot of money.

They drove across a bridge over a fast-running river, then through streets made cavernous by the huge buildings on either side. Here, in contrast to London, or at least Mayfair, there was poverty to be seen, men and women who seemed to have nowhere to go, and who stared at the taxi with thinly veiled hostility.

The taxidriver was also depressing. 'The Plaza,' he said disparagingly. 'Time was I had fares to the Plaza all the time. Not recently. You gotta be Europeans.'

'As American as you are, buddy,' Teddy told him.

'You came over on the boat, didn't you?' the man said, aggressively but triumphantly.

Julie thought they were going to have a verbal fight at least, but fortunately at that moment the car drew up in front of the hotel, an imposing building which had apparently been designed to suggest a

French château, and which overlooked Central Park. And once inside all suggestion of poverty could be forgotten. Here were soft-carpeted floors, obsequious under managers and bellboys, and some remarkable ceiling work.

'Your booking is open, Mr Longman,' the desk clerk remarked.

'Yeah. Well, we don't know how long we'll be staying.'

'Of course, sir. We hope you will stay as long as you wish. Will it be in order to present an account every week?'

'Any time you like,' Teddy said.

A bellboy accompanied them up to their suite. He was actually a good deal older than his uniform suggested. 'Anything you want, just ring,' he suggested.

'We'll do that. You accept English money?'

'Mister, I accept anything.'

Teddy gave him five pounds.

'Just ring,' he repeated, apparently dazed.

The door closed, and they were alone. 'You look nervous,' Teddy said.

'I'm scared stiff. Funny, I wasn't until we actually got here.'

'New York frightens people,' he agreed. 'But you're safe here, my sweetheart. If you want, you needn't leave this room until I get back.'

'Do you know, I think that's just what I'll do. Do you mean I can have all my meals here as well?'

'You can have anything you want up here.'

'Oh. When are you leaving?'

'Well . . .' he looked at his watch. 'It's just eleven. I thought I'd catch a train right after lunch. That way I can be in Boston this evening, see the folks, look up some people tomorrow morning and maybe be back by tomorrow night. Certainly the next day.'

'Oh, Teddy, make it tomorrow night.'

'Sure I will, if it's humanly possible,' he said. 'I'll give you a ring tomorrow morning, anyway.'

But his mind had already left her, she could tell over lunch. She couldn't blame him; he had a lot to think about. When he came back . . . She leaned across the table in the Persian Room to hold his hand. 'I'm going to miss you,' she said.

He blew her a kiss. 'Snap. But – thirty-six hours?'

'Thirty-six hours,' she said. 'Don't forget to ring.'

After he had left she stood at the sitting-room window looking down at Central Park, then she turned back to the suite, unpacked, undressed and lay down with one of the novels they had bought on board ship, and actually fell asleep. When she awoke she rang down for some tea, and then remembered that Teddy had told her the Americans didn't drink tea. Yet a perfectly English meal was delivered a few minutes later. When it was finished she wondered if she should dress for dinner – in her own suite? But she didn't want to become a slob. She did so, putting on her pale green evening-gown, one of those bought on the ship, rang for Room Service, and was given a most magnificent dinner, with three waiters in attendance, whipping silver plated covers off a succession of mouth-watering dishes. She wondered if the Plaza service was always like this, or if word of Teddy's lavish tip had got around?

'A liqueur, madam?' asked the wine waiter when she was finished.

It would make her sleep, she supposed. 'Yes,' she said. 'A brandy.'

'Of course, madam. Any particular name? Or vintage?'

She gazed at him. 'You choose one.'

He was back in ten minutes with a goblet of Hine Antique. By that time the dinner trolley had been removed, and when he closed the door she was alone, with a most remarkable feeling of well-being spreading over her. She sat by the window, sipping her drink, looking out at the park – it was still just daylight out there – and thinking of Teddy. He'd be confronting his parents by now. She wondered what they were really like, what their reaction to her would be, when she heard the suite door open behind her.

She supposed it was one of the waiters, although it was odd they hadn't knocked. But she was too relaxed to care. 'Forgotten something?' she asked, without turning her head.

'Well, hi,' the man said. 'You'll be Julie, I guess.'

CHAPTER 7

Julie leaped to her feet, turning as she did so, aware of a peculiar sense of *déjà vu*, in more senses than one – as usual she was a bedroom away from the automatic pistol.

Yet the man himself was not as alarming as what he had said. He was very tall, and powerfully built, but his thick head of hair was quite grey, and his big features surprisingly friendly; he was dressed in a rather old-fashioned tuxedo, which fitted him perfectly and yet seemed a size too small because of the huge shoulders and the barrel chest. He was carrying his fedora in his hands.

But he shouldn't have been there. And as for knowing who she was . . . 'How did you get in here?' she snapped.

'I asked for your suite.' He closed the door behind himself. 'You don't have to be afraid of me, Julie. Where's that layabout husband of yours?'

'Layabout . . .' her brain was back doing handsprings. 'Who are you?'

'Name's Hanson Pierce. Your daddy never told you about me?'

'No,' she said. 'No. I have never heard of you. My father is . . . he has never heard of you either.'

'He likes to play his cards close to his chest,' Hanson Pierce agreed. 'Sometimes I guess he forgets which of them are wild. But then, I guess maybe that's why he doesn't approve of your marriage. Where is that guy, anyway?'

Julie sat down again. Her knees would just not support her. 'He . . . doesn't approve of my wedding?' she whispered.

'You should've got his approval,' Hanson Pierce told her. 'So I'm to look him over.'

147

Julie licked her lips. I have gone mad, she thought. I have gone completely stark raving mad. 'My husband has gone to Boston,' she said.

'And left you here?'

'He had to see his parents,' she said, hardly believing it was her speaking. But she could only regain sanity by pretending she was sane, that this was a perfectly ordinary conversation. 'They don't know about the marriage, you see.'

Hanson Pierce nodded. 'A real spur-of-the-moment business. Don't hardly ever work out, Julie. Upsets everybody. What do his folks do?'

'His father's a lawyer,' Julie said. God, how can I be sitting here, talking . . . she could stand it no longer. 'Who *are* you?' she shouted.

'Hanson Pierce,' he told her again, frowning. 'You got any drinking liquor up here?'

'No,' she said. 'But you can ring for some.' Just to get someone else into the room . . .

'What's yours?' He picked up the telephone.

'Scotch. Scotch and water.'

'Now that sounds like a real drink. A bottle of Scotch and a jug of water,' he said into the phone. 'And a bucket of ice. Yeah, Mrs Longman's suite.' He replaced the phone. 'Nice hotel. Your hubby paying?'

'Yes,' she said. 'Yes.' All she had to do was keep him talking, until the bellboy got here.

'So when's he coming back?' He sat down on the settee, legs thrust in front of him, ankles crossed; he looked totally relaxed.

'To . . . tomorrow, I think.'

'I should hope so. Leaving you all alone, in New York. Christ, if MacGinnion got to know of it – he don't know about you, you see,' he explained.

'But you do.' She could find out who MacGinnion was later.

'I'm your daddy's right-hand man,' Pierce explained.

'Daddy's . . .' there was a knock on the door. Julie leaped to her feet, but Pierce merely called, 'Come.'

The bellboy entered with a tray. Julie had remained standing. 'Please,' she said. 'This man . . .'

'Mr Pierce,' the bellboy said.

148

'Mr . . .'

'Everybody knows Mr Pierce, madam.'

Julie opened her mouth and then shut it again.

Pierce was holding out a five-dollar bill, which the bellboy expertly palmed. 'Thanks, son. We don't want to be interrupted, see?'

'Oh, yes, Mr Pierce.'

'But . . .' before Julie could say another word the door was closed. She ran into the bedroom, seized her gun, turned to face the door, and lowered it. Pierce hadn't followed her.

'You're like a cat on hot bricks,' he commented.

Julie took a deep breath and went to the door, the gun levelled. He was at the table, pouring two drinks. 'Long on the water, I guess,' he said. 'For you.'

Julie took another deep breath. 'Pierce,' she said.

He turned, took in the gun, but did not seem the least alarmed. 'Now there's a fancy little toy,' he said. 'You got mice?'

She wanted to stamp her foot in anger; she had got all the menace she could into her tone, and into her expression. 'You had better start telling me who you are.'

'Well,' he said, 'if I ever had any doubt about who you are, little Julie, they'd be gone now. Real chip off the old block. Your daddy would be proud to see you standing there. You drinking?'

'After you've answered my questions.' But she knew she was losing control of the situation.

'So shoot.' He sat down, and smiled at her. 'I'm not speaking literally, of course.'

'Tell me who you are.'

'I told you that. I'm your daddy's chief clerk, you might say. I run things for him, when he's away, like now.'

That was at least possible, she thought. But . . . 'How did you know I was staying here? That I was with Teddy?'

'Can I put my hand in my pocket? Honest, I wouldn't try to draw on Julie Armitage.'

She presumed he was poking fun at her, and became angrier yet. 'What's in your pocket?'

'I'll show you. Two fingers.' He was as good as his word, thrust just two fingers into his pocket and extracted a sheet of paper, which he held out. 'You can read it.'

149

Cautiously Julie advanced across the room, took the paper, and retreated again until her back touched the wall. It was difficult to watch him and read it at the same time, but she stopped watching him altogether the moment she looked down. Because the paper was a telegram, which read:

JULIE ELOPED WITH YANKEE GOLDDIGGER NAMED
EDWARD LONGMAN STOP TRAVELLING BREMEN ARRIVING
NY SATURDAY STOP INVESTIGATE AND HOLD UNTIL MY
ARRIVAL STOP EDDIE

'Oh, God,' she said. 'Oh God!' Her knees gave way, and she slowly sank to the floor, still leaning against the wall, her gown gathering around her knees.

Pierce was across the room in a moment and kneeling beside her, holding her drink. He made no effort to take the gun from her hand. 'What the hell . . . you'd better drink this. For Chrissake, Julie, don't fade on me. I'm supposed to be looking after you.'

Julie raised her head. 'Until Daddy gets here.'

'Yeah.' He smiled. 'I'll put in a good word for you. Here, drink this.'

She wanted to. She gulped half of it, and would have swallowed the rest if he hadn't taken it away. 'Whoa,' he said. 'You don't want to get drunk.'

She had to think. Oh, how she had to think. This man had offered her no violence, had not as yet actually touched her. That put him in a unique class of men amongst those who had drifted into her life recently. And he seemed genuinely concerned. But what he was saying, or assuming . . . she pushed herself up, and straightened her skirt, while he watched her anxiously.

She got to the settee, sat down. Pierce gave her the glass, and she drank some more.

He stood above her, even more anxiously. 'I seem to have said something I shouldn't. Hell, Julie, if you'll tell me what it is, I'll apologise.'

This huge hulk was desperate not to offend her. Just like Alma Briden, she thought. Because they were both terrified of offending Eddie Armitage. Because they both supposed Eddie Armitage was still alive. But that couldn't be . . . 'It's just that . . . will you sit down, Mr Pierce?'

150

'Surely.' He collected a chair and set it in front of her, sat there looking almost comically solemn. 'Now, what's on your mind?'

She was trying to arrange the questions which were tumbling through her brain into some sort of order. It paid to start with the simplest. 'How did you know where to find me?'

'I had one of my boys meet the boat. That wire arrived three days ago. So he just trailed you here.'

And it had never occurred to them to look behind them, Julie thought. Poor Teddy; for all of his determination to help her he was just as much out of his class as she was. But . . . three days ago. Therefore it must have been sent the day after they left England. Again, all his elaborate precautions hadn't done them any good; there must have been someone watching his every movement there too, someone who had even trailed him into the shipping office. But considering that problem would have to wait.

'All right,' she said. 'You work for my father.'

'Sure thing.'

'Therefore you . . . you know what he does.'

'I'm his right-hand man,' Pierce repeated proudly.

'Yes,' she said. 'Okay. And he told you about me?'

'Well sure. Because . . .'

'You're his right-hand man. Therefore you know I have been living as Julie Allen.'

'Come again?'

'Daddy didn't tell you he has been pretending to be Edwin Allen, as my father?'

Pierce was looking too genuinely confused to be acting. 'Well, I knew he meant you to drop out of sight . . .'

'What do you know about me?'

'That you're his daughter, but that you're not involved in the Association, know nothing about it, in fact . . . but hell. You gotta know something about it.'

'Yes, Mr Pierce,' she said. 'I gotta know something about it. So hadn't you better tell me who sent you that telegram, really?'

'Telegram?'

She searched her memory of the movies she had seen. 'I think I probably mean wire,' she explained.

'Oh, yeah. Well, your dad sent it, Julie. It says so.'

Julie gazed at him. She was getting a very strong impression that

151

this large, perhaps none too bright, man was a devoted follower of her father's. In which case he might well provide the best protection in the world for her, right here in New York. And if he had been a close associate of Father's, he might even be the key to unlock the mystery, not only of why Father had been killed, but of what everyone was looking for. But she had to be sure. 'I don't know my father all that well,' she confessed. 'You know, only seeing him occasionally . . .'

'Yeah,' Pierce said. 'Three months a year is tough. If your mommy had lived . . .'

Julie sat up. 'You knew my mother?'

'Best man at your daddy's wedding, I was,' Pierce said proudly. 'Mind you, she didn't know nothing about the Association either. At least . . . I don't think she did.'

'What was her name? Her maiden name?'

Pierce frowned. 'Why . . . Goodwin, as I remember. You didn't know that?'

'No,' Julie said. 'Not until very recently. Do you remember when she died?'

'I wasn't there. That was in England.'

'Yes,' Julie said. He had to be what he claimed he was; he knew too much. 'Mr Pierce,' she said, 'I have some bad news for you. My father is dead.'

In any other circumstances it would have been amusing to watch the changing expressions flitting across Hanson Pierce's face. He registered every emotion possible in the space of about fifteen seconds – but the overriding one was disbelief. 'Eddie, dead?' he asked, when he could speak. 'He was as fit as a horse.'

'I know,' she said. 'But he didn't just die. He was murdered.'

Pierce looked horrified. 'Goddamn,' he said eventually. 'They got the killer?'

'No. The police think it was a tramp.' There was no use getting over-involved. 'But I know it was a deliberate murder. I want to find out who, and why.'

'You're damned right,' Pierce said. 'Eddie, gone. Christ almighty! MacGinnion! Has to be MacGinnion.'

'Who is MacGinnion?' Julie asked.

Pierce glanced at her, got up and poured himself another whisky.

152

'You are going to help me find Daddy's killer, aren't you?' Julie asked.

'You bet I am. Just how much do you know about the Association, anyway?'

'Only what I've managed to discover by going through his papers.'

'He never told you nothing?'

'No. As you said just now, I don't think he wanted me involved.'

'Yeah. He never wanted that.'

She leaned forward. 'But I am involved, now, Mr Pierce. And I am going to stay involved. So tell me.'

Pierce hesitated, then nodded. 'Yeah. You gotta right, now. Well, back in 1895 your daddy was sent to prison for embezzlement. That was in England. He was a kid of nineteen then, but they were real tough in those days, and because he tried to resist arrest they sent him to Dartmoor. I guess that's your equivalent of our Sing Sing. So he spent five years in that prison, breaking rocks on the moor. He told me about it.'

Father, in Dartmoor? But could she really be surprised by that? Could she really be surprised by anything this man was going to tell her?

'So when he got out, I guess he had a bit of a grudge against society, right? He and his cellmate, a big Mick called MacGinnion, came out together, and they decided to emigrate. So they came across here, steerage. They were bosom buddies by then. Hell, you'd think they were bosom buddies now, have been, all their lives. But I reckon your dad never did trust Big Pat MacGinnion all that much. Anyhow, they got over, and found the society here wasn't all that different to in the UK. So they reckoned they'd have to make their own way. They began small. I guess there were a few heists along the way, but the main business was protection.'

'Protection?' Julie asked.

'You know. We'd go along to a shopkeeper and say pay us a hundred bucks and we'll make sure your shop isn't done over. So the guy says, who the hell is gonna do my shop over? So we shrug, and say, you never know, buddy, you never know. Well, a couple of nights later the guy's shop does get done over. So the next time we call round he wants to pay. So we accept his money and we make sure he don't get done again. Simple, really.'

'And you "did" him in the first place.'

'Hell, that's part of the game, right?'

'Right,' she agreed. 'Were you involved then?'

'Oh, sure. I was one of your dad's first recruits. I'm kind of big,' he explained. 'And I can look menacing. Well, I can be menacing, too. I was twenty when your dad and I got together.'

'But why didn't the shopkeeper go to the police?'

'The police? Where would that have got him, save that the next time his shop was done he'd have been done as well.'

'Oh,' Julie said, faintly.

'Well, protection got us some dough together, so we expanded into girls.' He looked embarrassed. 'I guess you don't know about things like that.'

'Oh, I do,' Julie said.

'Is that a fact?' Pierce scratched his head, clearly unable to come to terms with modern youth. 'Well, we got a couple of girls and put them to work, and then a couple more so we was able to set up a house, and then another, and soon we had four houses. They was the best houses in New York City,' he said proudly. 'Still are.'

Julie swallowed some whisky.

'So that way we got some more money together, so we opened a gambling joint. Now there was real money. We had some spats with the police, but none we couldn't handle. Your dad had this smart lawyer on the payroll by then. Guy called Cerdo. Cerdo,' he said thoughtfully. 'Yeah, he'd be involved.'

'So he was never caught again?'

'Your dad ain't spent a single night in gaol since leaving Dartmoor,' Pierce told her. 'Meanwhile things were going good. This was just before the War, and it was then he met your mom. Fell in love at first sight. But he didn't want her involved. So he got married quiet like. Never a word to Big Pat. I was the only member of the Association who knew. He trusted me.' Once again his pride was evident.

'Then there was the war,' he went on, 'and after it, the Volstead Act. Julie, I am telling you, we thought we'd been doing pretty well before, but that guy Volstead took the lid off. Within a year after prohibition came in we had half a dozen speakeasies. Then there was more. We got twenty-five now, under our direct control, and we also control all the liquor that's sold in the state. And in Connecticut and Massachusetts. We've had some trouble with the Boston Irish, but they don't push us too hard.'

154

Julie poured herself another drink. 'And my father . . .'

'Eddie's the Boss. The Big Man. Everyone knows that.'

'And now he's been killed. And you think this man MacGinnion may have done it?'

'I'd bet my bottom dollar on that. He wouldn't have done it himself, of course. He'd have hired a hit. But he's the one.'

'Why would he have done it, if he and Daddy were such old friends?' She thought she knew the answer, but it was important to discover what Pierce knew.

The big man shrugged. 'Who knows? Maybe Big Pat figured it was about time he took over.'

It seemed certain that Hanson Pierce did not know the real reason Father had been killed – presuming money was the real reason. But there were things which didn't fit. 'Has MacGinnion taken over?'

Pierce frowned as he realised what she was driving at.

'Daddy was killed just on a fortnight ago, Mr Pierce. Has anything changed over here?'

'Not a goddamned thing. Hell—'

'So do you still think it's MacGinnion?'

Pierce looked genuinely disturbed. He got up and freshened his own drink. Then he gave her a hard look. 'How come nobody – but nobody – knows your dad is dead?'

'Simply because no one does know it. I told you, Daddy was using a false name, Edwin Allen, and he was killed as Edwin Allen. The British police are still trying to find out who Edwin Allen was, but they haven't got anywhere yet. I imagine they will, eventually. But right now, there are only a couple of people in the world who know Daddy is dead.' She wasn't going to tell him who they were, either; it was time she had some secrets of her own.

'Yeah,' Pierce said. 'Yeah. And MacGinnion can't come out and say so, and take over, until the news does break, because he knows that me and the boys would point the finger at him. He has to wait until it's official, then he can say, but hell, I was three thousand miles of water away from the scene of the crime. Yeah,' he said again. 'Well, we ain't gonna stand for that, are we, Julie?'

'No,' she said, without thinking. She couldn't afford to think, right this minute; what she had just been told about her father did not bear thinking about.

'Listen,' he said. 'I want you to meet the guys. I know they'll want to meet you. Whaddya say? I mean, the Boss dead, murdered . . . that's going to shake them. And then, the Boss's daughter, right here in New York, raring to go . . . that'll send them.'

Julie wasn't sure what 'send them' actually meant, but she gathered she'd be popular. 'Will this man MacGinnion be there?'

'Are you kidding? These are your dad's boys I'm talking about. Let me tell you, Julie, any one of these guys would drop dead for Eddie. They're gonna feel the same about you.'

'Ah.' My God, she thought, I came to New York in fear and trembling, and I may have unearthed a private army. So they're all crooks, and maybe worse. But so was Father. Father was the worst crook of all. And she was his daughter. 'Yes, Mr Pierce,' she said. 'I think I'd like to meet the boys.'

'Well, it's kinda late now. I'll have to make some phonecalls. Now say, anybody know you're in New York?'

'Not a soul, save you. And my husband, of course.'

'Yeah. Who is this character, anyway?'

'A very nice boy I met just after Daddy was killed, who helped me no end, and with whom I have fallen in love. Don't make any mistake about that, Mr Pierce. If anything happens to Teddy I am going to be very angry.'

Hanson Pierce raised both hands in the air. 'You're the boss,' he said. And grinned. 'Hell, I guess you are. Okay, if MacGinnion or nobody else knows you're in New York, you should be safe here overnight. I'll call for you eleven tomorrow morning. Okay?'

Julie opened her mouth to say yes, and then closed it again. 'Oh, my God!' she said.

'Come again?'

'Somebody else must know I'm in New York.'

'Like who?'

'Whoever sent you that telegram.'

'Holy Jumping Jesus,' Pierce remarked. 'I'd forgotten about that. But – hell, it don't make sense, Julie. The wire was sent to me. Everyone who knew Eddie would know I was his right-hand man. Would know that I wasn't gonna harm his daughter.'

'Yes,' she said, brain racing, but round in circles.

'It just don't figure,' he muttered. 'It could be some wise guy trying to be smart. You gotta get out of here tonight, Julie.'

156

'Tonight? But . . . the Plaza?'

'It's only a hotel. Trouble is, it's a real swank joint, and I can't move anybody in here to protect you. And like you said, somebody else does know you're here. So you gotta come somewhere I can protect you. You're dressed for it. Listen, leave all your gear here. Just come along with me, let the desk think you're out for the night. Which you will be. By tomorrow we'll know how the land lies.'

He's asking me to trust him, Julie thought. But hadn't she already trusted him? He could actually be kidnapping her but she believed that he was absolutely faithful to Father. And she had no one else, as usual. Oh, why had Teddy gone to Boston? 'Where would we go?' she asked.

'To my club – it belongs to the Association, but it's my baby. You'll be safe there.'

'Will I need the gun?'

Hanson Pierce smiled at her. 'If it makes you feel good, bring it along. But I'll be there.' He put his hand inside his jacket and brought out a rather larger version of hers.

'Does every American go armed all the time?' she asked.

'Those of them in our business sure do, baby. It's the only life insurance worth carrying. Let's go.'

She put on her white mink, placed the pistol in her handbag beside the travellers' cheques, and accompanied him downstairs. 'I'm just going out for a while,' she told the man at the desek.

'Of course, madam,' the man said, endeavouring not to look at Pierce, who was clearly old enough to be her father, and who was certainly not her husband.

There was a limousine waiting at the foot of the steps, and they climbed in and sat in the back, while a uniformed driver waited for instructions. 'Twice around the park,' Pierce told him, 'and then the Orange Room.'

'Yes, sir, Mr Pierce.' The car slipped away from the hotel.

'Why twice around the park?' Julie asked, beginning to get worried again.

'Just to make sure nobody's tailing me,' he explained.

'Oh. Do people normally tail you?'

'You never can tell, Julie. You never can tell.'

Driving slowly round the park in the dusk was extremely roman-tic. How she wished it could have been Teddy sitting beside her.

She and Teddy had never had time to be romantic – she remembered how he had been going to take her rowing on the Serpentine – and she had always wanted romance much more than sex – at least until she had discovered the joys of sex. And clearly there were quite a lot of other people who found the park romantic at night as well.

'I reckon more babies get conceived in this park than anywhere else in the world,' Pierce remarked, glancing at the courting couples.

'Are you married, Mr Pierce?'

'Sure. Thirteen kids.' He grinned at her. 'Every one in the same bed. Parks give me rheumatism,' he confided.

A total thug, with thirteen children. The two just didn't relate. 'Are any of them in the . . . the Association with you?'

'No way. You know something? One of my boy's a policeman. He's real smart.'

Clearly this was a world she could never have imagined could exist, were she not right in the middle of it.

'Okay, Joe,' Pierce said. 'We're clean. Let's go.'

They turned down Broadway, and then into one of the streets leading off, pulling to a stop before what looked like a warehouse. Certainly it was in utter darkness. Pierce held the door for her, and she saw what might have been a tramp, leaning against the wall and smoking a cigarette; for the first time she was truly glad to have the big man beside her.

'Gonna rain later,' Pierce remarked.

Julie looked at the sky. 'Do you really think so?'

'In there,' he said, and she realised a small door had opened in the warehouse wall.

She stepped into darkness, and felt him behind her. Her heart rose into her throat, then another door opened in front of her and she was in a dimly lit corridor.

'Straight ahead,' Pierce said.

'That man . . .'

'He's one of mine. Doorman, you might say. I was using the passwords, see? But he also keeps an eye open for a raid.'

'Do you get raided often?' She was walking in front of him, heels clicking on the tiled floor, her mind an odd mixture of terror and exultation.

'It happens. Whenever City Hall gets uptight about something. No hassle, really.'

158

Another door opened in front of her. She hadn't touched one of them. But now she was standing on a mezzanine floor, in a sudden blaze of light, looking down on a vast room which was completely packed with people and noise. On a dais on the far side a four-piece band played soft music, and on the small floor in front of them several couples danced. Along the top wall was a bar, glittering with a collection of multi-coloured liquors; white-jacketed barmen dispensed to the patrons in front. In the foreground, immediately beneath her, there was every conceivable form of gambling game, and this was the most crowded area, with men and women rubbing shoulders as they placed bets or threw dice. Everyone was in evening dress, everyone appeared to be very happy, and she suspected that almost everyone was at least tight.

'Good lord,' she said.

'It's a living,' Pierce explained. 'The office is along here.'

She continued along the balcony, and another door opened. Now she found herself in a most luxurious office, a place of huge desks and soft leather upholstery, from which the noise of the floor below was excluded, although a glass wall looked down on the players.

'One way,' Pierce explained. 'We can watch them, but they can't watch us.'

She was so fascinated she hadn't noticed the man behind the desk.

'On your feet,' Pierce commanded, and the sitting man hastily unfolded himself; he was somewhat tall, and thin.

'Who's your friend?' he asked.

'You'll find out,' Pierce told him. 'Which of the boys are downstairs?'

'Top, and Lenny. Arnie was there just now, but he may have left.'

'Well, fetch them up here. I want them to meet the lady.'

The thin man looked at Julie more closely. 'So what's your secret, apart from the big tits? He goes for blondes.'

'Shaddup,' Pierce snapped. 'And get on with it. I'm sorry about that, Julie. He has no class. None of the guys have class. Drink?'

'Yes, please,' Julie said. She desperately needed one. This was her father's world. He had created it, and ruled it – until someone had hit him over the head with a stone. Someone he had known? It had to be. A man with a reputation as tough as Eddie Armitage's would never just allow himself to be murdered; he had to have trusted his killer absolutely. Which was just one more terrifying thought to add to all the rest. When she had the time – and the courage – to sit down and think about them.

'This is the real McCoy,' Pierce told her, giving her a glass of Scotch. 'Not like the stuff we serve down there. Say, you know I knew that guy?

'Who?'

'McCoy. Ran rum out of Nassau. Great guy. Always delivered the best. That's how he got his name.'

Julie sat down. Her head was beginning to spin again. And she couldn't take her eyes off the people downstairs. Some of the women were exquisitely dressed, and some were really very beautiful, but all had the most desperate expressions flitting across their faces as they gambled and lost, or became almost childlike if they happened to win.

'Gets you,' Pierce remarked. 'I reckon I could set up as a psychiatrist with what I've seen and heard down there. You ever gamble?'

She shook her head.

'Yeah. You're your dad's daughter. Gambling is a mug's game. Getting hooked on ivory or cardboard is one hell of a sight worse than booze or snow. You've a cool head on those shoulders. Say, you ever heard of Queen Elizabeth?'

'Who?' She was totally surprised.

'Chick what used to rule the Limeys. Just a chit of a girl when she began. You know history?'

'I think so. I've read about Queen Elizabeth.'

'You know that story always got to me? Just a chit of a girl, and she had all those heavy guys, Drake and Frobisher and Hawkins and Leicester, all of them eating out of her hand. Made them all fall in love with her. Ain't that something?'

'Yes,' she agreed, wondering what on earth he was getting at.

'Course she had a real heavy dad, too, so all she had to do was keep things running. Like you.'

She stared at him, her jaw slowly slipping, then looked at the door as it opened. The tall man came in with three others. 'Trouble?' asked one.

'Trouble? Yeah. But you never know what's gonna turn up, do you? Julie, this is Top.'

160

She shook hands with a small, granite-faced man.

'Lenny.'

Heavy-shouldered and beetle-browed.

'Arnie.'

Blond and young and dashingly handsome.

'Closet you met.'

She glanced at the tall man. Closet?

'Well, hell, he spends all his time in here, see? Now, you guys . . .' Pierce surveyed them, savouring his moment. 'This here is Miss Julie Armitage.'

There was a moment of silence, then Arnie said, 'Well, Jesus wept.' He seized her hands again and kissed her on both cheeks. 'The Boss's daughter.'

The rest were crowding round to kiss and hug her.

'And she's one cute little lady,' Pierce told them. 'Always carries a gat, and ready to use it, too.'

Julie bit her lip; she wondered what he would say when he found out she had never fired a gun in her life.

'But it ain't all good news,' Pierce went on. 'You tell them, Julie.'

Julie drew a long breath, and told them. This time the silence was a trifle longer. Then Lenny said, 'Holy Christ! Big Pat?'

'That's what I figure,' Pierce said.

'That louse,' Top said. 'What're we going to do, Hanson?'

'Ask the Boss,' Pierce said.

Their heads turned as one, and Julie sat down.

'You serious?' Closet inquired.

'Look, we gotta crisis on our hands, right?' Pierce said. 'You know MacGinnion ain't no pal of mine. Or yours. With him as the boss we ain't gonna have it so good, if we have it at all. But we know why he's playing this one this way. There's too many of the guys loyal to Eddie. So his game must be to wait for the news of Eddie's death to filter through, and then appear completely surprised, like we all were, and completely innocent of the crime, and then kind of reluctantly take over because there ain't nobody else, right? And he will do all of that, because there ain't one of us with sufficient clout with the boys to take him on. Sure I got you guys and a few others, but nobody outside of this precinct really knows who I am. And the same goes for Jack McEvoy and Jimmy Standler. They're big in their own districts, but no place else. That's the way Eddie wanted

161

it. We gotta have a boss whose name is good to every man in the Association.'

'Yeah,' Top agreed. 'But a girl?'

'Well, Eddie didn't have no son,' Pierce pointed out. 'And this chick is a toughie. I told you.'

They stared at her again, while she desperately tried to get her thoughts under control. She was being invited to take over the greatest criminal organisation in the world. Little Julie Allen, who less than a month ago was saying, 'Yes, Mrs Simpson, No, Mrs Simpson' and anxiously trying to make sure her tie was knotted correctly.

Yet she wanted to do it. It was more than a desire to avenge Father's death and perhaps find out the truth about this money he was supposed to have stolen. It was more than just a feeling that here with these men she was safer than anywhere else in the world. It was a little – almost subconsciously – awareness that only by letting these men transfer their allegiance from Father to her could she in any way atone for the thirty years of brutal damage Father had inflicted on society. She didn't yet know how it could be done, and she did know that for any of these men, or any of their associates, to discover what she had in mind, would be horrifying. But if it could be done . . .

Teddy would be horrified right off. But she could tell Teddy what she had in mind. As for Cornwall, the thought of his reaction made her want to smile. And what of Mrs Simpson? She did smile. And Uncle Bob? Her smile faded. Uncle Bob was growing more sinister with every moment. Because who else could have sent that telegram. To hold her here until he arrived? And by his own admission, he was a man Father had trusted, absolutely.

But when he arrived he was going to get the shock of his life, because it would be her doing the holding.

The men had been watching her changing expressions. 'Maybe we should ask her,' Arnie suggested.

'Whaddya say, Julie,' Pierce asked. 'You gonna step into Eddie's shoes?'

She looked at them all, one after the other. Her boys. Five thugs, who were prepared to worship the ground she walked on. 'Yes,' she said. 'That's what I want to do.'

CHAPTER 8

The rest of the night passed in a whirl. They opened a couple of bottles of champagne and drank to her success and to the damnation of Big Pat MacGinnion, who she gathered would now be her sworn enemy. Then she was taken downstairs on to the floor of the club and given a guided tour, introduced to the various croupiers and barmen, all of whom seemed thunderstruck, but delighted, to shake hands with the 'Boss's daughter' – none of them was told at this stage that Eddie Armitage was dead.

Then they went on to another club, and then another, while her head began to spin more and more as her hands were squeezed and she was kissed by a succession of thugs. And then she simply knew nothing else until she awoke with a gonging headache, lying on the softest bed she had ever known. She opened her eyes, stared at the canopy, and then at the room, which was decorated in red and purple and gave the impression of being in one of the deepest pits of hell, save for the luxury with which she was surrounded.

For a moment she was too bemused to think, then the events of last night slowly came back to her. She sat up in alarm, groaned with pain and lay down again, and discovered she was naked. Then she did sit up in alarm. She had spent the night with Pierce. And Top, and Lenny, and Arnie . . . Arnie was the one she remembered most. And now . . .?

The door opened, and Julie gave a gasp and dived beneath the covers. But it was a Negress, tall and slender, elegant and utterly beautiful, wearing a blood-red housecoat and high-heeled mules, and carrying a glass of bubbling Alka Seltzer. 'You'll want this,' she said, standing by the bedside.

163

Julie wasn't going to argue about that. She drank greedily.

'Breakfast whenever you can stand it,' the woman said.

Julie blinked at her. 'Who are you?'

'Shana.'

Which wasn't very informative. 'Do you live here?' She didn't even know where here was.

'That's my bed,' Shana told her.

'Oh. I'm terribly sorry.'

'Why? I have another. And you sure needed that one.'

'Yes.' Julie licked her lips. 'Did you . . .'

Shana smiled. 'It was me. You don't think I'd let those punks paw you about? There's a new toothbrush in the bathroom. Join me when you're ready.' She gestured at the door. 'Use that robe.'

She went out, and Julie gazed after her for a moment. Back into a headspin. Maybe she'd feel better after breakfast. But she wasn't sure about that. Last night she had cheerfully agreed to be these men's 'Boss'. She must have been stark, staring mad. So now . . . she didn't know about now. But she had to find out, in a hurry.

'Where am I?' she asked Shana. They were sitting in a delightful boudoir – decorated in pastel shades as opposed to the bright colours of the bedroom – sipping coffee and eating waffles and bacon smothered in maple syrup. The housegown she had been given was midnight blue, and from the way it hung on her she presumed it also belonged to Shana.

'Your apartment,' Shana said.

'My apartment?'

'Well, actually, it belongs to Eddie.'

'Daddy's? Good Lord.' She ran to the window. They were very high up, somewhere in the very middle of the city, she thought. There were streets, way below her, and people like ants. The view made her feel giddy. She sat down again.

'No head for heights?' Shana inquired.

'No head for anything, right this minute,' Julie agreed.

Shana studied her. 'Your dad tell you about me?'

Julie raised her head from her coffee cup.

'Hanson told me you were a big girl,' Shana said.

Julie opened her mouth, and then closed it again.

164

'Maybe you're a racist, or just a prude,' Shana remarked. 'But men do need women. The right kind of women.'

'Yes,' Julie gasped. 'I'm neither a racist nor a prude, believe me, Shana. It's just that every day I find out more about Daddy, and everything I find out is so totally unlike how he always behaved around me.'

'Figures,' Shana said.

'Yes,' Julie agreed, and had a terrible thought. 'Who brought me here?'

'Hanson. And Arnie. About four o'clock. You were out. But really.'

'Yes. Did . . .' she licked her lips. 'Did they tell you anything?'

'Just that you're Julie Armitage. Shit, I knew that, by looking at you.'

Because, Julie realised, this room too was filled with photographs of her.

'They said you'd explain what you're doing here,' Shana added.

'Oh, God,' Julie said. 'Oh, God. Oh, Shana . . .' she gazed at her.

And a slow frown crossed the even contours of Shana's face. 'Oh, Jesus Christ,' she whispered. 'I knew it had to be something. How?'

Julie told her, and watched the beautiful face threaten to dissolve, and then recover. This woman had immense strength of character.

Shana stood up. 'So I guess you want me to leave.'

Julie caught her hand. 'Oh, Shana. I don't want you to go anywhere. I need you.'

'MacGinnion,' Shana said. 'You gonna get MacGinnion?'

'Yes,' Julie promised.

'I'd like to hang around until then.'

'I'd like you to hang around for just as long as you want,' Julie told her.

Shana studied her. 'You into girls?'

'Into . . . good Lord, no. I just want you to stay, as a friend.'

Shana looked uncertain for the first time, and Julie realised that in her world perhaps the word 'friend' had never existed.

'Actually,' she went on, 'I'm married.'

Shana sat down again. 'Are you now? Where's hubby?'

'He's . . . oh, my Lord!' Because now she too was living a double life, and Teddy had promised to call . . . 'I must get back to the Plaza.'

165

'And hubby?'

'He'll be there too. Maybe today. What time is it?'

Shana looked at a gold wristwatch. 'Pushing eleven.'

'Can we go there now?'

Shana considered. 'Maybe I should check with Hanson.'

'The hell with Hanson. I'm the boss now, Shana.'

'You?'

'Yes,' Julie said.

Shana considered some more. 'Why not,' she agreed. 'My car's in the basement garage.'

Shana drove a red and white Pontiac convertible with the top down and wore a red and white striped dress. None of her clothes would fit Julie, so she had been forced to put on her somewhat wrecked evening gown – she was going through clothes faster than she could buy them. She felt extremely conspicuous, being dressed like that at eleven o'clock in the morning, but no one seemed the least interested as they raced up Fifth Avenue, brakes squealing every time the lights changed.

'I want you to know,' Shana said, 'that Eddie was real good to me. I was fond of that guy.' A huge tear rolled down her cheek and fell with a gentle plop on to the steering wheel.

'Thank you,' Julie said.

'So I would sure like to be there when you shoot MacGinnion in the balls,' Shana said.

'Shoot him in . . .' she had been thinking of handing him over to the police, if his complicity could be proven. 'Yes.'

The car screamed to a halt in the forecourt of the hotel, and the door was opened for them. 'Park it,' Shana said to the attendant, and went up the steps. Julie followed, feeling very much the junior partner at the moment. She was also terribly embarrassed, as the hotel staff would know she had been out all night. However, that did not seem to bother the deskclerk, although he gave Shana a double take. 'There's been a telephone call from your husband, Mrs Longman,' he said. 'And I told your friends that you had gone out for the evening. They asked if you'd call them this morning.'

'Friends?' Julie asked.

'Ah . . .' he checked his notepad. 'Mr and Mrs Archibald. They came for you at ten o'clock last night, to take you to their party.

166

Seemed quite upset to learn that you'd gone out already. I've made a note of the number.'

Julie took the slip of paper as if she was in a dream. Maybe she was in a dream. She went into the lift, Shana at her elbow. 'I wondered if he was going to throw me out,' Shana confided. 'Not all these swank hotels go for coons. I'll bet he's on the phone to the manager right this minute. Who're these Archibalds, anyway? Hanson gave me to understand you didn't know anybody in New York.'

'I don't,' Julie gasped. 'I've never heard of anyone named Archibald.'

Shana looked at her, and the lift came to rest. 'I guess maybe we should've told Hanson what we were doing, after all,' she said.

'Should I telephone them?'

'Not on your sweet ass. We'll give that to Hanson. Meanwhile . . . what do you say we rush?'

They almost ran along the corridor, opened the suite door. 'Me first,' Shana said, and whipped out a small revolver from her handbag as she stepped into the room.

Julie wondered if she should do the same, then decided against it; she would feel too foolish.

'Clean,' Shana said, and she went in. The room was exactly as she had left it save that the maid had removed the drinks tray.

'Do you think I could have a shower?' Julie asked.

'If you're quick. I'll pack,' Shana volunteered.

'Oh, would you?' Julie agreed. 'I won't be a moment.'

'Go ahead,' Shana invited, and started opening drawers. 'Just don't drag your feet.'

Julie dropped the evening gown on the floor, stepped beneath the hot shower, allowed the water to bounce on her face and drive away some of the cobwebs. She towelled and put on clean underwear and a yellow sundress – the day was really quite warm. Then, cramming her dirty clothes into one of the cases, she carried it into the sitting-room, and suddenly remembered. 'But what about Teddy? My husband. When he calls back.'

'We'll leave your new number at the desk.' Shana closed the other suitcase. 'Let's go.'

'Who do you think the Archibalds were?' Julie asked.

'I'd rather not think. Come on.'

167

Julie looked around the bedroom, but she'd forgotten nothing. The hotel wouldn't be happy, as they'd only been here a day, but they would have to put up with it. Anyway, she would settle what bill there was. 'Right,' she said.

They lifted a case each, and gazed at each other as there was a knock on the door.

'Oh, God,' Julie said.

Shana pointed, indicating that she should get out of the line of fire, then moved towards the door herself, again drawing her revolver. She stood against the wall next to the latch, while Julie watched, heart pounding.

'Who is it?' Shana asked.

'Police. Open up, Mrs Longman.'

'Police?' Julie gasped.

Shana hesitated, then put away the gun, and released the latch. But her hand immediately returned inside the bag.

The door swung in, and two men entered the suite. They were in plain clothes, but they certainly looked like policemen. They gazed at Shana in amazement. 'Mrs Julie Longman?' one asked.

Shana looked at Julie.

'I'm Mrs Longman,' Julie said.

The men turned to look at her, then at the suitcases. 'Going somewhere?'

'What's it to you, big boy?' Shana inquired.

He glanced at her, then turned back to Julie. 'You'll have to give a raincheck to your friend,' he said. 'I have a warrant for your arrest. Put your handbag on the table.'

Julie could only gape at him; in fact the handbag fell from her fingers to the floor. She second man came over to pick it up.

'You got a charge?' Shana inquired.

'Who are you?' asked the first detective.

'I'm Shana Evans,' Shana said.

'And what're you doing here?'

'I'm a friend of Mrs Longman.'

The detective looked at Julie again, sceptically.

'The charge,' Shana repeated.

'Illegal entry into the United States will do for a start,' the detective said.

168

'Illegal entry?' Julie cried, and watched the other man empty her handbag on to the table. Just like that lout Baldwin. He picked up the gun.

'Well, whaddya know,' remarked the first detective. 'You gotta licence for that toy?'

'A licence?' Julie looked at Shana, who waggled her eyebrows.

'Lady,' the detective lieutenant said, 'you are in dead trouble.'

'Whaddya think of these, Lieutenant?' asked the other man, holding up the wad of travellers' cheques.

'Maybe she'll be able to raise bail,' the lieutenant commented. 'Let me see that passport, Tibbett.'

The detective handed the passport to his superior, who flicked the pages. 'This is a forgery.'

'A what?' Not even the creeping sensation of some unearthly *déjà vu* could stop Julie being aghast.

'You coming?'

Julie looked at Shana.

'Seems like you'd better,' Shana said. 'I'll look after your things, and I'll rustle up Hanson and some legal beef. Believe me.'

'Yes,' Julie said. 'Oh, yes.' Hanson had said Daddy employed a smart lawyer. But her brain was spinning out of control again.

She went downstairs beside the detective lieutenant; at least he hadn't wanted to handcuff her. 'Mrs Longman,' said the embarrassed deskclerk. 'The bill . . .'

'Maybe you'd better write them one of those cheques,' the lieutenant suggested. 'You have enough on your plate without being sued by the Plaza.'

Julie obeyed him without actually seeing the amount involved. She just did not know what she was doing, could only clutch at the few coherent thoughts which entered her mind. 'My husband will be back today,' she said. 'Or he may call again.'

'We will inform Mr Longman of the situation, madam,' the clerk said, more kindly now she had actually paid up.

But what was Teddy going to think? Of course there had to be a mistake. The detectives showed her into their waiting car, and they pulled away from the hotel.

'Please,' Julie begged. 'Please will you tell me what's going on? That passport can't be a forgery. It was issued in London. By the passport office. Only a few days ago.'

169

'Your name really Armitage?' the lieutenant asked.

Julie bit her lip. But of course it was on the passport. 'Yes. That was my maiden name.'

'And your father was Eddie Armitage?'

Another hesitation. But it would do her no good to lie about it. 'Yes,' she said. 'Is that important?'

'Baby, do you know who Eddie Armitage was?'

'I . . .' she sighed. 'Yes.'

The lieutenant nodded. 'And now he's dead, and you've come hustling over here to muscle in on the action, is that it?'

'I . . .' she opened her mouth and closed it again. He was dangerously close to the truth. 'I don't know what you mean.'

'It won't work, baby. You're gonna be deported on the next available ship.'

'Deported?' she shouted. 'But I haven't done anything.'

'Illegal entry,' he repeated. 'And Scotland Yard seem to think you know more about your daddy's death than you've let on. There's a detective on his way over now to pick you up and take you back.'

At the police station she was given into the care of a hard-faced woman constable, who took her to a cell. She was too bemused to protest, or even to feel revulsion at the surroundings in which she found herself, the stench of disinfectant, the latrine bucket, the way her fingerprints were taken and she was photographed from several angles. She was being treated as a criminal, but wasn't she a criminal, by the mere fact of being Julie Armitage?

It was the mix-up over her second passport that was so upsetting, even as she told herself over and over again that it was all a ploy on the part of the English police. Obviously they had at last unearthed Edwin Allen's true identity, had wanted to interview her, and found she had fled. So they had telegraphed New York to hold her on any trumped-up charge until they could come for her. But they had no right to do that unless they were meaning to charge her with a crime. And she had committed no crime.

She lay on her face on the cot, because she didn't want to have to look at the men and women who kept moving up and down the corridor, or to listen to the sounds of the station, the shouts of people being brought in, the rattle of typewriters, the gurgling of the coffee machine – these were all strange and frightening noises to her. She

170

had to put her faith in Shana and Hanson Pierce, people she had only met yesterday.

Then Julie rose to her knees in terror. She had forgotten whoever had sent the telegram to Pierce. That couldn't have been the police. There was someone else over there who knew all about her.

At one o'clock she was brought a tray of food, which wasn't at all bad, and she discovered she was quite hungry. 'Will my husband be allowed to see me?' she asked the woman, trying desperately to keep calm.

'If he wants to.'

She was suggesting that he might not when he discovered she was under arrest. But Teddy would know it was all a put-up job; he himself had procured her birth certificate from Somerset House. She simply had to keep calm. But would he be able to get her out of here? Did they have things like writs of habeas corpus in the United States? They had to.

'When will the English detective arrive?'

'Four or five days, I reckon.'

'Four or five days?' Julie could not stop herself shouting. 'You're going to keep me here for four or five days?'

'So don't you like the food?'

Julie threw herself down again. She wanted to shout and scream and cry. But she didn't. She lay and seethed for an hour, then rolled on her back and stared at the whitewashed ceiling. Four or five days. That would surely give Hanson Pierce, and Teddy, time to do something. They had to be able to do something.

She was very tired after her long night, and fell asleep. And awoke with a start as the key turned in her lock.

'Okay, Longman,' the woman said. 'You're free to go.'

Julie sat up. She couldn't believe her ears.

'Out,' the woman said. 'We don't run an hotel.'

Julie pulled on her shoes, brushed past her into the corridor, almost ran down it, gazed at a man she had never seen before, small and dark and so neatly dressed he might have been a mannequin in a department store window. He raised his hat. 'Dominic Cerdo, Mrs Longman. Let's get out of here.'

Julie wanted to kiss him, but was interrupted by the police lieutenant. 'Your handbag's over there,' he said. 'You want to check the contents.' He tapped the passport. 'I'm keeping this until the

171

man from Scotland Yard arrives. And the gun. Carrying a concealed weapon without a licence is an offence. There will still be charges to be answered. And let me tell you something, Julie Armitage: because you have a smart lawyer don't mean we are going to let you get away with anything. If we don't nail you on the gun charge, we are going to nail you on something. Remember that.'

'Ignore him, my dear,' Dominic Cerdo said, and ushered her outside to a waiting limousine. 'Home, Bert.'

Julie was far too euphoric to wonder where home was. 'Mr Cerdo,' she said. 'If you knew how grateful I am. But how did you get me out?'

'Writ of habeas corpus. I had to put up bail because of the concealed-weapon charge. But we'll wriggle round that one if we have to.'

'But if I'm in the country illegally—'

'How can you be in the country illegally, Mrs Longman? You are married to an American citizen. Besides, you were born here.'

'I was *what*?

'Of course you were, my dear. First thing I did when I was told of your predicament was to go along to City Hall to check out the details and obtain your birth certificate.'

'But that's impossible.'

'My dear girl, I know your father was never entirely honest with you, but you must believe that I have known him for a very long time. He was married right here in New York City, and you were born here six months after the marriage.' He gave her a brief smile. 'I think you could best be described as a child of love. But that is so romantic, don't you think? And after all, your parents did legalise the matter.'

Not for the first time Julie felt she was being sucked into the vortex of a never-ending whirlpool. Of course Daddy and Mummy had been married here. Hanson Pierce had said so. It had not occurred to her to ask Pierce anything more than that because she had known that six months later they had been in Epsom as Mr and Mrs Edwin Allen. But in the interim she had been born. Had that been the reason for Father's determination to set up a separate existence for his wife and child? Get them out of the firing line, so to speak? And had thus created an elaborate double life. Oh, Father, she thought. What a strange character you were; and I never knew you at all.

172

On the other hand, from what she had learned of her father these past couple of weeks, it was just as likely that he had already been planning to double cross his partners in crime.

But she was an American! She found that a strangely reassuring thought. She actually belonged somewhere. She belonged here, in this city.

'No need to be upset,' Cerdo said, watching her changing expressions.

'It's all a bit much to take in,' she said. 'Mr Cerdo, my husband will be going crazy trying to find me.'

'Your husband,' Cerdo said disparagingly. 'Yes. We'll see that he is informed where you are. But he will have to come to you. It really is necessary for you to be in a safe place for a few days, until we see the lie of the land. You see, the majority of your father's associates don't know you exist. And when they find out, they might just get the idea you have come to New York to interfere with his operations, which are their operations, if you follow me.'

'Yes,' she said. 'Mr Pierce explained that. He thought it might be a good idea.'

Cerdo raised his eyebrows. 'Hanson Pierce thought that, did he? I didn't know you knew him.'

'Yes. He was going to arrange a meeting for me with the various heads of the districts. He said the man to look out for was someone called MacGinnion.'

'Oh, indeed,' Cerdo agreed. 'Big Pat MacGinnion is the man to watch out for.' The car turned off the street and into the gloom of an underground garage.

'But wait a moment,' Julie said. 'If Mr Pierce didn't send you to get me out of gaol, who did? No one else knows I'm here.' The spinning sensation was back.

'I'll explain it upstairs,' Cerdo said.

Julie looked out of the window, and began to feel vaguely alarmed. 'Where are we?' she asked. 'I was going to stay at Daddy's apartment.'

'Too exposed,' Cerdo said. 'You'll be safer here. No one can get into this building, unless he, or she, belongs to the Association.'

'But . . . I would like to change my clothes, and have a bath, and—'

'Of course, my dear.' He opened the door for her and she got out.

'I'll have your clothes sent over right away. You'll be very comfortable here.' They were in a lift, and speeding upwards. 'Do they have elevators in England?' Cerdo asked.

'Well, yes. We call them lifts. But they don't travel half as far, or as fast, as yours.'

'The miracles of modern science,' Cerdo said. The lift had stopped, and they stepped out on to a carpeted lobby, to face glass doors covered in gold lettering, announcing that this was the home of the A & M Realty Company, Inc. A female receptionist smiled at them as they went in, and Julie's nerves began to settle. Cerdo ushered her along a corridor between closed doors from behind which came the hum of typewriters. Was all this Father's too?

They came to another door, and Cerdo gave a brief knock, and then opened it for her. She stepped into another huge, sumptuous office, only this one had windows which revealed a panoramic view of the city. There were two men in the room, one standing by the door, thin and hatchet-faced, the other behind the desk, huge and jovial. This man now came round the desk, arms outstretched.

'Julie Armitage,' he said. 'Geewillikins, if you knew how long I have waited for this moment. For crying out loud, I feel like bursting into tears. I'm Pat MacGinnion.'

Julie had guessed who he had to be the moment she had seen him. Her stomach had turned to lead and her brain had coagulated into a solid mass of terror. Now she took a step backwards, and had her arm gripped by Cerdo. And MacGinnion strode up to her, taking her hands to kiss them. 'Julie Armitage,' he said again. 'When I think what they've been doing to you my blood starts to boil. But you're safe now.'

I have got to get out of here, Julie thought. I have got to get *out* of here. But how?

MacGinnion had observed her expression. 'You don't have to be scared of me, Julie,' he said. 'Your daddy and I were partners for thirty-one years. Heck, more than that if you count the years we shared a cell. He was my closest friend. And now he's gone, you're my personal responsibility. And you and I are going to nail his killer. Right?'

Julie stared at him. We are going to nail you, she thought. You, you great thug.

174

MacGinnion glanced at Cerdo. 'She dumb?'

'I guess she's a little taken aback, Big Pat.'

'Yeah, well you'd better pour her a drink, Kaley. Sit down, Julie. Sit down.'

She was escorted to one of the deep leather armchairs, where her knees willingly gave way.

'The trouble is, Big Pat,' Cerdo explained. 'Seems she's been in touch with Pierce, and he has told her all sorts of weird things, like how she could take over the Association, being Eddie's daughter, and how the only person she has to worry about is you.'

'Did he now.' MacGinnion returned behind his desk, placed his elbows on it, and rested his chin on his hands to stare at her. 'How the shitting hell . . . oh, I beg your pardon, little Julie. It just slipped out. But how did you get in touch with Pierce?'

The man called Kaley was at her side with a glass of whisky. She observed that no one else was drinking, but she certainly needed a stimulant. She sipped. 'I didn't. He got in touch with me.'

'So that's who you went out with last night.'

'Are you Mr Archibald?'

MacGinnion grinned at her. 'You could say that, Julie. You sure could say that. But how did Pierce find out you were in New York?'

'I have no idea,' she said, truthfully.

MacGinnion's grin turned to a frown. 'You and me have to be straight with each other, Julie.'

'I am being straight, Mr MacGinnion.'

'The name's Pat. My friends call me Big Pat. And I sure hope you and me are going to be friends, Julie. I sure do hope that. So you went off with Pierce last night and he suggested you step into Daddy's shoes. I always wondered what that great hulk used for a brain.'

'Don't you like the idea, Big Pat?' She could do nothing but keep calm and try to dissemble until something turned up.

'Well, it'd be a kind of unusual situation, don't you think? And frankly, Julie, you're a sweet girl – I can tell that just by looking at you. But I shouldn't think you could hold down the job.'

'Hanson Pierce thought I could. And I want to get Daddy's killer. Including the man who paid for it.'

'Don't we all. What I would like you to do for me, first, Julie, is tell me the names of all the guys you met last night. All the guys who thought it'd be an idea for you to take over.'

175

'I really can't remember them,' Julie said.

MacGinnion gazed at her for several seconds, then he got up and came round his desk. 'Julie,' he said. 'I want to tell you a little story. A kind of cautionary tale. You come and sit over here.'

There was a leather settee against the far wall. Julie decided she had nothing to lose by going along with him. And equally that she didn't have any choice. She had to keep him talking, because as Cerdo had not been sent to get her out by Pierce, Pierce would still be working on it. She hoped. Therefore, when he got to the station and was told by the police she had left with Cerdo, he would come along here. She hoped and prayed.

For the first time she was happy that Teddy was out of town.

She sat on the settee, and MacGinnion sat beside her.

'Like I said,' MacGinnion told her. 'Your Daddy and I were close. The friends you make in prison, they're friends with a capital F. He was always the boss, and that was fine with me. I trusted him absolutely. So you'll understand what I've been finding out is upsetting. Hell, I'm not bothered about his sneaking off and marrying some little girl he'd made pregnant, although it would've been nice to meet her. And I can understand that he wanted his wife and daughter to be safe. I still reckon he should've told me about the double life he was setting up over in that place Epsom. Hell, that's what buddies are for. But okay, that's his business. It's the Association that was our real life, him and me. And when I learned that he had lifted twenty million dollars out of the Association profits . . .'

'What did you say?' Julie gasped.

'Twenty million. But you know that.'

Twenty million dollars, she thought. Good Lord! No wonder Uncle Bob and his henchman Baldwin had been going mad. And Teddy? Had he known of it too? But how could he?

'That hurt,' MacGinnion said. 'It hurt me, and it hurt the boys. So what we want, all we want, Julie, is our money back. Just hand it over, and we'll call it quits. Tell you what, we'll let you keep a million. That's a lot of dough. Buy a lot of pretty dresses. And what's more, if you want a job in the Association, you can have it. I'll make you vice-president. But no under-the-counter deals with Hanson Pierce or anybody else, and if we're gonna work together, I have to know just which of the guys was considering pulling a fast

176

one. You must be able to understand that. Now, what do you think? You ever heard a more fair offer than that?'

Julie had got her breath back. 'You think I know what Daddy did with the money?'

'Well, hell, Julie, a guy sets up a double life, and brings up his daughter to believe she's good class . . . of course he salted that dough away for you. Now I ask you, what the hell is a chick like you gonna do with twenty million dollars? You couldn't spend it. All that'd happen is that some guy will come along and marry you for it, fleece you of it, and leave you in the gutter.'

Julie's thoughts had careered quite out of control. Without thinking she muttered, 'So that's why you had him killed.'

MacGinnion's eyes narrowed. 'Come again?'

Julie glared at him; it was too late to turn back now. 'You did, I know you did.'

'Now, Julie, you really shouldn't go around making accusations like that.'

'If you didn't,' she said. 'How do you know that Daddy is dead? Nobody else does. Except those I told.'

'So you told me,' Dominic Cerdo pointed out.

'Maybe I did. But you weren't the least surprised or upset. And you didn't tell Big Pat. Because he already knew.' She was panting.

'For a lawyer, you don't have no more brains than a pea,' MacGinnion told his attorney in disgust.

'Well, Big Pat, I reckoned—'

'Ah, shaddup.' MacGinnion smiled at Julie. It was not a reassuring sight. 'Okay, Julie, cards on the table. I like that best anyway. Your daddy committed a crime against the Association. A very serious crime. When you're in the kind of business we are we gotta have absolute trust. If a guy, or a doll, can't be trusted, that's it. He has to go. But we didn't want to cause no upset in the Association, so we had it done as Edwin Allen. You know all that.'

'You can just sit there, and admit that, to me?' Julie whispered.

'Like I said, cards on the table. Now here are some more. Your daddy went off with twenty million dollars. There is only one possible reason for him to do that: to feather your nest. Maybe he intended to share it with you for a while, but that had to be the ultimate idea. Now as far as I can gather from my people in England, you have been playing real innocent. You've even

177

accumulated a husband. I have a pretty good idea why you wanted to do that: to get into this country quietly and legally, without having to admit you were Julie Armitage. Smart girl. And then the first thing you do when you get here is contact Hanson Pierce, your daddy's old troubleshooter, the one guy who might have the nerve to stand up to me. Again, smart girl. But Julie, you're moving in a world of smart men, now, and you have as much chance of pulling the wool over our eyes as a block of ice has of not melting in a hot oven. Now like I said, I don't blame anyone for trying to better themselves. It's what we're all doing, all the time, right? But there comes a time when you gotta realise you've gone as far as you can go, at least on that particular track. So I'm going to make my offer once more. I know you know where that dough is. I want it back. You give it to me and I am going to let bygones be bygones. I will give you a million dollars, but I don't reckon you can really come into the Association, not if you're going to bear a grudge about your dad.'

She had been trying to think. Obviously it would do her no good to keep repeating that Pierce had contacted her, not she him, and in fact the less that MacGinnion knew about what was really going on the better, but his last words stung her again. 'A grudge?' she shouted. 'You cold-blooded murderer—'

'Can it,' he snapped, and her head jerked at the sharpness of his tone. 'In fact, I don't want you this side of the ocean at all. Take your million and get out, and don't ever come back. Now give.'

'I wouldn't give you the last penny in my pocket,' she said.

'Julie, you are starting to make me mad.'

'But as it happens,' Julie went on, 'I couldn't give you the twenty million you claim is missing, because I don't know where it is. All right, I got the message that there was some money hidden, somewhere. And I've been looking as hard as anyone, believe me. But I haven't found a thing. And that is the truth.'

'You goddamned little broad,' MacGinnion shouted, and before she could defend herself his huge hands had closed on her throat. She gasped and tried to kick and strike him, but already stars were racing across her brain and she couldn't breathe. She thought she was going to die, but the other men were standing around her and talking to MacGinnion, and the fingers suddenly relaxed. She collapsed over the arm of the settee; her skirt was soaked from where

178

she had dropped her half-empty glass into her lap; it had fallen to the carpet beside her handbag.

She gasped for air and attempted to turn herself away from them. Dimly she heard MacGinnion's voice. 'Okay,' he was saying. 'Take her apart if you have to. But get me that dough.'

'You leave her with me, Big Pat,' Kaley said. 'Hey little girl, wake up.'

Julie raised her head, slowly. Every movement of her neck was painful.

She watched Kaley walk to the desk, pick up the phone. 'Tell Ricky and Mel to come in here,' he said.

'You gonna do it here?' Cerdo seemed alarmed.

'I'll take her upstairs. But you can come and watch if you like.'

Cerdo shuddered. 'And after?'

Kaley shrugged. 'That depends on her.'

Julie pushed herself straight. Were they talking about murdering her? Well, what would be surprising about that: they had murdered Father. As Uncle Bob had said, she had pushed her nose into something far too big for her. Oh, Uncle Bob, she thought: what would I give to have some of your brand of violence on my side right this minute.

The door opened and she thought of screaming. But that wouldn't do any good. This was Big Pat MacGinnion's empire. Even the nice-looking receptionist would be in his pay. She gazed at him. He had gone back behind his desk and was sitting down, still staring at her. Then she looked at the two men who had just come in. Neither was reassuring.

'We have a job,' Kaley said, and jerked his thumb.

The men grinned. 'Can't be bad,' one said.

'Yeah,' said the other.

'So take her upstairs,' Kaley commanded.

'Can she walk?'

'I should think so.'

One of the men stood above her. 'On your feet, baby.'

Julie obeyed. She didn't want him to touch her. But she was still dizzy from MacGinnion's attack, and she lost her balance. He caught her round the waist. 'Brother, this is going to be good,' he said to his partner.

'Use the stairs,' Kaley said.

179

She was pushed towards what she had supposed was a large cupboard, but which turned out to be a doorway leading on to a flight of stone steps. It went down as well as up, but she was pushed up. 'Let me go,' she gasped. 'I can walk.'

'Then do it, sister,' the man said, releasing her.

Julie held on to the iron bannister, and half pulled herself up. What am I going to do? she wondered. She was aware of a terrible fear, lurking in her subconscious. But for the moment she just could not believe that this was happening to her, that these men really meant to hurt her . . . She *had* told them the truth; she could not tell them more than that. She had a tremendous urge to turn and hurl herself at them, knock them aside and go tumbling down the stairs, down and down and down until she bounced out on to the street, fifty levels away. But she knew that wasn't going to work. That would merely give them the opportunity to manhandle her.

But weren't they going to manhandle her anyway?

There was a landing, and a closed door. The stairs continued upwards, but the first man said, 'Stop there,' and came beside her to unlock the door. 'Inside,' he commanded.

She stepped into a small, windowless room, which bore a remarkable resemblance to the police cell she had just left. Because that was what had happened; she had exchanged one prison for another, and this one was infinitely worse – if only because there was no woman warder.

She walked as far as the bed – it had a rusty iron bedstead, and there was no sheet on the mattress, and no pillow – and turned to face them, suddenly remembering she had left her handbag in MacGinnion's office with nearly fifty thousand pounds in it. But fifty thousand pounds wasn't going to interest men looking for twenty million dollars. They had taken up a position one on either side of the door, and now Kaley came in, and closed the door behind him. 'Real cosy,' he remarked. 'Now, little girl, you are going to have to give, or I am going to hurt you real bad.' He walked across the room towards her, while she watched his approach as a rabbit might watch the tongue of the snake reaching for it. He stood in front of her, put out his hand to stroke her cheek and the line of her jaw, and then suddenly tightened the hand and pushed her away from him, so that she fell across the bed and banged her head on the wall. 'Real bad,' he said again.

CHAPTER 9

Julie gasped for breath; her head seemed to have separated itself from her body. Yet her principal emotion was anger. These men had murdered Father. It was only just sinking in. And now they meant to murder her. The thought made her far more angry than afraid, whatever they were going to do to her.

Kaley stood above her. 'So where's the dough?' he asked.

She kicked, viciously, sideways. The toe of her shoe caught him beside the knee and he gave a squeal of pain and turned half round before falling over, on to the cot beside her. Hastily she sat up, but before she could move any further the two other men were standing above her.

Julie tried to get up, and the men caught her arms. Kaley had also pushed himself up, and she was turned and forced across the cot, on her knees. Her chest thudded into the mattress, and one of the men sat astride her shoulders to hold her down. The other was behind her.

'Bare her ass,' Kaley was snarling. 'Goddamn it, bare the bitch's ass.'

She tried to push herself up, but the weight on her shoulders was too great and now he grasped her wrists as well. While the other man was raising her skirt and tugging on her knickers. It was like being in Alma Briden's brothel all over again, but infinitely worse, because she realised there was no escape from this situation. These men knew who she was, and didn't care.

She raised her head and screamed, and had her hair grasped, and her scalp, and her face forced into the mattress so hard she thought she was going to smother. Then there was a stinging sensation from

181

her buttocks which made her body arch even with the weight on it; someone had struck her bare flesh with a leather belt. She gasped for breath, and twisted, as there was another blow, and then another. She tried to kick backwards, but that was useless, and the blows rained down until she seemed just a mass of agony from her waist to her knees. Then suddenly the weight on her shoulders was gone, and so were the stinging blows.

Julie had never even been spanked in her life, much less subjected to such a humiliating and painful assault. Tears flooded from her eyes and great sobs wracked her shoulders as she slowly subsided off the bed, on to the floor. But she couldn't sit, and instead moaned and turned on to her face, crumpling into a heap.

A toe nudged her shoulders and she rolled over on to her back, whimpering in agony, then turned on her side, gazing at the polished, pointed shoes in front of her face.

'You gonna kick again?' someone asked.

She inhaled slowly. No, she thought, I am not going to kick again. Not *kick* again.

She heard the door open. 'Good God,' Cerdo said. 'What have you done to her?'

'The bitch kicked me,' Kaley said.

'You had it coming,' MacGinnion growled. 'You asked her anything with these punks here?'

'We ain't heard nothing, Big Pat,' one of the men protested. 'Honest.'

'You better hope so,' MacGinnion growled. 'Out. Kaley, what have you got inside that head?' Julie heard the door close again. 'You want the whole world to know about that twenty million dollars?'

'I reckon those two boys are okay,' Kaley protested.

'Noboby, but nobody, is okay when that kinda dough is involved. Now let's see what you got here.' Fingers again dug into Julie's hair, and she was dragged into a sitting position.

MacGinnion's face loomed in front of her pain and tear-filled eyes. 'So give,' he said. 'Where's the money?'

She could see Cerdo standing behind him, so it had to be Kaley holding her hair; he was still panting from the exertion of beating her.

182

'I am going to kill you,' she sobbed. She remembered what Shana had recommended. 'I am going to shoot you in the balls.'

'You and the whole British army,' MacGinnion said contemptuously. 'Put her on the bed,' he commanded.

Her hair was released and hands grasped her shoulders instead. Cerdo took her ankles, and she was dumped on the bed, on her back, and held there, unable to keep still because of the pain, attempting to tense her muscles for some new and more ghastly assault, as MacGinnion bent over her.

'Little girl,' he said. 'I can destroy you. There isn't anyone ever going to finger me for that, but I can leave you ashamed that you're a woman, first. Now, you want to be ashamed that you're a woman?'

She stared at him through the tears. But she was finished dissembling. She wished she knew the right American words to use; she could only recall aspects of her English upbringing.

He grinned at her. 'Real chip off the old block, ain't you. But you ain't Eddie Armitage, baby. You're just a little girl.' He reached down and raised her skirt, which had fallen into place. Julie felt sick, and tried to bring up her legs, but Cerdo was sitting on her ankles.

'She's a looker, ain't she,' MacGinnion said. 'Who'd have supposed a crumb like Eddie would have a chick like this? That Mary Goodwin must have been a *broad*. Tie her wrists, Frank.'

Kalcy released her hands and she brought them down, but MacGinnion merely laughed and caught them in turn. She fought against him for several seconds, while he grinned, and then she subsided in exhaustion and despair. By then Kaley had taken some thin rope from the bureau in the corner and a moment later her wrists were secured to the bedhead.

'Now you guys can take a leg each,' MacGinnion said, and stripped her to the waist by simply bursting the two straps of her sun dress and tugging on the brassière. Kaley took one of her legs from Cerdo, and between them they pulled them apart; MacGinnion started to take off his pants.

Then Julie screamed, again and again as he hurt her, again and again. 'Help me,' she shrieked, until she ran out of breath, and could only utter huge, dry sobs, while a variety of visions, memories, drifted before her face. 'You are out of your league,' Uncle Bob had said. 'Those people will tear you limb from limb to get what they want.'

183

The weight was gone from her chest, and she could breathe again, but then Kaley wanted his turn. She no longer screamed. She couldn't. Now she could only dream of Shana, and Hanson Pierce, bursting in here . . . to shoot them in the balls. All of them. It had to happen.

Again she could breathe. And feel pain. And more hatred than she had supposed possible.

Fingers grasped her chin and shook her face to and fro. 'Wake up. Dominic don't go for girls. Now tell us about the money.'

Her eyes flopped open and she stared at them through a red haze. 'I don't know about the money', she whispered.

'Little girl . . .'

'I'll fix her,' Kaley said.

He stood above her, and she thought he was going to rape her again, but this time he never touched her. He stood straight, and from his pocket took a cigarette lighter. She gazed at him in apprehension, not immediately understanding what he meant to do. 'Filled this just this morning,' he said. 'Should be quite a lot in there.' He leaned over her, and she watched in horror as he slowly tilted the lighter, and allowed the fluid to drip on to her pubes. It reached her flesh in seconds, but he was moving it around to make sure she was thoroughly dampened; some of the liquid ran down the inside of her thighs.

'All gone,' he said. 'I guess I'll have to use matches.' He took a box from his pocket, struck one, held it in his fingers, above her. 'Little girl, you got any idea what will happen to you if I drop this match?'

She gasped, and now she did move, twisting from side to side so violently she almost tore herself free. But the rope holding her wrists was too strong, and MacGinnion himself now had charge of her ankles, grinning at her; Cerdo had retreated across the room in disgust.

'You wouldn't die,' Kaley told her. 'Leastways, I don't think so. You're a big, strong girl. But you'd sure as hell think twice about letting a man in there again. And guess what, you wouldn't be able to accuse us of rape, because you wouldn't have no evidence left. So, where's the dough?'

The match had gone out. Kaley dropped it on the floor, and struck another. This time he came closer. Julie watched him while

184

the pounding in her brain rose to a crescendo. 'I don't know,' she shouted. She would kill these men. She was more determined on that than on anything in her life. She would kill these men if it took her the rest of her days. But she had to survive them first. 'I don't know,' she screamed. 'Daddy never told me. As God is my witness, I don't know!'

Every muscle was tensed against the searing, humiliating pain she anticipated. But there was no pain. Instead her wrists and ankles were released. Immediately her knees came up and her arms came down, and she rolled on her side, trying to cocoon herself against the coming horror.

Kaley leaned over her. 'Think about it,' he suggested. 'You know what I'm going to do to you, when we come back. There won't be no second chances then. You'll be for the high jump. Think about it, and have your answers ready. For when we come back.'

Julie lay absolutely still, curled in her ball, until several minutes had passed. During that time she heard the door slam and the key turn, but she still didn't believe that they had left her alone, that they were not going to torment her again. Nor did she understand why they had stopped. If they believed, as they obviously did, that she knew where Father had hidden the money, they had had her nearer to breaking point then than they ever would again.

Or did they believe, did they know, that a few hours spent lying here, thinking of what was going to happen to her, would have an even greater effect?

She dragged up her knickers, attempted to sit, and had immediately to roll on to her stomach. They were right. If she thought about them coming back she would probably go mad. She tied her shoulder straps with granny knots – did it matter if she looked like a rag doll, now? She was the raggedest doll who had ever lived. But lying down, with only the pain and the memory and the fear, would allow her to realise what had happened to her . . . and that *would* drive her mad. She got out of bed, tried the door. But it was securely locked, and was made of solid wood. Then she hunted the walls, but there was no way out; the only connection with the outside world was a very small air-conditioning vent. At least they didn't mean her to suffocate.

She went back to the cot, lay down, found she was shivering

185

despite the heat of the room. This was only partly the shock and the pain and the degradation of the assault. It was also a growing awareness that there was no way out. She was going to have to wait here until they came back, and then . . . the thought of them touching her again was horrifying enough. The thought of what they were going to do to her . . . but if she thought about that they were going to win. She would be mad by tomorrow morning. She had thought she was close to going mad several times before during this past fortnight. But that had been all fun and games. Even Uncle Bob's assault could be seen to be fun and games in retrospect, compared with this. Uncle Bob! For all his denials he must have been in the Association with Daddy. It must have been him cabled Hanson Pierce, once he had discovered she and Teddy had fled. Uncle Bob could really be on her side. At least . . . twenty million dollars! Uncle Bob had to be interested in that. Hanson Pierce had not mentioned it, so maybe he didn't know about it. But Uncle Bob certainly did. Yet he had tried to arrange protection for her. She was sure of that. Maybe because he wanted her kept out of MacGinnion's hands until she found the money. But she was still grateful. It was the goddamned police muscling in that had landed her in this mess.

But how had MacGinnion and Cerdo known she was in New York at all? A traitor in Pierce's camp? Arnie, or Top or Lenny . . . or the sinister Closet? Or another informant from London? Or even Uncle Bob. She could be totally wrong about him. But if Uncle Bob had informed MacGinnion, who had informed Pierce? Or was Uncle Bob playing the two factions off against each other, hoping they would destroy each other in their efforts to get at the money through her? But Uncle Bob knew *he* wasn't going to get at the money except through her – he couldn't possibly risk her being dumped in the river.

But then, neither could MacGinnion afford to dump her in the river, so long as there was a chance that she might know where Father had hidden the money. But suppose tomorrow he decided she was telling the truth?

Her head was spinning again.

She looked at her watch. It was past seven now, and her stomach was beginning to remind her that she hadn't eaten for several hours. But they clearly did not mean to feed her. Why should they waste their time?

She rolled on her back, gritted her teeth – but the pain was at last

186

beginning to subside – and stared at the electric light bulb which hung from the ceiling. And then there was Teddy. Poor, innocent Teddy. Or was he innocent? He had lied to her about the birth certificate. How much else had he lied to her about? He had stumbled across an innocent girl, fallen for her – maybe with a little help from the suggestion that she might be, as he would put it, well heeled – and plunged into a maelstrom beside her. Well, she had wanted him to do that. She didn't know whether she loved him or not, but she had been desperate to belong, not only to a man, but to a family, and she had had no doubt that she *was* going to love him. But Teddy was himself out of his depth. He *must* have forged her birth certificate . . . but so quickly? Unless Cerdo had pulled a fast one. But she didn't see the New York police being hoodwinked, and besides, there was the Scotland Yard detective, a real one this time, on his way to arrest her. Poor Teddy also had been attempting to operate in a league far greater than anything he knew about. And if these thugs finally accepted that she didn't know about the money and killed her tomorrow, and dumped her body in the river as Kaley had suggested, he would never know just how lucky an escape he had had. Oh, Teddy! He wouldn't even have the fifty thousand pounds. MacGinnion had that too.

But, oh, Teddy, she thought. He'd be back from Boston by now. In fact, if he had called the hotel again and been told she'd been arrested he would probably have been back for some hours. He would have gone to the police station and been told she had been bailed out by a lawyer named Cerdo, and he wouldn't know who Cerdo was. He would be going half mad, trying to find her. Oh, Teddy.

And she was going to lie here, until tomorrow morning, when she was going to be tortured and horribly mutilated, and then dumped in the river. Because if they tortured her and she still did not tell them because she didn't know, they would *have* to decide she was of no more value to them. And there was no way they could let her go after raping her and then burning her in the way Kaley meant to. She was going to suffer the agonies of the damned . . . she sat up, driving her hands into her hair to stop herself from screaming. She would happily tell them where the money was, just to get out of here. To get out of here, and arm herself with a gun, or better yet a bomb, and come back, and blow them all to kingdom come. That was all she wanted to do.

But she had nothing to tell them. If she hadn't been looking for

187

twenty million dollars . . . Oh, Daddy, why so much? . . . she had certainly been looking for something. And had found nothing beyond an ongoing pay-off from a bunch of London brothels. Three hundred thousand pounds a year might be over a million dollars, but it would still take a very long time to add up to twenty million, and according to Father's bank statements he had paid at least a third of it into his Association account, as no doubt he had been supposed to do. So the money hadn't come from there, or gone there. But then, where had it gone?

For all Julie's fear, and her tumbling emotions, she fell asleep, and was surprised to awake some hours later. The electric bulb still glowed above her head. In fact nothing in the room had changed in any way, and yet she had been awakened.

By the sound of a key in the lock; no other sound had penetrated this room. She sat up, then dropped her legs over the side of the bed and stood up, instinctively straightening her skirt and the bodice of the sundress, feeling for her shoes with her toes. Her watch told her it was three o'clock in the morning. Could they possibly be coming back for her now?

She held her breath as the door slowly swung inwards . . . and she found herself gazing at Teddy.

For a moment she couldn't believe her eyes but there was no mistaking that crooked grin. Then she was in his arms. 'Teddy,' she gasped, hugging him close.

'Oh, sweetheart.' He kissed her mouth, her eyes, her nose, holding her tight. 'What have they done to you?'

Julie shook her head. 'Teddy . . .' she began.

'Let's get out of here,' he said. 'Explanations later.'

He released her, although he continued to hold her hand. With his other hand he drew a pistol from his jacket pocket, and stepped into the doorway. She followed, gazing at the darkened steps, and at something even darker lying in a crumpled heap on the landing. Instinctively she checked. 'Is he . . .?'

'One of the goons,' Teddy said. 'He was on guard, I suppose.'

'But is he dead?'

'I don't think so. I only hit him with the gun.'

She looked down at the unconscious face; he was the man who had pulled down her knickers, who had held her ankles while Kaley

188

had whipped her. Before she could stop herself she had kicked him in the groin, as hard as she could.

'What the . . .' Teddy was scandalised.

'I owe him more than that,' Julie said. 'But that'll do to go on with.'

'Come on,' Teddy said, and made to hurry her down the stairs. But she checked. She was amazed at how cool she felt, how calm; her brain seemed to be working for the first time in days. Big Pat MacGinnion had done that to her.

'That door,' she said.

'Eh?'

'It leads to MacGinnion's office.'

'Well, he sure won't be there now.'

'My handbag is there,' she said. 'With all our money.'

'For god's sake, Julie . . .'

'I want my money,' she said, and opened the door. Teddy remained standing in the doorway, watching her. The office was empty, as he had predicted, but it also smelt of whisky. No one had cleaned it since this afternoon. She went to the settee and looked down behind it. The handbag was still there, where it had fallen when MacGinnion had tried to throttle her. She picked it up. 'All right,' she said. 'Now we can go.'

'For God's sake,' he said again, held her hand, and hurried her down the stairs. It was a very long journey, down and down and down. She ran out of breath, but still hurried behind him, while her brain seethed, from the reaction of being freed, the reaction of having kicked Ricky – or was it Mel? – the understanding that it had satisfied some savage instinct even as it had horrified her to do such a thing, and the confusion of having Teddy here, rescuing her, like some fictional knight errant.

He came to a stop, and she bumped into him. 'Careful now,' he said, and slowly pushed against a bar. The steel door swung out, and they stepped into an alleyway, and breathed fresh air. She looked up at the stars, a cluster just visible between the towering buildings to either side.

'We'll walk a block, and take the subway,' Teddy said.

'Where are we going?'

'Penn Station. We'll take the first train up to Boston. You'll be safe there, and we can get a passage back to England in a week.'

189

He had been hurrying her along the alley towards the street, but now she checked. 'Boston? Back to England?'

'Julie, you are in deadly danger here. I would've thought you knew that by now. We gotta get out of here.'

'I'm not leaving New York,' Julie told him. 'I want to go to Fifth Avenue.'

'You what?'

'Fifth Avenue,' she said. 'I'll know the building when I see it. I'll be safe there.'

Teddy peered at her in the darkness. 'What did they feed you?'

'They didn't feed me anything. Please take me there, Teddy, or let me go on my own.'

He gazed at her for a few minutes longer. 'You know you're gonna be deported any second? And charged with God knows what?'

'No one is deporting me, Teddy'. Explanations, as he had said, would have to wait, and right now she owed him too much to be angry with him as well as everyone else, but he wasn't changing her mind.

Once again he hesitated, then he shrugged. 'Fifth Avenue is just a couple of blocks away. That way.'

She set off, and he hurried at her side. 'You wouldn't care to tell me what this is about?'

'When we get where we're going.'

She soon got her bearings, and reached the building a few minutes later. The doors from the street were locked, but there was a night porter who peered at them through the glass, and spoke into a voicebox. 'Who do you want?'

'Miss Shana Evans,' Julie told him. 'Tell her Julie's here.'

'You know the time?'

'I have a watch. Will you call Miss Evans?'

'Who the hell is Shana Evans?' Teddy demanded.

'Daddy's mistress. And my friend.'

'Your . . . and you reckon you'll be safe here?'

'Safer than anywhere else on earth,' Julie said.

Teddy scratched his head.

The porter was back, and keys were turning. 'She says you're to go up.' The man seemed bemused.

'Thank you.' Julie led Teddy to the lift and pressed the button. They gazed at each other. 'I think I owe you my life,' she said. 'Or at least my sanity.'

'For God's sake, you're my wife.'

'Yes,' she said. She kept forgetting that.

The lift stopped, and she stepped into the lobby, straight into a slender young man armed with a Thompson sub-machine gun, which he was pointing at her stomach.

'Hell . . .' Teddy's hand hovered over his pocket.

'Don't do it,' Julie snapped. 'You weren't here before.'

'I'm always here, Miss Armitage,' the young man said. 'You just didn't see me, before. Who's your friend?'

'My husband.'

The young man raised his eyebrows. 'Tell him to put his gat on that table.'

'No way,' Teddy said.

'Then back to the street, buster. No guns allowed in the Boss's apartment.'

'I wish someone would tell me what the hell is going on,' Teddy complained, but he obeyed, placed the pistol on the table.

The young man pressed a switch, and the door swung inwards. Shana stood there, wearing her crimson dressing-gown and her high-heeled mules, and clearly nothing else, but looking surprisingly fresh for four o'clock in the morning. 'Julie,' she said. 'Oh, Julie.' She took her in her arms. 'We thought you were gone.'

Julie had no doubt her emotions were genuine, and hugged her back. She was trying desperately to hold back the feelings of anger and shock. But there was so much to do. 'This is my husband, Teddy,' she said, when Shana had released her.

'Your husband?' Shana looked Teddy up and down. 'Where did he spring from?'

'He got me out of MacGinnion's place.'

'He did what? With who?'

'Alone, Shana.'

Shana looked at her incredulously, then at Teddy again. 'Sure your name ain't Dick Tracy?'

'It was perfectly simple,' Teddy assured her.

'He'll tell you about it in a minute,' Julie said. 'Shana, I have just got to have a bath, and something to eat. And I need some medication, I think. For severe contusions.'

'Sure. Your clothes are in the bedroom. Let me get you some ointment.'

191

Julie walked down the hall to the master bedroom, Teddy at her heels. 'Some pad,' he commented. 'And you know your way about it? You have some big explaining to do.'

'So have you,' she reminded him. She stripped off her filthy clothes and let them fall to the floor. Shana came in with some cream.

'Where's the damage?'

Julie bent over.

'Holy Jumping Jesus!'

Teddy was looking as well. 'Godalmighty,' he said. 'They did that to you?'

'A man named Kaley. You know Kaley, Shana?'

'I do. He's a thug.'

'At the moment,' Julie said grimly.

'What's that smell?' Teddy asked.

'Lighter fluid,' said Julie with a sob.

'Lighter . . .?'

'They wanted to . . . they were going to . . . burn me,' Julie told them.

'Honeychild, you have got guts,' Shana said. 'You go take a hot shower.'

Julie obeyed; waves of exhaustion were threatening to close in on her mind, as well as her body. But how good the water felt, bouncing off her skin. She dried herself, lay on the bed while Teddy rubbed the salving ointment into the weals, and inhaled the delicious scent of frying bacon from the kitchen.

'God,' Teddy said. 'That those brutes should do something like this to you . . . I guess I understand why you kicked that guy.'

'Yes,' she said, her voice under control again. You don't know the half of it, she thought; but that was her business. 'Now you tell me how you got on to me.'

'Well . . . I was half round the bend with worry when I called from Boston and was told that you'd gone out. I couldn't believe those thugs had lifted you. I mean, they didn't know where you were.'

'They did,' she told him. 'But they didn't lift me. Go on.' His fingers felt so gentle as they massaged her flesh. If he kept this up long enough she might forgive him – even if there was no way she ever wanted a man inside her again, as long as she lived.

192

'So . . . I called again yesterday morning, and then they told me you'd been arrested. I caught the next train down, and the police told me you'd been bailed out by someone called Cerdo. I was lucky there. The sergeant on the desk knew Dad, and I got him to tell me more. When I found out that Cerdo worked for MacGinnion, and that MacGinnion was known by the police to be your father's partner, even if they'd never been able to make a charge stick on either of them, I thought I was going out of my mind. I thought of telephoning Dad and asking for some muscle, but then I figured he would raise all kinds of objections, so I thought I'd see what I could do on my own. I bought myself a gun, and went along to Madison Avenue. It was real simple, because I had the inside dope. I used Cerdo's name to get into the building, and the gun to terrify the nightwatchman into telling me where you probably were. So I tied him up and started to hunt.'

He had stopped massaging. Julie pushed herself up and put on her dressing-gown, stood in front of the dressing-table mirror to brush her hair, while she gazed at the faces looking back at her. Her own, unmarked, either externally or behind the eyes, so far as could be told at a casual glance – and Teddy's, anxious and frightened. By what he had done?

'So who took on the mob single-handed then?' she asked, and smiled at him. He really had been incredibly brave. 'After telling me I'd be crazy to try?'

'Well, heck, Julie . . .'

'I'm your wife.' She turned to face him. 'Now tell me about the passport.'

'The . . .' he frowned at her.

'Scotland Yard have issued a warrant for my arrest because I applied for a passport with a false birth certificate,' she said.

'Oh, gosh.' He sat on the bed. 'You must think . . .'

'I'm waiting to think, Teddy.'

'Well, I . . .' he sighed, and his shoulders slumped. 'You're right. I couldn't find your birth registered at Somerset House. And I knew how upset you'd be, and that you wanted to leave England . . . so I went along to someone I knew . . .'

'A forger?'

'I guess so. A guy Dad had got off in Boston a good time ago. He did it for me.'

193

'Wouldn't it have been a better idea to tell me the truth?'

'Heck, I didn't know what to do. I love you so, Julie. I just wanted to make you happy.'

He looked genuinely upset. He was either a consummate actor or he was telling her the truth.

'What are we going to do?' he asked. 'But say . . .' his face brightened. 'You're married to me. They can't deport you.'

'That's right,' she agreed. 'But they can't deport me anyway.'

'Eh?'

'I'm as American as you are, Teddy.' She told him about Cerdo's discovery.

'Well, Holy Smoke,' he remarked when she had finished. 'That old man of yours was some character. But what do we do now? Mac-Ginnion's boys will be out looking for you. And me,' he added. 'Heck. We gotta get out of the country, Julie.'

'I'm not going anywhere,' Julie said. 'MacGinnion as good as confessed that he had Daddy killed. Well, no matter what kind of a thug Daddy was, he's going to pay for that.' And something else, she thought; those three. She went into the breakfast-room, where Shana was serving.

Teddy hurried after her. 'You mean you're going to the police?'

Julie drank coffee and ate bacon and egg standing up. 'What would happen to MacGinnion if I went to the police and accused Big Pat MacGinnion and his henchmen of murdering Daddy, Shana?'

'You'd be wasting your time, honey. Even if the cops believed you, Cerdo would have him out on bail in ten minutes, and the case would probably take five years to come to court, and even if he were convicted, there'd be another five years of appeals and by that time you'd have been pushing up a lot of daisies for a long time.'

'That's what I thought,' Julie said. She drank some more coffee, and felt almost human again, but so very tired. 'I'm going to have a sleep now. As soon as you think he'll be awake, I'd like you to call Hanson, and tell him I'd like to have a get-together with every member of the Assocation he thinks may be prepared to work for Eddie Armitage's daughter. Tell him to remember Queen Elizabeth.'

'Yeah,' Shana said. 'Oh, yeah.' Her eyes glowed.

'Just what in the name of God do you think you're doing?' Teddy asked in alarm.

'I'm going to start a war,' Julie told him.

194

'For God's sake . . .'

'There's nothing else I want to do right this minute, Teddy. I know I'm your wife, but you're not going to stop me. On the other hand, if you want out, that's all right by me. I'll look you up when Big Pat MacGinnion, and Dominic Cerdo, and Kaley, and his two goons, have all been buried.' She put down her coffee cup and went to the door. 'I'm going to stretch out. If you're with me, you can come too.'

He joined her five minutes later. 'You are one hell of a girl,' he said. 'I don't see how you are going to survive this, without at least going to gaol. But . . . I'm with you, Julie. To the end.'

His hand strayed to her breast. Julie tensed, reached for his hand and moved it away. Then she kissed Teddy gently. 'But if you lay a finger on me right this minute,' she said, 'I am going to cut your heart out.'

Julie stood on the band dais in the Orange Room, and surveyed what had to be the toughest collection of faces she had ever looked at. She had no doubt at all that they each concealed minds as vicious as those of Kaley or MacGinnion or their thugs, that any one of these men – even Hanson Pierce, beaming beside her – would happily, should the occasion arise, fill a girl's crotch with lighter fluid and set a match to it, but that made what she was determined to accomplish the easier for her to accept.

It was six in the evening, and the club had been temporarily closed for this meeting. Julie had had a good sleep, and done a lot of other things as well. She had kept at the forefront of her mind that image of Queen Elizabeth dominating all those 'heavy guys'. Well, from what she remembered of pictures she had seen of the Queen, she was physically far better equipped for the job in hand. What she needed was majesty. So she had sent Teddy out with a fistful of travellers' cheques to buy her some majesty, while once Shana had burned her sundress and underclothes – she did not ever want to see them again – the pair of them had got to work on what was already the most daring of her evening gowns, a blood-red sheath with a plunging *décolletage*. With scissors they plunged the *décolletage* even further, until her navel was revealed. Then they brought the slit material back together over her breasts, and secured it there with one of Teddy's purchases, a huge pearl brooch. Thus, naked flesh

195

above, discreetly revealed naked flesh below, and thrusting, partly concealed flesh between. 'Honey, you look good enough to eat,' Shana declared.

Teddy had been told to invest entirely in pearls, because Julie felt their glowing cream would stand out to best advantage against the crimson. So in addition to the brooch and her engagement ring, she wore a pearl choker and a huge pearl ring on her right hand, while there were pearl clips in her auburn hair. She thought Shana might be right; she did look good enough to eat.

But now they had to take control. These men might enjoy looking, but they would want more than that. And the moment was here. Yet she was totally confident. After what had happened to her in the past twenty-four hours she did not really think she could ever be afraid of anything again – and she had learned the art of lying with consummate artistry.

So she smiled at them. 'I think you all know who I am,' she said. 'I'm Julie Armitage, Eddie Armitage's daughter.'

There was a round of applause.

'But maybe you don't know why I'm here,' Julie said. 'I'm here to tell you that Eddie Armitage is dead.'

The hall wore the silence of total shock, disturbed only by a shifting of feet.

Julie had stopped smiling. 'He was murdered,' she said, in a voice of steel. 'By Big Pat MacGinnion.'

There was a rush of whispered comment. Julie gazed at them, waiting for them to subside.

'I know this,' she said, 'because Big Pat MacGinnion told me so himself, yesterday.'

Another balloon of sound.

'He kidnapped me, and intended to murder me as well, but I was rescued by my husband . . .' she glanced at Teddy, who was standing beside the dais. 'Now, there is only one reason for Big Pat to have killed my father: he intends to take over the Association himself.'

'Like hell he will,' someone shouted.

Julie smiled at him. 'That's what I feel,' she said. 'And I want to see my father's killer six feet down. You guys going to help me?'

'Yeah,' came a roar.

'You'll work for me?'

This time there was not quite such a reaction. Then someone asked, 'Just how old are you, Miss Julie?'

'I'm twenty-one,' Julie told him.

'Jees,' remarked someone else.

'But I am Eddie Armitage's daughter. If any of you doubt that, ask Hanson Pierce.' She glanced at Hanson, who nodded vigorously. 'Hanson is going to be my business manager. My chief of staff, if you like. So he'll be the real boss. But you'll be working for me. And you'll be bringing down Big Pat MacGinnion and his boys. And you'll be avenging Daddy.' She paused, and looked from face to face. But she had won, she knew. If only because the ideal was so novel, so sexually appealing. Oh, there would be second thoughts, fairly soon. But fairly soon was long enough.

'What's the play?' someone asked.

'The first play is MacGinnion. Not only because he murdered Daddy, but because with him gone the others will fall apart.'

'Christ, that building is like Fort Knox.'

'Doesn't he ever go out?'

'With a bunch of bodyguards.'

'Then what about his home?'

'That's pretty well guarded too. Besides, his wife and kids are there.'

'And it isn't done to involve the wife and kids, is that it?'

'Well . . .' the man looked embarrassed. 'I guess not.'

'But MacGinnion himself broke that rule, didn't he? I'm my father's kid.'

'Hell, she is,' Hanson Pierce roared.

'So we get him at home.'

'It'll take some planning,' said someone else.

She looked at Hanson. 'Can you do it?'

'Sure. But it'll be messy. I don't see the cops being able to look the other way after something like that.'

'Leave the cops to me,' Julie said.

They drank champagne in Hanson's office. 'You were great,' he said. 'Just great. You really swept them off their feet. And going after MacGinnion. That had them reeling.' He frowned at her. 'You know it's going to be tough.'

'I know,' she said.

197

'Well, the first thing we gotta do is to find a safe place for you. Because until he's dead, MacGinnion is sure going to be looking.'

'Boston,' Teddy said.

'Forget that,' Julie said. 'I'm not going any place. I intend to live at Daddy's apartment. You give me enough protection, and if MacGinnion tries to get at me there, we'll finish this business even quicker.'

'Save that he ain't gonna come after you himself,' Hanson pointed out.

'All right, so we'll flatten a few of his mugs.'

'Jees,' Hanson said. 'I sure hope you know what you're doing, Julie. There ain't never been a gang war in this city. The cops are just gonna have to react, and strong. The press'll make them.'

'I told you, leave the cops to me,' Julie said. 'You just make up the plan for getting MacGinnion'. She stood up. 'I'm for bed.'

'Just let me arrange some muscle,' Hanson said, and went downstairs, where his guests were drinking free liquor and discussing the amazing event of the afternoon.

'Julie,' Teddy said. 'You were terrific. You are terrific. But you really are stepping out of your league.'

'Am I, Teddy? I'm Eddie Armitage's daughter, remember? It must be in my blood.'

'So what happens when those goons out there find out about the money?'

'What money?'

'Well . . . what your dad has stashed away.'

'That's not going to interest this lot, even if they found out about it. And how can they? Are you going to tell them?'

'Of course not. But . . .'

'No one else on our side of the fence knows about any money. So forget it.' There was no way Teddy could know about the twenty million, because she hadn't told him yet – and she was quite sure MacGinnion didn't mean anyone except Kaley and Cerdo to know, either. 'Our business is to get MacGinnion and his friends. Those characters are playing for keeps.'

'And what are you playing for?'

'Keeps.'

'As Julie Armitage, the bandit queen. That's a short and bumpy road, however well you're doing at the moment.'

'You simply have to trust me, Teddy. As I have trusted you. Maybe more than I should have.'

'So you're gonna throw that birth certificate thing in my face for the rest of my life.'

'No,' she said. 'Not unless I have to.' She glanced past him to where Hanson was reappearing with Arnie and several other men. 'So leave it,' she advised.

He sulked all that night. But she guessed his main sulk was that she wouldn't have sex with him. That would be put right and soon enough – she hoped; maybe when she'd settled with MacGinnion. But she wasn't prepared to trust him again until MacGinnion *was* settled.

Next morning she went for a drive with Shana, Arnie, and two other heavies. Teddy was chagrined, but she would not relent. 'I'll explain it all,' she said. 'Just trust me.'

They drove down into the Bronx, and she made Shana stop at a call box, once she was sure there was nobody tailing them. 'I want to make a phonecall,' she explained.

'For God's sake, honey,' Shana said. 'We have telephones at the apartment.'

'This is a private call,' Julie said. 'Just make sure I'm not interrupted.'

By now she was well equipped with nickels and dimes, so she dialled and fed the coins in. 'New York District Attorney's Office,' said the girl's voice. 'Who's calling please?'

'I would like to speak to the District Attorney,' Julie said.

'Is he expecting your call?'

'I don't think so.'

'Then I'm afraid . . .'

'You tell him,' Julie said, 'that Eddie Armitage's daughter wants to have a word.'

There was a brief silence, then a series of thuds. Julie held the receiver away from her ear, and smiled through the glass window at Shana and Arnie and the hoods, who were all looking extremely worried.

'Zeidler,' said a voice. 'Is that really you, Miss Armitage?'

'Really and truly,' Julie said.

'And what can I do for you?'

'I think we should have a chat.'

199

'I couldn't agree with you more. Where and when?'

'Like as soon as possible,' Julie said. 'You name it.'

'Have you got company?'

'Lots and lots of company.'

'Can you unload it?'

'Given sufficient notice.'

'Well . . . how about tonight?'

'What time tonight?'

'Eleven o'clock.'

'Where?'

'Right here, Miss Armitage.'

Julie hesitated. 'I'll need to be sure I won't be arrested.'

'I don't bargain with people like you, Miss Armitage. If you have something to say to me, come along and say it, and we'll take it from there. If not, stay out in the dark and survive, if you can.'

Julie smiled at the telephone. Oh, but you do bargain with people like me, Mr Zeidler, she thought; when you hear what I have to sell. But she didn't say that. She said, meekly, 'I'll be in your office tonight at eleven.' She hung up.

It was a long day. Teddy was more morose than ever when she got back to the apartment, and everyone was tense, because Arnie was sure he'd spotted one of MacGinnion's boys on the street outside. In any event no one could doubt that MacGinnion knew where she had gone, if she hadn't fled the city. Then Hanson arrived in the middle of the afternoon with his plan of campaign. Julie didn't like it at all. 'It's MacGinnion we want,' she said. 'Not the whole goddamned neighbourhood.' How easily she slipped into the idiom of these strange new friends of hers.

'Little lady,' Hanson explained, 'it's kind of tricky to kill one ant without being bit by the others, unless you stamp on the whole lot at once. You're not getting cold feet now? That would sure disappoint the boys. Anyway, you don't have to be within ten miles of it.'

'Like hell,' Julie said. 'I'm coming with you.'

'You what?'

'That's nonsense,' Teddy protested. 'You've never been in a shoot-out.'

'Have you?'

He flushed. 'Well, no. But I'm a man.'

'That is quite irrelevant. I can't ask Hanson and his people to do something I'm afraid to do myself.'

Teddy looked at Pierce.

Who shrugged. 'She's the boss. And you know what, Teddy boy, I'm gonna feel happier knowing she's behind me than just about anybody else. Save for old Eddie himself. Goddamn, but he'd be proud of you, Miss Julie.'

He would probably bury me six feet under, alive, Julie thought, if he knew what I am going to do. The assault was planned for the following evening; no one complained when she opted for an early night. But Teddy naturally accompanied her. And now she had to trust him, at least to a certain extent. 'I need your help,' she told him. 'I want a distraction while I get out of here, at ten o'clock.'

'Are you out of your mind? MacGinnion's people are going to be all around this building.'

'They're not going to catch me,' she said. 'If only because there's nothing they'll expect less than that I would dream of leaving, alone and at night.'

'But where the hell do you want to go?'

'That's my business. You have to trust me, Teddy. When this is over, I'll revert to being a loving and obedient wife. I swear. But you have to let me do this the way I know it has to be done. I give you my word it is all on the up and up.'

'You know something,' he grumbled. 'You have changed, these last couple of days.'

'Well,' she said, 'if I hadn't, I'm not sure I would be here at all.'

He held her shoulders. 'And you're sure you know what you're doing?'

'Certain sure,' she promised.

He sighed. 'I thought I'd married a schoolgirl in trouble. Now—'

'You married Eddie Armitage's daughter,' she reminded him. 'And you knew that when you put the ring on my finger. But she's only a bird of passage. Julie Allen is waiting to be your wife. Just as soon as it can be done.'

He surrendered. He was the surrendering type. Yet with a streak of the heroic as well. When she thought of how he had just walked into MacGinnion's headquarters and out again, with her, laying out at least one man on the way . . . it was just unbelievable. But

201

it had happened. The luck of the innocent, she supposed. But it must have made MacGinnion mad.

She dressed herself in a pair of slacks and a heavy sweater, tucked her feet into the sneakers which Shana had insisted she buy – 'Everybody has sneakers,' Shana had said. So thank God for Shana's fashion sense; the rubber soles enabled her to move almost silently. At ten o'clock Teddy went to the kitchen for a glass of milk, and reported that everyone had left and Shana had gone to bed in the spare room. Julie then positioned herself by the stairway doorway, while Teddy went into the lobby, and had some kind of a fit. That brought Shana running from her room, the boy with the machine gun in from the front, and the other boy with the machine gun in from the stairs, almost flattening her against the wall as he threw the door open. But a moment later she was running down the stairs, and into the open air.

She stood against the wall of the building, watching the Avenue. At ten o'clock on a June night it was barely dark, and there were a great number of people about. Amongst them would certainly be some of MacGinnion's men. But she would have the element of surprise, as she had told Teddy. She was pleasantly surprised at the way, although her heart pounded, she was perfectly cool, perfectly sure of what she must do, and perfectly sure that she could do it, too. She waited until she saw an unoccupied cab cruising slowly up the avenue, then left the wall and ran into the roadway, waving her arm. He braked, and she scrambled into the back seat. 'The District Attorney's Office, and hurry', she gasped.

'What's up, doll?' asked the driver. 'You witnessed a murder?'

'Could be,' Julie said.

He drove faster, and got her there in ten minutes. And she was expected. Five minutes after entering the building, she was in Zeidler's office.

He was in his early forties, heavy-faced and equipped with big hands. But he looked immensely competent, even if somewhat hostile. 'Julie Armitage,' he said. 'There's a chair.'

She glanced at the other three men in the room. 'What I have to say is private.'

'You reckon?'

'You might prefer it to be so. You can search me, if you like. I'm not armed.'

He grinned. 'That would be a pleasure, Miss Armitage. But I'll take your word. Okay boys. Don't come in if you hear me screaming; I'm prepared to suffer.'

'And no tapes,' Julie said as they filed out. 'I want your word on that.'

'Are you running this show, or am I?'

'I'm about to make you an offer you can't refuse, Mr Zeidler. Play ball with me, and you could wind up as Governor of this State.'

He studied her for a few seconds, then reached beneath his desk and flicked a switch. 'So you've come here to make some kind of confession. Is that it?'

'What do you think I should confess about?'

'You are going to tell me, Julie. I figure you're on some kind of plea bargaining deal. But all I have on you is carrying a concealed weapon without a licence. Okay, that could carry a stiff sentence from the point of view of a pretty young girl. But I have a hunch you have something more on your mind.'

'I have,' she said. 'Tomorrow is going to see the start of the biggest gang war in history.'

He frowned at her. 'Over you?'

'In a way.'

'So you want protection.'

'No, Mr Zeidler,' Julie said. 'That is just what I do not want. I am starting the war, and I want to be able to finish it. So I want no interference from anybody. I know the press will give you a hard time, but you'll just have to ride it out. Because it'll be worth it in the end.'

Zeidler continued to study her. 'You're all nerve, Julie,' he remarked at last. 'So why should I do all this?'

'Because at the end, one half of my father's Association will be wiped out.'

'And you want immunity for the other half? Including yourself? No deal, Julie.'

'I will tell you what I want,' Julie said. 'Yes, I want immunity from arrest for past crimes for certain people I will name.' She took out a slip of paper and laid it on his desk. 'If they break the law again in the future, that's their look-out. I want the concealed weapon charge against me dropped. I want Scotland Yard off my back. And, as I said, I want no interference from the police for the next week.

203

But most important of all, I want you to make it clear afterwards that winding up the Association was Eddie Armitage's idea. That he planned it and intended it but that he was murdered before he could carry out his plan.'

'You sniffing snow regularly?' Zeidler inquired.

Julie smiled at him. 'In return for that, Mr Zeidler, I will deliver to you the books of the Association, the records of the Association, every goddamned thing you want about the Association, to close it down, once and for all. You have it in your power to put an end to organised crime in New York. At least until the next lot muscles in. But that won't have anything to do with the name Armitage.'

District Attorney Zeidler stroked his chin. 'You expect me to believe you can deliver that?'

'I do. What is more, I'll throw in a bonus. When it's done, my husband and I will leave the United States. As a matter of fact, I would be obliged if you would book us passages to France on the first available ship after the week is up.' She wrote out half a dozen of her travellers' cheques. 'These should cover it. Sailing from Boston, please. I will also need an American passport. A genuine one, please. I'm entitled to it.'

He looked at the cheques. 'You have it all thought out. But your terms are a little high.'

'My terms are a little low, Mr Zeidler. What do you have to lose? If I don't deliver the goods, it'll be because I am dead, and as no one else knows what we have said to each other here tonight, you will be free to take whatever action you wish against whichever members of the Association you can accuse of murder. If I do deliver the goods, you will have the vote of every citizen in this city for whatever office you wish to stand. Take your pick.'

Zeidler considered, still gazing at her. She gazed back. Again she knew that delicious feeling of winning.

'May I ask why you are doing this?' he asked. 'I would have thought, for Eddie Armitage's daughter, the world was her oyster, including the bad and the ugly as well as the good.'

'Mr Zeidler, up to less than a month ago, I had no idea I *was* Eddie Armitage's daughter. I thought I was the daughter of one of the finest men on earth, and that made me very happy. Now I've discovered that I am the daughter of maybe one of the most vicious men who ever lived. I suppose that makes me correspondingly unhappy. But he was still my father. I want to avenge his death. I want to rehabilitate his name – which is my name – and I'll be perfectly honest with you and admit that I have a personal grudge as well, against certain parties.'

'And you're quite willing to start shooting to accomplish that. Seems to me you've inherited a few of your father's characteristics.'

'Yes, Mr Zeidler, I am quite sure that I have inherited a great many of my father's traits. But it was MacGinnion who began the killing, because he thought he could get away with it. I'm going to prove to him that he can't.'

'You intend to take on Big Pat MacGinnion?'

'I am already doing so.'

'And have you any idea what he will do to you if he gets hold of you?'

'Yes, Mr Zeidler,' she said. 'He has already got hold of me once, as you put it.'

Zeidler looked her up and down, carefully, as if checking to make sure she still had five fingers on each hand, two ears, two breasts.

'That's why I intend to make sure he never gets hold of anyone else, ever again.'

Zeidler leaned back in his chair. 'And then you'll be satisfied.'

'Yes, Mr Zeidler, I don't enjoy being Julie Armitage.' She smiled. 'Well, actually, that's not true. I am enjoying being Julie Armitage. But I know I won't for very long. Believe it or not, I am not a criminal, and I do not wish to be. I also want, in whatever way I can, to . . . what does the cliché say? Repay society for my father's crimes?'

'Yeah,' Zeidler said drily. 'And then fade away into the sunset?'

'And then settle down to being Mrs Edward Longman the Third,' she said. And find that twenty million dollars, she thought. But he didn't know about that.

'And have you any idea what the boys who are on your side this minute would do to you if they discovered what you are planning for them?'

'I'll be putting them out of business. But as I understand what I have been reading in the newspapers, if your present governor, Mr Roosevelt, wins the forthcoming election, they're going to be out of business anyway.'

'If he wins,' Zeidler said. 'But they're still going to want to skin you alive when they find out. And enjoy it while they're doing it.'

She smiled. 'That's another safeguard for you, isn't it, Mr District Attorney? That when I say I am going abroad I mean it.'

Zeidler gazed at her for several seconds. 'You are a very unusual young lady,' he remarked at last. 'Eddie Armitage's daughter. Oh, yes. If I didn't quite believe in the hereditary principle before, I think you could change my mind. Okay, Miss Armitage, I am going to go along with you, for one week. I will quash the concealed weapon charge, and send that Scotland Yard detective home again. And I will give you my word that at the end of the week, if I have in my possession all the books relating to the Association, I will not proceed against . . .' he glanced at the sheet of paper, 'Hanson Pierce . . . holy shit. Do you have any idea what kind of a thug Hanson Pierce is?'

'He happens to be on my side, and he has a wife and thirteen children.'

'Is that a fact?' Zeidler went on reading. 'Arnie Lotman. Christ! He's guilty of at least one murder I haven't been able to pin on him. Shana Evans. Who's she?'

'A friend.'

He sighed. 'Okay. So you want them amnestied for any crimes which they may have committed, as revealed by those books. Right?'

'Yes.'

He nodded. 'You got it. How do you aim to make this handover?'

'I'll give you a date and a time and a place, when I know those things. Then I'll want one whole lot of muscle.'

He shook his head. 'Eddie Armitage's daughter,' he remarked again. 'Okay, Miss Armitage, you have a deal.' Then he grinned, surprisingly. 'You have to have the biggest nerve in the world. If I may say so, you are one hell of a girl. And I'll tell you, if, during, or right after this week, my people come across a large lump of cement at the bottom of the East River with your feet stuck in it, I think I may shed a tear for one hell of a brave girl too. But . . .' he pointed with his pen. 'If you fuck me about, Julie Armitage, I am going to send you to gaol for a hundred years. Remember that.'

CHAPTER 10

It was half past eleven by the time Julie got home, only to find the apartment, indeed the whole building, in an uproar. Hanson Pierce had been summoned, Teddy was seated in the lounge surrounded by armed guards as if he were a prisoner, which he was, and Shana was prowling up and down like a caged tigress.

All stared at Julie as she came through the door, escorted by two men with sub-machine guns.

'In the name of God,' Pierce exploded. 'Where have you been?'

'At the DA's office.'

'The what?

'I told you I'd square the cops,' Julie said. 'I have done just that.'

Pierce looked at her, then at Shana, then at Teddy. Teddy shrugged.

'Just like that,' Pierce said.

'Just like that, Hanson. So we can go ahead tomorrow with no interference. Now, I am awfully tired, and I'm going to bed. Would you mind ordering your goons to stop pointing their guns at my husband?'

Her cool authority, added to the magic of her name, as usual dominated their thinking, and the crisis was surmounted; Teddy joined her in bed a few minutes later. 'Don't you think you are living just a shade too dangerously?' he asked.

'It's only going to be for a couple of days,' she promised him.

'You reckon? Just what did you offer the DA?'

'I'll tell you that when the time comes.'

'But you intend to go ahead with this shoot-out.'

'Yes,' she said. 'If it's the only way I can bring MacGinnion to justice.'

'And you still intend to be there yourself.'

'I wouldn't consider it, otherwise.'

He shook his head.

'What about you?' she asked.

He gave his crooked smile. 'Where you go, I go, remember?'

Whatever his faults, he was her husband. 'So tell me,' she said – it was almost the first time they had had to talk. 'How did you get on with your parents?'

'I told them that I had married the sweetest little girl in all the world, only she was in a bit of bother. They're looking forward to meeting you.'

'Even if they find out my name is Julie Armitage?'

'Your name is Julie Longman,' he reminded her.

He wanted to make love, but she couldn't bring herself to do so. He didn't understand, as she had not told him what had been done to her, and became angry for a moment, but simmered down when she explained how exhausted she was, and how apprehensive too, about what was going to happen next. Nor was she telling a lie. She was as nervous as a kitten at the thought of the forces she had set into motion. She could look any of them, from District Attorney Zeidler, through Hanson Pierce, to Teddy himself, in the eye and appear as cool and calm and as tough as they now expected her to be. But she wasn't the least cool and calm and tough inside. She was terrified of the violence which was about to dominate her life. Yet she would not weaken. Big Pat MacGinnion had elected to draw the sword in every way. So maybe Father had double crossed his old friend; he was still Father. And nothing Father had done could excuse what MacGinnion, and his two henchmen, had done to her. Those that live by the sword shall die by the sword. So where did that leave her, now that she also was drawing the deadly weapon? She couldn't afford to think about that too deeply any more than she dared think about the way she was double crossing these men who had elected to follow her; she had to believe her cause was just.

Next day the tension in the apartment could have been cut with a knife. Even Shana was tense, and she was staying behind. It was not only the thought of the coming evening, it was the certainty that

208

MacGinnion had the building staked out, and that he would be laying plans of his own, and therefore might have planned an even more preemptive strike than theirs. But MacGinnion, as Julie was certain, was too much of a creature of the environment in which he had spent most of his life to break any of the rules. Not because he was afraid of hurting innocent people, but because he was afraid of stirring up the police by taking violence outside the narrow confines of the underworld. He would wait for Hanson and herself to go out to eat, or undertake some other time-honoured challenge to the opposition, before making his move. He didn't know he was fighting a rank amateur who didn't play by any rules.

Encouraged by her, Hanson had laid his plans on this basis. That evening at ten-thirty, three black limousines drew up at the apartment building and Julie – who was wearing her black dress this time – Teddy and Hanson himself got into the middle one, which also contained three other men, one of whom was Top. The other two cars were similarly loaded with six armed men, the first under the command of Arnie, and the other under the command of Lenny, and as the entourage moved away from the kerb, Hanson carelessly shouted to Shana, who had remained on the pavement, to call the Orange Room and tell Closet they'd be there in ten minutes. It was a simple little ploy; whether it would work or not no one knew as yet. They didn't much care if it failed; they were all too keyed up and ready to take on the world. Julie thought she was the calmest person in the car as they sped along Fifth Avenue, reached the Plaza, and swung right to take the Queensboro Bridge.

But even she wasn't all that calm. 'Is all set?' she asked.

Hanson nodded. 'Whoever's tailing us will have got the message now. But it ain't gonna do him no good. My boys cut the telephone wires round Oyster Bay an hour ago.'

Oyster Bay was where MacGinnion lived.

'And you know he's there?' Teddy asked. Teddy was certainly the most nervous.

'Went out at six, and hasn't budged,' Top assured them.

'And everybody knows my instructions?' Julie asked. 'We want MacGinnion, Cerdo and Kaley, and anyone else who points a gun at us. Nobody apart from those.'

'Sure, Miss Julie, sure,' Hanson promised her. 'But only MacGinnion and his bodyguards are out there right now.'

209

'He's the one to start with,' Julie said.

The picked up the Northern Boulevard and raced through Flushing, gradually increasing speed as they joined the North Hempstead Turnpike. It was quite dark by now, and there was little traffic. But about half a mile behind them the lights of a fourth car showed steadily. They were being tailed, but only by one car, and there was no way they could be stopped by a single car, as MacGinnion's men undoubtedly realised. They had taken their enemies by surprise.

They roared over Hempstead Harbour, and then swung off the turnpike into the lanes which criss-crossed the open country below Oyster Bay itself. They hurtled along at what seemed a breakneck speed on the narrow, unlit roadways; Julie was quite surprised when they suddenly emerged next to a beach, with the waters of Long Island Sound sparkling in the darkness. And not half a mile away were the lights of a large house.

Now they drove even faster. And now the following car, driven to desperation, began shooting from its windows. But the rear car of the motorcade returned fire from sub-machine guns, and suddenly there was a gush of flame and the screaming sound of exploding metal.

'Oh, my God,' Julie gasped.

'They had it coming,' Pierce told her.

She had to keep reminding herself of that.

The road bent in somewhat from the beach, and they swung down a drive, straight at a large pair of wrought-iron gates. These were closed, and there were men standing there, watching them, for a moment in amazement, and then reacting violently as they understood what was going to happen. Pistols emerged and they opened fire. But Arnie's men were also armed with sub-machine guns, and the defenders were literally blasted away from the bars, while Arnie's car continued to charge the gates at full speed, smashing into the iron with a tremendous explosion. Sparks flew, and men tumbled out to either side, just in time, for a moment later this car too was a blazing inferno.

Julie's car had pulled on to the verge, while she stared in total horror, too bemused to think, at the holocaust she had instigated. The third car raced by them, and stopped. Two men got out, a grapple attached to a steel chain was thrown, and lodged, then

210

secured to the bumper of the waiting vehicle, and the car backed off, dragging the blazing wreck away from the gates, which had sagged open. Julie's driver gunned his engine and drove at the collapsed steel. Arnie's men were already inside and crossing the lawns and flower beds. As the car raced past them Julie heard the barking of dogs, and a succession of shots. The barking stopped. Oh, my God, she thought again. Oh, my God.

The limousine screamed to a stop at the foot of a huge patio reached by wide steps. Several men stood there; even if they had rushed outside at the sounds of the shots, they were still taken entirely by surprise. Hanson himself led his henchmen from the car and opened fire, running up the steps as he did so. One of them came tumbling back down with a ghastly thud, blood pouring out of his dinner jacket. Teddy tried to restrain Julie, but she was out as well. She left her handbag behind, carried the new pistol Hanson had given her in her right hand, scooped her skirt up to her thighs with her left hand, and raced up the steps.

The front door had been knocked in, and Hanson's men were already inside. Here were men opposing them too. Whatever the code, MacGinnion had certainly kept himself well protected. But like those outside, they had been too totally surprised by the happening of the impossible, and they died almost before they could draw their weapons. By now the horror of seeing so much death and destruction was leaving Julie somewhat numbed. She looked up the stairs, and saw a woman running out of one of the rooms.

'Get back,' she screamed at her. 'Get back!'

The woman checked, looking down in amazement, staring at her, and the man standing beside her raised his gun. Julie knocked his arm aside. 'No women,' she snapped.

A bullet slammed into an occasional table beside her, scattering brass ornaments. She gasped, and turned, and gazed at MacGinnion, also standing on the balcony, levelling his revolver. 'You bitch,' he said. 'You bitch.'

She had to shoot him, but she just couldn't make herself squeeze the trigger. And it didn't matter. Before he could fire again a hundred sub-machine gun bullets had slammed into his chest. His midnight-blue smoking jacket exploded into flying crimson, and his body draped itself across the rail, before crashing to the floor six feet from where she stood.

211

'One down,' Hanson Pierce said, 'and two to go.'

Julie's knees gave way, and she would have fallen, had Teddy not caught her.

'I brought you a present,' Shana said.

Julie blinked at her. Had she really slept? Oh, she had slept. She had made sure of that by taking three brandies and four sleeping pills when she had returned to the apartment; she had not cared if she would never wake up again.

She stretched; the bed was empty, and Shana was just drawing the drapes to let a great deal of light in. Julie closed her eyes. 'What time is it?'

'Twenty past twelve.'

'Oh, good Lord.' She sat up, frowned at the black wig. 'What's that for?'

'I thought you might like to wear it next time you go out,' Shana said.

'What on earth . . .'

'There are some newspapers.' Shana indicated the two she had placed on the bed. 'You having breakfast, lunch, or brunch?'

'Ugh,' Julie said. She knew she couldn't eat a thing. Had she dreamed? It was difficult to be certain what might have been a dream, and what was ghastly fact. She picked up the first paper, and shuddered.

'**OYSTER BAY MASSACRE**', read the headlines.

At a quarter to midnight last night in his luxury home, Mr Patrick MacGinnion, well-known businessman and partner in the realty firm of Armitage and MacGinnion, was shot to death, along with several of his guests, by a band of armed men. Police are mystified by the ferociousness of the attack which left nine men dead and six seriously wounded. The District Attorney refused to comment on the possibility that this could be a gangland killing although as is well known Mr MacGinnion and his partner, Mr Edward (Eddie) Armitage have several times appeared before Grand Juries to answer questions on matters ranging from bootlegging to extortion, without ever facing indictment. However, efforts to contact Mr Eddie Armitage this morning failed; our reporter was

> informed by his housekeeper, Mrs Shana Evans, that
> he is at present vacationing in Europe.

Julie raised her head, and Shana shrugged. 'That's what I'm paid for, honey. Those guys don't seem to have heard yet that Eddie is dead.'

Julie picked up the other paper. **'RED HEADED WOMAN'**, it screamed at her.

> Mrs Florence MacGinnion, distraught widow of well-known Mr Big Pat MacGinnion, the realtor who was shot to death at his home last night, told police that the gang of murderers was led by a young woman with red hair, dressed all in black. 'She stood there, cool as a cucumber, directing operations,' Mrs MacGinnion told your reporter. Asked if she knew who this mysterious woman was, Mrs MacGinnion said no, but she felt sure her husband did, from what he said just before he died. The mystery woman, in addition to dark red hair, worn short, is well built and attractive. Police confess they have at this time no idea who this woman can be, nor what motive she had for perpetrating such a crime, although they agree that Mr MacGinnion's name has more than once been linked with organised crime in the state.

Julie dropped the paper and rolled on her stomach, burying her face in the pillow.

'What you want is some black coffee,' Shana recommended. 'It's right here. At least the woman described you as attractive. Oh, by the way, I burned the dress. You want to keep the undies?'

'No,' Julie said. 'Burn them, too.'

'Seems a waste,' Shana remarked, and left the room.

Florence MacGinnion. And three children, roused from their beds by the shooting, to stare at the shattered body of their father. Like her, they were the children of a thug. Would they grow up to be like her?

And all of those bodies. Only nine? She had supposed there were ninety. One of them was one of Hanson's men, shot as he climbed the steps in front of her. Two others had been wounded, and taken away to the private hospital which Father apparently kept on the payroll.

And those had been only the opening shots in the war.

She pushed herself up, drank the coffee, ran a hot tub, and sat in it. She should have bathed last night; she could smell the stink of cordite in every pore.

Teddy came in. 'How do you feel?'

'Ghastly. And you?'

'I'm not sure,' he said. 'Christ, what an experience. Hanson is over the moon. I reckon he's wanted to do something like that for a long time. Maybe we all did.'

Yes, she thought, maybe we did.

'Did you actually shoot anyone?'

He grinned, sheepishly. 'Nope. Did you?'

'I didn't even fire my gun.' She put on a dressing-gown, and sat on the terrace overlooking the city to have lunch. Hanson arrived.

'You read the papers?' he asked.

'Yes,' she said.

'Some notices, eh?'

Just as if I were an actress, she thought, and last night was my première in *Romeo and Juliet*.

'And you know what?' he went on, 'there hasn't been a single detective pushing any of my boys around. I gotta hand it to you, Julie. When you said you'd fix the DA, you sure did. You gonna tell us how you did it?'

'No,' Julie said.

'Okay. You're the boss. And how. But just in case . . . remember you was at the Orange Room last night, until three. You got there ten forty-five, you left at three. Everybody there's gonna swear the same thing, that they talked with you, that you walked around the tables. You had two glasses of champagne, and the second one was pink. It came normal, but you felt like pink and you sent it back to be changed. Logan the barman remembers it well, and he remembers it was just midnight when you did that. You don't have to remember the time; he'll do that. You got it?'

'I got it,' she said. But she had to get more than that; it was time to throw off the horror of what had happened and move on. Zeidler was keeping his end of the bargain; now she must keep hers. She gazed at Pierce. 'How do you think the boys will feel about me now, Hanson?'

'Baby, there ain't a man in the Association wouldn't climb up the

214

outside of the Statue of Liberty if you told him he had to do it, right this minute.'

'Okay,' she said. 'That's what I wanted to hear. Now, I intend to take the Association over properly. You with me?'

'Anything you want.'

'Right. I want to go through all the books. All the books, Hanson, from all the districts.'

He frowned. 'Some of the guys ain't gonna like that.'

'You mean because they've been cheating Daddy for years. Those days are done, Hanson. I want every book, and I want a record of every delivery of liquor, every account from every brothel, for the past six months. I also want the dates and type of every future delivery, for as far as they go. I want them accumulated in this apartment by the end of this week. Understood?'

Hanson Pierce scratched his head, and her heart went out to him. He might be a black-hearted murderer, but he was a nice guy, to those he didn't have to murder. And he clearly worshipped her. But then, she was a black-hearted murderer too. Only she was worse than that. She was a black-hearted betrayer.

'Okay,' he said. 'I'll tell them. I ain't promising nothing.'

'Oh, yes, you are,' she said. 'Because you'll also tell them that if they don't do as I wish they might get a visit from the red-headed woman. Right?'

Hanson gulped. 'Right.'

'Now, what about MacGinnion's books?'

'Well, I guess they're inside the A and M building. You aiming to storm that?'

She shook her head. Something like that would force Zeidler to respond. 'You telephone Cerdo, and tell him I want them, and that if he brings them over here he might just live till Christmas.'

'Jees,' Pierce said, and went off shaking his head.

Teddy was frowning at her. 'Just what are you at, Julie?'

'I'm not with you.'

'Okay, so you wanted to find out about your dad. I went along with that. You wanted to find out about his dough. I went along with that too. You came over here and you jumped with both feet into trouble. So you got tortured and beaten up and you wanted to get even with the guys who did it. By God, I went along with you on that one. Well, you've done that, at least with MacGinnion. He was the leader. So don't you reckon it's time to call it a day? We can sidle off out of here and be in Boston tonight.'

She gazed at him. 'And then?'

'Anywhere you like.'

'I'm sorry. I'm not yet ready to go to Boston.'

'You want to stay here and take over the Association.'

'I asked you to trust me.'

'And I'm not sure I can do that any more. Seems to me you're enjoying what you're doing.'

She made herself get angry; it was her only defence as she dared not tell him what her plan was until it was accomplished – he'd be so scared he'd certainly betray her, even if inadvertently. 'Maybe I am,' she snapped.

'Julie . . .' he leaned across the table to hold her hand. 'Are you nuts? Look, you have gotten away with murder, literally – for the time being. You have these punks following you like a flock of sheep – for the time being. Neither of those situations are going to last too much longer. And when people start waking up, you are either going to find yourself at the bottom of the river, or decorating the inside of a cell for the rest of your life – always supposing you don't get the chair. Have you thought about that?'

Julie pulled her hand free and stood up. 'If it's too hot in the kitchen,' she said. 'You'd better find some fresh air.'

'Where are you going?'

'Back to bed.' She looked down at him. 'I'd prefer to be alone, if you don't mind.'

She lay down, gazed at the ceiling. She was trembling, as she always did at moments of extreme tension. How she wanted to go back to him and put her arms around him and tell him everything was going to be all right – but he wouldn't believe her. And she couldn't change her mind now. She had to fulfil her end of the bargain, or she *would* wind up in the electric chair. Thus she had to keep herself at a level of white-hot fury, until she had all those books. And until she had killed Cerdo and Kaley? She didn't want to do that, any more. She had undertaken the execution of MacGinnion without knowing what was involved. She wasn't sure she could go through it again. She reminded herself that, as she was the Queen, she had the right to exercise the prerogative of mercy.

216

She dozed; she was still exhausted, both physically and mentally. And awoke to find Shana standing by the bedside. 'Sorry to bother you,' Shana said, 'but there's a phonecall for you.'

Julie sat up. 'For me?'

'I guess so. Guy asked to speak to Miss Julie Allen. When I asked who he meant, he said, "Just tell your mistress I want a word."'

Julie discovered both hands were clutching her neck. There was no one in America knew she had once been Julie Allen . . . save for Teddy and Hanson, and MacGinnion and his friends.

'You gonna take the call?' Shana asked.

Julie took a long breath. 'Yes.' She got out of bed, put on her dressing-gown, picked up the receiver. 'Hello.'

'Julie?'

Julie waited. She was sure she had heard the voice before, but she couldn't place it right away.

'You there?'

'Yes,' she said.

'Seems to me you and me should have a little chat.'

'What about?' she asked.

'Well . . . how does twenty million dollars grab you?'

Julie glanced around the room, but Shana had left. Shana was the soul of discretion. 'You'll have to repeat that,' she said.

'No games, Julie. It's late for games. Now the whole world has started falling apart I can market my wares elsewhere. Your daddy stashed away twenty million green ones. And you reckon it's yours. Maybe a few other people reckon it's theirs. Trouble is, none of you know where it is. But I do, and I might be willing to share. You wanna talk?'

Julie swallowed. Could this man possibly be telling the truth? MacGinnion had been certain only she would know where the money was . . . but Daddy could easily have confided in someone else . . . 'I might,' she said.

'When?'

'Right now.'

'Not on the phone. You know Jamaica Bay?'

'I should think I can find it.'

'Take Manhattan Bridge and Flatbush Avenue, but turn off before you reach the Floyd Bennett Air Station. That'll be on to Shore Parkway. It skirts the bay. Drive three miles along the

217

Parkway and you'll come to a lane leading to the water. Go down there and park. I'll be waiting for you. It should take you forty-five minutes to get there.'

'I'll be there.'

'And Julie . . . come alone.'

'I'm sorry,' she said. 'I can't. I don't drive.'

'Jesus Christ,' the man said in disgust. 'Okay, you can bring your hubby. I've been kinda wanting to meet that guy. Anybody else, no deal.'

'I'll bring my husband,' she said. 'In forty-five minutes.'

She hung up, found she was panting. Could it be true? If she could find the twenty million, and offer to give most of that back at the same time as she handed over the books . . . but of course it couldn't be true. It had to be a trap, to get Teddy and herself out on some lonely stretch of road, and either kill them or kidnap them and use them as a bargaining piece against Hanson. So . . . just not turn up? But just suppose it were true. And she could guard against a trap. They thought she was just going to walk into it, well, two could play at that game. If they wanted more trouble, they'd find out that Eddie Armitage's daughter wasn't quite the simpleton they took her for.

She ran into the kitchen. 'Shana . . . where's Teddy?'

'He went out.'

'Oh, damn. Did he say where he was going?

'Nope. I got the feeling he was in a bit of a huff.'

'Yes.' She bit her lip. She couldn't delay – but wasn't it really rather fortunate that Teddy wasn't here? For all the way in which he had rescued her from the A and M building, she still did not know how he would behave in a shoot-out, if it came to that. And all whoever was waiting for her could possibly know about her husband was that he was fair-haired. 'Can you get hold of Arnie?'

'I guess so.'

'Will you ask him to come here for me, just as quickly as possible. With some muscle. Heavy muscle. And the right kind of vehicle.'

Shana raised her eyebrows. 'Just what are you meaning to do now, honey?'

'It's terribly important, Shana. Get him here, please.'

Shana shrugged, picked up the phone. She had to try three numbers before she finally found him, at a gymnasium. 'He's

218

coming right over,' she said. 'I don't like what you're doing, Julie. And Hanson ain't gonna like it either.'

'So don't tell him,' Julie said. She'd be safe with Arnie and his gunmen, no doubt about that; she'd seen them at work. 'I'll go wait for him downstairs.'

'Nope,' Shana said. 'You wait here until he calls up.'

Julie hesitated, but she knew she was right.

'You gonna wear the wig?'

Again Julie knew she was offering sound advice. Between them they tucked up her hair – which needed cutting if she was going to maintain her pageboy – beneath the wig. 'Black hair suits you,' Shana said.

Julie made a face at her, but then the phone rang to announce Arnie's presence in the downstairs lobby. One of the permanent guards rode down with her in the elevator. 'Trouble?' Arnie asked, having looked at her twice to make sure it was really her; he wore a sweatshirt and tracksuit trousers, and gym shoes, and perspired profusely.

'There's someone I have to meet,' she told him. 'Urgently. But just in case it's a trap   '

'Yeah. I brought what you wanted.'

She accompanied him down to the garage. He was driving one of the big limousines which she knew was bulletproof, and there were two of his men waiting there, armed with sub-machine guns. 'You fellows are going to have to lie on the floor,' she said. 'I'm only supposed to bring a driver.'

They grinned at her. 'Anything you say, Miss Julie,' and got down out of sight. Julie sat in the front beside Arnie, and gave him the directions.

'Jamaica Bay?' he turned north. 'You know that's just a lot of nothing save birds?'

'So it'll be private.'

'And how. Am I glad you got me and the boys along.'

'I have a gun,' she said, and opened her handbag to show him the pistol.

'That peashooter?' he asked scornfully. 'Listen, if anything happens, you just get down on the floor and let us take care of it. Right?'

'Right,' she said.

219

'Who're you meeting, anyway?'

'I don't know yet,' she said.

'Sounds interesting.'

He exuded massive confidence, as he always did. If it was an ambush, the men waiting for her would get a shock. Of course she was taking a risk . . . Hanson and Teddy were going to be furious. But would she ever forgive herself if this was a lead to the money, and she passed it up?

Teddy wouldn't be too happy about that, either.

They crossed the bridge into Flatbush. By now the traffic was thinning, as they took the long, straight road towards the bird sanctuary. 'We're being tailed,' Arnie said, casually.

Julie looked back. There were three cars behind them.

'The second one back,' Arnie said. 'He's been with us since we left the apartment.'

'Who do you think he is?'

'Could be one of MacGinnion's mob. Although it seemed to us when we checked things out this morning that they'd been withdrawn. Or could be the police. You want me to lose him?'

Julie considered. To attempt to lose the tail would consume a lot of time, and she was already late. If it was the police, she had nothing to worry about; they would observe, and not interfere – unless she desperately needed them, when she would be glad they were there. If it was MacGinnion's men, surely she had enough muscle with her. 'How many?' she asked. 'Can you tell?'

Arnie slowed for a moment while he studied his rear view mirror. 'It's funny,' he said. 'But there seems only the one. The driver.'

Who could easily be coped with; certainly, going on the gangland pattern, a lone driver would not be an assassin. 'Let him come along,' she said. 'We're just meeting someone for a chat, and then going home again.'

'You're the boss,' Arnie agreed. Like all the rest of Pierce's men, including Pierce, he seemed to delight in reminding himself of that fact.

They swung on to the Shore Parkway, and Arnie checked his milometer. After three more miles, sure enough they saw the turning on their right, leading down through thick trees and tangled undergrowth to the lakeside.

Julie looked over her shoulder. The other car was still there, but it had dropped well back; as there was no other traffic at all now, the man would have to know they'd guessed his purpose.

'You happy?' Arnie asked.

'Yes,' she said, and it was not altogether a lie. It gave her such a magnificent feeling of confidence, almost of omnipotence, to be challenging the world with such a faithful band of followers.

He turned into the lane, and they bumped along it, for perhaps three-quarters of a mile, before arriving at the water, where the track ended in a dirty beach, from which there extended a dilapidated wooden shack. Alongside the dock was a punt, and moored a little way off the shore was a thirty-foot cabin cruiser. Behind the launch Julie gazed at nothing but a wilderness of brown water dotted with scattered islands, covered in trees and undergrowth. It was a most desolate spot.

There were no cars to be seen as Arnie braked to a stop at the head of the dock. 'You reckon we've come to the right place?'

Julie looked back along the lane. The other car did not appear to have followed them down it.

'Julie,' a voice called.

They both turned their heads left and right, but could see nothing. The men lying in the back stirred restlessly, and the tommy-guns were made ready.

'You're late, Julie,' the voice said. 'You wouldn't have tried to set something up, now, would you?'

'I had to find my husband,' Julie called. 'He was out. It took time.'

'Yeah. Well, you're lucky I'm a patient man. Step out of the automobile, Julie. You and Longman, and open all the doors. I have to be sure.'

'No way,' Arnie said.

'No way,' she called. 'You come out here and talk, if you want to.'

There was a moment's silence. 'Are we okay?' Julie asked, and took the automatic pistol from her handbag.

'This automobile is virtually a tank,' Arnie said. 'Even the gas tank is sealed with steel. They'd need to have a bomb . . . Jesus Christ!'

From the bushes to their left a man suddenly stood up, took a step forward and threw something that looked like a stone. It struck the earth three feet from the car, and rolled underneath.

'Out,' Arnie shouted. 'Everybody out.'

Julie was petrified, so he leaned across her, released her door, and

221

pushed her out. She fell to her hands and knees, as the tommy-guns started spitting fire, fortunately on the side away from her. But it was not fortunate for Arnie. He threw his door open and fell immediately, his sweatshirt dissolving into flying red. Julie was still rolling with the force of his thrust, and she found herself against a log of wood. Instinctively she rolled over this as well, landing on her face in the sand, winded and shocked, while the machine-guns still chattered, and as she drew breath, the Mills bomb exploded, right under the petrol tank.

She pressed her face and her body into the ground and put her hands over her head as a searing heat scorched her back for a moment and the noise seemed to have burst her eardrums, then discovered to her surprise that she was still holding her gun. Then the noise began to fade and she could hear the raucous call of thousands of seabirds as they fluttered skywards.

And voices. 'You reckon we got her?' someone asked.

'We sure got her husband,' said another man.

'It's the bitch we want,' said a third voice, and this one she recognised. 'Make sure.'

Julie was aware of a consuming anger more than fear. She had actually been considering calling it a day with the death of MacGinnion. Instead of which she had sent poor Arnie and his two sidekicks to their deaths – if they had got out of the exploding car they had certainly been cut down by the tommy-guns – and landed herself in one hell of a mess. For all her precautions and her arrogant confidence she had once again fallen into a trap. But if there was one thing of which she was determined, it was that she was going to take Kaley with her, wherever she was going.

The flames and smoke gushing from the car had started to die down, and she watched four men leave the bushes and approach her. Kaley was the fourth, and he was hanging well back. That was Kaley, all right. She tightened her hand on her pistol, wished she would stop shaking, and prepared to fire. At that moment one of the men saw her head. 'There she is,' he shouted, and sent a shot winging in her direction. She threw herself flat again, panting, realising that she had blown it, and heard the roaring of a car engine and another fusillade of shots. The men approaching her raced back to cover, all except one, who stopped to present his weapon to the approaching automobile, which was coming down the lane at a

222

tremendous speed. Before he could fire he was struck a glancing blow and hurled sideways into the flames, where he lay screaming in a most terrifying fashion.

Meanwhile the car was braking, and slewing sideways, to come to a stop almost against her log of wood, and the driver was leaping out and throwing himself in her direction, rolling over and over to reach shelter, as Kaley's men opened fire again and bullets crashed into this new target. A moment later that too exploded. This was much closer at hand, and Julie moaned as she again tried to burrow into the earth and beneath the log, and suddenly felt a searing pain in her back.

'Oh, God,' she screamed. 'Oh, God!'

The man grabbed her shoulder and rolled her over, with a force that sent her tumbling down the slope to the water. She screamed again and tried to stop herself, saw him coming behind her and tried to fend him off. But he seized her again and this time pushed her right into the water. 'Swim, goddamn you,' he shouted. 'Swim, or you're dead.'

Julie kicked off the waterlogged shoes and obeyed him. She had realised that they were still hidden to view behind the now two burning cars. And the water did something to ease the pain in her back. They were swimming towards the cabin cruiser, and in a few powerful strokes she was round the far side of it, panting and spitting water, with the man alongside her. Actually, the water was so shallow they found they could stand up, just.

'On board,' he snapped. 'We have to get out of here.'

She could only goggle at him, having the chance to see him for the first time. 'You?' she gasped.

'Regretfully, yes,' John Baldwin agreed.

Part Three

THE THIRD LIFE

CHAPTER 11

'Get on board,' Baldwin said again. Water dripped out of his hair, trickled down his face. Julie supposed she looked the same.

She gazed at the topsides of the launch, stretching some four feet above her to the deck stanchions. 'I can't climb up there,' she panted. 'I'm hit, I think.' The pain from her back was excruciating; but she couldn't climb up there anyway.

Baldwin had other ideas. Before she realised what he was doing, he had seized her round the thighs and lifted her, then shifted his hands, one to each buttock, and pushed. It was almost as violent an assault as any launched by Kaley and MacGinnion, and she yelped in distress as she was thrust up the side of the boat.

'Grab a stanchion,' he commanded.

She threw both arms round one of the iron uprights, and flailed with her legs. Wearing trousers her movements were free, and she actually got one up and tucked behind the next stanchion, but then she couldn't move, and hung there panting, while waves of pain seeped away from her back and waves of confused alarm from her mind.

He got up by what appeared to be a simple exertion of the muscles in his arms, swung himself over the rail, and reached back down for her. He tucked one set of fingers into her waistband and with the other held one shoulder, and simply lifted her over the rail as if she had been a toy. She gasped, and struck the deck so heavily she was winded.

Baldwin knelt beside her and rolled her on her face. For the moment she couldn't resist him, but then she heard ripping material and felt his hands on her back.

227

'You . . .' she tried to push herself up, and was forced flat again, while she felt his fingers releasing her brassière. Instantly some of the pain faded as the tight strap was freed, yet she wanted to fight him, but couldn't turn.

'You won't die,' he commented. 'Just a piece of burning metal. But it went right through your shirt. You're going to have a scar, Miss Armitage.'

He had released her. 'Thank you very much,' she said, and rose to her knees, hugging herself.

'Keep down,' he commanded.

She gave him as dirty a look as she could manage, but slumped against the cabin bulkhead; she was exhausted anyway. And now she could hear voices from the shore.

'Where are they?' Kaley was asking.

'They went into the water,' one of his men told him.

'Well, they should be floating, then.'

'Not if they made the boat.'

'Christ . . . bring that tommy-gun.'

'Oh, God,' Julie whispered. 'This boat is made of wood.'

'Let's hope it's thick wood. Where's your gun?'

'I dropped it.'

'Great God Almighty! You're one hell of a gangster chieftainess, you are.' He sat against the bulkhead beside her, took a box of cartridges from his pocket and his revolver from his waistband, and began filling the chambers. It was the biggest revolver Julie had ever seen.

'So where are your friends?' she asked.

'I have friends?'

'Who was doing the shooting when you came down in the car?'

'I was.'

'You? And driving?'

'Part of the training.'

'Oh, for heaven's sake . . .' She didn't know whether to admire him for his virtuosity or hate him for having got them into this mess. But he hadn't got them into this mess; she had. She watched water gathering about them as it drained out of her wig and blouse and slacks and underclothes, and out of his clothes as well, and sneezed.

'*Gesundheit*,' he remarked, and began crawling away from her.

'Where are you going?' she asked in alarm. He might be the most

228

hateful of all the thugs she had so far encountered, but she didn't want him to abandon her right now.

'I'm going to get this thing started, if I can do that without being shot. How many were there?'

'Four. I think. But you hit one.'

'Three, and a machine-gun,' he said lugubriously. 'You expecting reinforcements?'

'Nobody knows where I am,' she said.

'Goddamn,' he commented. He had reached the after end of the cabin roof, and now rolled over the coaming into the cockpit. There was no wheelhouse, but the steering position was half roofed.

Instantly there were several shots from the shore, and Julie gasped in terror. 'Are you all right?' she asked.

'You'd never know it. How'd you manage to stay alive this long, Miss Armitage?'

'Nobody asked you to butt in,' she snapped.

'If I hadn't, you'd be floating around the bay by now, on your face.'

She knew he was right, but that didn't make her any less angry. 'What are you doing here, anyway?'

'Trying to keep an eye on you. That's what I'm paid to do. And you know something? I wish to God I was somewhere else. Now shut up.'

She opened her mouth to retort, and then closed it again as she heard Kaley's voice.

'Okay, Julie,' he called. 'We know you're out there. Now you just drop back into the water and come ashore, and bring your boy friend with you, or we're gonna fill that boat so full of holes it'll look like a mosquito screen.'

'Keep them talking.'

'What are you doing?'

'Looking for the goddamned key. It has to be here somewhere. Talk to them, woman.'

Julie pushed herself away from the bulkhead and rose to her knees. She might not be seriously injured but her burned back was acutely painful, and every muscle ached.

'But don't show yourself,' he said.

She crawled to the forward end of the bulkhead, looked round the low cabin roof. 'What happens if I surrender?' she called.

229

'Why, you and I are gonna have a little chat,' Kaley said. 'Like we arranged on the telephone.'

'Damnation,' Baldwin said from the wheelhouse. 'There are no goddamned keys.'

'Oh, Jesus,' Julie said.

'You coming?' Kaley called.

'Let me think,' she replied. 'Baldwin,' she said urgently. 'What are we going to do?'

'You got five seconds,' Kaley said.

'Hope that this boat really is made of good wood,' Baldwin said. 'And try to reduce the odds.'

'You sure there are no keys?'

'What do you think I've been doing this last five minutes?' he inquired. 'Praying?'

'Can't you start the engine by hand?'

'A big diesel? You have got to be joking.'

'Time's up, Julie,' Kaley said. 'I'll say so long now.'

Baldwin stood up in the cockpit, levelled his revolver, and fired. He had obviously already selected his target, and the man next to Kaley, the one with the tommy-gun, spun round and crashed to the ground.

'God,' came the scream. 'God, I'm hit. God, Mr Kaley, I'm dying.'

Baldwin threw himself out of the cockpit and on to the deck beside her, with the cabin between them and the shore.

'Where did you learn to shoot like that?' she asked.

'Something else they teach you in my profession.' He raised his head to look over the cabin roof, and fell flat again as a shot rang out. 'They've taken cover, goddamn it,' he said. 'Wait for it.'

The wounded man was still screaming, but was apparently being ignored by Kaley and the remaining hood, and now even his cries were drowned out by the chatter of the sub-machine gun. The motorboat trembled as the shots slashed into the hull, but the impacts all seemed to come from below them.

'Thank God they can't shoot,' Julie said.

'They can shoot,' Baldwin told her. 'They're aiming at the waterline.'

And as he spoke she heard the gurgling from beneath them, and felt the boat begin to list.

230

'What are we going to do?' she wailed in terror.

'She'll probably capsize somewhat, and expose us,' he said, thoughtfully. 'I'm sorry, Miss Armitage, but it's back into the water. Quickly, now.'

'But when she sinks . . .'

'She isn't going to sink,' he pointed out. 'Not in five feet of water.'

'Oh.' She'd forgotten that.

He grinned at her; it was the first time she had ever seen him smile – he had splendid teeth. 'They've forgotten that too,' he said.

Still the bullets were smashing into the hull, and now the list was becoming pronounced. Julie inserted her legs beneath the grab rail, clung on to the stanchion, and allowed her body to slide down the topsides and into the water; in the excitement she had forgotten about her back and she whimpered with pain as the wood tore across the burned flesh. Baldwin was beside her a moment later. Now the boat was definitely turning away from them, and her anti-fouled hull was exposed, along with a shallow keel and the propellor.

Julie was standing, up to her neck, and as before the water somewhat cooled the burning in her back, but did nothing for the burning in her brain. The firing had stopped, Kaley could see that the boat was sinking – but then she stopped moving, as the hull settled into the mud. And she remained a formidable barricade.

'Goddamn, Mr Kaley,' the gunman remarked. 'It's too fucking shallow.'

'I can see that,' Kaley snapped. 'That dame has the luck of the devil.'

'So what are we going to do, Mr Kaley? I reckon Billy's dead.'

He had certainly stopped screaming.

'You reckon we should pull out, Mr Kaley?' the man asked.

'No way,' Kaley told him. 'We got that bitch pinned down, and she's gonna stay that way until I can put a bullet up her ass.'

'But how we gonna get at them, Mr Kaley? That guy has a gun.'

The voices died as Kaley apparently considered the situation. Baldwin began to edge towards the stern of the sunken boat, to see if he could get another shot.

'For God's sake be careful,' Julie begged.

'Part of the training,' he reminded her, but a burst of machine-gun fire sent him back beside her. 'Trouble is, they don't use live bullets at Hendon. Or machine-guns,' he added thoughtfully.

231

There was still no sound from the shore, and he went the other way, this time being very cautious not to expose himself. 'Oh hell,' he commented.

'What?'

'Listen.'

She heard a car engine. 'Could it be . . .?'

'No. It's Kaley or his henchman going for help. He doesn't mean to let you leave here alive. See what happens when you start a gang war?'

'Shut up,' she said. 'You don't know how much I owe that bastard.'

'There are some debts better left unpaid,' Baldwin commented. 'You know this town better than me. How long do we have?'

'If he uses the first available telephone, he could probably have an army here in an hour.'

'Well, we'd better not be around when it arrives. Listen, how well can you shoot?'

'I've never fired a gun in my life.'

'And you know the police think you're a red-hot momma? All right, Miss Armitage. Watch this.' He leaned against the hull, took a deep breath, stepped round the listing bow, the revolver held in both hands, and fired at the shore. Instantly there was a burst of fire back, and the water became pitted, while more bullets slammed into the hull.

'God,' Julie gapsed. 'Are you all right?'

'So far. And I've spotted his position. He's on the other side of that log of wood where you were hiding when I found you. That's better than I'd hoped. Now . . .' he reloaded his revolver. 'What I want you to do is take this gun, hold it in both hands, because it has a kick, and level it at that log of wood. You can just see it without exposing yourself too much. You with me?'

Julie took the revolver and leaned against the hull. She could see the log; behind it wisps of smoke were still rising from the burned-out automobiles. 'I can see it,' she said. 'What are you going to do? Swim across the bay?'

He grinned at her. 'I wouldn't get back in time. But it's only about forty yards to the shore, I think. I can hold my breath that long. I'm going to launch a direct assault.'

'You can't do that. He'll kill you.'

232

'Not if you shoot him the moment he shows himself. Can you do that?'

She gazed at him. 'Yes,' she said. She had to. 'But I wish you wouldn't.'

'It's that or nothing. Miss Armitage . . . I have never trusted my life to a woman before. Don't let me down.'

'I won't let you down, Mr Baldwin,' she promised.

'Good girl.' He took off his sodden jacket and tie, draped them on the hull, then made his way to the stern of the boat, looked back at her, gave a thumbs up sign, and sank out of sight.

Heart pounding, she gazed at the shore, body pressed against the hull as if that gave her more protection, revolver held in both hands as he had told her, resting on the wood in front of her. John Baldwin. Bob's employee? That made sense if Uncle Bob had sent Pierce that telegram. He wanted her protected, kept alive, no matter what. But why? Only if he still believed, like everyone else, that she was the key to a fortune. Twenty million dollars. But how did Uncle Bob know about that?

She saw ripples on the water between the boat and the shore, and held her breath. Now was no time to think about anything except Kaley. Kaley who had whipped her and made her beg, and had then thrust himself into her. Kaley . . . the hate started again, and her fingers curled round the trigger of the gun.

The ripples became more pronounced as Baldwin entered really shallow water. And Kaley saw him. 'Goddamn!' he shouted, and stood up, the tommy-gun thrust forward. Baldwin reared back on his knees, and Julie fired. The bullet missed, but Kaley was distracted, half turned away and did not immediately shoot. Baldwin was on his feet and charging him. But Julie had him in her sights again, and squeezed the trigger. Kaley spun right round and crashed to the ground, the tommy-gun rolling away from his fingers.

Julie leaned against the hull and panted, the revolver loose in her fingers. She heard the splashes coming towards her, and still could not move. Her body felt drained of blood, of strength.

'Miss Armitage?' Baldwin came round the boat. 'My God that was a good shot. You just about blew his head off.' He came closer, peered at her. 'Miss Armitage? Julie?' He took the revolver from her hand and stuffed it into his waistband below the water. Then he put on his jacket, put his tie in his pocket, and gently pulled her away from the hull. She let him do it. She still couldn't move herself.

She floated, on her back, while he towed her to the beach. When the reached the shallows he put one arm under her knees and the other under her shoulders, and carried her ashore. Out of the water the pain started again, and she moaned, while great shivers tore through her body.

'Hell's bells,' she heard him mutter. 'Julie. Julie, wake up.'

She hid her head in his shoulder. She didn't want to look at the thing lying on the ground, the other dead men, Arnie . . . once more she had provoked a massacre.

Baldwin went on walking, into the trees. Obviously they couldn't stay by the shore, waiting for Kaley's men to come back. He carried her for what seemed an eternity, until she knew his arms must be aching, then he laid her down. She opened her eyes, gazed at bushes surrounding them, trees forming a canopy overhead, and through the trees the blue sky and the sun, which was still high and deliciously warm. But yet the shivers wracked her body. She was cold, and she was in pain, but far more than that, she was in shock. Last night, and then today, were too much for her brain to accept. And now she had killed as well, physically.

'Julie,' Baldwin said urgently. 'Julie!'

She had rolled on her side to keep her back from the ground. Now she gazed at him. He had saved her life. But he was one of them. Everyone was one of them. She had no one she could absolutely trust. Except maybe Teddy. But could she trust Teddy? Even if he had saved her from MacGinnion and Kaley, there were so many unanswered questions . . . Anyway, Teddy was mad at her now, and thought her a killer. Well, wasn't he right?

'Julie, you have to pull yourself together. Julie . . .' he slapped her face.

She gasped, and tried to sit up, and he put his hand on her chest and pushed her flat again.

'You . . .' She struck at him.

'That's the spirit,' he said. 'Fight me.'

She struck at him again, and to her surprise he didn't defend himself. Her hand slashed across his face and his head jerked, and she stared at him, panting.

234

He wiped a trickle of blood from his lip, grinned at her. 'You were slipping into hysterical shock.'

'Was I?' She attempted to do something about her torn shirt, which had been all but dislodged in their brief tussle.

'It would be better if you took everything off, for a while. Let them, and you, dry.'

'You'd like that.'

'It's an odd thing,' he remarked. 'But rape is not something they teach at Hendon.'

'Why do you keep banging on about Hendon, Baldwin? I know you're not a policeman.'

'Is that a fact?' he remarked. 'I can still give you good advice. Strip, and let the sun dry you and your clothes. I'm going to wander off and do the same.' He grinned at her. 'I'll keep out of sight of you.'

'I thought we had to get out of here?'

'We have half an hour, still. Now . . .'

They heard the growl of a car engine. Several car engines, coming down the lane. 'Jesus,' Baldwin said.

'Half an hour?'

'Well, your friend Kaley obviously had help available much closer than Manhattan.' He snapped his fingers. 'Of course. He would have had some heavies standing by just in case you had come supported. I imagine they didn't work out who I might be until I was past them. Come on.' He held her hand and pulled her to her feet, hurried her further into the bushes. Branches whipped at her shoulders while thorns and pebbles tore at her bare feet, but she plunged along behind him until the car engines stopped, then he pushed her to the ground and lay beside her. 'Don't make a sound,' he whispered.

The noise of her panting was as loud as an express train, she thought. It was a still afternoon. So still they could hear the exclamations of the men as they surveyed the holocaust on the shore.

'Think they're still behind the boat, Mr Cerdo?' someone asked.

'I doubt it,' the attorney said. 'But you two guys take a look, anyway. They gotta be around here some place. They ain't had time to get too far. Spread out and find them. Remember, if that dame gets away we've all had it. She's poison.'

235

The undergrowth started to crackle as men moved through it. Julie raised her head to look at Baldwin, and then inhaled sharply as she began to sneeze. Instantly his hand whipped out and his thumb and forefinger closed on her nose, so tightly she thought he was going to pull it off. She punched him on the chest and he let her go; the sneeze had died. 'For Christ's sake keep quiet,' he whispered.

'Aren't they going to find us anyway?' she whispered back.

'It's a big wood,' he pointed out.

She lowered her cheek to the earth, nestled her body, spread her legs. Her back was in agony, and these might be the last few moments she was going to spend on earth, and she had just killed a man . . . and yet she was strangely relaxed. Obviously exhaustion, mental and physical, was about to take her over completely. But there was more than that. She gazed at Baldwin, and he gazed back at her. Then he stretched out his hand and pulled off her wig. 'I like you better natural,' he said.

She had forgotten she was wearing it.

'How's your back?' he whispered.

'Hell.'

'Well . . . you've got more guts than any woman I have ever met, little lady. And most men.' His hands moved across the ground to hold hers. 'Squeeze that, hard as you like, if the going gets rough.'

She curled her fingers around his, and they lay still, as the crackling sound came closer. His right hand held the revolver, lying on the ground in front of him. He intended that they should sell their lives dearly, if they had to. But she didn't want to die, however she might deserve to. She wanted to lie here forever, with these strong fingers wrapped around hers.

The feet came closer still, and then were past them, and moving on. Julie raised her head, and he shook his. 'They have to come back,' he whispered.

She lay down again, staring at him, and he blew her a kiss. She felt an ant runing across her back and gave a wriggle, and he blew it away. She heard the feet again, but again they went by; as Baldwin had said, it was a big wood.

The noise receded. 'They ain't no place in there, Mr Cerdo,' one of the men said.

'Jesus, Jesus, Jesus,' Cerdo remarked.

'What are we gonna do, Mr Cerdo?' asked someone else.

236

'Get the hell out of here,' said a third voice.

'Now, boys,' Dominic Cerdo protested, but he wasn't Mac-Ginnion and he wasn't Kaley. They were both dead.

'You can come if you like, Mr Cerdo,' they offered.

Five minutes later the car engines started again, and after another five minutes even that sound had died. Julie sat up. The shirt remained stuck in the earth, but that hardly seemed to matter now; mind and body felt startlingly aware. So maybe she was in a kind of reaction, but it was there. She had felt, after her rape, that she would never again be able to look at a man without a shudder. Not even at Teddy, much less a strange man whom she disliked anyway. But Baldwin was no longer a strange man, and he had saved her life, and as with Teddy, or Uncle Bob, when they had first met, she could feel his strength flowing over and enveloping her, strength she so badly needed.

'I think it might be a good idea for us to follow their example,' Baldwin said. 'Before someone else comes along and finds that battlefield and calls the cops. They'd *have* to do something about that. But it's going to be a long walk.'

'Yes,' she said.

'Can you make it without shoes?'

'I'll have to,' she said, and stood up. The shirt trailed from her fingers, and he looked at her for a moment, then took his jacket off and gave her his shirt. It hung on her like a nightdress.

'I suspect we may be arrested for indecent exposure', he remarked, putting his jacket on again.

'Oh, God,' she said.

'What now?'

'My handbag! It was in the car. It went up in the fire.'

'It didn't have anything valuable, I hope?'

'Oh, Jesus,' she said.

'The family treasure?'

'Forty thousand pounds in travellers' cheques, all but.'

'Always travel light, I say.'

'But Baldwin . . . John . . .' she wailed, tears springing from her eyes. That money had given her a sense of power, the knowledge that it was there a psychological boost.

She was in his arms, her head resting on his shoulder, while she nestled against his naked chest.

237

'It's not the end of the world, Julie,' he said, stroking her hair. 'I have enough for a taxiride into Manhattan, if they'll accept wet notes. And if your money was in travellers' cheques, you can always reclaim it.'

She supposed she could. Teddy had kept the various forms. But she could only reclaim it in England. She was penniless, in New York.

She moved her head back to look at him. 'I'm broke until I can get to London.'

'You're Julie Armitage. You have got to be a millionairess a hundred times over, on either side of the Atlantic.'

She gazed at him. Presumably he was right. She hadn't even thought of looking for her father's bank account here.

'Is that better?' he asked.

Her head flopped up and down.

'So blow your nose.' He took a still sodden handkerchief from his hip pocket.

She blew, and sighed. 'You must think I'm a nut.'

'I think you are the most deliciously inept hoodlum I have ever encountered.' He grinned at her. 'But the accent is on the word delicious.' He kissed her on the nose, and she took his face between her hands and kissed his mouth. She had discovered the power of that kiss, and there was only a thin shirt separating their respective torsos.

Her arms were round his neck, but he grasped her wrists and moved them, then held her away. 'You *are* a nut,' he said.

'Am I?'

'Let me present you with a little evidence. Item One: you hate my guts. Item Two: you are a married woman. Item Three: you are the boss of the world's biggest crime syndicate. Item Four: you have just killed a man. Item Five: you have just started a gang war. Item Six: I am a policeman. As your hubby might say, how does that grab you, baby?'

She gazed at him. She was no longer the least afraid of him. While he was holding her wrists she wasn't afraid of anything. 'May I present a defence?'

'If you can.'

'Item One: I owe you my life. Item Two: my husband and I are not getting on very well at this moment, and I don't know if we ever

238

shall again. Item Three: my heading the world's biggest crime syndicate is a purely temporary measure. Items Four and Five: Kaley, and Pat MacGinnion, between them organised the murder of my father, and then each raped me. That's what this killing is all about. Item Six: as I have told you before, I know you are not a policeman, John Baldwin.'

His turn to study her. Then he said, 'Is all of that true?'

'Cross my heart and hope to die.'

'And how do you know I'm not a policeman?'

'Scotland Yard didn't own you.'

'They told you that?'

'Well . . . they told Teddy.'

'You were there?'

'I was in the same room. He telephoned, just after you had been pushing us around in the London flat.'

'He telephoned,' Baldwin said. 'What number? Whitehall 1212?'

'I don't know. He looked it up in the book.'

'So you don't actually know what number he telephoned. Or who he spoke to.'

She stared at him, while her jaw sagged. Because if that were so . . . she didn't know who she had spoken to at Balliol. Or even if it had been Balliol. Teddy had given her the number. And Teddy had forged her birth certificate – to enable her to get a passport and come to America. Where a good many people had been waiting for her.

But Teddy was also the man who had risked his life to come and rescue her, and had done so magnificently.

'Yes,' Baldwin said. 'I think you want to think about that. Come on, let's make a move.'

'But Baldwin . . .' she caught his arm as he would have set off. 'What am I to do?'

'I don't know what you intend to do. What's this about getting out from the Association?'

'Just as soon as I've done what I came here to do.'

'I'd say you've just about done that. Now you have to get out of the States before they slap a first-degree murder charge on you.'

'I'm not finished yet,' she said.

'You really are sticking that pretty little chin out, you know,' he told her, 'and saying to the world, come hit me just as hard as you can.'

'Baldwin,' she said. 'Do you believe I was telling you the truth?'

'It's stupid of me, but I do, yes. In so far as you know it.'

'Then will you help me?'

'I thought I'd done my boy-scouting for the day. But I'll see you back to your apartment. I'm told you're safe when you get there. I'm not coming in with you, if that's what you mean. They don't teach us suicide at Hendon, either.'

'But if I can wriggle out of my mess, will you help me?'

'I'm a police officer, Julie. That sort of limits my freedom.'

'Okay,' she said. 'Okay.' She couldn't blame him for being suspicious. She fell into step beside him as they walked back towards the road. But within five minutes she had got a thorn in her foot, and after extracting it, he was carrying her again. She put her arms round his neck and rested her head on his shoulder. He had the most comforting shoulder. If only she could trust him . . . 'Will you tell me what you're doing here?' she asked when he had to stop to rest.

'I thought you knew. When we discovered you'd forged your birth certificate in order to get a passport, I was sent to bring you back. Oh, a woman constable accompanied me; we're very proper at the Yard. But when we got here, I was told that I couldn't touch you on that charge, because you have turned out to be an American after all. So that was that. But I bear grudges. I sent WPC Andrews home, and decided to take a fortnight's leave, and hang about. I've been watching your apartment ever since.'

Pierce's men would probably have mistaken him for one of MacGinnion's people.

'Why?' she asked.

'Because your father was killed on our patch, Julie. We had just found out that he was an international crook. We wanted him. We were putting together a case against him. Then someone came along and hit him with a stone. So we wanted to know why, and we wanted the killer. And it seemed to me, and my superiors, that you, with a little prodding, might be the one to lead us to those goals.' He turned his head and grinned at her. 'We had no idea you were suddenly going to go mad.'

'You weren't interested in the money?'

'Only in so far as it seemed to provide a motive. But we soon discarded that idea. Five hundred thousand or so is one hell of a lot, but these people are playing with millions.'

240

'You think my father has half a million pounds hidden away?'

'I think it could well be as much as that.'

She held his arm, turned him to face her, and kissed him again. She thought she had never felt so happy in her life. Because he had become the answer to her prayer; at last someone she could trust.

'I know it sounds fabulous,' he said, 'but I don't think we're going to let you hold on to it. When we find it.'

'I don't want to hold on to it,' she said. 'But I have just realised that you are telling me the truth. And to think I thought you worked for Uncle Bob.'

'Uncle Bob?'

'Major Roberts, to you.'

'Oh, yes. Another very slippery customer, Julie. You want to watch him.'

'How much do you know about him?'

'Not as much as we'd like to. We haven't been able to connect him to any of your father's criminal activities. But there is no question that he is, or was, a very close friend. They saw each other several times whenever Armitage was in England. And Roberts seemed to use the flat while your father was away; at least, he would go there fairly often.'

'Yes,' she said. She was back to where she had started, with that strange feeling about Uncle Bob, that he was absolutely genuine, even down to claiming he had fallen in love with her as a girl from her photographs and what Father had told him about her. That he was so determined to protect her and care for her he had sent that telegram to Hanson Pierce to make sure MacGinnion didn't get his hands on her . . . but yet that, in some way she just could not understand, he was against her as well.

But she didn't have the time to think about it, right now, as Baldwin lifted her and set off again. All too soon they could see the road.

'So what happens next?' Baldwin asked, setting her on her feet.

Now she had to think. But she wanted to, where it involved him.

'Listen,' she said. 'Have you spoken with District Attorney Zeidler?'

'I'm afraid District Attorneys seldom have the time to chat with visiting police sergeants.'

'Okay. When you've changed, after we get back, you go down to his office and you tell his secretary that Julie sent you. He'll see you then. You tell him that a week today is D-Day. That I want him to come to my apartment at six o'clock next Tuesday.'

'To fight another war?'

'I'll have the place open by then.' She didn't know how she was going to do it, but she was sure she could. 'And then, you say I would like him to tell you what I'm doing.'

He frowned on her. 'Do you mean that? That you're working with the DA?'

'We have a bargain. My end of which I now have to carry out.'

'And that means going back to Hanson Pierce and Longman.'

'Yes. At least for a while.'

'Julie . . . do you have any idea how dangerous that could be? These fellows play rough.'

She kissed him. 'So do I, now. Right? Anyway, you may not like the guy, but Teddy is on our side. And he's my husband.'

He scratched his head. 'You are the damnedest little girl.'

'So what I would like from you are two promises.'

'Try me.'

'First, when I leave here, and it may be in a hurry, I want to return to England. Can you get back over there just as fast as possible and arrange that?'

He frowned. 'There's no policeman in Great Britain who wants you back over there – but I'll fix it. If you'll tell me why.'

'I can't do that,' she said. 'You have to trust me. If the District Attorney of New York can trust me, then you can. If he can persuade you that I'm on the up and up, then you just believe me when I say it's all part of what I'm trying to do.'

He studied her face. 'And the second promise?'

'That if I, and it has to be me in person, ever telephones Whitehall 1212, some time soon, you'll come running.'

He grinned. 'On roller skates. Here's a car.' He waved his arm.

'What are we going to tell him?'

'That our boat sank in the bay. Julie . . . What happens if you don't telephone Whitehall 1212, some time soon?'

'As they say over here, I'll be at the bottom of the East River with my feet stuck in cement.'

He held her shoulders. 'I wouldn't like that to happen.'

'I don't think I go much for the idea, either.'

242

'So you be careful. I'd hate never to get that telephone call.'

'You'll get it, Baldwin. I always deliver the goods.'

He kissed her on the nose. 'I'm counting on that.'

The car scraped to a halt beside them. 'Jesus,' remarked the driver. 'You guys okay?'

'We,' Julie told him, 'are fine.'

'Holy Mary Mother of God!' Shana remarked.

Hanson Pierce appeared speechless for the moment. So did Teddy. But then, so were the guards; Julie had feared the one on duty in the downstairs lobby – his cover was selling newspapers from a kiosk by the door – would have a heart attack when she had entered the building. She and Baldwin had picked up a taxi in Flatbush, and by the time she had regained Fifth Avenue her clothes had dried, but she was still barefooted and looked as if she'd been through a washing machine; fortunately they were all so surprised by her reappearance no one had troubled to look too closely at Baldwin's shirt.

'I would like a hot bath,' she said.

'You got it,' Shana agreed, and hurried for the bedroom.

Julie followed her, and the men followed Julie.

'Where the hell have you been?' Teddy demanded.

She sat on the bed. She had never been so exhausted in her life. And yet, for all the leaden feeling that she had led three more men to their deaths, there was a lurking happiness. She had an ally. More than that she dared not consider.

'I had a date,' she said.

'With Arnie? Where is that guy?'

'My date was with Kaley,' she said.

'Kaley?' Pierce shouted, at last finding his voice.

'That's right. He telephoned here and asked for a meeting. So I went.'

'By yourself?'

'I took Arnie, and all the muscle he could raise at short notice.' She looked at their faces. 'None of you guys was available.'

'Christalmighty! And you're alive?'

'Yes,' she said. 'But Arnie is dead. So are the others.'

Pierce stared at her. 'Arnie? Christ, I liked that boy. When I get hold of Kaley . . .'

243

'Kaley is dead,' Julie said.

There was another silence. Then Pierce said, 'Arnie got him? Well, hallelujah. I always knew that boy would die well.'

'No,' Julie said. 'Kaley killed Arnie. I shot Kaley.'

This time the silence was longer.

'You shot Kaley?' Teddy asked at last.

'Through the head. And three others.' She had no intention of telling them about Baldwin, and the more kudos she could gather the better.

'Well, I'll be damned,' Pierce said admiringly. 'Eddie's daughter. Well, I'll be damned!'

'The cars got burned out,' she told them. 'So I had to walk several miles to find a lift back to town. I am very tired and I have a sore back. So if you fellows would like to leave Shana and me alone . . .'

'Sure thing, baby,' Pierce said. 'Come along, you guys. The Boss wants to be alone.' He herded them from the room.

Teddy stayed. Well, she supposed she couldn't really expel her husband.

'Bath's just right,' Shana announced.

'Great. Will you take a look at my back?'

The shirt had stuck to the burn, and taking it off was agony. Shana helped, while Teddy peered at her. 'Holy Smoke,' he commented.

'You've lost a couple of layers,' Shana said.

'Can't you put something on it?'

'Yeah. Got to keep the air out, I guess. I'll smother you. Wait a moment.'

Julie got up, stripped off the rest of her clothes. She had to keep Teddy distracted until she could get rid of the shirt.

He sat on the bed to watch her. 'You are quite something, my darling girl. You figure on keeping up this dangerous living?'

'No,' she said.

'Where's the gun?'

'I dropped it. I think I was sort of shocked.'

'I should say. It'll have your prints on it.'

'If they ever find it. Teddy . . . I've lost the money.'

'Eh?'

'It was in my handbag, and went up with the car.'

'Oh, Christ,' he said, and she realised that losing the money

244

might have been a stroke of fortune after all, because whatever doubts he might be beginning to have about the truth of her story vanished immediately – he knew how much store she had set by that money. As long as Shana made no comment about the shirt she should be all right.

'But you have the numbers, don't you?'

'Yeah. Yeah, I guess we can reclaim . . . in England.'

'I know. I thought of that. But . . . why shouldn't I just tell Pierce I need money?'

'He'll want to know what for.'

'Will he? I'm the Boss, remember?'

He gave one of his crooked grins. 'I keep forgetting.' Then he put his arms round her thighs to bring her against him and kiss her stomach. 'Jesus, Julie, I love you so. When I think of the risks you took . . .'

She looked down on his head. Turn out right, she thought. Oh, please turn out right. He might never be as reliable as John Baldwin, but he was her husband, and she thought she could well love him for the rest of her life . . . if he could only be honest with her.

'Let's have you,' Shana said. She had some very heavy ointment with which she smothered the burn. 'I'll put some more on after your bath,' she said.

'Thanks,' Julie said, and nudged her discarded clothes with her toe. 'Shana, will you burn all of those? I don't ever want to see any of them again.'

'Christ,' Shana remarked. 'I've read of guys like kings and millionaires who give their shirts to their valets after wearing them once; I have never heard of a gal who burns everything she takes off.' She bent to scoop them up, and hesitated.

'All of them,' Julie repeated. 'They're filthy.'

Shana gave what might have been a little shrug. 'Sure,' she said again.

After her bath Julie lay on her face while Teddy recoated the wound. 'This is gonna take a little while to heal,' he commented.

'So I'll skip backless dresses for a week.'

He dried his hands, but a few moments later they were back, sliding over her shoulders and down to her buttocks. She enjoyed that; she needed a massage. 'Julie . . . you are so beautiful.

245

Julie . . . I'm sorry about this morning. Losing my temper. If I did, it was because I was scared – for you. Julie, you've killed four men. And started a war. You can't mean to keep this up. The cops are going to get you, eventually, if MacGinnion's lot don't.'

'MacGinnion's men are finished,' Julie said.

'And you have a deal with the cops.'

'That's right.'

'Don't you think you should tell me what it is?'

She pushed herself up, turned on her knees to face him.

'I'm your husband,' he said. 'And I'm on your side.'

'So trust me, Teddy. Trust me.' She held his face and brought it forward for a kiss. 'I trusted you.'

His face hardened. 'Meaning you don't any more.'

'Meaning I'm asking for a quid pro quo. For just a week.'

'A week?'

'That's a promise.'

'And during that week you're going to go charging round the country being shot at?'

'No,' she said. 'Never again. That's a promise too.'

He grinned. 'Well, that's something.' His hands slid over her shoulders and down to her breasts. 'Julie . . . you've killed both the bastards, and I have missed you so . . .' another grin. 'We are honeymooning.'

'I know.' She held him close.

'You needn't hurt your back,' he whispered. 'You could come down on me.'

'I know,' she said. She wanted to be close to him. But she was just too exhausted – mentally and physically. 'Not now,' she whispered. 'Later perhaps, after I've had a rest.'

Pierce came to dinner. As instructed, he brought with him a hundred thousand dollars in cash; he had raised not an eyebrow when Julie had demanded the money. 'I've let word of what happened to Kaley circulate,' he said. 'Among the boys.'

'Was that a good idea?' Teddy asked.

'I reckon so,' Pierce said. 'I have to say they were a bit reluctant to let the Boss have all their records. Even the Boss. Hearing about how she fixed Kaley, coming on top of Big Pat, will do the trick. You wait.'

'Well, thank God for that,' Julie said, and listened to the telephone ringing.

Shana answered it. Shana had been magnificent, had uttered not a single comment about the strange shirt – a man's shirt. But for that very reason, Shana – making sure that Shana came to no harm – was a worry for the future. Now she gazed at them, eyebrows expressive. 'Dominic Cerdo,' she said, her hand over the mouthpiece. 'He wants to speak with Miss Julie.'

'No way,' Pierce snapped, getting up.

'Relax, Hanson,' Julie said. 'I'll take it.'

Pierce pointed. 'No more private meetings.'

Julie blew him a kiss. 'Those aren't necessary any more.' She knew Cerdo was beaten, and terrified. He had lost control of his own mob, and he had to know that he was on her list; even if he had hardly touched her, he had been in the room, watching. She took the receiver. 'Good evening, Dominic.'

'Julie? Christ, where were you, this afternoon?'

'Watching you, Dominic. Unfortunately, I'd run out of bullets. But I've reloaded my gun, now.'

She could hear him panting on the other end of the line. 'Now, say Miss Julie, I wanna talk.'

'You mean you want to call it a day.'

'I never wanted a fight in the first place. I never even wanted you hurt. You know that, Miss Julie. I was against those guys messing you around.'

'Were you, Dominic? How I wish I'd known that at the time. But you can surrender, if you like.'

'Surrender?'

'That's what I said. Surrender yourself, and the Armitage and MacGinnion Realty Building. Now listen to me very carefully, Dominic. Hanson and I are going to be over in twenty minutes to take possession. We will not be alone. You pull your people out. Send them home. But you stay. I want the complete records of the Association, Dominic. And you are going to stay there and hand them to me. And if, so help me God, there is one item missing, I am going to shoot you in the balls. Personally. You understand me?'

'But . . . Miss Julie . . .'

'Those are my terms. Then you can go back to your law practice. But not for the Association.'

She listened to his gulp. Without the Association he didn't have a law practice.

'Twenty minutes, Dominic', she repeated, and hung up.

'Think he'll go for it?' Pierce asked.

'I know he'll go for it.'

'Oh, boy. Then we'll – you'll – have the whole Association in your hand. You know something, Julie, I don't think even your dad ever managed that. Queen Elizabeth. I knew you was just like that dame.'

Why, yes, Julie thought; maybe I am. Because she had managed to make them all fall in love with her, from Uncle Bob to the DA, she felt. And Arnie and the other two men who had died for her. And John Baldwin? There was a prize.

'I thought you were exhausted,' Teddy grumbled. 'And were going to bed.'

Julie blew him a kiss. 'I'm not that exhausted,' she said. 'Bed will have to wait.'

Teddy had to wait for longer than she had supposed. Next morning she woke with a high temperature. She hadn't got to bed until nearly dawn, as she and Pierce had taken charge of the Association's books, with Cerdo hovering anxiously at their shoulders. Julie had been tempted to take the little man aside and warn him not to mention the twenty million, but had decided against it. She did not wish to give him any handle with which to stir the pot, and for the moment he was so terrified the money was forgotten. By the time he began to think straight again he'd be in gaol; he wasn't on her list of immunities.

When they were finished they had filled the building with their own people. By then, however exhausted, she had been satisfied. She had brought all the books back to the apartment, and she reckoned that when the accounts from the other districts arrived she would have everything Zeidler could possibly need to shut down the Association for good, enough evidence to send all the remaining district bosses to gaol for a long time together with Cerdo. She had collapsed into a deep sleep, which even Teddy had not been prepared to disturb. But now . . .

'It's the burn,' Shana told her. 'Nobody can go around hurting themselves like that and expect to get away with it. You know you're

248

scarred for life? Four by three in black flesh, and I'm talking in inches. Now if it had been me, that would've been white. Drink this.'

Julie looked at the liquid suspiciously. 'What is it?'

'Just ground-up aspirins. It should bring the temperature down. You wanna get well, don't you?'

I must get well, Julie thought. In a hurry. D-Day was rushing at her.

She slept, and awoke bathed in sweat, but Teddy and Shana were there to sponge her off. 'Oh, my darling girl,' Teddy said, and gave one of his grins. 'At least I know where you are, some of the time, nowadays.' He was anxious too. To get out of here while they still breathed. And go looking for her inheritance. She wondered what he was going to say when he discovered just how big an inheritance it was.

'When do you think I'll be able to get out of bed?' she asked Shana, the next time they were alone.

'Three, four days. But you ain't gonna be one hundred per cent.' She sat beside her. 'I guess you're in a hurry to die.'

'I want to live forever.'

'Then you sure are going about it in a strange way. Trying to pull the wool over the eyes of people like Hanson Pierce, or even your hubby, could be a dangerous business.'

Julie watched her through half-closed eyes. My brain should be sounding danger signals, she told herself; but she was too tired. But it would be a good idea to appear even more tired than she was.

'The shirt?' she asked, drowsily.

Shana gave a faint shrug. 'He must've been a big guy.'

'He was,' Julie said.

'And a tough one.'

'How do you figure that?'

'Honey, you didn't shoot four men. Maybe you shot Kaley. I guess you had cause enough for that. But you ain't no hoodlum. Any fool can see that.'

Julie sighed, and smiled. 'I'm glad of that. But . . . *any* fool?'

'Any fool. So Teddy and Hanson aren't thinking very straight at this moment. But they'll get around to it. I've never met a husband who could stand having his wife wandering around in another guy's shirt. And I can tell you that Hanson ain't gonna like the idea that

249

you have some private muscle hidden away, especially the kind of muscle that can destroy Kaley's lot.'

'Umm,' Julie said, and abandoned trying to appear drowsy, because she was now very wide awake indeed. 'How do you feel on the matter?'

Shana's face was expressionless. 'How should I feel?'

'You must have some ideas.'

'Sure.'

'Maybe you could share them.'

Shana considered, then gave another of her little shrugs. 'I reckon you aim to pull the rug, sometime soon.'

'And if I do, where do you stand?'

'Now that, I reckon you should tell me.'

Julie took a long breath. 'Do you have somewhere to go?'

Shana almost smiled, a rare sight. 'People like me always have some place to go, honey, even if some of them ain't very nice. But it would have to be far away if I was going to make sure of not meeting Hanson again, on a dark night.'

'Would . . .' twenty million dollars, she thought. But she was committed to giving it back, to somebody. Well, nearly all of it. 'Would fifty thousand dollars take you far enough?'

'Fifty thousand dollars would take me all the way, honey.'

'You'll have to take my word that I'll get you the money, afterwards.'

'I think you are the only person in this world whose word I'd take on that, Miss Julie.'

If you only knew, Julie thought. If you only knew. But this was her business, Queen Elizabeth's business, making women as well as men fall in love with her. 'Then you'll back me, if I need you?'

'You got it. But for Christ's sake be careful. Hanson ain't quite as dumb as he looks.'

'I'll be careful,' Julie promised, and closed her eyes. She was well on the way to creating an army of her own. And these were *people*.

She slept the sleep of utter relaxation, awoke, had a light meal, and slept again. Hanson Pierce called to look at her with an alarmed expression. 'You ain't gonna die on me, little lady?' he asked.

'No,' Julie smiled. 'I'm not going to die, Hanson.' And wanted to weep at the thought of what she was about to do to him.

But the illness, as she began to recover, was also very useful. It

gave her time to think, and remember. Remembering was important, because it had begun to dawn on her that the key to the puzzle
of Daddy and the money had to lie somewhere in everything that
had happened, simply because nothing else *had* happened. Every
movement Daddy had made on his English journeys could be
accounted for, yet he had never reached Epsom with the money he
must have been carrying across the Atlantic. But she just didn't see
how he could have unloaded the money . . . until she started to
think about John Baldwin. She had been reluctant to do so, and not
only because the mere memory of those moments of madness made
her feel guilty; to remember John was to remember Arnie and the
others, hoodlums, murderers, but her faithful followers to the end.
Yet the memory of Baldwin was so reassuring she found herself
trying to recall everything they had done together, or said
together . . . and suddenly she realised that she had found the
answer to the mystery, and it was so simple it would have been
laughable had it not been surrounded by so much tragedy.

So now it was just a matter of getting well and working out how to
distract Pierce's goons when it was time for Zeidler and his men to
arrive, the other books had by now been accumulated. Teddy spent a
lot of time with her each day, but with Shana always hovering they
couldn't talk about anything serious. Nor did she want to: she was
determined to keep her secret for the time being, but she knew she
would need his help for the coup she was planning. He wouldn't
share the bed with her while she was ill, but by the fifth night her
temperature was back to normal. She refused aspirins that night,
began to tense up again, and awoke at three in the morning to find
him alongside her. She felt absolutely one hundred percent fit.
Which was just as well, because D-Day was rushing at her. She was
in a strangely ambivalent frame of mind. One half of her being was
filled with a fierce exultation that she should almost have reached
the end of this particular journey, that Daddy's name was going to
be at least partly cleared, however dishonestly, that she was going to
be free, to resume her quest for the last part of the puzzle. But the
other half felt unrelenting regret for the fact that she was about to
betray Hanson, and Closet, and Top, and all the others who had so
faithfully supported her, and indeed, risked their lives for her. She
could only take comfort in the thought that if Roosevelt did win the
election, they were going to be put out of business anyway.

251

And she could afford no regrets. She had made an undertaking to Zeidler, and now to Baldwin as well, and she couldn't backslide. Now was the time to bring Teddy at least partially into the picture, she thought, raising herself on her elbow to look down at him. Besides, before all hell broke loose, and she broke free, it was terribly important to be certain that she did want him to be a part of her search, and her life, whatever games he had tried to play in the past.

She switched on the light, moved the sheet and crawled on to him. He slept on his back, and she sat astride his thighs, watching his mouth, faintly open as he breathed, close as he started to wake up, watching his eyelids flicker, and feeling the movement beneath her as consciousness returned.

'Julie?' He wasn't sure. 'You okay?'

'Okay,' she said. 'Okay.'

He brought her down to kiss him, and she stretched her legs and lay on him, kissing him and fondling him, making sure she would be as aroused as he when he was ready, and heard the bedroom door open.

'Christalmighty,' Hanson Pierce said. 'The boss's daughter. Now there's a chick, eh?'

Julie gave a squawk of alarm and rolled off Teddy, reaching for the sheet in the same movement and sitting up. 'What the hell are you doing in here?'

The upstairs guard was at his back.

Hanson Pierce grinned at her. 'I've come to say goodbye, Julie.'

'Goodbye?' She had no idea what he was talking about.

'Sure,' he said. 'You and lover boy are leaving us, today.'

'We are what?'

Pierce grinned at her. 'You're gonna take a little ride. Down to the river.'

CHAPTER 12

Julie could only stare at him in a mixture of consternation and horror. She had been planning to double cross him, and all the time he had been planning to double cross her – but he didn't mean just to let her retire.

By now Teddy was also sitting up, gazing at the two men in a bemused manner. 'Are you out of your mind, Pierce?' he demanded. 'This is the Boss.'

Pierce grinned. 'Yeah. She's a real cutie. The name we had to have, for a while. But look at it this way, Miss Julie, thanks to you we've got rid of MacGinnion and Kaley. Cerdo I can settle any time. And all without any interference from the cops. I don't know how you squared them, but you sure did a good job there. And the boys have accepted me as your business manager. So if you was to disappear, and turn up in a week's time kind of waterlogged, I'd be the obvious guy to take over. Because you set it up. And you know what? You even got rid of the one guy who might've objected. Arnie.'

Julie was panting. She knew just how deadly this big man could be. 'And you don't think the boys will know who put me in the river?'

Pierce grinned at her. 'Sure they'll know. Some survivors from Kaley's mob, avenging their boss. Come along now, we don't want to wake anybody up. There's no need to dress. Clothes ain't gonna do you no good where you're going.'

Julie bit her lip. She wanted to scream. To have come so close to success . . . but she had never been close to success. Pierce must have had this in mind from the moment she had told him of

253

Father's death. In fact, he had spelled it out almost right away: he needed the Boss's name to hold the Association together, and settle with MacGinnion – and she had not troubled to look beyond that. But now she had to think, very clearly and very fast, because Teddy was clearly incapable of doing so. He was in fact starting to get out of bed.

'Hands high,' Pierce commanded. 'And turn round.'

Teddy obeyed. His face was working as if he was in anguish. Well, no doubt he was.

'Okay, Sam,' Pierce said.

The guard laid down his tommy-gun, stepped forward, took a pair of handcuffs from his pocket, pulled Teddy's arms behind him, and snapped the cuffs on his wrists.

'Now you, little lady,' Pierce said. 'Just move nice and slow. I gotta lot of time for you, Julie, and I'd sure hate to have to hurt you. Nice and slow. But move!' His voice suddenly rasped.

Julie let the sheet drop and got out of bed. As he had commanded, she moved nice and slow. Maybe by looking at her he'd lower his guard. But even if he did, how could she take on Pierce and another man physically? Teddy was now helpless. And he wasn't going to lower his guard; she remembered Closet's remark that first night, that he preferred blondes even to big-breasted redheads.

But if she didn't have the physical strength to defeat him, and she didn't have the sex appeal to vamp him . . . she still had to have the better brain. And the more knowledge.

'Turn around,' he commanded. 'Sam.'

Julie turned around, and the man named Sam pulled her arms behind her back in turn. As the handcuffs clicked she gazed at Teddy, who was gazing at her. He looked ready to burst into tears. 'Julie . . .' he begged.

'You're being a fool, Hanson,' Julie said, keeping her voice as even as she could.

'Yeah,' he agreed. 'Now listen. We're gonna ride down in the elevator to the garage, right? If either of you tries anything or makes a noise, you are going to get belted one. Like I said, I sure don't wanna have to do that to you, Julie. When you gotta go, it's best to go decent like. Right?'

Julie took a long breath as she turned to face him. 'And what about the twenty million?'

254

Pierce gazed at her, brows slowly drawing together in a frown. 'The what?'

'You kill me, Hanson,' she said, 'and you'll never see a cent of that money.'

'You trying to hoodwink me?' he demanded.

'I never try to hoodwink anybody,' Julie asserted, with some truth. 'I always deal my cards face up. For God's sake, what do you think this whole thing is about? Why do you think I came to the States? It was to find out about the money. Why do you think MacGinnion kidnapped me? It was to find out about the money. Why do you think I wanted all the Association books? It was to find out about the money.'

Pierce looked at Teddy. 'She on the level?'

'It's the money we're after,' Teddy said, loyally. What he must be thinking she did not know.

'That's all, Hanson,' Julie said. 'You can have the Association. We're on our way back to Europe the day after tomorrow.'

Pierce scratched his head with the hand holding the gun. But that was no risk with them both handcuffed. 'You expect me to believe that? Twenty million . . . Jesus . . . whose money are we talking about?'

'The Association's,' Julie told him. 'Money Daddy embezzled, at the rate of two million a year, for ten years.'

'Holy Christ!' Pierce sat on the bed. 'And MacGinnion found out.'

'That's right. So he had Daddy killed, figuring he'd get it out of me easier than out of him.'

'Because you know where the dough is?'

Julie took another deep breath. 'Yes, Hanson, I know where the dough is.' To her own surprise, she realised that this time she wasn't lying. She was sure she did. Or at least, who had it.

'So?'

'Take off the cuffs, let Teddy and me get dressed, and we'll talk about it.'

'Yeah? Suppose I just beat it out of you.'

'MacGinnion tried that, and it didn't work.' Yet her voice had given the slightest tremble.

'I ain't MacGinnion, little lady.'

'But I am still Julie Armitage, Hanson. You'd do better to make a deal.'

'Such as?'

255

'Half for you, and half for me. In return I will promise never to set foot in America again. And you can have the Association. You won't do better than that.'

Pierce gazed at her. Then he grinned. 'You're a real cutie, Miss Julie. You got guts where other gals just have flab. But you ain't gonna hoodwink old Hanson. Not you, little girl. I reckon I'll worry about the money after I'm running the Association. If there is that kind of dough knocking about, I'll find it. Without your help.' He stood up again. 'Let's go. It'll be light in an hour.'

Julie couldn't believe her ears. She had been so sure of success, there. But Hanson Pierce was actually the smartest of all the people she had come into contact with during this last unforgettable month – with maybe one exception. And now she had lost, and was going to die. Horribly, with the cold water of the East River embracing her naked body and forcing itself down her throat. She had to bite her lip to stop the tears.

'Hell, I know it's tough,' Pierce said sympathetically. 'Losing is always tough. But . . . someone has to, right? Now walk.'

Julie stepped forward, and gazed at Shana, who suddenly filled the doorway, behind both the men, wearing her blood-red dressing-gown, and holding an automatic pistol in both hands, levelled in front of her. 'Hold it, Pierce,' she said.

'Christ, the nigger,' Sam snapped, and started to turn. Shana only moved the gun six inches, and blew his head off. Blood and brains scattered across the room and Sam dropped like a bag of cement.

Pierce had also turned, and died a second later; Shana shot him through the heart.

'Oh, God.' Julie dropped to her knees; they had just given way. She would have fallen right over if Shana hadn't dropped the pistol and rushed forward to catch her.

'It's okay, honey,' she said.

'Okay? God . . .' She was now responsible for eighteen deaths. Or had they really all been responsible for themselves?

Shana propped her against the bed, knelt beside Pierce, and began going through his pockets. She seemed perfectly oblivious to the blood gathering about her knees as she was to the various odours which had suddenly filled the room. But this was her world. She had grown up in this milieu of violence and terror. Julie knew it could never be *her* world.

256

'Here we are.' Shana found the keys, unlocked Julie's handcuffs. 'What about big boy?'

Teddy stood as if turned to stone, staring at the carnage in front of him.

'Please.' Julie pushed herself up, hugged herself; she felt as chill as if she had indeed been dragged from the river. She pulled on a dressing-gown. 'I need a drink.'

Shana released Teddy in turn, then went into the lounge. Teddy rubbed his wrists. 'God,' he said. 'You are a dangerous woman, Julie. Did you know Shana was there?'

'I knew she had to be, some time.'

'And she was on the payroll, all the time.'

'I'm not in the suicide business,' Julie told him, quoting Baldwin. Because she was slowly pulling herself together. It was as necessary as ever to be Julie Armitage, for one last crowded hour, now.

Shana returned with a brandy, and she drank greedily. All she had to do was steady her nerves.

'So what do we do next?' Shana asked. 'This building is full of Pierce's men.'

'But I'm still the Boss,' Julie said. 'And it's time to finish it.' She stepped over Pierce and into the cleaner air of the lounge, flicked through the telephone directory, found the number she wanted, picked up the telephone and dialled.

'You're not calling the police?' Teddy was horrified.

'Why not?'

Teddy looked at Shana, and Shana shrugged. She was willing to let Julie take over again.

The phone rang, again and again. Julie drank some more brandy. Then a woman said, sleepily, 'Who is it?'

'I'd like to speak with Mr Zeidler, please,' Julie said.

'At this hour? Mr Zeidler is asleep.'

'Then wake him up. Tell him Julie's on the line.'

There was a series of low noises, then Zeidler came on the line. 'Julie? Julie Armitage?'

'Julie Armitage, Mr Zeidler. I thought you'd like to know that I have managed to tie things up for you sooner than expected. If you can bring your people here, in an hour's time, you'll find everything you need.'

'And just how do I get in, without blowing up half of Manhattan?'

257

'You walk in, Mr Zeidler. Nobody's going to stop you.'

'Well, I'll be damned. And what is Pierce going to be doing?'

'Nothing. Because when you get up here, you will find Hanson Pierce and one other, very dead.'

'Great God Almighty! You?'

'In a manner of speaking.'

'You mean he found out?'

'I mean we fell out.'

'And you're going to be there?'

'No. That's why I want you to give me an hour. I shall be on my way to Boston. I know I'm a couple of days early, but I am just going to disappear for those days. Then I'm going to disappear forever as far as you're concerned. Did you see my messenger?'

'Yes.'

'And has he left yet?'

'No. I think he wanted to stay here and see how things turned out.'

'Can you contact him?'

'Yes.'

'Then will you do so, immediately, and ask him to get on with it. My husband and I must be allowed entrance into Great Britain.'

'Yes,' Zeidler agreed. 'I will do that. Will I see you again?'

'No, Mr Zeidler. Do you want to?'

There was a brief hesitation. Then he said, 'I guess it would be a mistake. Okay, Julie. You have one hour to be out of town. Your steamship tickets and passport are waiting for you at the office of the Hamburg–America line in Boston. So . . . I'll wish you good luck.'

'Thank you, Mr District Attorney.'

'And Julie – take care. There'll always be a lot of people interested in Julie Armitage.'

'I'll remember,' she said, and hung up.

Shana and Teddy gazed at her.

'Holy Jesus Christ,' Teddy said. 'You planned that, from the beginning? That was your bargain with the DA? The Association in exchange for your revenge?'

'Yes,' Julie said. 'I made him promise an amnesty to Hanson, though. I guess I am just an innocent little girl, at that.' She glanced at Shana. 'But you're amnestied too, Shana.' She went back into the bedroom, tried not to look at the two things on the floor, took fifty

258

thousand dollars from her handbag. 'I owe you more than that. Maybe one day I'll be able to pay you more.'

'Then I'll keep in touch,' Shana said. She took Julie in her arms, hugged her close, kissed her on both cheeks, and then on the mouth. 'Knowing your old man was a privilege,' she said. 'But if I had never met you, Miss Julie, I wouldn't ever have found out what life is all about. How're we gonna clear the building?'

'There's only the backstairs guard and the fellow in the lobby. Bring them in here.'

'You gonna do them too?'

'Not unless I have to. You take the tommy-gun, Teddy. But don't shoot unless I say so.'

There was no question of shooting. The two guards were brought into the bedroom. The backstairs man had heard the shots, and was already in a state of alarm, but Pierce, as Julie had surmised, had not taken him into his confidence; the downstairs man had no idea what was happening.

'Mr Pierce?' they gasped together. Sam was apparently unimportant.

'Yes,' Julie said. 'I just discovered that he's double crossed us. Now, going by what he said before I shot him, the DA is going to be here any moment with half the New York police force. So we have to get out, but fast. I'll contact Closet and we'll get together as soon as the coast is clear. Right?'

'But we can't abandon you, Miss Julie? Mr Pierce said—'

'Mr Pierce is dead,' Julie told them. 'I'm the boss, right? And I can take care of myself.'

There was no way they could argue with that; they had the evidence.

'So make yourselves scarce. I'll be in touch.'

They hesitated. But she had given them orders they were happy to obey; they didn't want to have to stand up to the NYPD. 'You're the boss,' one said, and a moment later they were gone.

'I have to hand it to you, Julie,' Shana said. 'You sure you don't really want to take over the Association?'

'Quite sure,' Julie said. 'Now you have to get out of here too, Shana.'

'Shame,' Shana said. 'Those guys wouldn't have stood a chance. You take care, eh?'

259

She hurried off to pack.

'We'd better do the same,' Julie said. 'We only have an hour.'

'But Julie . . .'

'We'll talk on the train.'

'I was only going to ask, why Boston?'

'Why, to visit with your folks, like you wanted.'

'Heck,' he said. 'I'd forgotten.'

The monotonous rattle of the rails made her sleepy all over again. But again, also, she supposed she was in a sort of shock. It was difficult to believe that she had only been in New York a week, that her arrival should have stirred up such an upheaval, such a bloodbath, and that it should now be behind her.

Was it behind her? Through lowered lids she gazed at Teddy, sitting opposite. Teddy had a lot on his mind, but he couldn't talk about it yet, because there were too many other people in the carriage, just as there had been too many people around all the time at Pennsylvania Station while they had waited for the first train north. They had not in fact left New York until after the hour had elapsed. By the time the train pulled out Father's apartment would have been crawling with policemen, and newspapermen. But if Zeidler kept his word, none of them would ever even know she existed. So the district bosses she had addressed and whose allegiance she had won would certainly denounce her when they were arrested, but by then it would be too late – if Zeidler kept his word. She had no doubt that he would.

Would she ever come back? She would like to. As a plain tourist. No, she could never be a tourist in New York. She had been born here, had as much right to be here as anyone on the street. But if she came back, it would have to be as Mrs Edward Longman the Third. That was the most important question she had to face at the moment, even more important than the money.

The train stopped at a station, and several passengers got off. For the moment their part of the compartment was empty; it was still very early.

'You awake?' Teddy asked.

'Yes.' She sat up straight.

'Julie . . .' he leaned forward and held her hands. 'My mind is spinning.'

'Join the club.'

'Did you really come to America to . . . well, to destroy the Association?'

'Maybe I did. I didn't come here to kill anybody. A week ago I still thought in terms of police, and justice. But I suppose when I found out that people like MacGinnion could always beat justice . . .' she sighed. 'The rape was the last straw.'

'The rape?'

She raised her head. 'I never told you. MacGinnion and Kaley raped me in that room. God . . . it's something you read about like . . . like somebody else falling under a bus, and you say to yourself, well, that can never happen to me. And then it does.' She gazed at him. 'I'd never known the meaning of the word hate before then.'

'And you never told me.'

'It would have been one more thing to upset you, Teddy.'

'You are out of this world.' She wasn't sure whether he was praising or criticising. 'So you went ahead and hoodwinked Pierce and the boys into gunning down MacGinnion, while you made that deal with the DA, and then you went and got Kaley yourself, all without telling a soul. If you weren't my wife, you'd frighten me. Maybe you frighten me anyway.'

'Do you want a divorce, Teddy?'

He frowned at her. 'A divorce?'

'Well . . . even if you knew my name, I think you thought you were marrying Julie Allen. I think you were, too, at the time. Now you're married to Julie Armitage.'

'So do you have anyone else lined up for a short life?'

'No,' she said. 'I hope not, anyway. I hope and pray not. But . . . I still have things to do.'

'Yeah,' he said. 'Like finding your dad's fortune.' He grinned at her. 'That was a stroke of genius, telling Pierce it was twenty million dollars. Jesus!'

Julie studied him. She had known this moment had to come, and had still not decided how to handle it. He was her husband. He had saved her life at least once in their brief partnership, and he seemed to love her dearly . . . and there were times when she thought she could love him back. Yet she couldn't bring herself to trust him as she should. Because of the forged birth certificate? Or because of the doubts Baldwin had sown?

261

She should tackle him on that here and now. But she didn't want to do that, and the reason was not merely the fear that he might not be able to answer her convincingly. It was more a secret feeling that the less he knew of what she knew, the less he would be able to cheat her.

Or should she be more honest with herself and admit that her reluctance to be absolutely straight with him was less because he hadn't been straight with her in the past than because of the as yet unknown factor her strange encounter with John Baldwin had injected into her emotions?

But there could be no second thoughts on the twenty million dollars. If Teddy had married her for what he thought he could get out of her rather than for love, the less he knew of that the better. So she said, 'Yes, wasn't it?'

'Mind you,' he said. 'It would be nice if there was that kind of dough lying around, and we knew just where it was. I mean, since you lost the travellers' cheques, and now you've given Shana fifty thousand . . . was that necessary?'

'We had a deal.'

'Oh. Well, in that case . . . but we're down to fifty thousand, with steamship tickets to buy, and—'

'The steamship tickets are bought and paid for,' she told him. 'They, and my passport, are waiting for us in Boston.'

'Holy Cow! Say, just what else have you done this past week and forgotten to tell me?'

She smiled at him. 'I'll try to remember.'

'Do that.' He was definitely annoyed at being left out of so many of her plans. 'But the fact is we don't have all that much to play with, do we?'

'Fifty thousand dollars should keep the wolf from the door until we can reclaim on those travellers' cheques. And if we run short, perhaps your dad could lend us some.'

'Oh,' he said. 'Ah well, the fact is, Julie, I was going to ask you if you could let me have ten thousand.'

She raised her eyebrows.

'Well – I borrowed it off the old man already, you see. And frankly, in these times, even the law ain't a very lucrative profession. I know he had to dip into his savings to give me the money. I sure would like to pay him back.'

262

'Of course you'll pay him back, Teddy,' she said. 'But in the name of God, what did you need to borrow ten thousand for?'

'I didn't know how much we'd need. When I heard how you'd been arrested, I thought maybe they'd have confiscated your money, and, heck, I didn't know what to think.'

He was looking as woebegone as only Teddy Longman could look. 'Relax,' she said. 'I understand. But what did you spend it on?'

'Well, actually, it was a damned good thing I had it. I had to buy the gun, and then . . .' he sighed, and grinned at the same time. 'I didn't really bust my way into the A and M building. I bribed the janitor.'

'You mean you didn't hit that goon over the head?' she cried. Was another dream about to be shattered?

'Oh, I did that.' Another grin. 'I didn't have any money left to bribe him with. Anyway, he didn't look the type.'

'He wasn't,' she agreed. 'Oh, Teddy, if you weren't such a liar, I could adore you.'

'Meaning you don't adore me now.'

'Meaning I don't know whether to laugh at you or cry.' She opened her handbag, took out a wad of notes, and gave him some. 'There's your ten thousand.'

'Gee,' he said. 'I don't know what I'd do without you, Julie. My folks are going to be so happy to meet you.'

She wondered if he meant that they might not have been had he not repaid the loan – with her money.

He telephoned them from the station. Julie would have taken a cab, but he didn't want to appear suddenly, he said. It was now quite late and she was more exhausted than ever, so that Mrs Longman quickly decided that what she needed was supper and bed. Mrs Longman was tall and thin like her son, as was her husband, and they both seemed very neat, quiet people, even if, to Julie's surprise, they lived not in a house but in an apartment, and a curiously new apartment, she felt. They had done their best to turn it into an instant home, with family photographs and old furniture heirlooms, yet she couldn't escape the feeling that they hadn't been here very long. But she didn't want to pry; perhaps the Depression had made them sell their house, and they were even more strapped than Teddy had indicated.

263

She also didn't know how much Teddy had told them about her, because he hadn't told her, and with so much else on her mind she had forgotten to ask. Certainly they seemed to have no inkling of what had been happening in New York, or of who she really was, or even that her father had been killed . . . although they seemed to know he had died suddenly. Fortunately she was in her bedroom with Teddy before she could give herself away. Then she did ask him.

'Well, to tell you the truth, I thought it best to tell them as little as possible at this stage,' he said. 'So I said your father had just died, kind of sudden, and that you're an orphan, and that we met, and . . . I decided to get married instead of going back to Oxford.'

'Oh. Don't they have to find out the truth, sometime? What about my arrest? Didn't you have to explain that?'

'They don't know you've been arrested.'

'But when you asked for the ten thousand . . .'

'I told Father I'd had to borrow the money for our passages and the honeymoon.'

'Oh, God,' she said. 'If you would only try telling the truth, straight down the middle, you'd find life one hell of a lot easier. You mean you never asked him for help from his friends. You never had any intention of doing that.'

'Well . . . I was going to. But it would have needed too many explanations when I heard of your arrest. I just knew I had to get back down and get you out of gaol as rapidly as possible.'

She gave up. 'Have you repaid him the money?'

'Yeah. Julie . . .' he held her hands. 'Don't be mad at me. I did what I thought was best, honest.'

She hesitated, then smiled. 'Okay, Teddy. I know you did. But tomorrow we come clean, right?'

'No, please.'

'Why not?'

'Because it would upset them too much. They really went for you. I could see it. But they went for Julie Allen. To have them discover you're Julie Armitage, and everything else, the deaths, the rapes . . . that I was involved in anything like that . . . God, it would crucify them. I'm their only son, you know.'

She gazed at him. Of course what he was saying this time could be true. But . . . 'You mean I, we, have to live a lie as regards your parents for the rest of our lives?'

264

'Just give it time, Julie. Please.'

She sighed. 'All right. Now I just have to lie down or I'm going to fall down.'

'So nothing for hubby again tonight.'

She kissed him. 'I'm not quite the iron woman you seem to think I am, Teddy. I really am played out, in every way. My back still hurts and, well . . .'

He put his arm round her shoulders. 'The rapes.'

'Yes,' she said. 'The rapes.'

'God, if I'd known—'

'You'd have got your head shot off trying to avenge me? I've been avenged.'

'Yeah, but you had to settle Kaley yourself. When I think of that . . .'

'It's done. Done, done, done. Teddy, just give me a few days.'

He kissed her on the forehead. 'You can have all the time you want, sweetheart. Just so long as one day Julie Allen comes back to me.'

She could do no wrong in his eyes at the moment. Because she was Julie Armitage and he was afraid of her? She hoped not. Or because they had not yet found her father's fortune? She hoped that even less.

But it was very necessary to make a decision about it, because as her brain became less tired and she began to attempt to put the thoughts and ideas which had drifted through her mind into some kind of order, she realised there was no way she was going to succeed in her quest without constant and close help. Baldwin would certainly help, and how she would love to be able to summon him to her aid – but as he had explained, he was a police officer and he would have to take a different view to her as to whom the money really belonged.

There was no one else, except Teddy.

The decision slowly hardened, and became easier to make as the next couple of days went by. If she could not become the least intimate with the senior Longmans, partly because of the lie she was living as regards them and partly because of their obviously reduced circumstances, Teddy, on his home ground, was the old Teddy of their first days together in London. The hesitancy that had character-ised his dealings with the mob – how had he found the guts to storm the A and M building, even with the support of ten thousand dollars? – had disappeared, and he was as knowledgeable and masterful as

265

when he had first attracted her. And Boston was his own home town, and had a history longer than any other part of the United States, save perhaps Virginia.

He drove her into the country, out to Concord, to show her the bridge where the 'shot heard around the world' had been fired, and he explored the old town with her, and took her across to Bunker Hill, where the famous battle had been fought, and he showed her over the *USS Constitution*, Old Ironsides, at her permanent berth in the Charles River. 'One always feels that English people coming here feel, well . . . squashed,' he said. 'But heck, you're an American.'

Even if an exile, she thought, as from tomorrow. But he was trying so hard; the newspapers were beginning to reveal that there had been a series of massive police raids on various offices, apartments and speakeasies in New York, undoubtedly related to the Long Island Massacre as it was already known, and perhaps also to the Battle of Jamaica Bay, as the scene had been described by the first officers to get there. The news that Eddie Armitage was dead, as well as his right-hand man, Hanson Pierce, had also been released. But there was no further mention of the 'red-headed woman in black', and no mention at all of either Shana Evans or Teddy Longman; Zeidler was keeping his side of the bargain just as long as he could, and she was grateful for that.

That night she at last let Teddy make love to her again, and realised that it was the first time she had lain in his arms since their last night on the *Bremen*, and thus the first time they had ever slept together on American soil. But she did not confide in him until they were actually at sea, after a tearful farewell from Mr and Mrs Longman.

'Cherbourg?' Teddy demanded as the ship steered past Deer Island, and he examined their tickets for the first time. 'How're we going to find your dad's money in France?'

'We're not, I shouldn't think. But I have to make sure I'm going to be allowed back into England.'

'You're Mrs Edward Longman the Third.'

'I'm also née Armitage, on my passport, and very unpopular, I understand, with Scotland Yard. Don't worry, I have someone working on it.'

He frowned at her as they went down to their cabin; the North

266

Atlantic was choppy today. 'You're not up to your secret deals again? Who's working on it?'

'Zeidler is setting it up,' she said. So, she was now the one who was lying. But to tell Teddy about Baldwin right now would provoke a row. If he had lied about Baldwin not being a true policeman, she was going to have to wait for him either to confess it or give himself away and at the same time tell her why.

'Zeidler? You mean you have another deal with him?'

'Not really.'

'Then why is he the least interested in you now? He's got the Association, and you're out of the States. What more does he want?'

Julie lay down and stared at the iron deckhead above her, felt the slow roll of the ship as she met the waves, the occasional shudder as she plunged into the troughs; she loved being at sea. It relaxed her. But this was the crunch; she couldn't afford to be relaxed.

'He would like to find out about Daddy's money, I think,' she said.

'Oh, yeah? So he can stick his finger in?'

'Well I don't know about that. It's rather a lot of money.'

'Yeah?' He was interested. 'How much?'

'How much do you reckon it should be?'

'If he'd been salting away something like seventy-five grand a year for, ten years . . . heck, that's three-quarters of a million pounds. Holy Cow! You are rich, after all.'

'Yes,' she said. 'I could be. But there's a little more than that involved.'

'More? How much more?'

'How would twenty million dollars grab you?'

He had been lying down as well. Now he slowly sat up.

'You see,' she explained, 'I wasn't lying to Hanson Pierce. MacGinnion did kill Daddy for the money, because he reckoned he could get it out of me. I think he was afraid of Daddy, for all his size and bluster.'

'You mean your dad was embezzling from the Association?'

'I'm afraid so.'

'Well, goddamn . . . twenty million! You sure it's that much?'

'That's how much MacGinnion said it was. And I can tell you that he was deadly serious.'

'And you know where it is? You must've known all the time. And you say you can't trust me?'

267

'I don't know where it is, Teddy. And I didn't know all the time. But I'm beginning to have a pretty good idea. There are still one hell of a lot of things about this business I don't understand, but there are some of them which seem to make sense.'

'Such as?'

'Well, let's go through it from the beginning. Daddy gets killed by a tramp. We know it wasn't a tramp, but a hit man sent across by MacGinnion. I don't suppose we'll ever find out who the actual murderer was, but I don't suppose that's important now, either. MacGinnion killed Daddy because he was sure I knew where the money was, and I am pretty sure he put someone on to tailing me wherever I went. I think it was that man I saw at the inquest. I've never been so sure of anything in my life. Anyway, I didn't go and get the money, because I didn't know anything about it. I don't know what MacGinnion would eventually have done – he certainly was aware of almost everything that happened in England between Daddy's death and our departure for the States – but in any event when he was told we were on our way, he decided to stop trailing me, and to torture it out of me if he had to. I would say he was getting just a little panicky then, because you had turned up, like the joker in a pack of cards. He couldn't place you, and he didn't know what you were after. And when we got married, it must have put the wind up him, because suddenly I was no longer a lonely little girl. Make sense so far?'

'Yeah,' Teddy said. 'Supposing he knew we were married.'

'Oh, he knew,' she said. 'He knew everything. Anyway, we got over there and he promptly tried to kidnap me. Only Hanson Pierce got there first. But because I didn't know what was going on, I blundered out of Pierce's custody and into MacGinnion's. And was in dead trouble until you came along once again.' She squeezed his hand, because she wanted him with her all the way, now. 'Mind you, I think he slipped up there. The way they suddenly stopped mauling me and just pushed off for the night. But of course, he had no idea that I could possibly be rescued.' She gave his hand another squeeze. 'He thought you were a negligible quantity.'

'Yes,' Teddy said thoughtfully.

'Okay. So then I thought I was using Pierce to avenge Daddy, and myself, and Pierce thought he was using me to take over the Association, and bingo. But the one factor, the only factor, that has remained constant from beginning to end, is that no one over here save MacGinnion, Kaley and Cerdo knew anything about the twenty million. MacGinnion wouldn't even let any of his goons stay in the room while they were asking me about it. Now, if we accept what seems certain, that Daddy didn't share his secret with them, but that they somehow found out, it means Daddy didn't share his secret with anyone, right? Because he certainly didn't share it with me.'

'I follow that. But I don't see how it helps us.'

'Simply this. MacGinnion found out that Daddy was living a double life and was mad as hell. I found out that Daddy was living a double life, and was horrified. But neither of us could see the wood for trees. Daddy must actually have been living a *third* life, unknown to either of us. And which had nothing to do with either of us, too. Because I just know you were right in the very beginning: if Daddy had meant that money to come to me he would have left some pointer. But he didn't. So it must have gone to someone else.'

'Holy Smoke. He was some character. But it doesn't make sense, Julie. I traced his movements, remember? New York, London, Epsom, London, New York. Regular as clockwork. So where was this third home he was maintaining?'

'I didn't say it was a home, Teddy. I said it was a life. A life can be many things. We think of it as conventional, home, wife, kids, car, pets, garden, but those are just aspects of a certain kind of life. A life is what we are actually doing with our brains and our bodies and our resources, the goals we have, the ambitions we mean to achieve.'

'I'm still not with you, sweetheart. Because apart from running a criminal empire, which we know about, and fathering you, which we also know about, your daddy seems to have done nothing but travel in ships or trains. That's a life?'

'Agreed. But you can live a life vicariously as well, you know.'

'Come again?'

'A general in an army is a soldier, right? But once he's a general he doesn't actually hold a gun and rush into battle. He sits behind the lines with his maps and his staff officers and tells other men where to go and get killed. Yet fighting the battle is his life, probably more so than for the men in the front line.'

Teddy scratched his chin, but he was frowning thoughtfully. 'Like you said, he has his staff officers.'

269

'And Daddy had his.'

He raised his head.

'Think of this. Who picked me up in Switzerland? Who knew more about me than I knew about myself? Who claimed to be in love with me although he had never actually seen me? Who swore that he had nothing to do with Daddy's criminal organisation, however much he knew about it? Who felt he had to protect me, even to the extent of cabling Hanson Pierce that I was on my way to New York and would need protection, but who had to send the cable as Daddy because Pierce would never have heard of him? He also didn't know Pierce would try to double cross me, but that was my fault, for telling him Daddy was dead in the first place.'

'Holy Smoke!'

'And who,' Julie went on, 'has been trying to stop us looking for the money from the start? That's where I went wrong. I thought he was interested himself. But of course he knew about it all the time, and about where it was. Just as he knew it wasn't intended for me. What surprised him, and misled us, was that Father had apparently left no provision for me at all, beyond the house and the few thousand in the bank. And he couldn't understand that.'

'Yeah,' Teddy said. 'You know something, Julie – your dad comes across as pretty much of a heel.'

'To you and me. Because I was never important to him. I thought I was. He was the most important thing in the world to me. But I understand now that to him I was just an appendage he had picked up along the way, to whom he felt he owed a certain duty. Nothing more than that. Okay, so that makes me feel just wonderful. It doesn't matter now. But I don't think even the Association meant that much to him – not after he started embezzling. I think for the past ten years Father has only been interested in this third life. Nothing else.'

'And now your Uncle Bob has it all.'

'We don't know yet what it is.'

'But Uncle Bob does.'

'Yes,' she said, and smiled at him. 'It gives us a target, anyway.'

CHAPTER 13

Suddenly it was like the voyage across. They had left everything unpleasant behind them, and were honeymooning, and were again engaged on a great adventure. Which they thought they could handle. But this time she was far more confident. Because if she was right about Uncle Bob, then they now held all the secrets, and he didn't know that. That was a whole different ball game.

She understood that Teddy's euphoria was at the thought of all that money, waiting to be found, and she reminded him that it was her intention to give it all back.

'You're kidding,' he protested.

'I was never more serious in my life.'

'Who're you going to give it back to?'

'I don't know. Some charity or something.'

'Okay,' he said. 'Okay. That's a great thought. But twenty million dollars . . . there's no charity in existence could absorb that much all at one go. Give them some. You gotta keep some for yourself.'

'Well, maybe a little,' she agreed. She would like to send Shana some more money as well.

'And what about Uncle Bob?'

'That,' she said, 'depends on Uncle Bob.'

When she had left England, only a fortnight before, she had been an innocent girl. She was returning a woman who had killed, and who had learned how to hate – and to manipulate. Uncle Bob didn't know those things yet.

Did Teddy, fully? He was rapidly becoming his old, masterful self, and she was letting him get on with it. She liked masterful men, even if she now knew Teddy could never actually master her. He

271

clearly thought that once they found the money, he would take charge, humour her a little as regards her weird idea of doing some good with it, and have the larger part to live on for the rest of his days. If he had married her for her inheritance, he had watched it grow from perhaps a few hundred thousand through three-quarters of a million, to a quite unimaginable total, all in a month. No wonder he was euphoric.

And he had no idea that she understood all of that, that she even understood all of his machinations. Clearly the Baldwin deceit had been simply to stop her ever inclining towards surrendering all her knowledge to Scotland Yard. The odd thing was that while she thought of the two times he had lied to her – and she wasn't sure he hadn't lied to her about the ten thousand dollars either, but had needed the money to settle some long-standing debt of his own – made her angry, she knew that had he not lied she would not be where she was today. Had he not convinced her the police knew nothing about her father, she might very well have surrendered and given them everything she knew and be left with just the house in Epsom and four thousand pounds. And had he not forged her birth certificate she would never have gone to the United States, and become, just for a week, the Queen of the Mob – and caused eighteen men to be shot dead. And she knew that, for all the horror involved, she wouldn't have missed a moment of her adventure. Except the little room above MacGinnion's office. She could have done without that. Yet in some ways that had made her what she was now, a woman who could take care of herself.

None of that resolved her dilemma with Teddy. But it made her more confident that she could deal with it. However often he had deceived her, as long as she always knew when he was doing it he could cause her no harm. And if he had married her for her money, she intended to keep control of that – and he *had* married her. He was her husband, the only man with whom she had ever willingly shared a bed, and he was everything she could imagine of a man in bed. Well, perhaps not quite, if she ever allowed the memory of that afternoon in the woods by Jamaica Bay to intrude. But she was old-fashioned enough to feel such thoughts were immoral.

While the impassioned exuberance of their first few days together had faded slightly, she felt that in time she could establish a far more important, and loving, relationship with him. That she had to do, because beneath all the superficial toughness she had been forced to develop, the ruthlessness with which she had sought her goals, she was terribly aware that there still remained only a lonely young girl, without a relative in the world, save for this odd man who had so strangely swum into her life. She couldn't afford to let him go.

It was the first time she had been able to think about her situation so objectively, but her thoughts were still overlaid with the excitement of the quest that lay ahead of them. As were Teddy's, which was probably just as well. He talked of nothing else. 'You say Zeidler is smoothing your entrance into England,' he said. 'What then?'

'We go back to the apartment,' she said. 'As if we have spent the past couple of weeks honeymooning. No one is going to know any different, except for one or two Scotland Yard policemen.' She glanced at him. 'Does that bother you?'

'Not if it doesn't bother you. And then what?'

'Well, George isn't going to suspect anything, that's for sure. So we just sit tight, and wait for Uncle Bob to turn up.'

'And?'

'I'm inclined to play it straight. Uncle Bob doesn't have Daddy's money. I'm sure of that. But he knows where it is, and he has helped Daddy set up whatever the money is being used for. I'm sure of that too. So if we make it plain we know all about it, I think he will decide to negotiate.'

'I wouldn't be too sure of *that*. We may have to use a bit of muscle.'

'If we have to, we will.'

'Yeah,' he said. 'I'd enjoy using a bit of muscle on that character.'

'Only if we have to,' she reminded him. 'And I'll decide when.'

'You're the boss,' he said with his disarming grin.

They docked in Cherbourg and found an hotel. Fortunately there was no telephone in the room, so she waited until Teddy was taking a bath then went downstairs to the booth, and put through a call to London, her heart pounding as she asked for the magic numbers: suppose they did say there was no one by that name at the Yard? But five minutes later she heard a familiar voice on the line. 'Baldwin?'

'I owe you one shirt,' she said.

'Julie!' His voice was excited. 'Where are you?'

273

'Cherbourg.'

'Hell. When did you arrive?'

'A couple of hours ago. When did you get back?'

'Yesterday. We've cut it pretty fine. How did it go in New York?'

'Blood everywhere,' she said. 'But the deed is done. I want to come to London tomorrow.'

'Ah. How?'

'Cross-channel ferry to Portsmouth.'

'Hmm,' he said. 'Right. I'll be there to make sure there's no trouble. But Julie, there's a small complication.'

'What?'

'I can't explain it over the phone. I want to see you the moment you reach London.'

'It'll be tricky. Teddy is with me.'

'That golddigger? I thought you'd have unloaded him.'

'He's my husband, Baldwin. Where I go, he goes. Okay?'

A brief hesitation. She wondered if he'd say, like everyone else, you're the boss. Instead he said, 'And you reckon you're on the trail of something.'

'Yes.'

'What?'

'I'll tell you when I work it all out. But it is essential that I return to England. You promised.'

'And I'm going to keep my word. It's just the thought of you and that louse—'

'Are you propositioning a married woman, Sergeant?'

She heard him smile into the mouthpiece. 'Could be.'

'Well, I have your telephone number. You'd better keep your fingers crossed.'

'Joking apart,' he said. 'Use it. The moment you get to London.'

'Is it serious?'

'Very, from your point of view.'

She hesitated. But she did want to see him again. 'All right,' she said. 'I'll be in touch. Baldwin . . . I enjoyed wearing your shirt.'

'I enjoyed lending it to you. I'll be waiting to hear from you, Julie.'

The phone went dead, and she leaned against the wall and took several deep breaths. Flirting with Baldwin was fun – if she was flirting. And what was this important matter he had to see her about?

274

Had they found out something more about Daddy? That would be too good, or maybe too bad, to be true. But maybe it was just an excuse to see her. She hoped so.

'Where the devil have you been?' Teddy demanded when she returned to the room.

'Ringing London.'

'For Jesus' sake! Who?'

'The contact Zeidler gave me. Everything's okay. We go across tomorrow.'

'I'm not sure I like the idea of you working quite so close with the DA,' he grumbled. 'Does he have tabs on us?'

'Not so far as I know,' she said, and took him in her arms. 'He trusts me. Maybe you could try doing the same.'

Baldwin was as good as his word, and when they disembarked at Portsmouth there were no questions asked. She kept looking around her, expecting to catch a glimpse of him, but she didn't. They took the train to London, and arrived just after five, to the delight of George. 'Miss Julie! Mr Longman. Did you have a good honeymoon? I must say, you're looking well.'

'It was a lovely honeymoon, George,' Julie said. 'Have there been any callers?'

'Not really. Major Roberts dropped by once or twice to see if I knew when you were coming back. But nobody else. But the fact is, Miss Julie, I haven't heard from your dad, either. I'm getting kind of worried.'

Julie had already chosen her tactics for this one; it was very unlikely George ever read any American newspaper, and there was little chance that Eddie Armitage's death, or indeed his connection with London's underworld, had yet been revealed in England. 'That's all right, George,' she told him. 'We honeymooned on the continent, and Daddy was able to join us for a couple of days. He's been delayed, but he'll be back in a week or two.'

'Oh, that does relieve me so, Miss Julie.'

'Did Major Roberts say if he would be dropping by again?'

'Why, no, miss. But I expect he will.'

'I'm sure. But the next time he comes, George, do telephone me before you let him up.'

'He has his own key, miss.'

275

'I'm sure he does. And that is fine when Father is living in the flat. But the last time he came he walked in on me in my bath, and I really don't want that happening again. So please, stop him down here and give me a call first, will you? You can tell him those are my instructions.'

Teddy watched her with his crooked grin, and when they had shut the flat door behind them he said, 'You are a far better liar then I could ever be.'

'I'm not.'

'How do you reckon that?'

'Simply because I think you sometimes believe yourself. I haven't made that mistake yet.'

'It's making the other guy believe you that counts,' he said. 'Glad to be home?'

'Oh, am I. I think I'm going to make this our permanent address.'

'Can we afford the rent?'

'I think so. I intend to tell the situation to Cornwall just as soon as we've sorted out Uncle Bob, and get the whole thing cleared away. I'm both Julie Allen and Julie Armitage, and I can prove it. Thus I'm entitled to the four thousand odd down in Epsom, and the house, and whatever is in Daddy's bank account. Five thousand pounds, isn't it?'

'And you reckon the police are going to let you keep that?'

'It's mine.'

'What about the London racket?'

'I'll give them what I have on that too, and they can do what they like with it.'

'You have it all thought out,' he said. 'But just in case, I intend to start tomorrow on reclaiming those travellers' cheques.'

'Then we'll have more money than we know what to do with.'

'With twenty million to follow. Yippee.'

'A little of it,' she reminded him.

'A little bit of twenty million is still a lot of dough. Sweetheart, I hate to say it, but stumbling over your dad's body was the best thing that ever happened to me.' He held her shoulders. 'I hope you feel that I was at least some compensation for being orphaned.'

She kissed him. 'Some.'

But she was genuinely happy, genuinely relaxed, it seemed for the

276

first time in her life. The traumas were behind her, she was sure. Certainly there could never be another trauma to compare with what she had experienced in New York. Alongside Big Pat MacGinnion, Uncle Bob had to be a teddy bear. And once she had been afraid of him!

But first, there was Baldwin, and the thought of that was making her just as happy.

'Where'll we eat?' Teddy wanted to know.

'Anywhere you like. But I simply have to have my hair done first,' she said. 'It needs cutting and washing, and I know I look a perfect sight.'

'You gonna find anywhere open at this hour?'

'I think so. There's a salon just round the corner which I noticed stayed open fairly late, when last we were here. Tell me where we're eating, and I'll meet you there.'

'Okay. There's an oyster bar just off Dover Street.'

'Great. See you there at seven-thirty.' She hurried off before he could argue. A bride of hardly a fortnight, deceiving her husband. And so happily. But it was all helping towards their reaching the goal which was the most important thing in life for them both, at the moment. She didn't think they could settle down to being happily married until Daddy and his money were finally laid to rest. Then she would say goodbye to Baldwin, and turn her back forever on Julie Armitage – because Baldwin only belonged in Julie Armitage's world. He had nothing to do with Julie Allen. Or with Mrs Edward Longman the Third, really.

She hurried along the street, and slowly became aware of a peculiar sensation, that she was being followed. She knew it had to be sheer guilty conscience, but she couldn't shrug it off. She didn't know anything about being tailed, and she accomplished nothing by doing what she had seen in movies, like stopping to look in shop windows or suddenly turning round; everyone behind her seemed to be going about his or her legitimate business. She didn't know whether to be alarmed or not; it could not conceivably be Teddy. But there were so many ramifications in this business and she still had no idea what was on Baldwin's mind. She decided it would probably be an idea to take no risks, so she abandoned the idea of using a phonebooth, and did indeed go to a beauty parlour.

Which happened to be open. 'But,' the receptionist said, 'I'm afraid we're fully booked this evening, madam. I can make you an appointment for tomorrow morning.'

'Actually, what I would like to do is use your phone,' Julie said.

'Our phone, madam?'

'There's a man following me,' Julie told her, not sure whether she was lying or not. 'And I wish to ring my husband. He's a Scotland Yard detective,' she added.

'Oh,' the girl said, suddenly entirely co-operative.

Julie dialled.

'Are you at the flat?' Baldwin asked.

'No. A beauty parlour two blocks away.'

'Just off Curzon Street,' he said. 'I know it. Does Teddy know what you're at?'

'Of course. But I have the strangest feeling I'm being followed.'

'That wouldn't surprise me. There are still far too many people know you as Julie Armitage. All right. Wait for ten minutes and then go out of the back door of the shop. That should fox whoever it is. Turn right at the next street and you'll find yourself in Berkeley Square. Wait on the corner and I'll pick you up. Ten minutes.' He hung up.

'Is there a back way out?' Julie asked.

'Well, I suppose so,' the girl said.

'Thanks a million,' Julie said, and was taken through the salon, past a row of women with their heads encased in driers, and an assistant having a cup of tea, to a door leading on to an alleyway. 'Which way is Berkeley Square?'

'Just turn right at the street.'

'Great. Oh . . .' Julie took out a five-pound note. 'If anyone were to ask, would you tell them I'm having my hair done?'

The girl looked at the money. 'Why not?' she agreed.

Baldwin was waiting for her on the corner as promised, driving a nondescript-looking car. 'Everything all right?' he asked.

'I think so.'

'What about your tail?'

'I don't even know if there was one. But if there was I've got rid of him.'

'That's my Julie.' He was watching the traffic.

'It's so good to see you again,' she said.

'Ditto. But Julie . . . my bosses aren't.'

'They let me in.'

'Because I convinced them they should. But they want co-operation, or they're going to put you back out.'

'Can they do that?'

'I'm afraid they can. You're an American citizen, and you are known to have been involved in criminal activities in New York. If not here.'

'But Baldwin – you know that's not true.'

'Julie, I know that it is true, as regards New York.'

Her shoulders slumped. She had been so looking forward to this meeting. 'So what happens now? Baldwin, we are close. I know we are close, to finding out about the money. And Baldwin, it's no matter of just half a million pounds.'

'I rather gathered that,' he said, still watching the traffic as he followed the stream. 'We've located your father's private deposit account.'

'Have you?' She was excited. 'Is there much in it?'

'Close to a million.'

'Good Lord,' she said. But it had been too much to hope Daddy would have had the twenty million in an English deposit account. 'Daddy seems to have been a regular magpie.'

'You don't seem very impressed.'

'Well . . . he has another twenty million dollars tucked away somewhere.'

Now at last he looked at her. 'What did you say?'

'It's a fact. That's what all the ruckus has been about really. Why he was killed. He stole it from the Association. What's that, about five million pounds, right?'

'Yes,' he said.

'So that's what we're looking for. You can't expect me to go through the roof at a mere one million.'

'Goddamn,' Baldwin said. 'I wish you hadn't told me that, Julie. I'm going to have to report it.'

'So? Make your bosses jealous.'

'Julie, they don't feel you are entitled to that money. Any of it.'

'I know that.'

He continued speaking as if what she had said had not immediately registered. 'They think that if you want to settle in this

279

country you should make arrangements to dispose of the money in a suitable way.' Then the penny dropped. 'You know that?' he cried.

'Of course I do. Although what your people are saying sounds very much like blackmail to me.'

He grinned. 'Governments don't blackmail people, Julie. They make certain proposals.'

'Do I get any of it?'

'I think a modicum can be arranged. Enough for you to live on.'

'Teddy is just going to love that. And if I say no deal, it's on the next boat back to the States, eh?'

'I'm afraid so. With full publicity. And Julie, there are a lot of people in the States who must be feeling they owe you one.'

'I know that,' she said. 'Besides, Zeidler and I have a deal; if I turn up there again he puts me in gaol as well. All right, Baldwin, your non-blackmailing government wins. As I said, I wasn't going to keep the money anyway. Well, not all of it. But – I haven't even got the twenty million yet. You can have the rest to go on with, but you may have to wait a while for the lot.'

'But you have an idea where it is.'

'I have an idea who knows.'

'Who?'

She hesitated.

'You must co-operate, Julie.'

She shrugged. 'I think Uncle Bob knows. In fact, I'm sure of it. And I think I can get it out of him. But Baldwin, no muscling in by any flatfooted bobby.'

'Meaning me?'

'Or any of your pals. Uncle Bob isn't going to tell anybody but me.'

'And then you're going to tell me.'

'When I've got the money.'

He shook his head. 'Sorry, Julie. Look at it from our point of view. I might trust you, but to the Home Secretary you are merely a red-handed murderess, the type of person we can do without in this country. He's prepared to go along with my superiors for the time being, and they are prepared to go along with me, because I have promised them that you will be one hundred per cent co-operative. The moment you find out where that money is, you have to tell me.'

280

Julie considered. Then shrugged again. 'Okay. You're sure I'm going to get something out of this?'

'Something. So we'll be keeping an eye on you.' He drew to a halt, and she discovered that they were back in Berkeley Square. 'If you go back to your beauty parlour, you will have fooled the world.' He squeezed her hand. 'We'll be keeping an eye on you. And I'll be looking forward to hearing from you.'

'I love you too,' she said, and got out, stood on the pavement to watch him drive away. Of all the goddamned cheek, she thought. Stay in Britain, but hand over six million pounds for that right. Then she laughed out loud. What did it matter, compared with having Baldwin keeping an eye on her?

She went back to the scandalised beauty parlour, and emerged from their front door. 'Well, heck,' Teddy said when she got to the oyster bar. 'You don't look a bit different to me.'

'I'm not supposed to look different,' she told him. 'Only to feel different. That's the secret.'

Teddy as usual was raring to go next morning, and set off with the travellers' cheques' numbers. Julie slept in, lazily – she had not been allowed to sleep much during the night – nor had she wanted to. Now she was sated, content, happy and secure. She was in partnership with the British police. It wasn't possible to feel more secure than that. Her resentment had faded – in fact she felt quite excited about it; the only problem was going to be breaking the news to Teddy. That, she decided, would have to wait until they had actually found the money.

When she got up she made herself some coffee and boiled an egg, then sat in her dressing-gown enjoying the sunlight drifting through the window. This apartment couldn't compare with Daddy's pad in New York but it was one hell of a lot safer.

Simply because in England things happened on a smaller scale. When the telephone rang, she knew who it had to be, but she also knew no one was going to come charging through the door behind a machine-gun, and equally that Uncle Bob would have no suspicion of the sort of welcome he was going to get.

She picked up the receiver. 'Yes.'

'Good morning, Mrs Longman,' George said formally. 'You asked me to inform you when Major Roberts called. He's here now.'

'Thank you, George,' she said. 'Ask him to come up, will you?'

'Right away, miss.'

Julie went into the bedroom, checked her pistol. Then she unlatched the door, and stood beside it against the wall, as she remembered Shana doing at the Plaza. She breathed slowly and deeply, and her muscles were tensed, but she was neither afraid nor overly apprehensive of the coming minutes.

There was a knock.

'It's open,' she said.

The door swung inwards, and Uncle Bob stepped into the lobby, stood there for a moment, then took another step forward. 'Julie?' he called.

Julie closed the door and slipped the latch in the same movement, using her left hand. Then she brought the hand back on to the pistol to join her right, and held it levelled before her face, arms extended. Uncle Bob had heard the noise and started to turn. 'Just don't move,' she said. 'Or I will blow your head right off.'

'You – Julie?' But he didn't turn. She had won an initial victory.

'Go into the lounge,' she ordered. 'Then sit on the settee. But Uncle Bob . . . I don't know if you are armed, but if you are, I wouldn't put a hand near your pockets.'

He hesitated, then again obeyed, walking across the carpet with his hands held away from his sides. When he reached the settee he turned, immediately looking for her. But she had already slipped into the kitchen, and had taken up a position at the hatch, where she could keep him in her sight but was only half visible herself. 'Sit down,' she repeated.

Slowly he lowered himself on the cushion. 'Your idea of a game, Julie?'

'Yes,' she said. 'I play it every day now. It's called survival.'

'So you've learned about things like that.' He had to know where she was now, but he was looking straight ahead.

'I'm here, Uncle Bob. Would you like to know what I've been doing this past fortnight or so?'

'I read the papers, Julie. Seems to me you've learned a great deal. Most of it bad.'

'Well, I didn't have much choice,' she told him. 'But I also learned about the twenty million, from Pat MacGinnion – before I killed him.'

282

'You killed MacGinnion?'

'And Kaley, Uncle Bob. And Hanson Pierce, when it became necessary.' Nor, she reflected, was she entirely lying. Without her they would all still be alive, torturing helpless girls.

'Jesus Christ.'

'So, as the saying goes, in for a penny, in for a pound.'

He continued to stare straight ahead of him. But she knew he wasn't as calm as he pretended; there were beads of sweat on his forehead. 'You will probably find that the British police aren't quite as relaxed about that sort of thing as your American friends.'

She smiled. 'I'm on very good terms with the police, Uncle Bob. Now tell me about the money.'

'What money?'

'The twenty million that Daddy stole from the Association over the past ten years.'

'I have no idea what you're talking about. Twenty million dollars? That's an enormous sum of money.'

'Oh, it is, Uncle Bob. But how did you know I was talking about dollars? I didn't say so.'

He began to turn his head, then checked the movement. 'I made an assumption.'

'So give.'

'I know nothing about any money, Julie.'

'Uncle Bob, you're pushing your luck. Let me tell you about the money. I had a chance to go through the Association's books while I was in New York. Seems Daddy was the overall finance manager, and because he was Eddie Armitage, the Boss, and everyone was afraid of him, he could virtually do what he liked. So back in 1920 he began to siphon off two million dollars a year, out of cash receipts. He did this every year right down to this one, when at last MacGinnion found out what he was doing, and had him murdered. You with me so far?'

'It's a very interesting story, Julie.'

'I'm glad you're enjoying it. MacGinnion had this crazy idea that he could get the money back from me where he wouldn't have dared try to accuse Daddy of embezzling. Well, he was wrong, and now he's dead. But that doesn't answer the question of what Daddy did with all that money. And everyone who was looking for it, including me, made two basic mistakes: we all assumed that Daddy actually

283

cared about me, wanted to leave me set up for life. He didn't. And we all – never having had money like that ourselves – assumed that Daddy would use some very elaborate and safe way of getting the money to wherever he wanted it to go. But Daddy had so much money it never meant anything to him; leaving it lying about didn't bother him at all. The strange thing is that I knew this from the very first day I came to this flat, but it didn't register. There was a suitcase containing fifty thousand pounds just sitting on the floor, and George said that the suitcases came pretty regularly, so sometimes there must have been three or four of them just stacked here, waiting for Daddy to turn up, and it never concerned him in the slightest, apparently. And that money was peanuts compared with what he was bringing across the Atlantic, in his suitcases, in cash. We worked that one out, but we couldn't work out what he did with it when he got here. He went to his club once or twice, and then he went down to Epsom, with one of his cases stuffed with paper. Somewhere between leaving the ship at Southampton and arriving in Epsom he unloaded something like a million dollars a trip. But how, and to whom? We couldn't find any answer to that, and we couldn't find any bank account into which it had gone. It never occurred to us that the money hadn't gone anywhere. He just unpacked that suitcase here, Uncle Bob, didn't he? And left the money in a drawer or some place, and went away, knowing it would all be gone by the time he came back. It would have been removed by the man whose business it was to remove it. The man, the only man, who had a key to this flat and could come and go as he pleased, and who therefore would come once a week or so, and just take as much money as would comfortably fit into his pockets, and walk out again. That's why you had to leave me and rush up here the day of the funeral, isn't it, Uncle Bob? You weren't investigating Daddy's background, you were anxious to get the rest of the money out of here. Only you were too late. Someone, one of MacGinnion's men, I suppose, had already burgled the flat and taken what remained. Did you lose a lot?'

'Do you seriously suppose your father would have trusted anyone – even me – so completely?'

'Yes, Uncle Bob. You virtually claimed that he did, right after he was killed. And you were confounded to discover that, while he had let you have the disposal of all that money for so long, he had made not the slightest provision for me. I appreciate your concern, believe me, even if at the time I thought you were after whatever inheritance I had for yourself. And I appreciate your keeping tabs on me and cabling Hanson Pierce so he would look after me in New York, even if you made a big mistake there: Pierce was only ever interested in looking after Pierce. So when all is said and done, it seems that I have to make provision for myself. I don't know why Daddy trusted you so implicitly, but I do know that you took the money, and did something with it. I want to know what that was, and I want it back. So you had better start telling me the truth.'

'I'm sorry, Julie. I can't do that. And it wouldn't do you any good if I did. It's where you can never touch it.'

'And that's how Daddy wanted it to be?'

'Yes.'

'Well, it's not how I want it to be, Uncle Bob. Daddy may have been a friend of yours, but I have discovered he was never a friend of mine. Maybe it assuaged his conscience to play the loving father for three months in every year, but I was just a toy to him. He didn't leave me anything save a memory, a memory which became more and more hideous the more I probed into it. But he overlooked one thing: he also left me an inherited character. Everyone I've met this past month has been afraid of Eddie Armitage. Well, by God, those of them that are still alive are now afraid of Eddie Armitage's daughter. Uncle Bob, I want that money. Not for myself. I want to use it for some purpose to make up for some of the things Daddy did. And I'm going to get it, no matter who I have to trample on.'

At last he turned his head. 'Are you serious?'

'I'm always serious nowadays.'

He hesitated, and she almost thought she had won. Then he shook his head. 'I can't give you the money, Julie. I have not got the power to do that.'

'But you can tell me where it is, because you know.'

'Yes, Julie, I know. But I can't tell you that, either. At least . . . you will have to give me time.'

'How much time?'

'Ah – a week. At the end of that time, I may be able to tell you where the money is. But the word is *may*. I'm not promising anything.'

'Uncle Bob, I've grown up,' Julie said. 'In a week you could have disappeared forever, with the money.'

285

'You will have to trust me, Julie. Your father did.'

'That's the worst possible recommendation,' she pointed out. 'No way.'

He hesitated, then stood up. 'So shoot me.'

She stared at him, the pistol levelled, watched him walk to the door and open it.

'One week, Julie,' he said, without turning his head, and closed the door.

She bit her lip so hard she nearly drew blood. Because he had called her bluff, and got away with it. How could he? If he had read the newspapers? But he had known she wasn't going to shoot him in cold blood. After all, he had put his faith in Julie Allen.

'Goddamn him to hell,' she growled. She had thought she could terrify anyone . . . but she had not been able to terrify Uncle Bob. She threw the pistol across the room in disgust, threw herself on the settee, glowered at the photographs of herself which filled the room. Stupid frightened cow, she thought. Now he was gone. He wouldn't be coming back. A week! God, she was hopeless.

There was a rap on the door. Julie stared at it for a moment, then rushed across the room to regain her gun. Had he come back? She stood against the wall as before, released the latch. 'Come in,' she called.

Teddy stepped into the room.

'Oh, Teddy!' She pocketed the pistol, and he closed the door, grinning at her.

'So what did he have to say?'

'He . . . you knew he was here?'

'Sure. I figured he'd do the same as last time, wait to make sure I was out of the way before coming to call. So I kind of hung around.'

'Oh, Teddy!' She was even angrier with him than with herself. 'If only you'd come up.'

'I figured you could take care of yourself, now.'

'You reckon?' She repeated their conversation, as best she could remember it.

'He's a cool customer,' Teddy agreed, and went to the bar to pour two whiskies and water. 'But we have him now.'

'We'll never see him again, you mean. Or the money. He was the only lead we have.'

'And he's all the lead we need. I'm not just a pretty face. I figured out exactly what was going to happen this morning, and I also figured that not even you were going to be able to frighten anything out of him, so . . . I went along and hired a private eye.'

'A what?'

'A detective, sweetheart. Not one of your police heavies, but a private operator. Guy I used to know once upon a time.'

He seemed to have known so many men once upon a time, from recently-ordained clergymen to forgers; presumably a private detective fitted into the middle.

'Had a stroke of luck there,' he confessed, 'because this guy was available. So we hurried back here, and got here just as Uncle Bob was leaving. He's on his tail now. He'll fill us in.'

'Oh, Teddy, I don't know what I'd do without you.'

He grinned at her. 'You don't have to do without me.'

'So what do we do now?'

'Wait for my man to report. Simple as that. Why don't you get dressed, and we'll nip out for a spot of lunch?'

She was back in control, thanks to Teddy. He had this most remarkable habit of turning up trumps whenever she really needed one. She had been tempted to telephone Baldwin to bring him up to date, out of despair, but she quickly abandoned that idea. Not only would it be terribly disloyal to Teddy, but she didn't have the time; when they got back from lunch, George said, 'There's a gentleman here to see you, Mr Longman.'

'Ah,' Teddy said, 'Where?'

'Right over there, sir.'

They turned together, to look at the featureless, nondescript little man who was seated on the upholstered bench on the far side of the lobby, and was now getting up.

'But,' Julie cried. 'I know you. You were at the inquest—' She bit her lip before she told George too much.

'That's right, Mrs Longman,' he said. 'The name's Hart. Calvin Hart.'

Julie gazed at him, then looked at Teddy, who gave one of his grins. 'I'll explain it upstairs,' he said.

Julie felt as if steam was coming out of her ears. She led them up to the flat, slammed the door. She was feeling the first pangs of indigestion.

287

'Now, sweetheart,' Teddy said. 'Don't be mad. Like I said, I've known Calvin for years.'

'You mean you were actually telling the truth this morning?'

'Well, mostly. But you see, I didn't cotton on to Uncle Bob from the beginning. You know that. So almost the first thing I did after that assault on you here was to contact Calvin and ask him to keep an eye on the guy. He was doing that at the inquest.'

'But you couldn't tell me?'

'I wasn't sure just how far you'd gone off him. I didn't want to upset you.'

'Upset me,' she snorted. 'So he actually trailed Uncle Bob here this morning.'

'That's right. And away again, I hope. Did you, Calvin?'

The detective had been waiting patiently. 'I did, Mr Longman.'

'So?'

'He returned to his club, where he stays when he is in London, and packed a bag, and then took a taxi to Victoria Station, and there took the train to Folkestone. He purchased a ticket for Boulogne.' Hart smiled. 'It is a route I know well.'

'Oh, big deal,' Julie said. 'So we know he's in France. Have you looked at a map recently? It's one hell of a big country.' She was furious, but she didn't know whether it was with Teddy for his continuing deceit or still with herself for having let Uncle Bob get away.

'Indeed, Mrs Longman,' Hart agreed. 'But we will soon know where Major Roberts has gone. I have a partner, Osbert Lewis. We were both on duty this morning, and my partner has undertaken the task of following the major wherever he goes. Then it will simply be a matter of Mr Longman and yourself visiting that place, if you wish.'

Julie gazed at Teddy, and Teddy grinned at her. 'Oh,' she said. 'Well . . . thank you very much, Mr Hart.'

'My pleasure, Mrs Longman. Mr Longman?'

'I think we owe Mr Hart some money, sweetheart,' Teddy said.

'Oh, oh yes. How much, Mr Hart?'

'Well, I can't say, Mrs Longman, until my partner gets back. There'll be expenses, of course. I think five hundred pounds should cover it. If it does not amount to that, I shall of course refund the difference.'

'Oh. Oh, yes.' She paid him.

'Thank you,' he said, riffling the notes. 'I'll be in touch as soon as I hear from my partner. Good day.'

The door closed behind him, and they looked at each other. 'I hate you,' Julie said. 'I loathe and despise you.' She threw both arms round his neck. 'But oh, how I love you as well.'

'Teddy,' she said, assuming her favourite posture of lying on his chest. 'I would like you to promise me something.'

'Name it.'

'That you will never ever again tell me a lie, or do something without telling me exactly what you're aiming at.'

'That's a tall order.'

'I have to be able to trust you,' she pointed out.

'And right now you don't feel you can?'

'Well, there are so many things.'

'Tell me one of them.'

'Well, what about Baldwin?'

He frowned. 'Baldwin? Uncle Bob's sidekick?'

'No, Teddy. Detective Sergeant Baldwin of Scotland Yard.'

His frown deepened. 'I'm not with you.'

'Teddy, I met Baldwin in New York. Met him! He was the man who saved me from Kaley. He'd been sent across to bring me back here, and he was tailing me. Thank God!'

'So who's the deceitful one now?' Teddy said. 'You never mentioned a word of this to me.'

'Because I didn't know how to. But he is an English policeman. And you said he wasn't.'

'How do you know he's an English policeman? He show you his badge again?'

'I sent him to District Attorney Zeidler. And he is the man who arranged our entry into this country. So you lied to me when you said he didn't work for Scotland Yard. I think I know why you did – you didn't want me surrendering and handing everything I knew over to the police, but it was still a terrible thing to do.'

He gazed at her for several seconds with an expression she had never seen before; it contained a mixture of annoyance and a sort of wistfulness. Then it dissipated in his crooked grin. 'Okay,' he said.

289

'I promise. Never again.' He squeezed her down on him. 'You're just too smart, I guess. Or too lucky.'

There were other things she wanted to tackle him about, like the ten thousand dollars, but she was happy to have surmounted this crisis without a quarrel. 'Lucky,' she said. 'I have to be, lucky.'

They spent an utterly quiet two days. They couldn't entirely relax, because they were waiting for Hart's telephone call, but they pretended, played cards, made love, and on the second morning took a walk up to the park, where Teddy at last fulfilled his promise and rowed her on the Serpentine. It was a hot day and absolutely blissful. 'Teddy,' she said. 'Are we still honeymooning?'

'No,' he told her. 'We haven't started to honeymoon yet. We'll honeymoon when we've found the dough.'

She knew he was joking, but she wished he wouldn't. She was coming to the stage where she hardly cared whether they ever found the money. But when they got back to the flat Calvin Hart was waiting for them. He looked thoroughly dejected. 'I've heard from Lewis,' he said.

'Oh, that's splendid,' Julie cried.

'I wish it were, Mrs Longman. He trailed Major Roberts, by train, right across France and into Italy.'

'Italy?'

'Yes. The train was for Milan, and there Major Roberts changed for a slow stopper into the mountains. Well, Lewis followed him on to that without difficulty, but,' he sighed. 'Well, Lewis was on the alert and when the train halted at a village he saw Major Roberts get off. Of course he followed, but he had to get off the other side of the train so as not to be seen, and wait until it had pulled out before he could cross the track. By the time he had done so, Major Roberts had disappeared. Literally.'

'Disappeared?' Teddy shouted. 'From an open station?' Just how big is this village?'

'It is a tiny little place, Mr Longman. According to Lewis, only a couple of streets.'

'What's it called?'

'San Giorgio del Monte. It sits right at the base of some fairly steep foothills of the Alps, apparently. Well, it's all rather odd, and rather sinister, too. Poor Lewis . . . he's very upset. You see, Mrs

Longman, he felt pretty sure that he would pick up the major's trail without difficulty in such a place. Well, there was a garage, so he went there, because it contained the only taxi in the village. But the garage people hadn't rented their car to anyone. So he began making the rounds. He went to the police station, and asked the constable there; there was only one constable. And he went to the local bar restaurant, and he even tried some private houses. And not a soul had seen or heard of Major Roberts. He had stepped out of the train, and in fifteen seconds had vanished into thin air. In a totally strange community. It's not possible. But there it is. I'm terribly sorry.'

'Well, don't be,' Teddy told him. 'I think Lewis has done a great job. It's as plain as the nose on your face that Uncle Bob has to be a regular visitor to this place San Giorgio, because he must be known to the villagers, and in fact he's so well known they closed ranks around him.'

'Good heavens,' Hart said. 'I never thought of that.'

'But . . . some remote Italian village?' Julie asked. 'And Uncle Bob would stand out in a crowd as an Englishman, a stranger. Why should they want to help him?'

'Wouldn't you, if he's been stashing away the kind of loot we think he has, for the past ten years?'

'God,' she said. 'I never thought of *that*. But – in this little village?'

'Almost certainly not. I think we will find that Uncle Bob has some estate in the vicinity of San Giorgio, and is regarded there as the patrone. Calvin, you've done a great job.'

'Thank you, Mr Longman. What instructions shall I give Lewis? He's calling me back this afternoon.'

'Tell him to come home,' Teddy said. He grinned at Julie and squeezed her hand. 'I think this is where we take over the hunt, eh, sweetheart? What do your people shout when they put up a fox?'

'Tally ho,' she said. 'Oh, tally ho.'

Once again, excitement, and endeavour, and more important, total partnership. Besides, now all doubts were swept aside. They had Uncle Bob, and therefore the money, in their sights.

CHAPTER 14

Julie's only problem was how to let Baldwin know. Teddy wanted to leave immediately and catch the afternoon boat, and she was entirely in favour of that. So, she thought, Baldwin will just have to wait. She would contact him as soon as she could. He couldn't blame her if she was unable to do so right away. And besides, while she had no intention of cheating the British Government – or more important, him – she thought it might not be a bad idea for her to find Uncle Bob first. She had no doubt she was going to do so. And Baldwin would want to interfere, with all the heavy efficiency of the police, and start telling her what she couldn't do because it was illegal.

But how reassuring was the memory of that massive, protecting confidence he had exuded. Which was horribly unfair on Teddy, she told herself. Had she been at his side when he had raided the A and M building she would have seen him in a similar light. And besides, Teddy was her husband, and Teddy was turning up trumps, as he always had when the going got rough, and once again they were adventuring together.

Now was the time to put Baldwin out of her mind. The excitement was building inside her all the time as they packed, one suitacase between the two of them, and lunched on the train to Folkestone. This was surely the last lap. If only she could find what she wanted to find. Something like the set-up Teddy envisaged, with Uncle Bob some kind of Italian lord of the manor, owning mile upon mile of countryside? That would be acceptable, because she felt she could handle that without remorse or compunction, but it didn't make sense. The only logical reason for Daddy to have stolen

292

twenty million dollars, if he hadn't intended it for her, was that he intended it for himself, and the only logical reason for him to need that kind of money was that his third life required such a lifestyle. Therefore the vast estate they were about to uncover was probably populated by a wife and children and dogs and yachts and expensive cars, a life from which his 'love-child' was to be forever excluded – because of course while his trips to and from England seemed to have left him no time for such an arrangement, they had no proof that he had not absented himself from New York on other occasions, and maybe taken a ship direct to Genoa. When she thought that she became angry. But at the same time she knew she was not going to be able to handle such a situation. Because she *was* a 'love child', hastily and perhaps lovelessly legitimised. These people she was now seeking would be the legitimate Armitages, or whatever name he had used. They might not, almost certainly did not, know the true identity of the millionaire they assumed to be their father, but had she any right to spoil their happy dream, simply because hers had been so cruelly torn to pieces?

Teddy was studying her as the train ground towards Folkestone. 'You don't look happy.'

She raised her head. 'Maybe I'm not. Teddy, if there is another family, if Uncle Bob turns out to be one of Daddy's agents, looking after Daddy's legitimate wife and family and estate . . . we just melt away into the sunset. Right?'

He grinned at her. 'Let's cross that bridge when we come to it.'

'I'd rather cross it now.'

'Like I told you once, you're too good to live.'

'I want a promise, Teddy.'

He grinned, and shrugged. 'So you got it. It's your dough. But what will we do then?'

'I have enough for us to live on until you finish law school. It won't be as exciting as tracking down twenty million dollars, but we couldn't do that for the rest of our lives, anyway. Then you'll just have to try supporting me for a change.'

'In the manner to which you have become accustomed.'

'No,' she said seriously. But she was suddenly happy. To be planning the future together, as husband and wife, brought a touch of sanity to this crazy summer.

But it wasn't over yet, because she wasn't going to give up the quest until she knew all the answers. And some of the answers were still unanswerable; when she stepped off the train at Folkestone she saw John Baldwin's face at one of the compartment windows.

Instinctively she turned towards him to make sure – he had appeared at a compartment some distance down from theirs – but he hastily pulled back and she lost him.

She glanced at Teddy, whose face was grim. 'I saw the louse. You still reckon he's a policeman?'

'I know he's a policeman. But why?'

'He's tracking you, sweetheart.' He hefted the suitcases and escorted her towards the ferry. 'I guess the British police are still interested in that money, and they figure you are still going to lead them to it. Don't tell me you really thought that guy arranged your re-entry into this country as an act of friendship?'

She bit her lip. She was more concerned with the realisation that if Baldwin, and presumably his detectives, were keeping her under constant surveillance, it had to be because he still didn't trust her – and he was absolutely right. 'What are we going to do?'

'Lose him when we get to France. I'll sort it out.'

He was being masterful again. One of his peculiar traits was that he could switch on the masterful male image whenever he chose – and the odd thing was that however his usual bumbling and uncertain behaviour made the act laughable, he had proved that it actually wasn't an act. When he wanted to prove it.

But she also knew he could be quite ruthless. And the last thing she wanted was a fight between him and Baldwin – while she also had to prove that she was keeping her word. 'Teddy,' she said. 'I have just got to go to the toilet.'

'For God's sake,' he complained. 'Can't it wait until we're on the ship?'

'I don't think so. I think the sight of that man has got me going. There's a Ladies right there. I won't be a moment.' She hurried inside, shut herself in a cubicle, pulled out several sheets of toilet paper, and wrote with her lipstick:

FOR GOD'S SAKE LAY OFF. TEDDY IS ON TO YOU. WE ARE GOING TO SAN GIORGIO DEL MONTE, ITALIAN VILLAGE NORTH OF MILAN. I WILL CALL YOU AS SOON AS SOMETHING TURNS UP. JULIE

She went outside, found the attendant.

'Is everything all right, dearie?' the woman asked, having watched her dash for the cubicle. 'You look a little pale.'

'I'm fine,' Julie said, and held out the toilet paper and a five-pound note. 'There is a man behind me, off the train. Big with a broken nose. Will you give him this message for me?'

'Is he your husband, dearie?'

'Oh, no,' Julie said. 'That's my husband waiting outside the door.'

'Ah.' The woman took the note and the money. 'You'll be in the *News of the World* next. I'll deliver your message.'

'Bless you,' Julie said, and hurried back outside.

'That was quick,' Teddy commented. 'Feeling better?'

'A lot. Must have been something I ate. Baldwin around?'

'Nope. I guess he'll keep out of sight now, and sneak on board at the last moment.'

But they saw nothing of him on the crossing, or in Boulogne, and Julie could allow herself a sigh of relief; her friend must have delivered the note. 'Maybe he was just checking that we were leaving the country,' she suggested, as Teddy was obviously brooding on it.

'Maybe,' he said grimly.

They caught a fast train for Paris, where they changed trains and stations, hurrying by taxi down to the Gare du Lyons for the Milan express. Teddy had reserved them a first-class sleeper, and he saw her to it before wandering off to, as he put it, check things out. He returned just before the train was due to leave. 'Can't find hide nor hair of him,' he said. 'I guess he didn't come across after all.'

Julie had never felt so relieved in her life. Her digestion – which had indeed been acting up – started to settle down again, and it was great sitting opposite Teddy in the dining-car as the train pulled out of the station and began chugging south. Except that then she began to remember the last time she had sat in a dining-car on a continental train. Then Uncle Bob had sat opposite her, and she had felt so secure, even with the knowledge that Daddy was dead. Then she had had no suspicion of the terrifying forces which were whirling about her.

But she had encountered those forces, and she had triumphed. And now she was the hunter rather than the intended victim.

'Another brown study?' Teddy commented.

'I suppose all my studies are brown, right about now.'

'I know,' he said seriously. 'When you finally climb off the back of the tiger, you are going to have a little trouble adjusting.' He grinned. 'Aren't we all?'

'I know,' she said in turn. 'I only hope I'm worth it.'

He picked up her hand and kissed her knuckles. 'You're worth it. Now we have to have an early night. I gather we make Milan at dawn.'

And then? She didn't expect to sleep, but she did. She had always been good at sleeping while travelling. Before she knew anything more there was a rap on the compartment door, and the guard called, '*Monsieur, madame, Milan dans trente minutes.*'

They dressed, hurriedly, closed the suitcase, went along the corridor to the carriage door, waited. Milan Central at six o'clock in the morning was chill and windswept, but the arrival of the Paris express caused it to be extremely busy, even if it seemed most of the passengers were staying in their couchettes, en route for Venice. Teddy waved a porter away and himself hefted the suitcase as they checked the information board and then found their way to an almost deserted platform to wait for the early train into the hills.

Now it was really chill and windswept, and Julie hugged her coat tightly around her; she had dressed very sensibly, she thought, in a thick skirt and blouse with cashmere sweater on top, equally protective stockings and sensible low-heeled and laced walking shoes. She wore a beret and a matching blue cloth coat. She knew all about walking around the Alps, even in the height of summer, and she had no idea how much she would have to do.

The train arrived at a quarter to seven, and they got into a very bare and not terribly clean carriage. There were only half a dozen other passengers, but several sacks of mail were thrown into the guard's van. Then they were off again, chugging north, seeming to stop every ten minutes at odd little places, sometimes with not a house in sight.

An hour after leaving Milan, when the hills were already begining to rise steeply about them, they saw the sign, 'San Giorgio del Monte'. 'Here we go,' Teddy said, and helped her down. A mailsack was heaved beside them by the guard, and a moment later the train had pulled away, and they were alone on the platform, across which

296

an even chillier breeze was sweeping. Julie shivered, and pulled her coat tighter.

Teddy grinned at her, and threw his arm round her shoulders. 'So far, no change from what this fellow Lewis told us. Now I guess we do what he did, and wait for this place to wake up.'

He lifted their suitcase, and they walked to the steps leading down from the station. The scene was exactly as Lewis had described it to Hart. In front of them was a street, stretching perhaps a hundred yards, with houses, one or two small shops, and a bar restaurant. At the far end of the street there was a garage, and then the street became a rough road, leading up into the hills, which began about half a mile away, and against which the mountains in the distance formed an immense backdrop. Off the street, to either side, there were two cross streets, or lanes, and down one of them could be discerned the steeple of a church. But that was it. There was not a living thing in sight save for a mongrel dog, which barked once or twice at the movement from the station, and then went back to sleep.

'I have a sensation of having been marooned on a desert island,' Julie remarked.

'Yeah. I think we may as well stay here,' Teddy said. 'There's a bench.'

They sat down, and he put his arm round her again. She rested her head on his shoulder and tried to think, and wait for her nerves to settle. Presumably eight o'clock in the morning was the worst possible time to see anywhere for the first time, but it made no sense to her to invest twenty million dollars in creating a paradise in this bleak and windswept spot when there was all of southern Italy waiting with its warmth.

She then tried thinking about Uncle Bob, who had been here only two days ago, and had stood at the top of those steps, and then disappeared. In fifteen seconds, according to Calvin Hart. He could not have got beyond the first two houses, which waited in such curtained disinterest. But they had been interested in Uncle Bob. They had to have been.

'There,' Teddy said, and she watched a door opening in one of the houses halfway along the street. 'The postman, I'll bet. Do you speak Italian?'

'Pretty well,' Julie said. French, German and Italian had been spoken at Mrs Simpson's Academy – she realised with a start of surprise that she was actually within half a day's drive of the Academy. Had Daddy been within half a day's drive of her all these years?

'Then it's all up to you,' Teddy said.

The man came slowly up the street, and the dog slunk off. He reached the foot of the steps, and glanced at them. 'Good morning,' Julie said, in Italian.

'Good morning,' he replied.

'Perhaps you could help us,' Julie ventured.

'There is an hotel at Carloponto,' he said. 'It is fifteen miles from here. It is where the skiers go. In the winter,' he added, as if unable to understand why anyone should wish to go up to Carloponto in July. 'There is a taxi.'

'Oh,' she said. 'Thank you. We shall go there. But actually, we're looking for a man named Major Roberts. My uncle,' she added, as the man glanced at her.

He continued to inspect her for some seconds, and she remembered that of course he would be one of the people the man Lewis would certainly have questioned, two days ago.

'It is very important that I speak with my uncle,' she explained.

'There is breakfast,' the man said. 'At the restaurant.' He walked down the steps.

'But . . . Major Roberts?' Julie asked again.

'I know no one of that name,' he said, and trudged up the street.

'Surly bastard,' Teddy commented. 'Any joy?'

Julie repeated the conversation.

'Well, I'm certainly for breakfast,' Teddy said. 'And afterwards, if we get no response, we'll jolly well go up to this place Carloponto. Maybe they'll be more helpful there.' He lifted the suitcase and went down the steps.

She hurried behind him. 'Yes, but . . . if what Lewis said is true, these people simply have to know Uncle Bob.'

'I haven't forgotten that. But I think better on a full stomach.'

They had to bang on the restaurant door for several minutes before it was opened. 'I'm terribly sorry to disturb you,' Julie said to the woman. 'But the postmaster told us we could get breakfast here. We're on our way to Carloponto,' she added. 'From the train.'

'You want breakfast?' the woman asked.

'Oh, yes, please.'

'Half an hour,' the woman said, and stepped aside to allow them in.

It was warmer in the restaurant, marginally, and she lit a couple of oil lamps for them; there was apparently no electricity. She then departed for the kitchen, and Julie repeated their conversation.

'Heck, what a bunch,' Teddy commented. 'But we gotta keep trying.'

Julie nodded, and listened to a motorbike start up outside and then ride off into the hills. That disturbed her, but when the woman returned with steaming black coffee and a plate of cakes, she went into her routine. 'My husband and I are looking for my uncle,' she said. 'Major Roberts, an Englishman, who came down here two days ago. It is terribly important that we find him as quickly as possible.'

'I know no Major Roberts,' the woman said.

'We know he got off the train here,' Julie explained. 'Who should we ask about him?'

The woman shrugged.

'Would he have gone to Carloponto?'

'Perhaps,' the woman said. 'You should go to Carloponto. There is the taxi.'

'They sure seem to want us to go to Carloponto,' Teddy said. 'I guess to get us out of their hair.'

'Or to get us to use their taxi,' Julie said. 'They're probably all related to the taxidriver.'

'Well, we'll do that thing. When we've eaten.'

They paid for the meal and then walked up the street to the garage. By now it was past nine, and they were aware that they were being watched by what seemed everyone in the village, either from corners or from behind draped windows. 'This place gives me the creeps,' Julie confessed.

'Don't worry. They're probably far more afraid of you than you of them,' he said reassuringly. 'Where's your gun?'

'My gun? I left it behind.'

'For Jesus' sake!'

'Those days are done, Teddy.'

'They can't be done, sweetheart, until we have that twenty million. You don't think Uncle Bob is going to hand it over without some persuasion, do you?' He squeezed her hand. 'Anyway, I have mine. Hopefully that'll be sufficient.'

'Teddy! You can't possibly start shooting here. This isn't New York.'

'Could be a lot tougher. But I promise I won't. Unless I have to. Chat these guys up.'

They had reached the garage, where three mechanics were surveying their approach. No, they had never heard of a Major Roberts. But if they wished to go to Carloponto in the mountains, the taxi was available.

'What do you think?' she asked Teddy.

'I think we had better do that. We are obviously going to get no change here, and we have to have somewhere to use as a base. Besides, if this place is a tourist resort, even out of season, they are probably going to be more co-operative. They may even speak English.'

'We would like to go to Carloponto, yes,' Julie said.

'Now,' one of the mechanics said.

It was not a question, and one of the others was already opening the door of the somewhat ancient saloon. Julie got in, Teddy beside her, and their suitcase was strapped on to the luggage grid. The man they had spoken to got behind the wheel, one of his assistants cranked, and they drove out of the yard and indeed out of the village.

'Thank God for that,' Julie commented. 'I suppose this hotel at Carloponto *is* open? I am going to have a hot bath before we start doing anything else.'

'Sounds a great idea,' Teddy said. 'Could be quite pretty up there.'

She looked out of the window, as the road began to wind upwards. The slopes rose steeply to either side, covered now in multicoloured wild flowers, but it was easy to imagine them covered in snow in the winter. And always the mountains rose higher and higher in the distance. She looked over her shoulder, but the village had already disappeared from sight. Indeed there was nothing to be seen at all except a few goats, grazing some distance away; she could see no shepherd.

The road dipped down, and then rose sharply again, and then bifurcated. Julie gazed at the sign, which read: Carloponto–Monte

300

Giorgio, and frowned as they turned right instead of left. 'Teddy,' she said, 'We're not going to Carloponto.'

'Eh?' He sat up.

'This is the other road.'

'Heck. Ask him what he's playing at.'

Julie tapped the driver on the shoulder. 'Where are we going?' she asked. 'We want to go to Carloponto.'

'This is a short cut,' he explained, without turning his head.

Julie translated.

'Well, he had better be right,' Teddy said, and put his hand in his pocket. 'Now, aren't you sorry you didn't bring your gun?'

Julie bit her lip. But she *was* feeling frightened. She had thought physical violence was behind her . . . but could it ever be behind Julie Armitage?

Teddy grinned and squeezed her arm. 'Don't look so scared. No bunch of Italian peasants is going to get the better of Teddy Longman. Or Julie Armitage. Right?'

'Right,' she agreed.

'So what the devil is that?'

They turned another corner and the road, now hardly more than a track, with the hillside rising steeply on their left and falling away equally steeply into the valley on their right – there would be no room to pass another vehicle, supposing there could possibly be one up here – led to a massive building set into the hillside. There was a bell tower, and the windows were little more than slits, at least where they overlooked the road.

'It has to be some kind of monastery,' she said. 'Teddy, I don't like the look of this.' Because the car was slowing, and as they watched, the great solid gates swung inward; the road led straight up to them, and nowhere else. 'We've been kidnapped.'

'By a bunch of monks?' he asked incredulously.

The men waiting for them were certainly wearing black robes.

'If they start anything,' he muttered, and drew his pistol.

'Put it away, for God's sake,' she snapped, praying the driver hadn't seen it.

Apparently he hadn't, and the car drew to a stop just inside the gates, where the doors were immediately opened for them. Julie stepped down, and found herself facing a tall, thin man in the habit of an abbot, who held her hand and squeezed it. 'You'll be Julie,' he

301

said, amazingly in English. 'Do you know how much I have wanted to meet you, my dear child? And you'll be Teddy.' He shook Teddy's hand; Teddy appeared quite bemused, but he had taken both hands from his pockets, to Julie's relief. 'I am Father Michael,' the priest said. 'Welcome to Monte Giorgio. Come in, come in. My people will see to your bag, and Uncle Bob is waiting.'

Julie dared not look at Teddy, and she knew it would be futile to think right this minute. They followed the priest into a door let into the solid stone walls of the monastery, and along a corridor, to reach a rather pleasant little sitting-room, where there was a carpet on the floor and some antique carved wooden chairs, and a window, looking out at the courtyard and therefore much wider than any of the external apertures. And there, waiting for them, was indeed Uncle Bob, standing in front of the presently empty fireplace.

'Just how did you know we were coming?' Teddy demanded.

'Pepe in the village informed us almost the moment you stepped off the train,' Uncle Bob said.

Julie snapped her fingers. 'The motorbike.'

'But we were expecting you, anyway,' Father Michael explained. 'We are presuming the man who followed the major from England was in your pay?'

'I'm afraid he was,' Julie said.

'You're becoming quite formidable, Julie,' Uncle Bob said.

'Yes,' she agreed.

'And have you brought your automatic pistol?'

'No,' she said. She did not mention Teddy's.

'Well, sit down, please,' Father Michael said, and rang a little brass bell. 'Brother Paul will prepare some coffee.' He sat down himself, and after a moment's hesitation Julie did the same. Teddy followed her example, but Uncle Bob remained standing. 'Major Roberts and I,' Father Michael explained, 'have been at odds ever since the death of your father. I didn't learn of it for some time, of course, not until the major himself came to see me. Then my instinctive reaction was to invite you here to put you into the picture, you might say. But the major was equally instinctively against that. I think it had something to do with, if you will forgive me . . .' his gaze drifted from Julie to Teddy, 'the young man you had acquired, and whom he did not trust.'

302

'The tense is present,' Uncle Bob said.

'In any event, he did not find the time to come to San Giorgio until after you had left for America,' Father Michael said. 'I suggested he return to England and see you again, but I had to leave him full discretion, never having met you myself. But he tells me you threatened him with a gun.'

His choice of words was curiously unpriestlike, Julie was realising – but she did not feel he was hostile. On the other hand, she had not felt Hanson Pierce was hostile. 'Perhaps he has never told you how he has in the past beaten me up, Father Michael,' she said. 'How he can't keep his hands off me whenever we are alone together. I felt I needed the gun, believe me.'

Father Michael sighed, and glanced at Uncle Bob, whose ears were red. 'He has always been a lecherous bastard,' Father Michael observed.

'Now hold on, Mike,' Uncle Bob protested. 'I have always loved this girl. Christ—'

'Would hardly approve,' Father Michael said, quietly but severely. 'However, Major Roberts also told me that you surprised him by saying that you did not want your father's money for yourself, but would give it to a suitable charity.'

'Well . . .' Julie glanced at Teddy, 'something like that.'

'I was so relieved to hear that,' Father Michael said. 'I immediately instructed Major Roberts to return to England and bring you here, but when he pointed out that he had been tailed from London, we realised that you would soon be coming of your own accord.'

'Just how did you manage to lose Lewis?' Teddy demanded.

'I stepped into the first house,' Uncle Bob said. 'They all know me in the village.'

'Ah, coffee,' Father Michael said, as one of the monks entered with a laden tray.

Julie looked at Teddy, who waggled his eyebrows. But she could tell he was reaching a peak of exhilaration. In these most peculiar circumstances, they had reached the end of their quest. 'The money?' she asked.

'Eighteen million dollars,' Father Michael said. 'What a splendid figure. And what a shame Eddie did not reach the milestone of twenty before he died; I know he wanted to do that. And the major tells me you personally avenged his death.'

'With a little bit of help from my friends,' Julie acknowledged.

'That must please Eddie wherever he is,' Father Michael said. 'And do you know, despite all, I have a certain hope that he will be in heaven.'

Teddy moved, restlessly.

'So my father brought all the money he embezzled from the Association to you, here,' Julie said. She wasn't prepared to worry about a two-million-dollar discrepancy at this moment.

'Well, he sent it, via the major.'

'Holy cow,' Teddy said. 'And you never palmed any of it?'

'I am not a thief,' Uncle Bob said with dignity.

'Major Roberts is my agent,' Father Michael explained. 'He is absolutely trustworthy.'

'And the money is here?' Julie asked.

'Well, there could hardly be a safer place for it to be accumulated. Your father did not trust banks, whose secrets can be learned. Our secrets are truly secret. Except for someone like yourself, who possessed, shall I say, inside information. But I am sure you will not betray us, either.'

'Of course not, Father. But . . .' Julie gazed at him. 'I would like my money, please.'

'Eighteen million dollars,' Father Michael said again, and sipped his coffee.

'You mean he just accumulated the stuff?' Teddy asked incredulously. 'In cash?'

'In a manner of speaking, yes.'

'With no idea of doing anything with it? Just letting it lie?' He glanced at Julie. 'For Julie?'

Oh, Father, Julie thought; and I was coming to hate you.

'Well, not exactly,' Father Michael said. 'I think I had better tell you how it all came about. I'm afraid in my youth I was a criminal.' He smiled at their faces. 'We all begin our journey towards grace in strange ways. I was not a very successful criminal, and I was caught out and sent to prison for armed robbery. I served seven years in Dartmoor.'

'And there you met Daddy?' Julie cried.

'Exactly. He was, even then, a formidable man to cross. I never did cross him, but it so happened that being an Italian I was made the butt of the other prisoners' humour, and on more than one

304

occasion he intervened to save me from a beating. I was grateful. In time I think I came to love your father. We never shared a cell, unfortunately – he was with MacGinnion. And he was released two years before myself. He then disappeared, and sadly, as I later learned, he determined to return to a life of crime. I did not. I returned to my native country, and entered the church.' He smiled at Julie. 'I think it is fair to say that, in our different professions, we both prospered.'

He put down his coffee cup. 'I did not ever expect to see Eddie Armitage again, but to my amazement we encountered each other in the summer of 1919, when I visited England on church affairs. We recognised each other immediately, even if twenty years had passed since we had last met. We talked. I told him of my success in the church, and he, after some hesitation, and after swearing me to the secrecy of the confessional, told me of his success in America.

'He had a reason for doing this, which was not immediately apparent, but which came out in the course of conversation. Your father had indeed done well in his chosen profession and, as you undoubtedly know, was already the boss of New York's biggest crime syndicate. He was, in his professional dealings, a hard – indeed a ruthless – man, who had several murders to his discredit. However, he was still a man, and some nine years earlier, he had met and fallen in love with a girl in New York.'

'My mother,' Julie said.

'Indeed. Perhaps you are aware . . .' he hesitated.

'I am aware that I was conceived out of wedlock, Father.'

'Yes. Perhaps it was the knowledge that his wife was pregnant encouraged Eddie to marry her. I know he loved her; events proved that. But he feared to involve her in his activities. When he did marry her, he determined that his life with her and his life as boss of the syndicate should never mingle, and thus he set up the Epsom existence. And might have maintained this, unchanged, for the rest of his life. But in 1918 your mother died.'

'Yes,' Julie said.

'Can you remember how affected your father was?'

'I . . . no,' she said. 'I wasn't seeing all that much of him, even then.'

'He was shattered,' Father Michael said. 'He had built an entire

305

life around that woman, and now she was gone. He took it as a divine judgement, and I know he considered suicide, and might have committed it, but for the necessity of caring for you. Still, he was in a bad state when he and I met again. He poured out his heart to me, his old comrade-in-arms, and asked me to help him. He wished to make some atonement for his crimes, some offering, perhaps, for the memory of his wife. It was basically a pagan desire, but in my business we are required to cater to all aspects of human nature.

'However, it transpired that he was not ready to give up his other life with the syndicate, however much his grief, and the two situations appeared to me to be irreconcilable, until I hit upon this scheme, that he should divert as much as possible of the Association's profits to me.'

'For God's sake,' Teddy remarked.

'Indeed, my son. Eddie was reluctant at first, because he feared being detected by his associates. Nor did he feel that there would be sufficient funds available to make it worthwhile. But the very next year Prohibition was enforced in America, and the Association profits overnight became astronomical, while there was so much money arriving from so many different sources Eddie found it perfectly simple to withhold large sums. These sums, as you undoubtedly know, he carried across the Atlantic in cash, and left at his London apartment for the major to collect, and bring to me here.'

Julie was speechless.

'So you reckon the money is all yours,' Teddy said.

'It was given to me, yes,' Father Michael agreed.

'And you don't reckon Julie has a say?'

'Of course she has a say. She is Julie Armitage, or was until she married you. And it happens that we have just over a million dollars right here in the monastery, awaiting disposition. As there does not now seem any likelihood of that being increased in the future, I think we should come to a decision as soon as possible as to its utilisation, and I would very much like Julie to be associated with that decision.'

'A million?' Teddy demanded. 'What happened to the other nineteen?'

'All the other money has already been disposed of.'

306

'Disposed of? You can sit there and tell us that you have calmly spent nineteen million dollars of somebody else's money?'

'My dear young man,' Father Michael said. 'The money was always disposed of strictly in accordance with Eddie's wishes. I would not have dreamed of doing otherwise.'

'It was spent on what?' Teddy shouted, now getting very agitated.

'You keep using the word, spent. It was put to work, not spent.'

'You—'

'Oh, be quiet, Teddy,' Julie snapped. 'Let Father Michael finish. Put to work, Father?'

'It was your father's wish that his money, whenever he had accumulated sufficient, was to be used to achieve some worthwhile objective. I'm afraid he always did have delusions of grandeur, and I suspect that he envisaged himself as playing God. But I was content to go along with him where the end result was so important. Thus we needed to accumulate considerable funds to put it to much use. You may remember the monsoon floods in Bengal two years ago? There was a mystery million dollars for the relief of the victims.'

'Daddy did that?' Julie whispered.

'Oh, indeed. And there were others, whenever a great cause arose. His first big act was to send four million dollars to the Japanese earthquake relief, after the Tokyo disaster of 1923. And then there was the Mexican volcano catastrophe – as I say, I think he felt he was buying himself security in the afterlife. And who knows, if it is possible to do that, then he may well have done so.'

Oh, Daddy, Julie thought, and felt tears spring to her eyes.

'You mean he gave all of that money to charity?' Teddy asked. His voice was also hushed; he was clearly scandalised.

'I suppose he did, yes.'

Julie looked at Uncle Bob. 'And you never told me?'

'Eddie made me swear that I would never reveal his secret to a soul,' Uncle Bob said.

'Even after he was dead?'

'Even after he was dead. As you know, I was shocked by the way he had neglected to make any provision for you, and in fact I have been discussing with Father Mike the possibility of letting you have some of our accumulated funds . . .'

'No,' Julie said.

'Come again?' Teddy demanded.

307

'I don't want a penny of that money,' Julie said. 'As you say, Father, we'll decide where it can be put to best use, as Daddy might have wanted.'

'Are you nuts?' Teddy shouted.

'I damn near got myself killed trying to atone for Daddy's crimes,' Julie said. 'And you. And I did get a lot of other people killed. Maybe they all deserved it. But as far as I'm concerned Daddy wasn't such a louse after all.'

'Even if he just left you holding an empty bag?'

'He left me holding a lot of pride,' Julie said.

'My dear girl,' Father Michael said, and came across the room to squeeze her hands. 'Now I know that you are truly Eddie Armitage's daughter. I am proud of you. And as you say, we will devise a use for the money which would have gladdened Eddie's heart. Eh, Bob?'

'Oh, indeed,' Uncle Bob said.

Julie hugged him. 'I'm sorry I was so hateful.'

'I suppose I had it coming. Oh, Julie . . .' he looked past her at Teddy, and then released her.

'Now, of course, you'll spend the night here,' Father Michael said.

'Here?'

He smiled at her. 'We are allowed to offer shelter to women, properly chaperoned. There is a train back to Milan this afternoon, if you insist, but we have a lot to talk about, have we not?'

Julie looked at Teddy.

Who gave one of his crooked grins. 'I guess we have,' he said.

They were shown to a cell, which contained two cots and a washbasin, and in which their suitcase had already been placed, to wash up for lunch. And for all his apparent acceptance of the situation Julie braced herself for a crisis. But Teddy was remarkably relaxed. 'So you reckon you've bought yourself a little bit of heaven too,' he said.

'If that's how you wish to look at it, yes.'

'Okay. So be mad at me. I just couldn't believe what you were doing. But it's your dough.'

'Teddy! Aren't you *mad* at *me*?'

'I don't stay mad at you very long,' he said.

She was in his arms and hugging him close. 'Oh, Teddy . . . I am so happy. It'll work out, you'll see. Just as I told you it would. And you'll be a lawyer. Your Dad will be so proud of you.'

'Yeah,' he agreed. 'That'll be fun.'

She knew he was really acting, that he was bitterly disappointed and still couldn't believe she had done such a thing, but he was accepting her decision, and that was what mattered.

Lunch was a jolly affair, which surprised her – 'Communion wine,' Father Michael explained with a smile. 'We have our own vineyard in the next valley.' – served by one of the brothers, and in the afternoon they were taken on a tour of the monastery. 'It has been a monastery for well over a thousand years,' Father Michael explained. 'But of course, in the early days, it had of necessity to be a fortress as well, and the monks had to be able to defend themselves. Nowadays, we keep very much to ourselves, and have little contact with the outside world.' He gave another of his private smiles. 'But we are still prepared to offer succour to the weary traveller who may have traversed the Alps, or like yourselves, journeyed up from the south.'

The place was certainly built like a fortress, with walls several feet thick, and huge cellars in which were vast stores of wine and cheese, reached by a single huge steel trapdoor set into the courtyard. 'Once upon a time, the ultimate refuge when the barbarians swept down from the mountains,' Father Michael explained. 'Nowadays it serves to protect our produce from any weaknesses of the flesh. And this is all our own produce. In addition to growing our own grapes, we also farm our own goats. You may have seen some of them as you approached.'

'We thought they belonged to the village.'

'No, no, my dear, the village belongs to us. They are our tenants.'

'Oh,' Julie said humbly.

'Some set-up you guys have here,' Teddy said. 'So self-contained. I admire that. You'll be telling me next you're not on the telephone.'

'But of course we are not on the telephone, Mr Longman. We cater to our own requirements.'

'There has gotta be an emergency some time, Father.'

'Should there be anything we cannot handle ourselves, then one of my brothers rides his bicycle into the village. There is no

309

telephone in the village either, of course, but there is Marco's taxi, which if it is truly necessary, can drive one of us down to Milan. It is a long and bumpy road, so it has to be truly necessary.'

'What about this place Carloponto?'

'Why, the same. Carloponto entertains tourists in the winter, skiers you know. But it is necessary to book by letter. The postman goes up once a week.'

'Some set-up,' Teddy repeated. 'Say, would you guys object if Julie and I took a little walk in the hills? They sure are beautiful.'

'Why, Teddy,' Julie said. 'I never put you down for a nature-lover.'

'Walking is my second favourite sport,' he said, and grinned at her. 'If I hadn't been so keen on walking, I wouldn't be here now, right?'

'Right,' she said, as she remembered how he had found Father's body.

'Supper is at seven,' Father Michael said. 'And this evening we will make a decision on the money.'

'Yeah,' Teddy said. 'I'll just fetch my binoculars.'

The gate was opened for them and they took the track, and then climbed the next shallow hill. From there they found they could look down on both the monastery and the road, which swung away to the left side of the hill. By now it was four o'clock, and the afternoon was cooling off, but there was no breeze, and the stillness was almost tangible.

'Oh, Teddy,' Julie said, putting both arms round his waist to hug him. 'I am so happy!'

'Yeah,' he said. 'I guess you are.' He looked down at her, smiled, and kissed her on the nose. 'Let's walk. I've been sitting down too long already.'

He slung his binocular case and they climbed down a shallow hill and then up another one, even higher. She was quite out of breath by the time they reached the top, but he was amazingly fit. 'Boy, what a view,' he enthused.

It certainly was spectacular. The road stretched below them for several miles in either direction, and in the distance they could just make out the houses of the village, some five miles away. To the north the road wound its way along the valley out of sight.

'Why don't you take a rest?' he said. 'I want to have a look around.'

Julie sank to the ground, warm and dry from the day's sun, then lay back, using her beret as a pillow, while she drowsily watched Teddy

310

open his binocular case and begin to sweep the hills and the valley beneath them.

'What do you see?' she asked.

'All kinds of nice things,' he said. He put the binoculars on the grass, beside his case, and knelt before them with his back turned to her, taking something else from the case. She closed her eyes, and actually fell asleep, but only for a couple of seconds, then woke up again with a start at what she at first supposed had been a lightning flash. But there was not a cloud in the sky.

She sat up, gazed at Teddy, who was standing, half turned towards the afternoon sun, and half turned towards the village, holding something that looked like a woman's vanity case in his hand. And with that . . . there was another flash of light, and then another.

Julie rose to her knees. 'What on earth are you doing?'

'This is a heliograph,' he explained.

'A what?'

'You never read any military history? In the days before telephones, and radios, bodies of soldiers would use these two little mirrors to catch the sun's rays and throw it, oh, ten miles maybe. That way they could communicate with each other, using Morse code.'

'Good lord. But who are you communicating with?'

'Some friends of mine I've spotted down in the valley. Just where they should be . . .'

'Some . . .' she scrambled to her feet. 'Teddy! What are you doing?'

'You don't think I am going to walk away and leave a million dollars sitting in some crummy monastery, do you? Okay, so I was looking for twenty times that. But a million will keep the wolf from the door for a day or two.'

'You . . . you are going to make me very angry, Teddy,' she said. 'I won't allow it.'

He sent another flash of light into the valley, then lowered the mirrors and grinned at her. 'You, baby? You had just better start keeping a civil tongue in your head, or I might just wring your neck here and now.'

She stared at him with her mouth open.

'Behave, and I'll think about letting you live. And your friends. Remember that, now.'

Blood seemed to pound through her arteries and fill her brain. Oh,

311

she was Eddie Armitage's daughter. She leaped at him, and he laughed and caught her wrists before she could reach him, swung her round and pushed. She staggered forward, tripped over a loose rock, and fell. For a moment she was winded, then she rose to her knees, turned on them, and felt the rock again. She knew she had to have a weapon to fight him with, and she was so furious she didn't at the moment mind whether or not she hurt him. She picked up the rock and rose to her feet.

'I mean it, Teddy,' she said. 'I am not going to let you steal that money. If I have to knock some sense into your brain, by God, I will.'

He grinned at her. 'When you are going to hit a guy with a rock, Julie, you don't ever talk to him first. You just go up to him, and wham, before he knows what's happening. That's how I did your dad.'

CHAPTER 15

'You . . .' Julie stared at him, too bemused to think for a moment. 'You killed Daddy?' she whispered.

'Sure. I had to set the ball rolling.'

'You . . .' she hurled herself forward, the stone swinging at the end of her fingers. But he evaded her easily enough, caught her shoulder to half turn her towards him, and delivered a perfect right-handed punch on to her jaw. She didn't know whether she lost consciousness or not, found herself lying on the grass with the whole world rotating about her, with her head opening and shutting in great claps of thunder, and with waves of nausea racing away from her stomach – but the sickness was not entirely caused by pain.

Teddy sucked his knuckles and grinned at her, standing above her. 'If you knew just how long I've wanted to do that,' he said. 'Every time you started to act the great Julie Armitage. Now you just lie there, or I am going to hit you again.'

Julie gasped. She couldn't have moved right that minute even if she had dared. And to compound her problem tears started flooding from her eyes. But they were tears of anger and disappointment more than fear.

'You're such a fool', Teddy said contemptuously. 'But so are all your friends. The police down in that one-horse village have got to be the dumbest in the world. You know they never once suspected that the guy who "found" the body could have put it there in the first place. Simply because I'm a nice-looking chap and I had no motive. Even that dummo lover boy of yours, Uncle Bob, only ever thought I was after your tits or your bankroll. Well, I'll tell you something, baby, your tits and those ants you have in your pants were a bonus.

313

When Kaley told me I'd be squiring some virgin from school, I thought to myself, Christ, she has got to have cross eyes and buck teeth. But you never know your luck.'

Some of the pain was starting to recede, but it was being replaced by a lot else. Julie inhaled. 'May I sit up, please?'

'Sure. Just don't try anything.' He stepped back so there was no risk of her grappling his legs. He had a gun and he was bigger and stronger, but she was still Julie Armitage, she thought. He was a murdering punk but he was afraid of her. And he had killed Daddy.

But Baldwin would soon be here, despite her note. Perhaps he was here already. Or was he waiting for her call?

'But you were as dumb as any of them,' Teddy went on, enjoying her changing expressions. 'Checking me out! When you called "Balliol", that was my old friend Johnnie Stevens you spoke to. You remember Johnnie Stevens?'

Oh, my God, Julie thought. Oh, my God! 'You mean we're not even actually married,' she muttered. It was painful to move her jaw sufficiently to speak.

'Christ, no. Marry you? I'd need my head examined.'

Julie felt she had been kicked in the stomach as well as punched on the jaw. For all of her recurring suspicions of his motives, of himself, she had clung to the one solid rock in her life, that he was her husband, that for all his faults he had taken upon himself her love and protection for the rest of *his* life.

'And the way you fell for that envelope,' Teddy grinned. 'I stuck it in the drawer while you were calling your crummy friend Cornwall. And it just never crossed your mind.'

She wanted to scream and shout. She wanted to roll on the ground and tear at the grass with her teeth in her despair. But there were so many things she also wanted to know. 'You worked for Kaley?' she asked.

'I'm one of his bright boys,' Teddy said, proudly. 'Or was. He knew I could handle it. Oh, sure, I know you never had a clue as to what was going on. The fact is, neither did he. He thought he did. Make that chick fall for you, he told me, and find out about the money. Then he, or I guess Big Pat MacGinnion, started to get impatient. So when I wired him to say I wasn't getting anywhere this end, he came up with the idea that I should "marry" you and bring you to the States. He thought he could beat it out of you. He never

314

figured Uncle Bob or someone would lose his head and involve Hanson Pierce. My business was to leave you alone in the hotel suite where they could lift you, and bingo, they lost you. But even that could've worked out all right; you're so dumb you walked right back into their arms. Only Kaley, well . . . he was always trying to think too far ahead. When he realised you were tougher than he had estimated, he got this idea that I should play the big hero and get you out of the A and M building, when you were real frightened and upset, and that maybe you'd realise you were out of your league and lead me home. The only guy didn't like that idea was Mel; his bop on the head had to be for real. But you – Christ, baby, didn't you realise that nobody, but nobody, could get in and out of that building without MacGinnion's say-so?'

Oh, God, she thought again. Because she had suspected all of those things, at the time – and yet had refused to consider them seriously enough. 'And then you betrayed Kaley as well,' she said.

'Well, baby, when I saw the way things were shaping up, I had to do a rethink. You weren't running anywhere. You wanted to fight a war. Oh, you have guts. I won't ever deny that. And my orders were just to follow, for a while, and see where you went. I didn't like the idea of you getting your head blown off, at least, not until we had found the money. I told you so at the time. But then I realised, heck, you mightn't have much grey stuff between your pretty little ears, but you sure were Eddie Armitage's daughter. So I decided to kind of let things take their course. Mind you, am I glad I wasn't around when you went on that crazy date with Kaley. I reckon he was getting the message by then that I could've changed sides.'

Yes, she thought. Bring your husband, Kaley's spokesman had said on the phone; I want to meet the guy. His word for execution. Poor fair-haired Arnie. But then, Kaley had meant to destroy them both anyway.

'And it all worked out pretty good. You even fell for my dad and mom, and that rented apartment in Boston.'

'For which you needed the money to pay,' she said. God, how stupid she had been.

'Well, heck, without Kaley to foot the bill I was running a little short. But by then I knew you weren't gonna give up. Although I didn't know just how much we were after until you told me; Kaley had never named a figure. Then it was just a matter of contacting

315

Calvin, and letting him know that instead of us both working for Kaley, we were now working for ourselves, as equal partners. And here we all are.'

'So what are you going to do to me?' she asked in a low voice.

'Well, baby, that could well depend on you. When Calvin and Lewis get here, we are all going back down to the monastery. The story is we met these guys, see, and invited them back for the night. So long as you go along with that, your Uncle Bob and Mad Mike the Monk will buy it.'

'And if I don't?'

'Then I guess we'll just have to shoot our way in. Calvin is coming prepared for that.'

'I suppose he was on the same train as us, last night.'

'Well, of course. But you were so upset at seeing that copper in Folkestone you never thought to look. Only Calvin didn't catch the stopper; you would've had to notice him then. Lewis was waiting for him with an automobile, and I told them to drive out here, by-passing the village, and park and wait for my signal. I didn't know where we were going to wind up, but I knew it had to be someplace in these hills. Listen.'

She could hear the growl of a car in low gear coming up the road.

'So if you don't play ball, a lot of those guys are gonna get hurt,' Teddy said.

'And if I do play ball?'

'Well, we'll just take the money and go. Oh, we'll do one or two other things as well, like immobilising Marco's taxi. That'll give us a good head start, and the Swiss border ain't all that far.'

'And you think you can run forever?'

He grinned. 'Far enough, baby. Far enough.'

But not with her, she knew. Not after what he had just told her. And he would know that even confessing to the murder of Daddy would be less dangerous than confessing how contemptuously he had treated her love. So once he and his friends were out of the monastery with the money she would be expendable. Yet she had to go along with them, on their return, or they would, she knew, murder as many of the monks as necessary without the slightest hesitation.

'You won't get away with it,' she said futilely. 'The police are already on our trail. Baldwin . . .' Oh Baldwin, she thought. Wha would I give to see you coming over that hill now? He simply had to be close.

'Yeah,' Teddy said. 'Baldwin. You can forget Baldwin. Here they are.'

The open tourer bumped to the side of the road and stopped. Calvin Hart stepped down, and a man she had never seen before, considerably larger than his partner and with a busy moustache who she presumed must be Lewis.

'You made good time,' Teddy said.

'Yes,' Hart said, as precisely as ever. 'Well, let's do what we have to do and get out of here.'

'No rush,' Teddy said. 'The train comes back around now, and it could be late. We wait until it's long gone, right? We play it real cool, take our time, enjoy the hospitality that's gonna be offered us, and when we're ready, bingo.'

'You have got to be out of your mind,' Calvin said. 'We're likely to have the whole world on our doorstep at any moment.'

'How come?'

'Because that Scotland Yard detective you hit on the head in the toilet in Paris is dead, that's how come.'

Julie's knees gave way and she sank to the grass. If the bruise on her jaw was still throbbing, and her stomach was still churning, she now felt that she had just been shot through the heart.

'Holy shit!' Teddy commented. 'You kidding?'

'It's in the afternoon papers in Milan. Scotland Yard man found dying in Gentlemen's Lavatory at the Gare du Lyons. I knew you shouldn't have hit him so hard.'

'Well, he must have a soft skull,' Teddy remarked.

Oh, Baldwin, Julie said. Oh, Baldwin. Someone else she had led to his death. But Baldwin wasn't someone else. He was Johnnie Baldwin. Now the tears came flooding down her cheeks. Because now she was absolutely alone in the world. Save for Uncle Bob and Father Mike. But they had no idea of the sort of people they were about to have to face.

But had Baldwin? She had supposed so, after the way he had handled Kaley. And she had been wrong.

'Anyway,' Teddy said. 'What's the panic? So a British bobby gets done in a French lavatory. No one knows who did it. We'll just go home via Germany, that's all.'

317

'They say it don't pay to kill a British bobby,' Lewis muttered.

'So what are these guys? Better than the Feds? They're cops. And I can tell you, when you blow a hole in a cop, he bleeds just like anybody else. There ain't nobody in this whole world will know I had any cause for stopping Baldwin. Save for the boss, here.' He nudged her with his shoe. 'Say, Boss, time we were moving.'

Julie raised her head. I am going to kill you, she thought. Oh, God, I am going to kill you, even if it is with my last breath on earth. But she didn't say so. If he had so completely fooled her for so long, her only hope of survival, even for a little while, was to be as devious.

She pushed herself to her feet, made no attempt to brush dust from her skirt or even from her hair, allowed her shoulders to slump. Actually, to appear different to that would have been the act.

'Is she all right?' Hart asked.

'Yeah. I just had to teach her who is really the boss around here. I think she got the message. Let's go.'

He made her sit in the back beside him. 'Show her what you got there, Calvin,' he commanded.

She knew before he even opened the suitcase. Two sub-machine guns.

'So remember,' Teddy told her. 'There is no reason for anybody to get hurt. Only you can make that happen.'

'If . . . if I co-operate, will you swear not to shoot anyone?' she asked.

He grinned, and ruffled her hair. Her beret had come off. 'Sure I swear.'

She bit her lip, and watched the road unfolding in front of them. They swung round the bend and looked at the monastery. 'Hell's bells,' Lewis commented. 'We can get into that bastille?'

'Easy as pie,' Teddy assured him. 'Give them a toot, Calvin.'

Hart blew the horn, but there was no immediate response. They stopped in front of the gate, and a small square window was opened.

'Do your stuff, sweetheart,' Teddy said. 'But remember . . . Calvin speaks Italian.'

Julie drew a long breath . . . but she didn't dare risk anything here. 'It's Mrs Longman,' she called.

A moment later the gate swung open, and the car drove in. Father Michael and Uncle Bob emerged from the main building. 'Julie?'

They peered at her as Teddy helped her down, holding her arm. 'What has happened?'

'She ain't feeling too good,' Teddy explained. 'She took a fall, down one of those hillsides.'

'My God!' Uncle Bob hurried forward.

'Nothing broken,' Teddy assured him. 'She just wants to lie down for an hour. But say, padre, these two guys happened along and gave us a lift. I reckon the least we could do is ask them to stay for dinner.'

'Of course,' Father Michael agreed. 'You are welcome, gentlemen. The priory of San Giorgio is always open.'

'That's very kind of you, Father,' Calvin said, and shook hands. 'The name's Calvin Hart, and this is my friend, Osbert Lewis.'

'My pleasure,' Father Michael said. Uncle Bob didn't look so sure, but he was more concerned about Julie.

'Are you sure you're all right?' he asked.

Teddy's fingers were tight on her arm, and his right hand was in the pocket of his jacket, while Calvin was carrying the suitcase with the tommy-guns, and she knew how quickly he could open it. 'I think so,' she said. 'I'll be fine once I've had a little rest. Father Michael . . . do you think I could have a bath?'

'Of course, my dear. I will instruct Father Paul to draw you one.'

Teddy escorted her along the corridor to their cell, closed the door. 'You're doing all right,' he remarked. 'Just keep up the good work.'

Julie turned away from him, washed her face, and felt better. But only marginally. The words kept searing through her head: Baldwin is dead. Hit on the head and killed, just like Daddy. The only man she had ever loved, and the only man she thought she ever could have loved, both murdered, by that grinning hoodlum behind her. The man to whom she had given her body and her trust. Well, what did that make her?

'Lie down and relax,' Teddy said. 'Say, I don't suppose you feel like a tumble? You look real good when you're mad.'

'You touch me . . .' she whispered.

He grinned. 'Okay. Maybe it wouldn't work, anyway. We both have a lot on our minds. When we've done the job.'

He lay down himself, but with his eyes open, watching her, and he had taken the pistol from his jacket pocket before hanging the garment up. Julie removed her skirt and blouse, which were both

319

filthy anyway, and lay on the other cot. She closed her eyes, and then rolled on her side, away from him. She couldn't think with him grinning at her. And she had to think.

But what about? She could only think about Baldwin, and that was disastrous. She had to think about what was going to happen next. But she couldn't do that, either, to any purpose. She only knew that if she started something a whole lot more people were going to get killed, and this time they wouldn't be hoodlums or policemen but monks. She just could not take that responsibility. Far better to let Teddy and Hart and Lewis have the money and go. For the time being. She'd track them down, Teddy at any rate, if it took her the rest of her life; she now had two murders to avenge, and hadn't he raped her just as much as MacGinnion or Kaley – even if she hadn't realised it at the time?

There was a knock on the door.

'Yeah?' Teddy called.

'I have Signora Longman's bath ready,' Father Paul said, un-luckily in English.

'Oh, great. She'll be right along.'

Julie had already got out of bed. Now she finished undressing, took her dressing-gown and slippers from the suitcase, watched him also get up. 'You aren't coming,' she said.

'Of course I am, baby. You think I'm gonna let you out of my sight?'

'And you don't think that'll get the monks wondering?'

'It'll get them excited, sure. But you're my wife, not some little girl they've picked in off the hillside. Come along now.'

He had put on his jacket again, and the pistol was in his pocket. She opened the door, and Father Paul smiled at her. If he had discerned anything unusual in the conversation he gave no sign of it. They followed him down the corridor until he opened another door and showed them into another cell, this one completely empty save for a large tin tub in the centre of the floor, filled with steaming water. The only other furniture was a single chair with a towel draped across it. 'Is good?' he asked.

'Is great,' Teddy told him.

Brother Paul went to the door, hesitated.

'That's okay,' Teddy told him. Brother Paul looked at Julie, then stepped outside and closed the door. 'They'll have an animated supper,' Teddy said. He dropped the towel on the floor and sat down. 'We don't want to be too late.'

Waves of utter helplessness swept over Julie. If she could pick up the tub and brain him with it . . . but she couldn't, and that would, in any event, still leave Hart and Lewis. But perhaps . . . she had to think, straight. She had to think like Julie Armitage, for one last time. Even with Baldwin dead, with the future stretching futilely in front of her, she had to be Julie Armitage, at least until she had avenged Daddy – and everything else. The fact that he still found her attractive had to be a weapon.

'I can just see you curdling there,' he said. 'You'll give yourself ulcers. Come along now, or we'll scrub the idea.'

Julie dropped the dressing-gown on the floor, and stepped into the tub. It was hot enough to send a tremendous goose pimple through her body, and when she sat down there wasn't room for her legs, so she had to drape them over the side.

'Christ,' Teddy said, watching her. 'You know, it'd be a real shame to have to float you down a river.'

'Maybe you won't have to,' she said.

She didn't dare look at him, as she picked up the soap. The fact that he had not immediately replied was encouraging.

She soaped her arms, slowly, languorously. 'Maybe I over-reacted, out there on the hill. But you sure sprang something on me.'

'Yeah?'

She turned her attention to her legs. 'Well . . . no girl likes to be deceived, quite that much. I mean, what the hell, about Daddy? He was a thug. He'd killed, and he'd robbed, and he'd cheated, and one day he had to die. He'd even cheated me. I hated him for that. Maybe, if he'd lived, I would have killed him myself when I found out. But to pretend to marry me – that was unforgivable.' At last she looked at him. He was looking at her. 'And stupid,' she pointed out. 'So what are you going to get out of this? A third of a million dollars? What's that, maybe eighty thousand pounds? By your own reckoning Daddy has maybe ten times that in an account some-where. And it's all mine. You can't touch it without me.' She finished her legs and stood up to soap her body. 'Maybe you'd like to do my back.'

He was breathing quite heavily, watching her massaging her

321

pubes. Now he put the pistol in his pocket, and stood up, came towards her.

'How's the scar?' she asked.

He touched it, and she gave a little shiver.

'Does it still hurt?' he asked.

'Yes. Underneath. But I suppose it's healing.' She gave him the soap over her shoulder.

His hands slid over her flesh, down to her buttocks, went between, then came round the front and up her body to hold her breasts. 'It sure would be a shame,' he muttered in her ear. 'To lose all of that money and all of this flesh.'

His body was almost touching her. 'You ever done it on a bathroom floor?' she asked.

'Jesus,' he muttered, and the soap fell into the water. She could not see him, but she just knew he was taking off his jacket. She would never have another opportunity. She took a long breath, and then struck backwards, turning as she did so and kicking with all of her strength, while she brought her hands together into a swinging club which caught him across the side of the face. He gasped and fell to one side, and she leapt over him, hesitating, water rolling down her body. Her dressing-gown was on the far side of the tub. But the chair was her only weapon. She reached for it, picked it up, turned, found that he was already back on his knees, his face distorted with anger in a way she had never seen before. And knew that she was not going to succeed.

But she had to succeed. She swung the chair with all of her strength, and he grunted, and caught it. She panted, and tried to raise it again, but he retained his hold of it, and with a twist of his wrists tore it from her grasp, and threw it to one side. She ran for the door, and tried to leap the tub, but he fell forward and caught her ankle. She went into the water with an enormous splash, and hit herself on the iron rim with a force which left her breathless. And he was still holding her ankle, his fingers eating into her flesh, as he raised the limb higher yet, making her more and more helpless. Panting and sobbing, she tried to kick him with her other leg, supporting herself on her hands, but he just laughed, and then twisted his leg, so that she turned over, and hit the floor, on her back, once again winded and gasping.

322

'You are something,' he said, and knelt above her. 'No,' he grinned, 'I've never done it on the bathroom floor.'

She struck at him, and he caught her wrist. 'Now listen,' he said. 'You lie there, or so help me God, I am going to hurt you.'

She knew he meant it, and in any event she was too exhausted to continue the fight. She had failed. Because she wasn't really Julie Armitage. For all the great charade in New York she had depended on other people's muscle, and now she had none left. Julie Allen was indeed out of her class.

Teddy grinned as he took off his jacket and tossed it where she couldn't possibly reach it. 'I ought to hurt you anyway,' he said. 'But you sure do turn me on.'

Her only hope was that someone would have overheard the fight. But no one came in. When he took her outside, her mind a seethe of bitter agony and hatred, Brother Paul was certainly there, but merely looking embarrassed.

'I'm afraid we made a bit of a mess,' Teddy said. 'My wife ain't that used to tin tubs.'

Brother Paul smiled and bowed.

Teddy pushed her into their cell. 'Okay,' he commanded. 'Get dressed. Wear that pretty dress you brought.'

She stepped into her dark blue cocktail dress, put on flesh-coloured stockings and black courts, and brushed her hair. If she felt bruised and battered, and sick and angry – far more so than even after she had suffered MacGinnion and Kaley – there was no external sign of it. Her chin was slightly discoloured, but less so than she had supposed, and indeed hoped.

'Powder it,' Teddy commanded.

She obeyed. For the moment she was defeated, and it might be the last moment. But she had failed, and there was no way she could call for help without precipitating another bloodbath; she couldn't face that. When she was ready he escorted her down the corridor to Father Michael's sitting-room. Hart and Lewis were already there. They had left their suitcase in their cell, but she couldn't doubt that, like Teddy, they were carrying pistols.

'My dear Julie,' Father Michael said. 'You look as pretty as a picture. But that mark on your chin—'

'She hit it when she fell,' Teddy explained.

323

'Do you know you have said hardly a word since coming back?' Uncle Bob remarked.

'Speaking is a little painful,' she told him.

'I can imagine. Would you like some medication? Father Mike keeps quite a store here.'

'Oh, yes,' Julie said. 'Shall I come with you?'

'Of course . . .'

'I don't think medication is a good idea,' Teddy said.

Uncle Bob gazed at him. 'Why not?'

'I don't believe in it,' Teddy said, blandly. 'I'm a believer in faith healing.'

Uncle Bob opened his mouth and then closed it again, glanced at Father Michael, who did not seem the least disturbed. 'I do not think anything I possess can heal much, Mr Longman,' he said. 'All we were thinking of was relieving your wife's discomfort.'

'She'll get over it,' Teddy said.

'Why, you lousy little . . .' began Uncle Bob.

'Uncle Bob, please,' Julie said.

The men glared at each other.

'What are we waiting for?' Calvin asked.

'Yeah,' Lewis said. 'Let's get the hell out of here. That train has to have gone through by now.'

Father Michael looked from one to the other. 'Is something wrong?'

'Not a lot,' Teddy said. He grasped Julie's arm, and plucked her away from the centre of the room. Hart and Lewis also backed away, and all three men drew their pistols.

'My word,' Father Michael remarked.

'Just don't try anything,' Teddy said. 'You won't believe it, Calvin, but this character is an ex-hood. Told me so himself. Don't even think about it, Major,' he added, as Uncle Bob looked about to explode.

'I assume you want the money,' Father Michael said.

'That's right. Now.'

Father Michael sighed. 'So you were right, after all, Bob. And I was wrong. It saddens me.'

'And if we refuse to give it to you?' Uncle Bob inquired. His big hands were curled into fists.

'We'll shoot you,' Teddy said. 'And anybody else who gets in our way. And we'll find the dough, eventually.'

'You're talking nonsense.'

'Please believe him, Uncle Bob,' Julie said. 'He means it. They have tommy-guns in their luggage. Please give them the money.'

Uncle Bob stared at her. 'Are you in this, Julie?'

'Of course she is,' Teddy said. 'Ain't you, sweetheart?' His fingers bit in to her arm. 'Ain't you?'

'Yes,' she said. 'Yes.'

'And you gotta admit it really is her dough,' Teddy said. 'Now, you guys gonna play ball?'

Father Michael and Uncle Bob looked at each other. 'I don't think we have much choice,' Father Michael decided. 'There is no money in the world worth dying for. It is in my office.'

'Which is where?'

'Across the courtyard.'

'Oh, yeah? Okay. Nobody move. Cal, get your gear in here.'

Calvin hurried from the room.

'How many monks you got here, padre?' Teddy asked.

'There are twelve of us.'

'Well, that sure ain't gonna be no hassle. Okay, Cal?'

Hart was back with the suitcase, which he now opened to take out the two tommy-guns.

'Talk about overkill,' Teddy said with a grin. 'But it pays to be safe. Okay, you two guys. We're gonna walk across the yard and get the dough. All of us. Just remember that blotting you lot out will be easier than stamping on an ant.'

'Please,' Julie said, as Father Michael and Uncle Bob exchanged glances again. 'He means it. This money has already caused God knows how many deaths. Please just give it to him.'

'To you, you mean,' Uncle Bob said. 'Seems to me you've caused as many deaths as the money.'

'Yes,' she said, her shoulders sagging.

Teddy pulled her to one side of the doorway. 'Let's go. You first Uncle Bob.'

Uncle Bob hesitated, then moved forward.

'He's all yours, Ozzie,' Teddy said. 'And you can blast him any time he steps out of line.'

Lewis followed; he had pocketed his pistol and carried one of the tommy-guns.

'Now you, padre,' Teddy said. 'He's yours, Calvin. And padre, try to remember; one burst from that tommy gun will have your entire monastery banging on St Peter's door.'

Father Michael went through the door, Hart and the other tommy-gun behind him; Hart carried the now empty suitcase in his other hand.

'Okay,' Teddy said, and pushed Julie forward. 'Just remember you're expendable too, baby. And if I have to shoot you, then I have to shoot everybody else. You got that?'

Julie didn't reply. She stumbled along the corridor and into the open air. It was still perfectly light, although the sun had dipped behind the mountains to the west. Uncle Bob and Lewis were halfway across the yard, and Teddy called out, 'Hold it there, Ozzie. Just wait by the car. Major, you stand over there by the wall, right?'

Julie's heart was pounding with a mixture of despair and apprehension. She knew that Uncle Bob was going to explode any minute, and that Teddy was actually willing him to do so.

'We won't be five minutes,' he said.

Father Michael hesitated, was nudged in the back by Hart's gun, and opened the office door. There had been only one of the monks in the yard when they had emerged, but now several others gathered, staring at them and the guns, muttering to each other.

'You'd better talk to them, Julie,' Teddy said. 'And you'd better talk good and sensible.'

They were at the office door, and he was still holding her arm, while Lewis surveyed the monks, and Uncle Bob, moving the muzzle of the tommy gun slowly to and fro.

'Please,' she called in Italian. 'Please do nothing. These men are killers. Please.'

'How're you doing, Calvin?' Teddy called.

'There is a great deal of it,' Calvin replied. 'Place them in the bag, Father.'

Teddy grinned. 'Hallelujah.'

It took some five minutes for the money to be transferred from Father Michael's safe to Hart's suitcase. It was the longest five minutes of Julie's life. The tension in the courtyard of the monastery was greater even than in the car on the way to execute MacGinnion. And she didn't know what she wanted to happen. If in some way these black-robed figures could get the better of their captors . . . but she knew there was no way; they could only die.

'Eureka,' Hart said, emerging behind Father Michael.

'Dump it in the back of the car,' Teddy told him. 'Okay, you guys.' He counted. 'Ten. Where are the other two? Ask them, Calvin.'

'Where are the other brothers?' Hart demanded.

'About their duties,' Father Michael said.

'Well, get them out here.'

'Brother Paul,' Father Michael called. 'Brother Primo.'

There was no response.

'You had better try again, padre,' Teddy said. 'And hope they obey you, or we are going to start shooting.'

Father Michael called again. 'Come into the courtyard,' he said. 'There is nothing you can do.'

A few moments later the two remaining monks emerged. Julie sighed. Again, perhaps, she had been hoping for a miracle.

'Now you're sure that's everyone, padre,' Teddy said. 'Because let me tell you something; if I come across anyone else, man or woman, I'm gonna blow his or her ass off. Right?'

'There is nobody else, my son,' Father Michael said.

'Okay. So down you go, into the wine cellar.'

They hesitated, and he pointed with his gun.

'Suppose we refuse?' Uncle Bob demanded again.

'Then you get it, in the gut. You, buster. You'd better tell your pals, padre.'

'Into the cellar,' Father Michael said, and the monks slowly obeyed him.

'And you, Uncle Bob,' Teddy ordered.

Uncle Bob glared at him.

'Please, Uncle Bob,' Julie said. 'For God's sake.'

'I'll be looking,' Uncle Bob said. 'For you both.' He went down the steps.

'And you, padre.'

Father Michael paused at the top of the steps. 'I know you are being coerced, Julie,' he said. 'I will say a prayer for you.'

He disappeared, and Lewis gave a shout. 'Yippee!' He ran forward, closed the trap, and shot the bolts. 'They ain't coming out of there for a while.'

'What about Mrs Longman?' Hart asked. 'You don't suppose she should be in there with them?'

'I reckon she should get one,' Hart said.

Julie looked from face to face. They're talking about me, she thought. My life. But does it matter?

Teddy grinned. 'She comes with us, for the time being. I'm not done with her yet.' He was thinking of the million pounds, she knew. Did that represent a chance for her? She was too beaten and dispirited to think about it.

'I think you're crazy,' Calvin said. 'But it's your funeral. Where now, Switzerland?'

'The village, first.'

'Come again?'

'That taxi is their only link with the outside world,' Teddy told them. 'We take that out, and they gotta wait for tomorrow morning's train. By then we'll be in Germany.'

'Good thinking,' Calvin agreed.

Oh, God, Julie thought, as she was bundled into the back of the tourer. There was to be more shooting. She wanted to start fighting him, to see if she could wreck the car, to force him to shoot her . . . but she couldn't risk dying until she could be sure of taking him with her. She would have to be patient. She would have to be Julie Armitage, Eddie Armitage's daughter, for yet another while longer.

They drove out of the courtyard, and stopped to let Ozzie close the gates. 'Must leave it looking real natural to anyone passing by,' Teddy said. It was just after nine and the dusk was beginning to close.

'Now, we want a quick in and out,' he reminded them. 'Leave the locals wondering what hit them. The garage is this end of the street.'

'We stopped there to fill up before joining you,' Calvin told him, and put the car in gear, then braked, as bumping down the road towards them there came a saloon.

'Looks like the cab's come to us,' Ozzie said.

'That's not the cab,' Teddy snapped; behind the first car there came another. 'Christalmighty! Back up.'

Julie tried to get up and he threw both arms round her waist. Calvin grated the gears as he engaged reverse and sent the tourer back while Ozzie jumped out to open the gate. The oncoming cars had also braked, doors opening as they did so to allow uniformed men to tumble out. 'Goddamn!' Teddy shouted. 'Fucking police. Get this crate inside.'

The gates were open, and the tourer was hurtling backwards. Teddy was reaching for the tommy-gun Ozzie had left behind, and Julie threw off his arm and stood up to look at the quaintly uniformed civil guards, who were drawing their revolvers and preparing to open fire as they saw the sub-machine gun. There were seven of them, but there was also an eighth man, a big, aggressive looking man with a broken nose who had already drawn and levelled his gun, but was lowering it again as he saw her.

John Baldwin!

The gate slammed shut and Ozzie slammed the bolts. 'Holy shit!' Teddy snapped. 'You said that guy was dead.'

'Well, that's what the papers said.'

'Some kind of put-up job,' Ozzie suggested.

He's alive, Julie thought, her brain singing. Baldwin is alive, and there, as she had always known he would be. Just a little late, but he was there. She listened to banging on the cellar door. Uncle Bob was trying to get out. Teddy was caught between two fires.

'Yeah,' Teddy was saying. 'But how the hell did he know to come here . . .' he gazed at her. 'You little bitch,' he said. 'I ought to break every bone in your body.'

'An excellent idea,' Calvin agreed. He had got out, and was peering through the small window. 'But just what are we going to do then, Teddy?'

'Get the dame for a start,' Ozzie growled.

Julie stared at Teddy, whose immediate anger had faded with remarkable suddenness. 'I think we'll hang on to her for a while,' he said. 'That guy Baldwin wouldn't shoot when he saw her. She could be our passport to safety.'

'Well, I guess they can't get at us in here,' Ozzie said, picking up his tommy-gun. 'I reckon this place can stand a siege, and we got the metal.'

'So you aim to become a monk?' Teddy asked. He held Julie's arm and forced her out of the car.

'We certainly can't stay here very long,' Calvin said, still peering through the aperture. 'Listen.'

They heard the growl of an automobile engine.

'Reinforcements?' Teddy asked.

'Soon will be. They're sending one of their people back in one of

329

the squad cars. We'll have the whole damned Italian police force up here come morning.'

'So how many are there now?'

'Seven. Only one went.'

'And what are they doing?'

'Talking, mostly.'

'Yeah,' Teddy said, and looked at the sky. It was half past nine, but still fairly light, although the sun had gone. He drew his pistol, tightened his grip on Julie's arm. She was hardly thinking any more, only aware that Baldwin was there, that she had a chance to live . . . and that she had something to live for. But then she felt the pistol muzzle jamming into her right breast. 'Now you listen to me,' Teddy said. 'You want to survive you just behave. Or I am gonna blow this tit right off. Now give. What's with you and Baldwin?'

She gazed at him. 'He's on my side,' she said.

'And how.' He grinned at her. 'Cuckolding the old man, eh? And you not even married a month.'

She didn't trouble to deny it. The more he had on his mind the better.

'So how'd he know to come here?'

'I told him,' she said.

'How?'

'I left a message at Folkestone.'

'Goddamn,' he said. 'The fucking toilet.' The gun jammed into her flesh, and she winced. 'I ought to let you have it right now. But how'd he know to come up here? You only knew we were making for San Giorgio.'

'I imagine he asked after us in the village,' Julie said.

'What I'd like to know is how he managed to reach here so quickly,' Calvin said. 'After you knocked him out in the toilet in Paris.'

'Yeah. I guess we'll have to ask him that, one of these days. But he's a cutie, putting it out that he was dead.'

'Because when you hit him you tipped your hand,' Hart pointed out. 'He wanted you to think you'd got away with it. While he rounded up all the force he could. He must have come down by airplane. We may have a problem, Teddy. This chap seems to have all his marbles.'

'So what. The guy is fond of you, eh, Julie?'

'He's on my side,' she repeated. 'He has been from the beginning.'

'Is that a fact. So I guess it's you he's been hurrying behind, not us and not the dough. Okay, Calvin, open the gate.'

'Are you mad?'

'I told you, this little chick is our passport to freedom. You guys be ready to move out.'

The banging had ceased from the cellar; no doubt Father Michael and Uncle Bob were listening and trying to decide what was going on.

Calvin pulled the bolt, and the gate swung back a few feet. Teddy pushed Julie into the aperture.

'Stop right there, Longman,' Baldwin called. 'Throw your gun down, and come towards us, slowly, with your hands up. Tell your goons to do the same.'

'What about the chick?' Teddy asked.

'If you harm her, by God . . .'

'I don't aim to,' Teddy said. 'Unless I have to. Heck, she's my wife. But a guy has to look out for himself. I don't aim to spend the rest of my life in an Italian gaol, or a British one. Now you listen to me, Baldwin. My pals and I are coming out, with Julie. We are gonna drive past you, nice and slow, and then we are gonna take off and not trouble you no more. Now I'll tell you. You try to stop us, in any way, and I'm gonna give you Julie with her tit shot off. Remember that. You co-operate, and make no trouble, and I'll leave her for you at the border. Unharmed. You got that?'

'I heard you,' Baldwin said.

'So is it a deal?'

Julie held her breath. She wanted to kick down and hit backwards with her elbow but she knew that in the mood he was in Teddy might well carry out his threat. And now she no longer wanted to die, however much she was still determined to avenge Daddy's murder.

'It's a deal,' Baldwin said.

'Then maybe you'd better tell your friends.'

Baldwin obviously didn't speak Italian, but equally obviously he was accompanied by an English-speaking policeman. The two men exchanged a brief word, then the Italian began translating. Julie stared at Baldwin, and he stared back. 'You all right, Julie?' he called.

331

'Yes,' she said. 'Yes. I'm all right.'

'And we all aim to see that she stays that way, right?' Teddy asked. 'Okay, you guys,' he said, without turning his head. 'Bring the automobile back out.'

'You think this is going to work?' Calvin asked.

'I know it's gonna work. Come along.'

The gates swung even wider, and the engine growled. The tourer braked beside them, and Teddy pushed Julie into the back seat. 'Stand up,' he snapped as she would have sat down. He remained standing as well, both arms round her waist, the pistol still held against the underside of her breast. 'Nice and slow, Calvin,' he commanded. 'We want these guys to take a good look.'

The car moved slowly forward. The policemen were standing in a group to one side of the road; Baldwin was with them. They stared at the tourer and its occupants, faces grim. 'We'll be behind you, Longman,' Baldwin said. 'And so help me, if you don't leave Julie at the border . . .'

'She'll be there,' Teddy promised. The car moved past the men, and was alongside the remaining policecar. 'But you won't,' he muttered. The pistol stopped pressing into Julie's flesh as he aimed at the nearest wheel and fired.

The front tyre exploded and Teddy then put a shot into the rear one as well. He was an excellent marksman. But for that quick second the gun was no longer pressing into Julie's flesh. Now she did strike behind her with her elbow with all of her strength. Teddy gasped, and lost his balance, falling backwards over the front seats to cannon into Hart. As he was still holding Julie's arm she went with him.

Hart gave an exclamation of alarm, but the two bodies descending on his shoulders and into his lap in a flurry of arms and legs made him lose control of the car. It swung to the left, teetered for a moment, and then went down the slope. Julie knew it was going to go over, and Teddy had lost his grip on her arm. She pushed down on Calvin's head and threw herself sideways, hit the ground with a jolt which knocked all the breath from her body, and went rolling, unable to stop herself, listening to a cacophony of sound as the car crashed down the slope beside her.

She landed in a hollow, on her back, bruising herself on a large stone, arms and legs and skirt scattered, and mind too, as she stared

332

at the darkening night sky and thought she was going to choke before she could get her breath back. Then she sat up, to gaze at the tourer, which had come to rest only a few feet away, upside down, wheels spinning feebly in the air, at Calvin Hart, on his hands and knees, making moaning noises as he clutched a broken wrist, and at Ozzie Lewis, who seemed unhurt, but who was staring down the hill with a most pitiful expression, as he watched the cloud of paper drifting away from the burst-open suitcase which continued to roll and slide down into the darkness. She almost wanted to laugh, until she saw Teddy.

He also seemed to be unhurt, and was on his knees, looking up the slope. He did not know where she was, obviously, but he was watching Baldwin leading the Italian policemen down the slope towards them, and he held one of the tommy-guns in his hands. She gasped in horror, because Baldwin was shouting her name, and in the gloom they obviously where not sure where anyone was. And Teddy was levelling the gun, a look of the most vicious hatred on his face.

Julie sucked air into her lungs, picked up the stone, and lurched forward. She tripped as she did so – the rock was much heavier than she had supposed – and went flying towards him. Teddy turned in alarm, and the stone crashed into the side of his head, just above the ear. He fell without a sound, and Julie fell beside him, panting and weeping, watching the blood drifting away from his shattered temple.

Feet clumped around her, and Baldwin pulled her to her feet. 'Are you all right?' he panted.

She hid her face in his shoulder. He had such a reassuring shoulder.

One of the policemen had knelt beside Teddy. Now he stood up. 'That man will be dead in an hour,' he said. He signalled two of his people. 'Carry him up to the monastery, and see if Father Michael can help him.' He fumbled at his belt, and produced a pair of handcuffs. 'You are under arrest, senora.'

Julie goggled at him. 'On what charge?'

The police lieutenant shrugged. 'I think there will be several charges. But the principal one may well be murder.'

Church bells, shrouding Milan with their melodious sound. Presumably it was Sunday. Julie had lost track of the days since she had been brought here. Since the morning after Teddy's death, when she had been examined by the magistrate. She had not felt like defending herself. She had only wanted to close her eyes, and sleep, as if a nightmare was over, and her exhausted brain and body could at last relax. She had not seen Baldwin again. She was not sure she had wanted to. As he had reminded her more than once, he was a policeman, and necessarily looked at things from a policeman's point of view – and she had killed a man before his very eyes. Her husband. There had been no time to tell him that they had never actually been married, nor was she sure how to set about proving that.

Or even if she wanted to.

Since then the days had rather drifted together. She gathered that the wheels of Italian justice ground rather slowly, and that it might be months before she came to trial. Months in which she would be confined in this cell, apart from the other prisoners on remand, as she was so dangerous a woman, and exercised in private as well. The wardresses were very kind, even sympathetic, but they were no company. Not that she wanted company. Because she was Julie Allen. For a brief crowded hour she had become Julie Armitage, had lived on a scale and at a pace she would not have supposed possible had she not experienced it. No doubt she had been mad, from the moment Uncle Bob had come to Mrs Simpson's Academy, to the moment she had hit Teddy with the stone and killed him. She had no regrets about that, even if the Italians locked her up for the rest of her life. She had at last avenged Daddy.

But with the blow had come sanity again.

So, another day, another . . . the key scraped in the lock and she sat up. Her suitcase had been brought down from the monastery, but the prison supplied its own nightgowns and these she was required to wear, drab lengths of cotton cloth primly secured at the neck with cotton cord.

The head wardress smiled at her. 'Good morning, Julie,' she said. 'Will you please get dressed?'

'Now?' They had taken away her watch but she knew it was still early in the morning.

'There are some gentlemen to see you,' the wardress explained.

The moment had arrived. She was about to be placed on trial. Well, it would at least relieve the monotony of her existence.

She pulled on her clothes, the same clothes she had worn on the day they had visited the monastery, and followed the wardress down the corridor to the interview room. She stepped inside, and found herself gazing at Mr Cornwall.

'Julie,' he held her hands. 'How very good to see you at last.'

She frowned at him. Her brain seemed to be working very slowly. 'Have you come to defend me, Mr Cornwall?'

He smiled at her. 'I have come to take you home, Julie.'

She stared at him, and slowly sat down on one of the straight chairs. 'Home? But – Teddy's death?'

'It has been decided not to prosecute you. It has taken a great deal of time, but we have depositions from the two other men involved, Calvin Hart and Osbert Lewis – who are both to be tried, incidentally, for the assault on the monastery – that you were coerced by your husband into assisting them, and a deposition from Father Michael and Major Roberts to the same effect, and one from Detective Sergeant Baldwin that you were definitely saving his life in striking Mr Longman.'

'Oh,' she said. 'Oh. Is John – Mr Baldwin – here?'

'No. I'm afraid he had to return to duty. He did give me a message for you, however, when last we met.'

'Yes?'

'It was merely to remember his telephone number. Whitehall 1212.'

'Oh,' she said. Baldwin! Despite it all, he wanted her to call him. Oh, Baldwin!

'However, I doubt you will have to use it,' Mr Cornwall went on. 'I have also been in touch with the Home Office about all the ramifications of this case, and they have decided to allow you to live in Great Britain, if you choose to do so, providing you report regularly to the police, and ah . . . generally behave yourself.'

'Yes,' she said. 'Oh, yes.'

'Unfortunately,' he continued. 'They are insisting you stand by the bargain you apparently made with this man Baldwin, to donate the balance of your father's funds to charity. I must say, I would be inclined to fight that in the courts. I mean, no matter what sort of life your father lived – and I will admit that I was quite shocked to discover the true facts of the case – that is your money. There is no law in England allowing them to sequestrate the funds.'

'But if I fight them they'll just deport me.'

'Well, I suppose they will. But still, a million pounds . . . that

335

would set you up very nicely in America. And you are an American citizen. No one can deport you from there.'

He was obviously still in the dark about the American end of things. 'I can't go back to America, Mr Cornwall. Not for a long time.'

'Indeed? May I ask why?'

'It's a long story. Give them their money.'

'Yes. Well . . . I'm afraid it doesn't leave you all that much, you know. Unfortunately my fees, well . . . there has been a great deal of expense. With careful husbandry you should be able to live on the income from what is left, but there is no possibility of you being able to retain the Mayfair flat. That is very expensive.'

'Yes,' she said. She would have to get used to being poor again. But she had only been rich for less than a month.

'So if you would care to fetch your things . . .'

'Yes,' she said. 'Yes.' How unimportant it all was. Baldwin had left a message. And she had said, when she called, he should come to her. On roller skates.

Father Michael and Uncle Bob were there to say goodbye. 'I am truly sorry about your husband,' Father Michael said.

'Don't be. We weren't married,' Julie told him. 'I thought we were, but that was part of his deception. He made me a complete fool.'

'But it was he perished at the end,' Father Michael pointed out. 'It is a pity that all that money had to be lost . . .' he sighed.

'Yes,' she said. 'Isn't it?' She gazed at Uncle Bob. 'You were right, and I was wrong, from the beginning, Uncle Bob. I'm sorry.'

'Julie . . .' he held her hands. 'I know I behaved very badly, at times. But—'

She shook her head. 'It wouldn't work, Uncle Bob. It couldn't. It couldn't have, anyway, I don't think. But now it would be impossible.'

He sighed in turn, and nodded. 'I suppose you're right. But Julie, to think of you all alone in the world, and with such memories.'

'I'll manage,' she said.

Mr Cornwall wanted her to go down to Epsom, but she decided to spend a last couple of days in Mayfair, before it was placed on the market. George was there to greet her. 'Oh, Miss Julie,' he said. 'Mr Cornwall told me, about Mr Armitage, and Mr Longman. I am so very sorry.'

'Thank you, George,' she said. 'You understand that I couldn't tell you about Father before.'

'I'm sure you did as you thought best, Miss Julie,' he said, carrying her bag upstairs for her, and opening the door.

She stepped inside, inhaled the familiar scents, looked at the photographs of herself, and wanted to burst into tears. In the oddest, most crazy way, she had been happy here. 'George,' she said, 'you know I am going to have to sell the flat.'

He was carrying the bag into the bedroom for her. 'Oh, surely that won't be necessary, Miss Julie.'

She followed him slowly. 'I can't afford it any more. Simple as that.'

'You can't afford this flat, miss?' George frowned at her.

And she saw the two suitcases, waiting by the bed. 'George,' she said, 'what are those?'

'They belonged to your father, Miss Julie. So now they belong to you. In fact, he gave me specific instructions that, should anything ever happen to him, they were to be delivered to you personally. I think he wished to bypass things like lawyers and probates and death duties, if you understand me.'

Oh, God, Julie thought. 'George, do you know what is in those cases?'

'Why, yes, Miss Julie. Mr Armitage and I were the very best of friends, so when he gave me the money, it was for me to place in a safe deposit box where no one would ever know about it until it was needed. I took it all out the moment Mr Cornwall told me Mr Armitage was dead, and brought it here to wait for you.'

Julie sat on the bed; her knees felt weak. 'The money? How much money, George?'

'Well, miss, I'm not absolutely certain, but I think you'll find approximately a million dollars in each case.'

Two million dollars, she thought. The discrepancy between what MacGinnion had said was stolen, and what Father Michael had actually received. For her?

'Mr Armitage also gave me a message for you, Miss Julie, whenever I should have to deliver the money. He said to tell you that if you never revealed you possessed it, to anyone, you could be the happiest woman on earth. And then he said, tell her, George, that I loved her, as much as I loved her mother.'

337

The tears rolled down Julie's cheeks.

'So you won't have to sell the flat, now, will you, Miss Julie?'

'No,' she said. 'No, I won't have to sell the flat, George.'

George went to the door. 'And you needn't worry about me, Miss Julie. Mr Armitage left me well provided for.' He winked. 'I haven't told anybody either. Not even the wife.'

The door closed, and Julie remained gazing at it for several seconds. Dear Father, she thought; he had been Eddie Armitage to the very end. His daughter could inherit two million dollars – if she had the gumption to find out that she was his daughter. Otherwise, she could live on a pittance for the rest of her life.

But she was Julie Armitage, even if she intended to be Julie Allen for the rest of her life. Well, at least most of the time. Because, as Father had said, she need not tell anyone about this money. Not anyone at all.

But that needn't stop her being the happiest woman in the world.

She went into the living room, dialled 1212. After a few connections a voice said, 'Baldwin.'

'Baldwin,' she said. 'How about dinner tonight?'